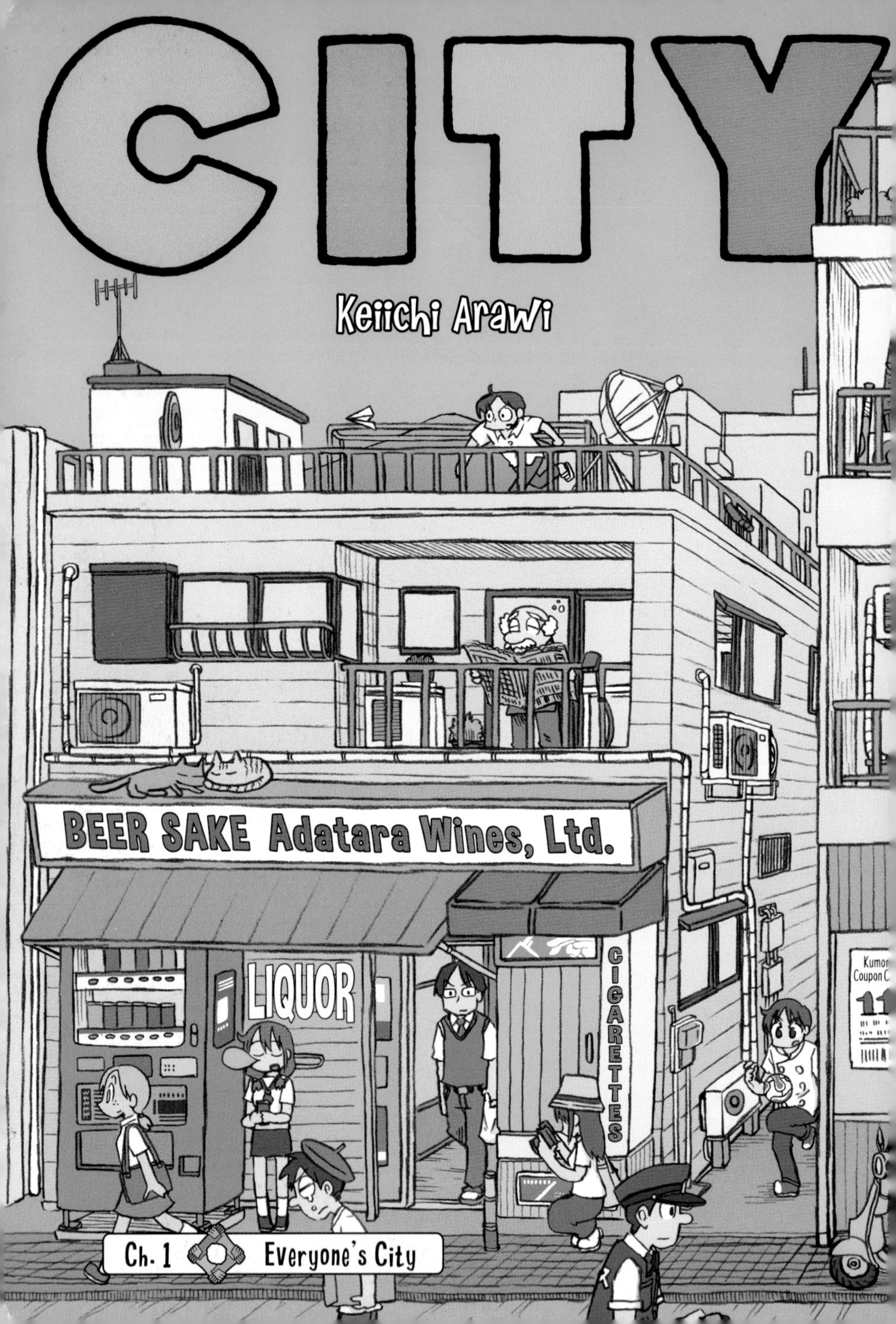
CITY
Keiichi Arawi
BEER SAKE Adatara Wines, Ltd.
LIQUOR
CIGARETTES
Ch. 1 Everyone's City

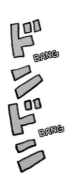

ド BANG

ド BANG

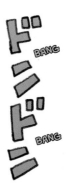

ド BANG

ド BANG

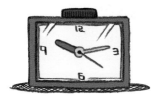

CONTENTS

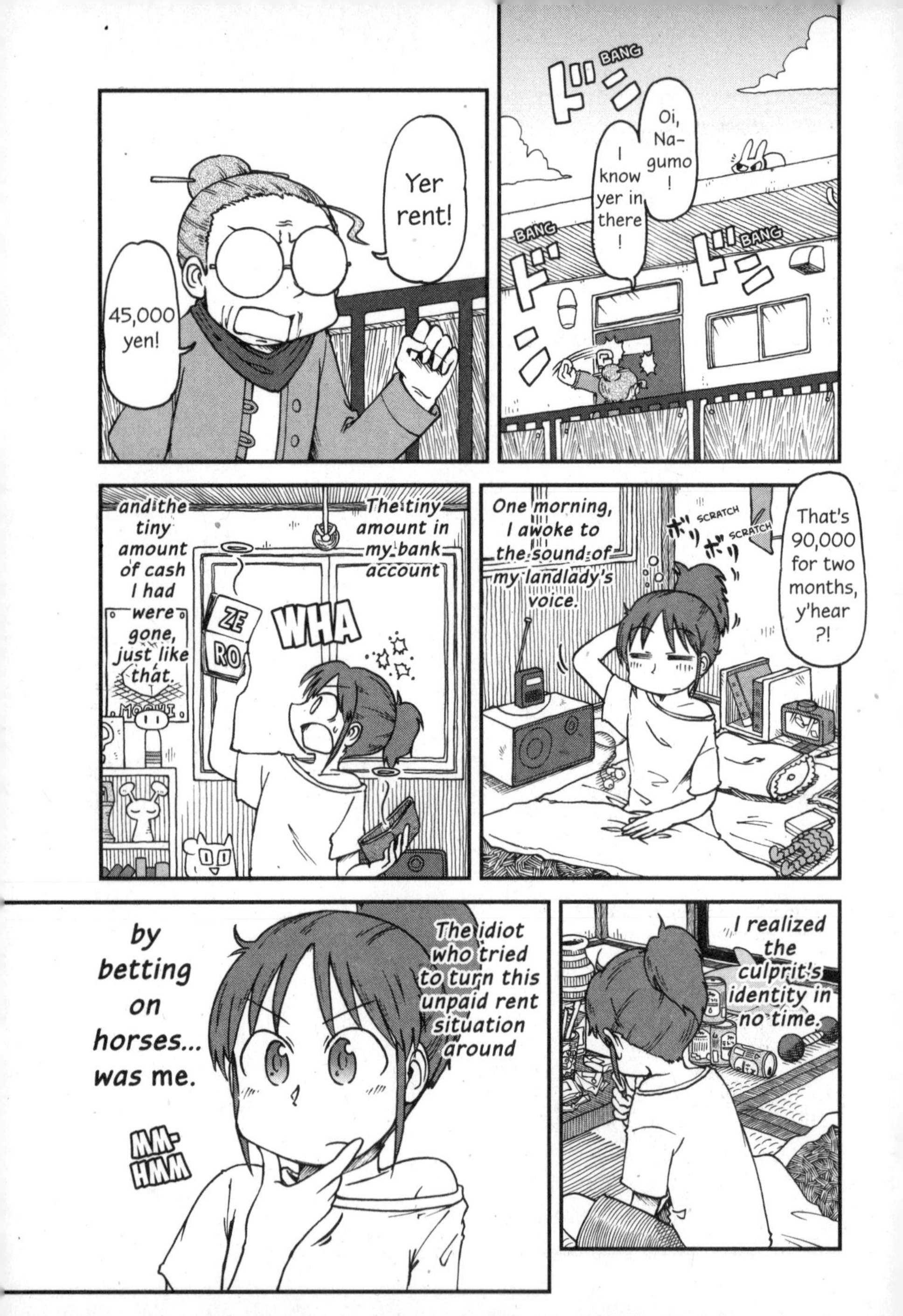
BANG
Oi, Nagumo!
I know yer in there!
BANG
BANG
Yer rent!
45,000 yen!
That's 90,000 for two months, y'hear?!
SCRATCH
SCRATCH
One morning, I awoke to the sound of my landlady's voice.
The tiny amount in my bank account
and the tiny amount of cash I had were gone, just like that.
ZE RO
WHA
MOCHI
I realized the culprit's identity in no time.
The idiot who tried to turn this unpaid rent situation around
by betting on horses... was me.
MM-HMM

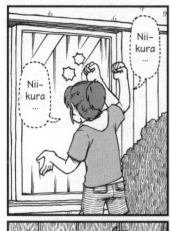

Nii-
kura
...

Nii-
kura
...

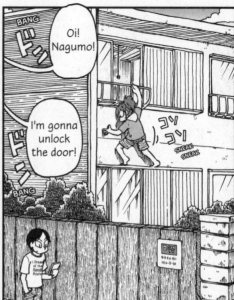

BANG

Oi!
Nagumo!

I'm gonna
unlock
the door!

BANG

SNEAK.
SNEAK.

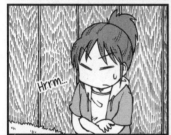

Hrrm...

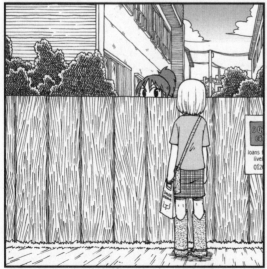

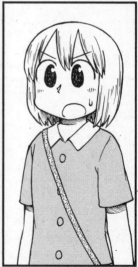

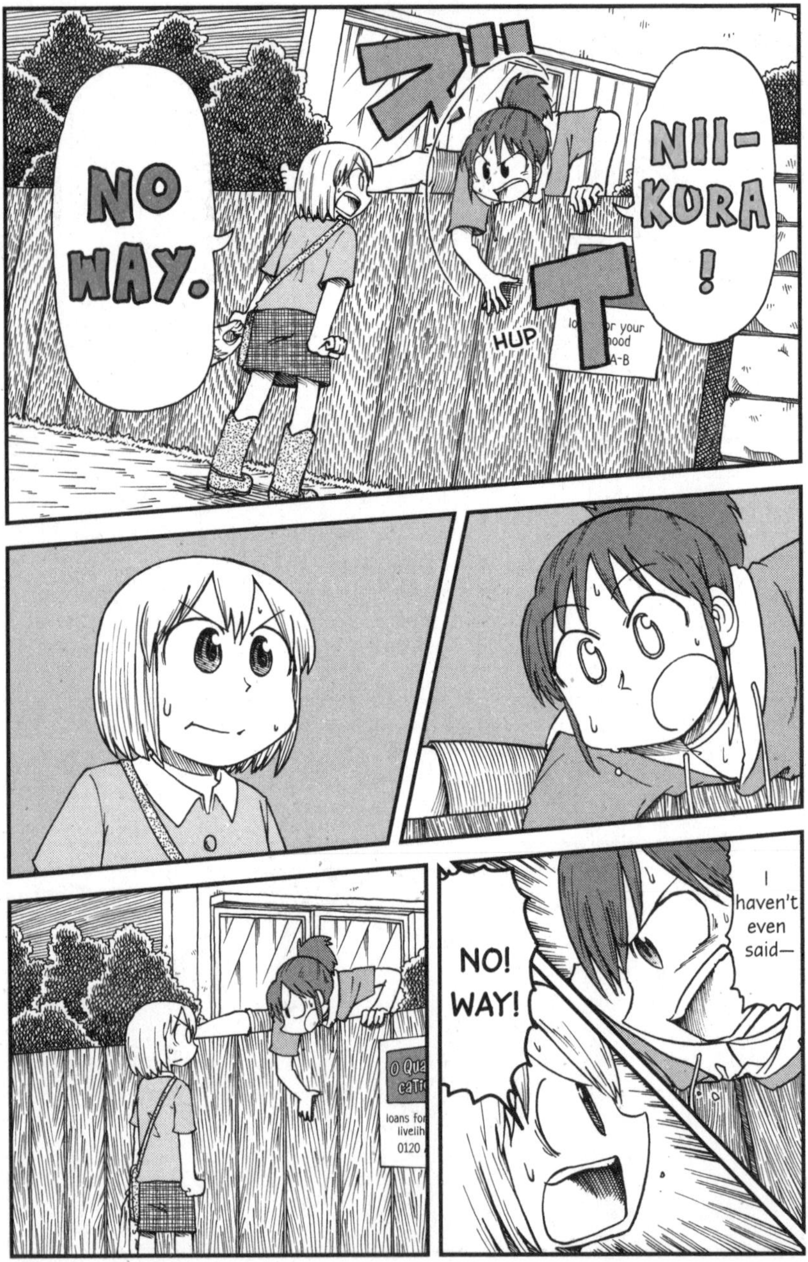
NII-KORA!
HUP
NO WAY.
I haven't even said—
NO! WAY!

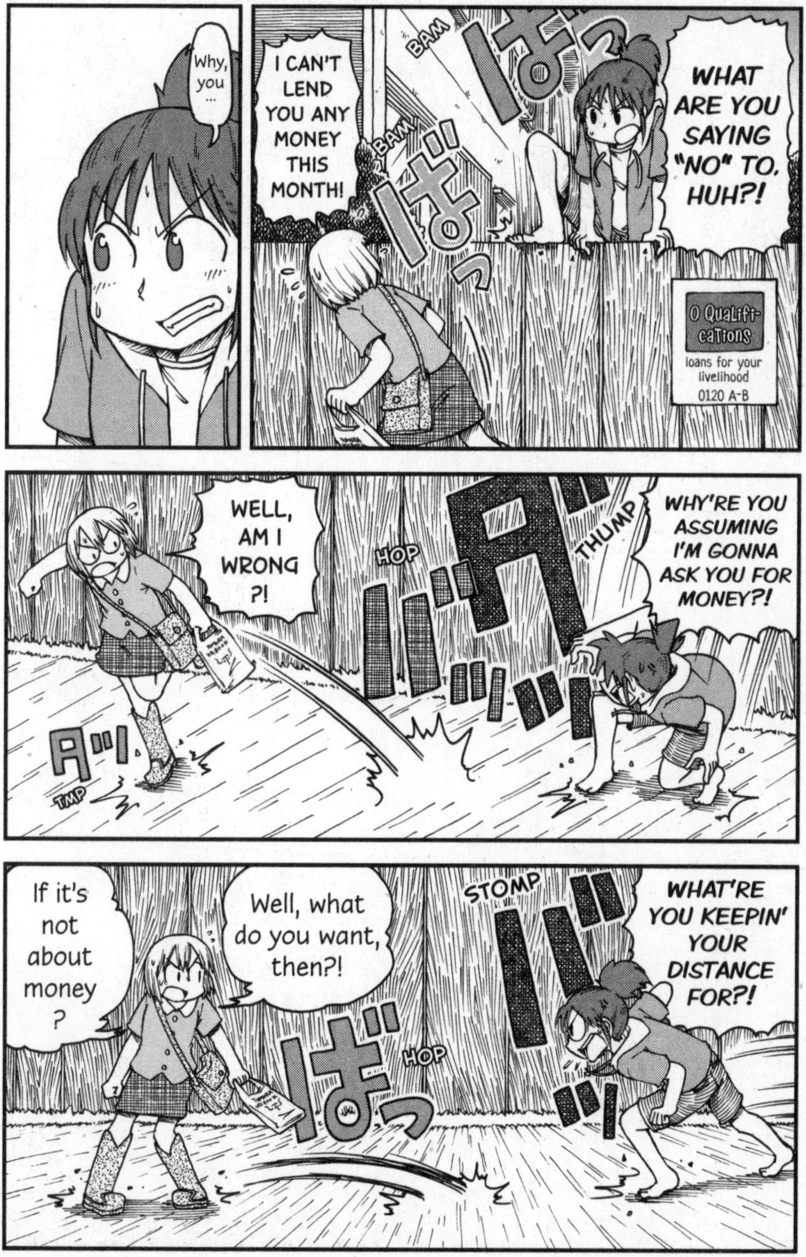

WHAT ARE YOU SAYING "NO" TO, HUH?!
ばっ
BAM
ばっ
BAM
I CAN'T LEND YOU ANY MONEY THIS MONTH!
0 Qualifi-cations
loans for your livelihood
0120 A-B
Why, you ...
WHY'RE YOU ASSUMING I'M GONNA ASK YOU FOR MONEY?!
ダ
THUMP
HOP
WELL, AM I WRONG ?!
TMP
WHAT'RE YOU KEEPIN' YOUR DISTANCE FOR?!
STOMP
ばっ
HOP
Well, what do you want, then?!
If it's not about money ?

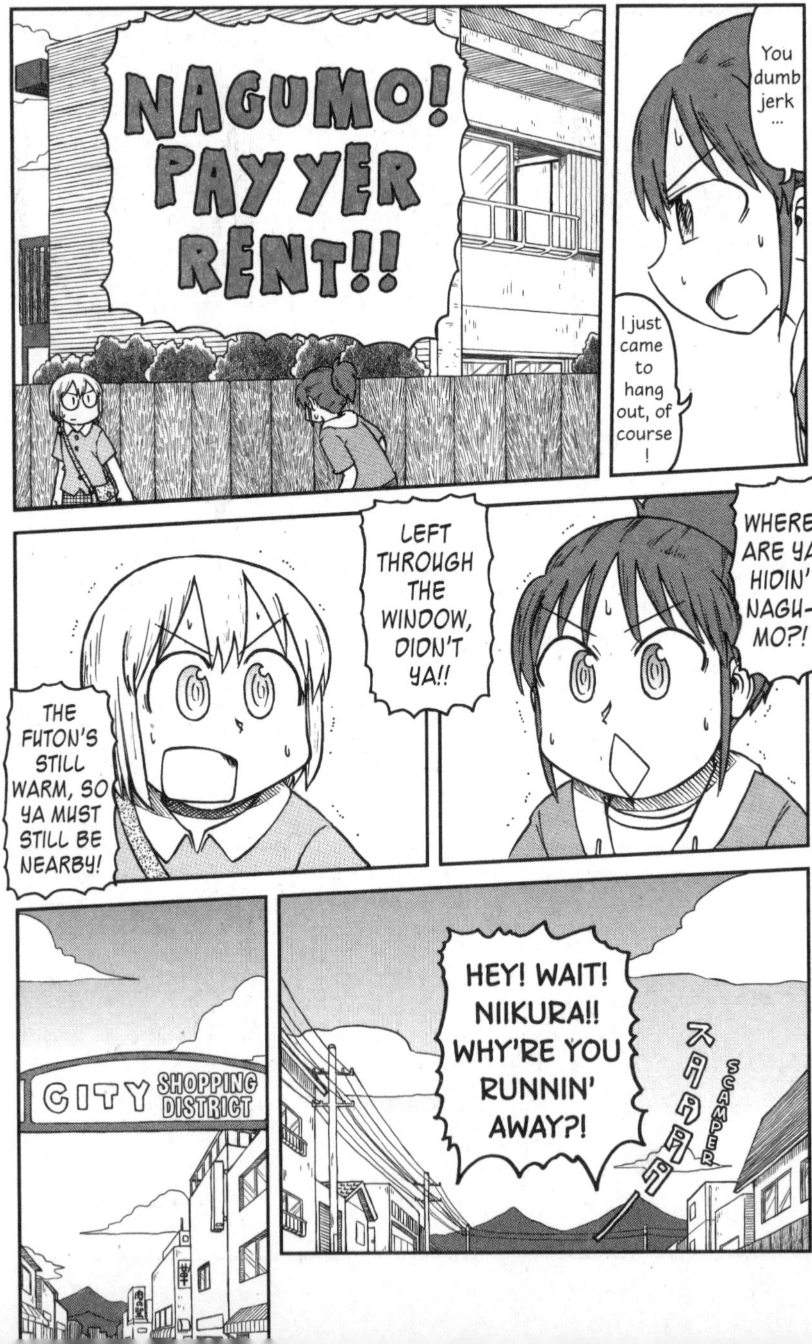
You dumb jerk ...
I just came to hang out, of course!
NAGUMO! PAY YER RENT!!
WHERE ARE YA HIDIN' NAGUMO?!
LEFT THROUGH THE WINDOW, DIDN'T YA!!
THE FUTON'S STILL WARM, SO YA MUST STILL BE NEARBY!
HEY! WAIT! NIIKURA!! WHY'RE YOU RUNNIN' AWAY?!
スタタタタ
SCAMPER
CITY SHOPPING DISTRICT

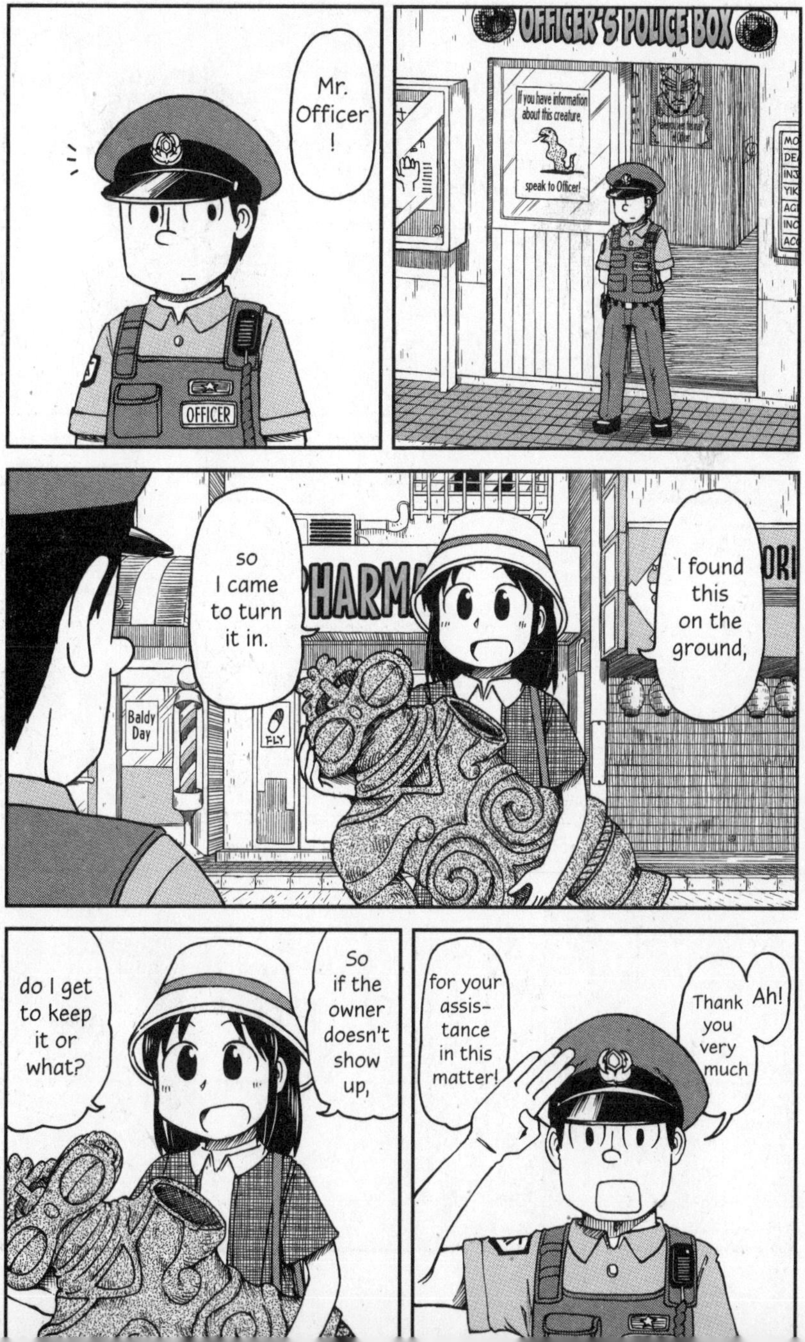
OFFICER'S POLICE BOX
If you have information about this creature, speak to Officer!
Mr. Officer!
OFFICER
I found this on the ground,
so I came to turn it in.
Baldy Day
FLY
Ah!
Thank you very much
for your assis-tance in this matter!
So if the owner doesn't show up,
do I get to keep it or what?

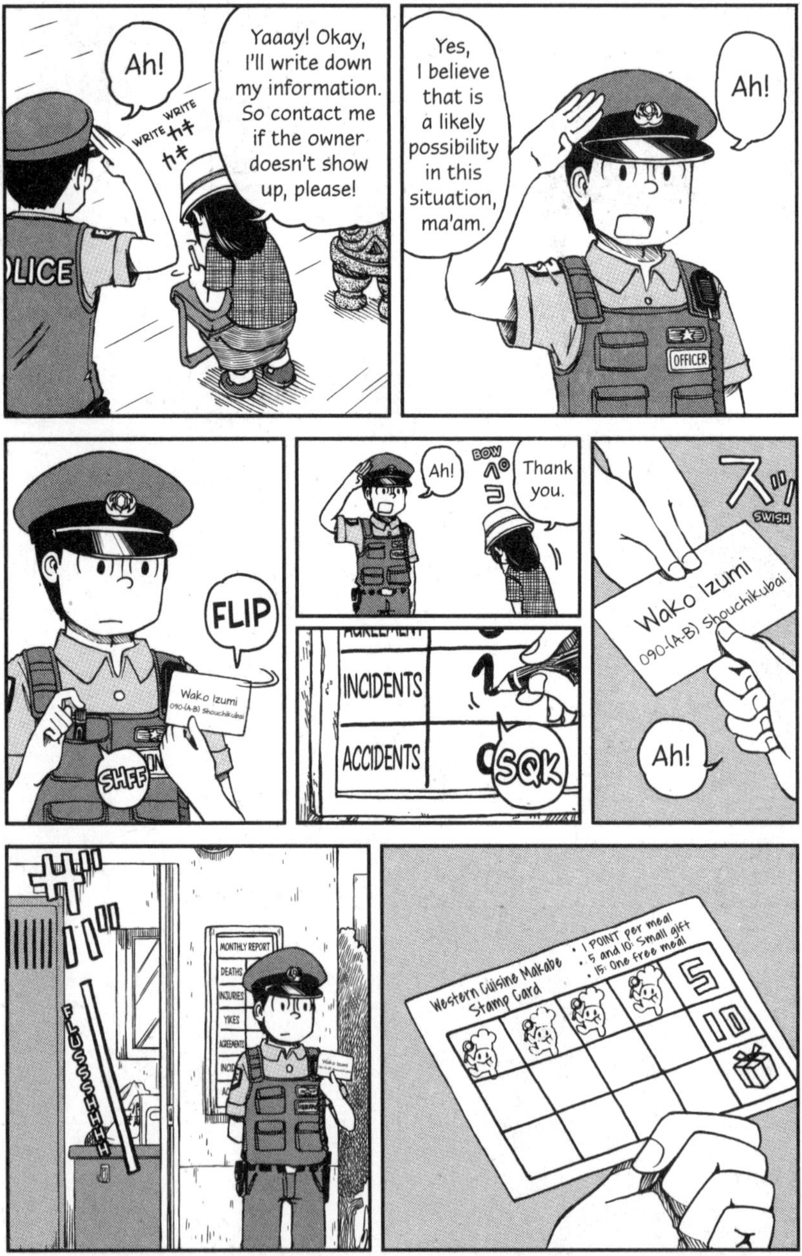
Ah!
Yes, I believe that is a likely possibility in this situation, ma'am.
OFFICER
Ah!
WRITE WRITE カキカキ
Yaaay! Okay, I'll write down my information. So contact me if the owner doesn't show up, please!
スッ SWISH
Wako Izumi
090-(A-B) Shouchikubai
Ah!
Thank you.
BOW ペコ
Ah!
INCIDENTS
ACCIDENTS
SQK
FLIP
Wako Izumi
090-(A-B) Shouchikubai
SHFF
Western Cuisine Makabe Stamp Card
• 1 POINT per meal
• 5 and 10: Small gift
• 15: One free meal
5
10
ザバ
FLUSSHHHH
MONTHLY REPORT
DEATHS
INJURIES
YIKES
AGREEMENTS
Wako Izumi

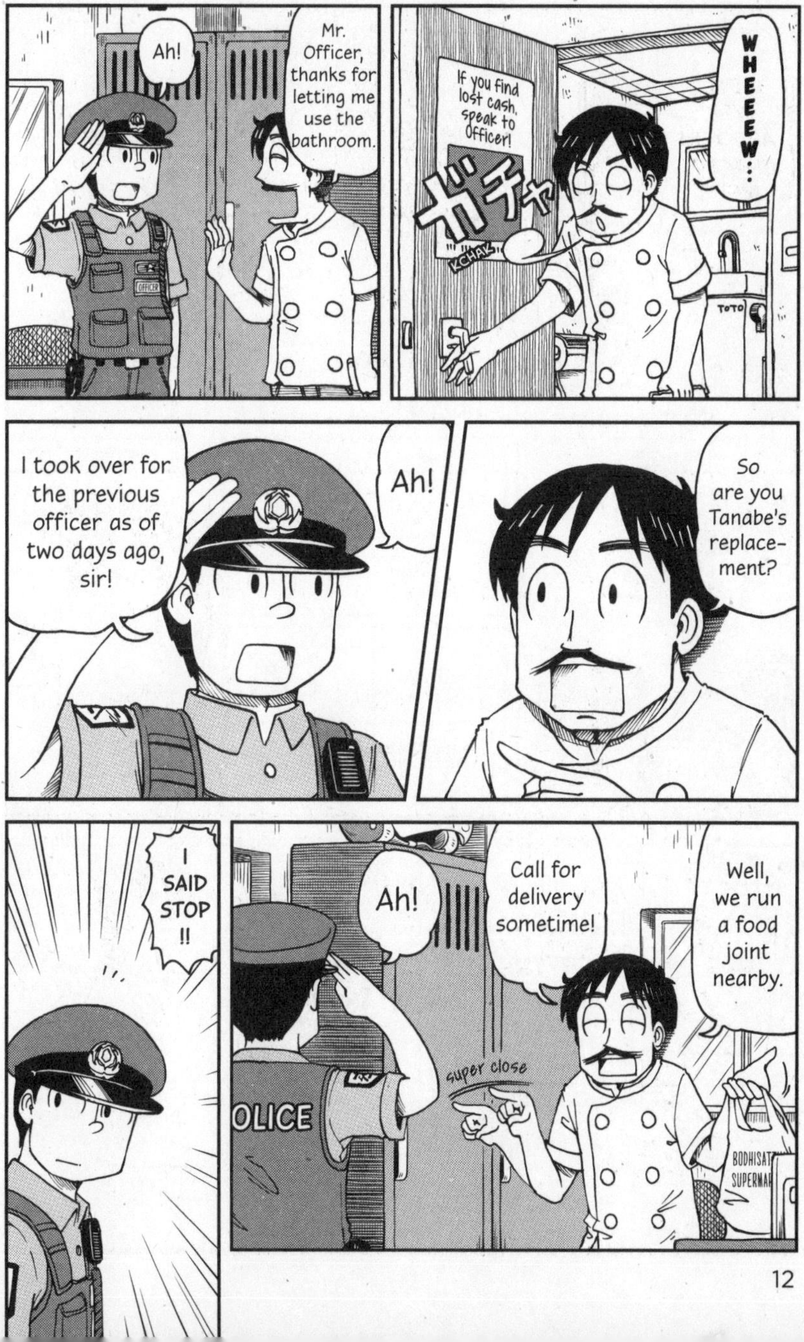
WHEEEW...
If you find lost cash, speak to Officer!
ガチャ
KCHAK
Mr. Officer, thanks for letting me use the bathroom.
Ah!
So are you Tanabe's replacement?
Ah!
I took over for the previous officer as of two days ago, sir!
Well, we run a food joint nearby.
Call for delivery sometime!
Ah!
super close
TOTO
I SAID STOP !!

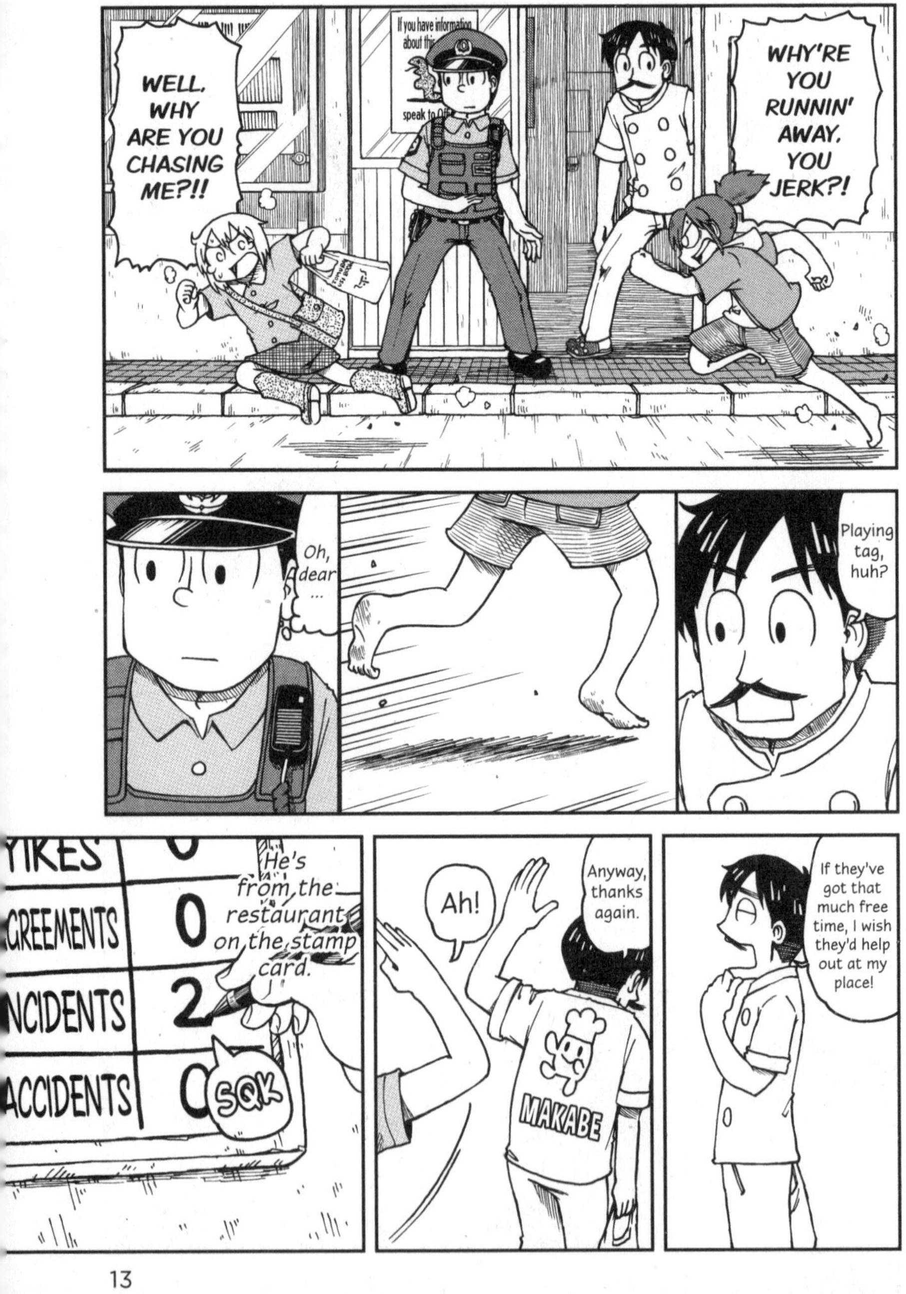
WHY'RE YOU RUNNIN' AWAY, YOU JERK?!
WELL, WHY ARE YOU CHASING ME?!!
If you have information about this
Playing tag, huh?
Oh, dear ...
If they've got that much free time, I wish they'd help out at my place!
Anyway, thanks again.
Ah!
MAKABE
YIKES
GREEMENTS 0
NCIDENTS 2
ACCIDENTS 0
He's from the restaurant on the stamp card.
SQK

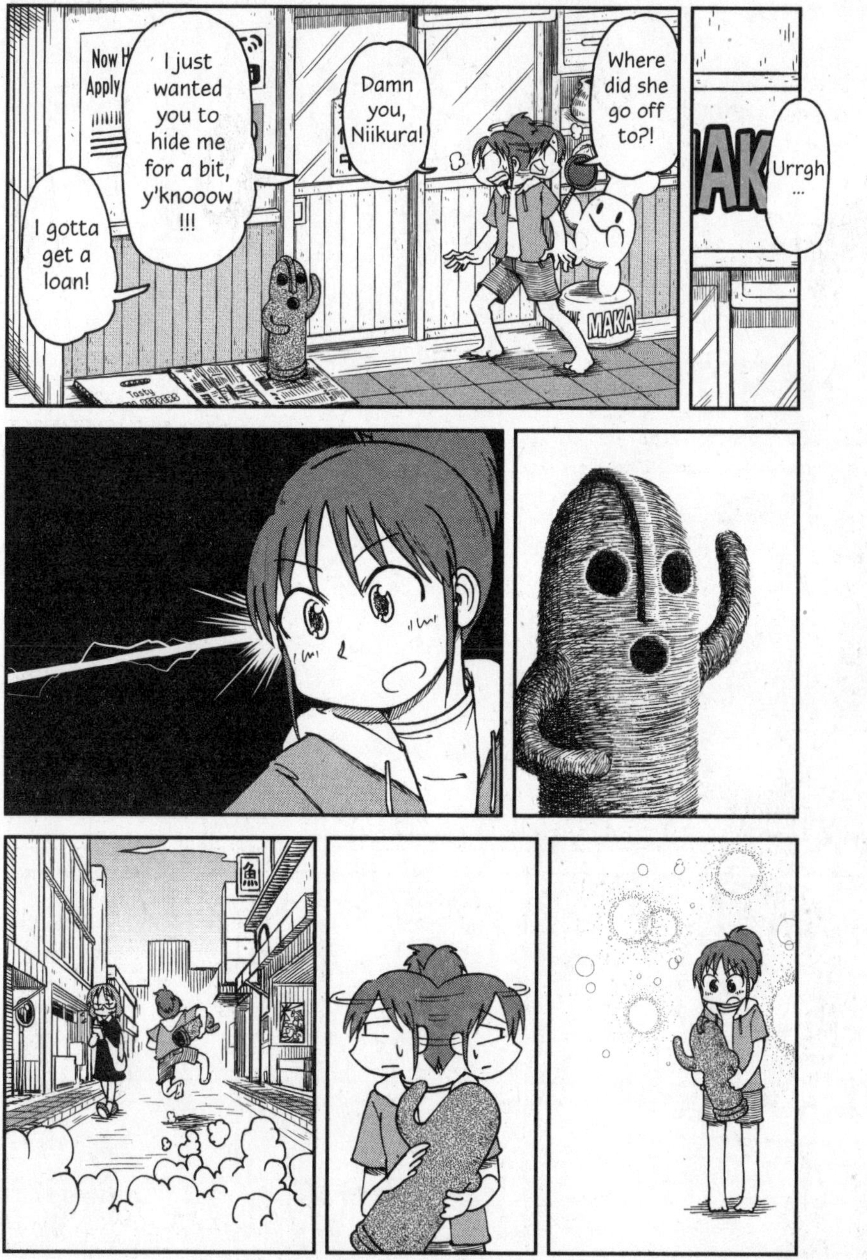
Urrgh ...
Where did she go off to?!
Damn you, Niikura!
I just wanted you to hide me for a bit, y'knooow!!!
I gotta get a loan!
MAKA
魚

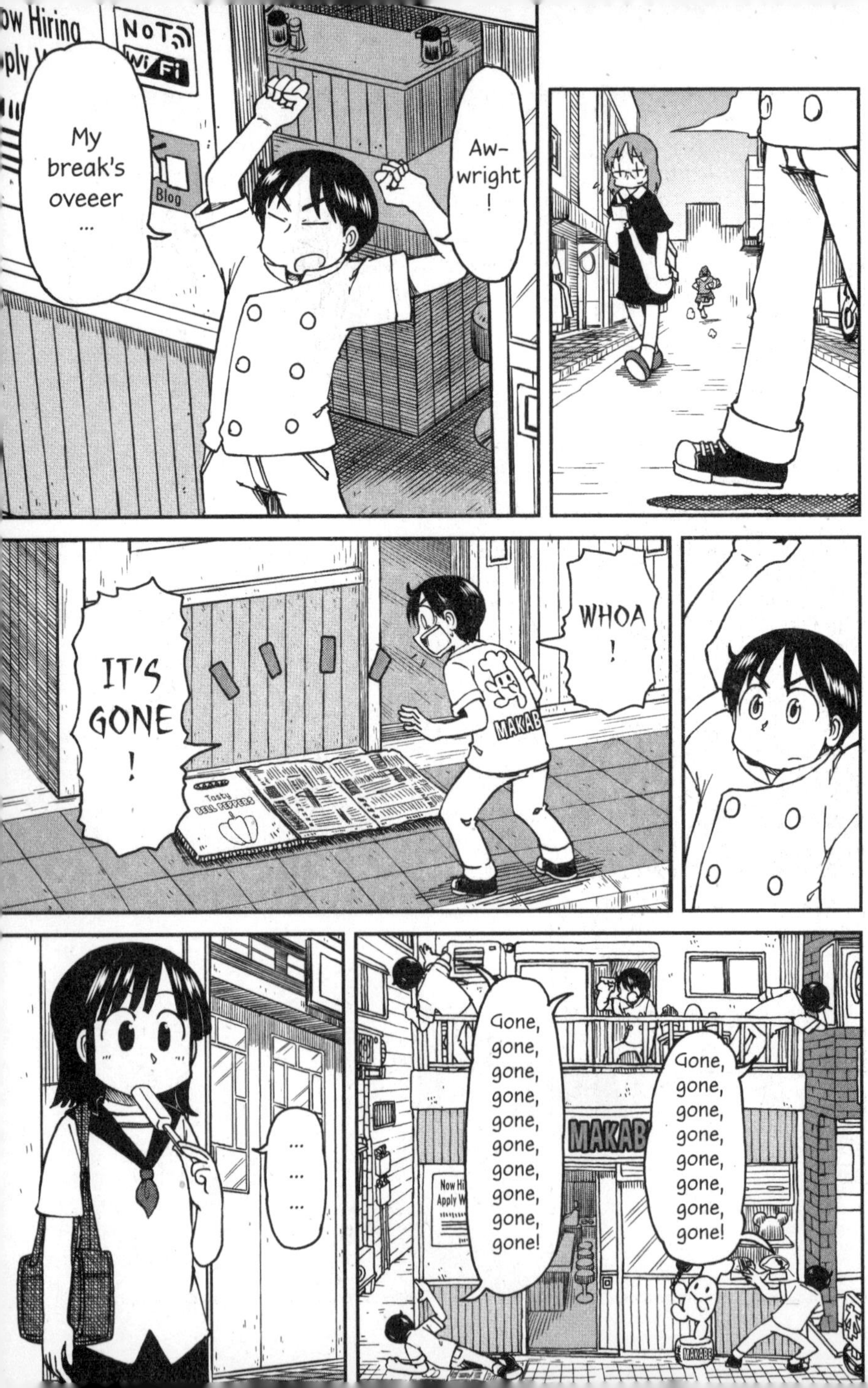

Aw-wright!
My break's oveeer...
NoT Wi Fi
Blog
WHOA!
IT'S GONE!
MAKAB
Tasty BELL PEPPERS
Gone, gone, gone, gone, gone, gone, gone, gone!
Gone, gone, gone, gone, gone, gone, gone, gone, gone, gone!
MAKAB
MAKABE
... ...

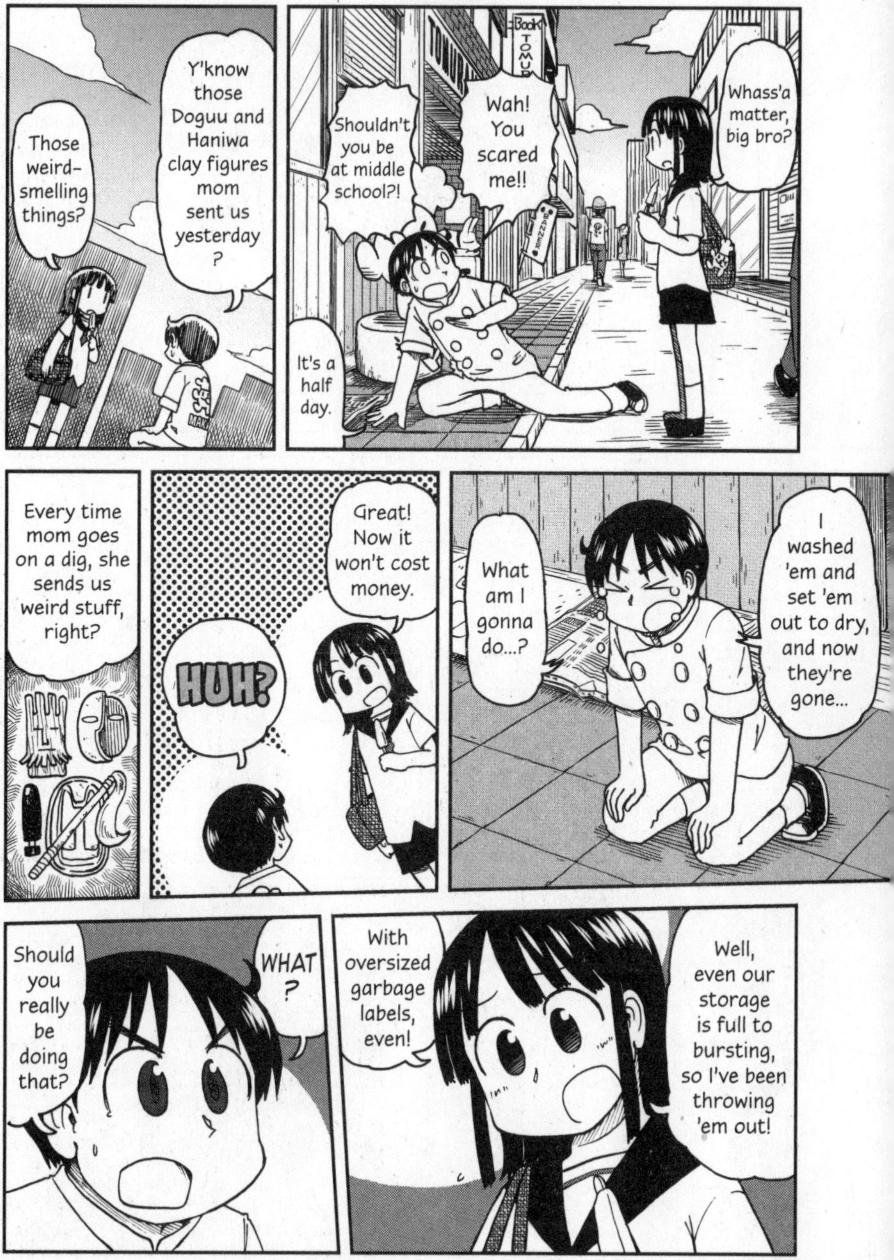
Whass'a matter, big bro?
Wah! You scared me!!
Shouldn't you be at middle school?!
It's a half day.
Y'know those Doguu and Haniwa clay figures mom sent us yesterday?
Those weird-smelling things?
I washed 'em and set 'em out to dry, and now they're gone...
What am I gonna do...?
Great! Now it won't cost money.
HUH?
Every time mom goes on a dig, she sends us weird stuff, right?
Well, even our storage is full to bursting, so I've been throwing 'em out!
With oversized garbage labels, even!
WHAT?
Should you really be doing that?

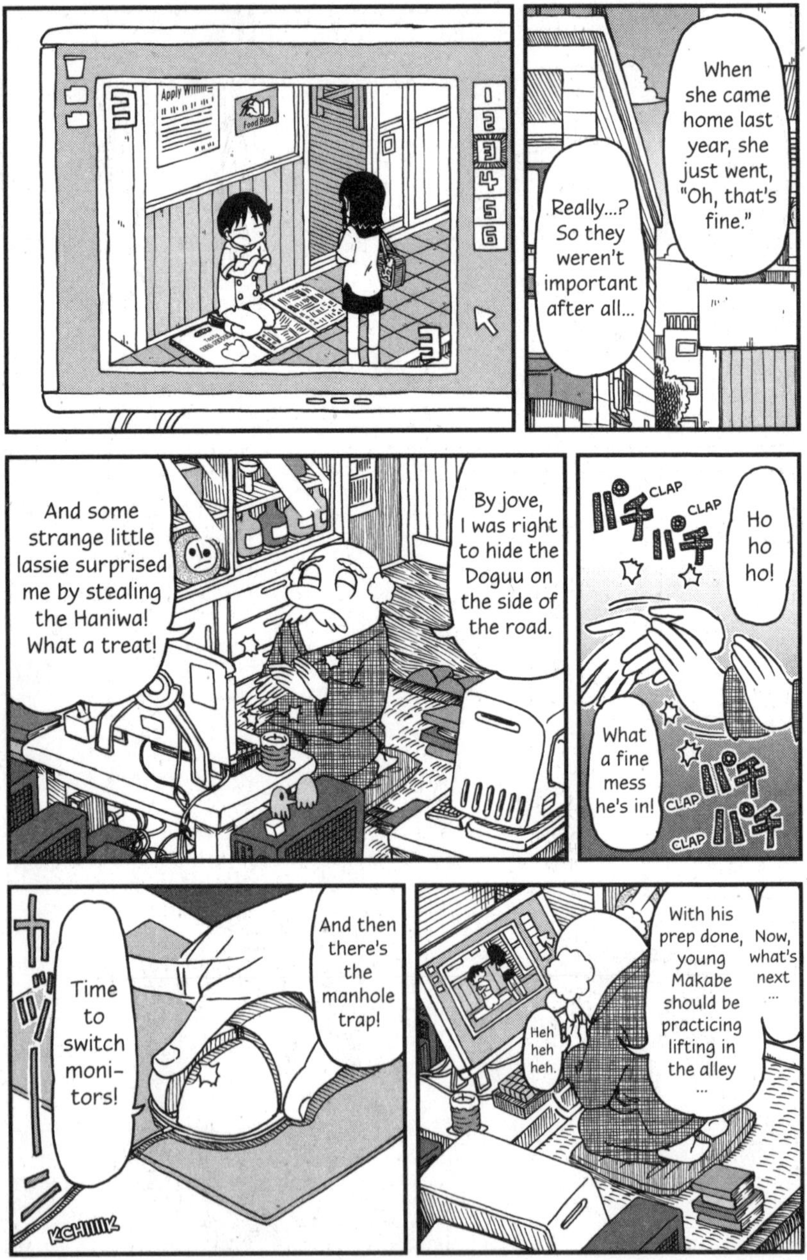
When she came home last year, she just went, "Oh, that's fine."
Really...? So they weren't important after all...
Apply Within
Food Blog
パチ CLAP パチ CLAP
Ho ho ho!
What a fine mess he's in!
パチ CLAP パチ CLAP
By jove, I was right to hide the Doguu on the side of the road.
And some strange little lassie surprised me by stealing the Haniwa! What a treat!
Now, what's next ...
With his prep done, young Makabe should be practicing lifting in the alley ...
Heh heh heh.
And then there's the manhole trap!
Time to switch monitors!
KCHIIIK

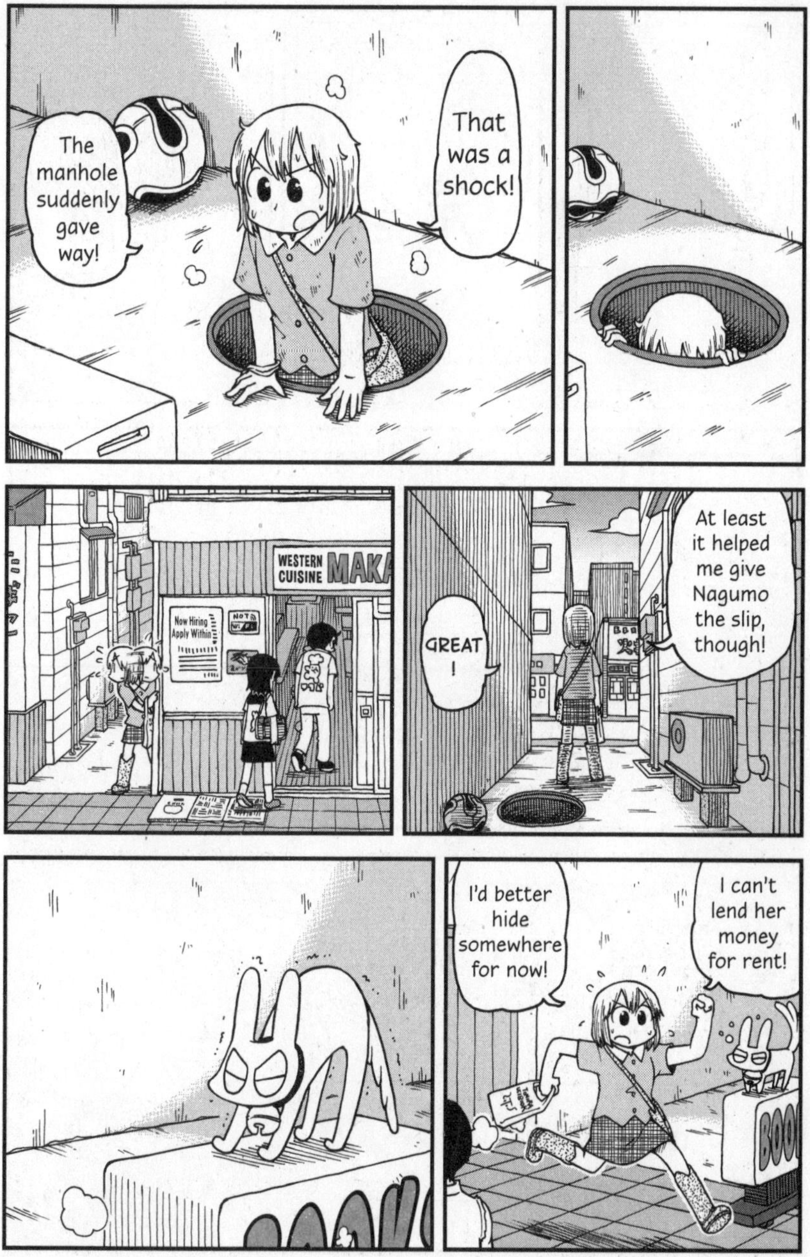
That was a shock!
The manhole suddenly gave way!
At least it helped me give Nagumo the slip, though!
GREAT!
WESTERN CUISINE MAKA
Now Hiring Apply Within
I can't lend her money for rent!
I'd better hide somewhere for now!

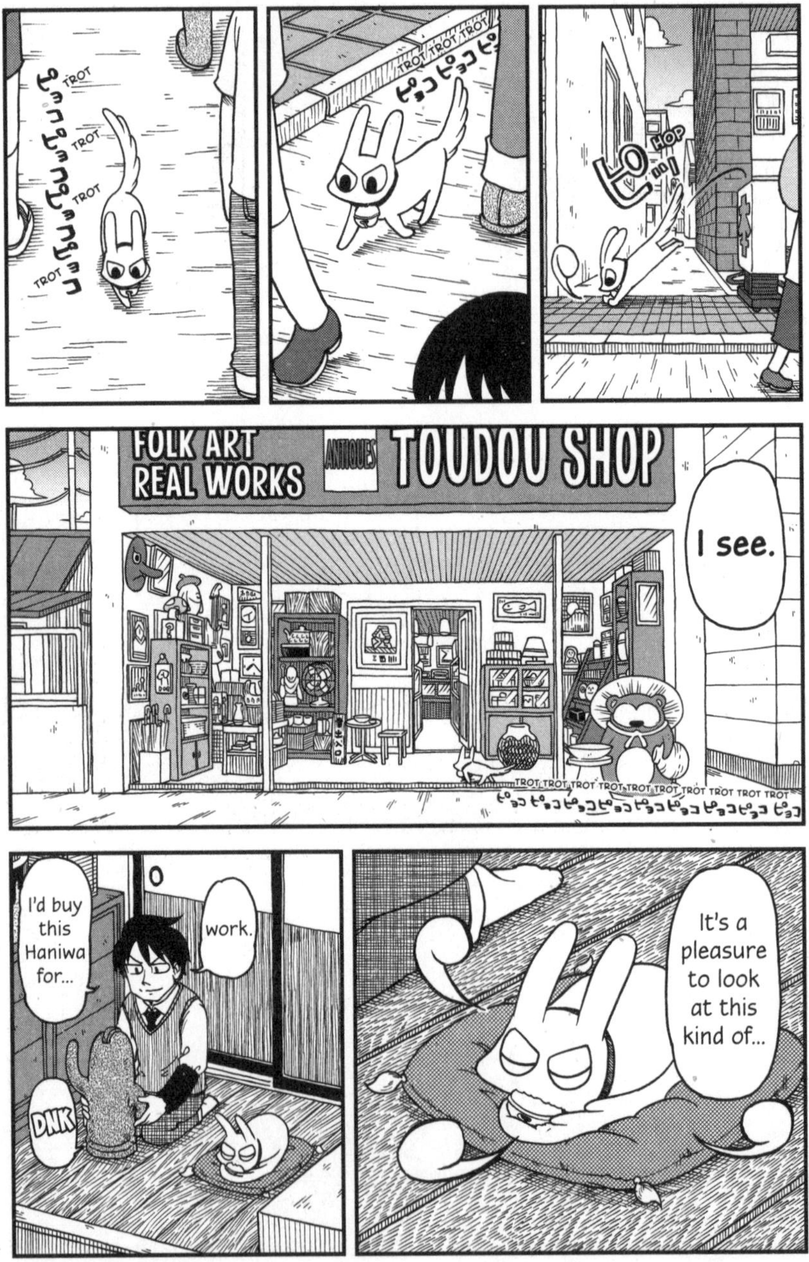
ピョン
HOP
TROT TROT TROT
ピョコピョコピョ
ピョコピョコピョコピョコ
TROT TROT TROT TROT
FOLK ART
REAL WORKS
ANTIQUES
TOUDOU SHOP
I see.
TROT TROT TROT TROT TROT TROT TROT TROT TROT
ピョコピョコピョコピョコピョコピョコピョコピョコピョコ
It's a pleasure to look at this kind of...
work.
I'd buy this Haniwa for...
DNK

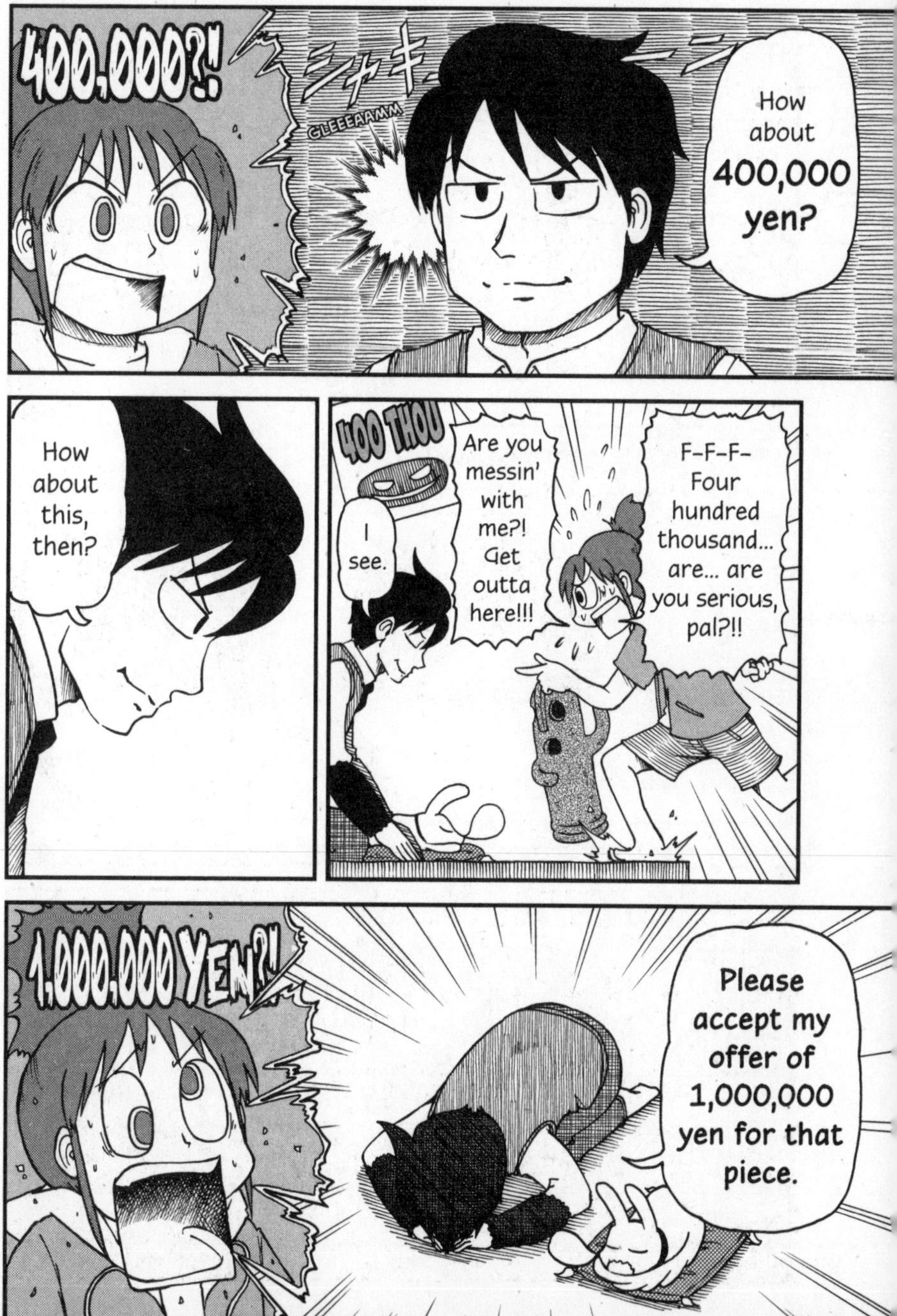
How about 400,000 yen?
GLEEEAAMM
400,000?!
F-F-F- Four hundred thousand... are... are you serious, pal?!!
Are you messin' with me?! Get outta here!!!
400 THOU
I see.
How about this, then?
Please accept my offer of 1,000,000 yen for that piece.
1,000,000 YEN?!

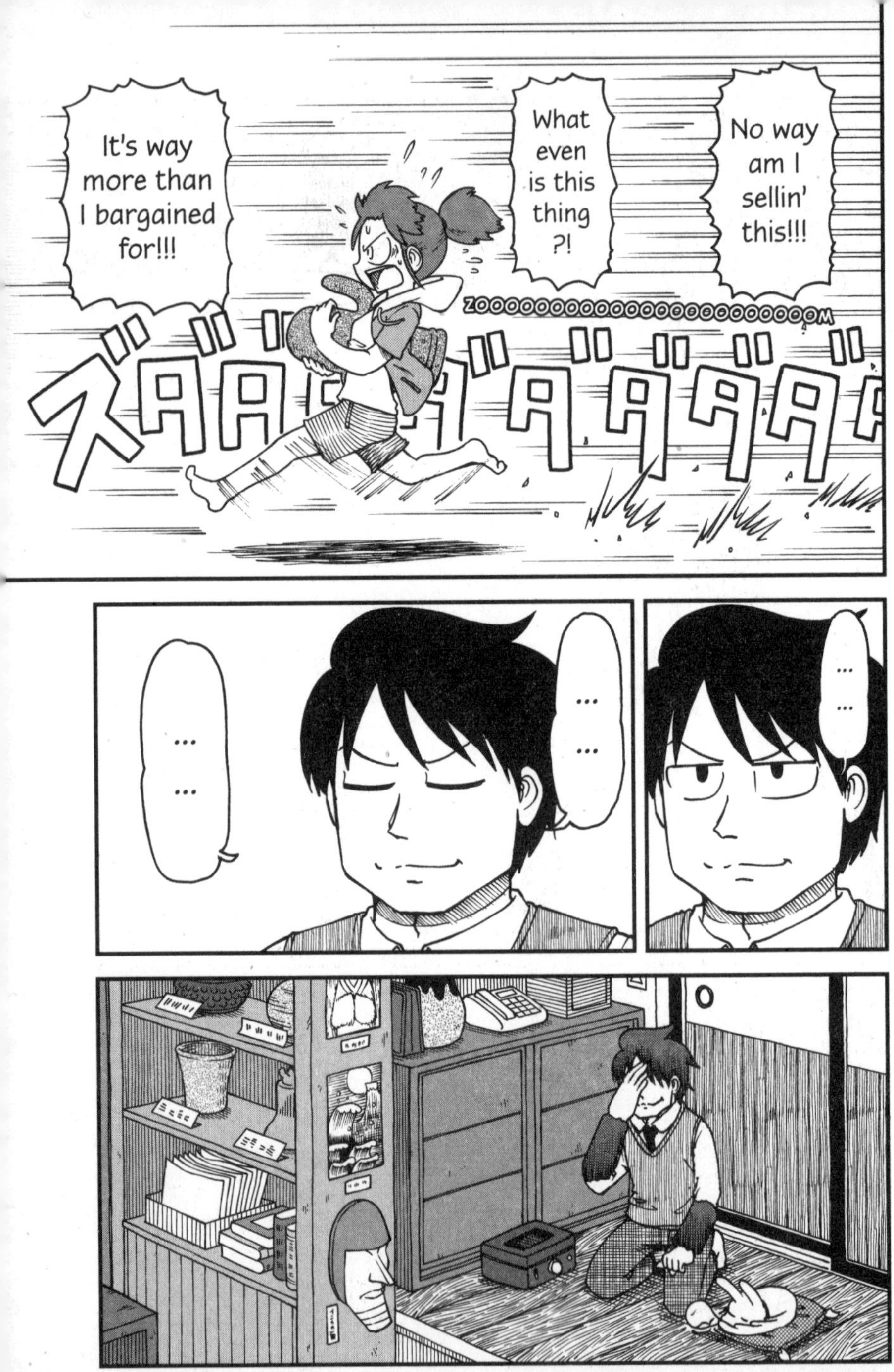
No way am I sellin' this!!!
What even is this thing ?!
It's way more than I bargained for!!!
ZOOOOOOOOOOOOOOOOOOOOOOOOOM
ズダダダダダダダダ
… …
… …
… …

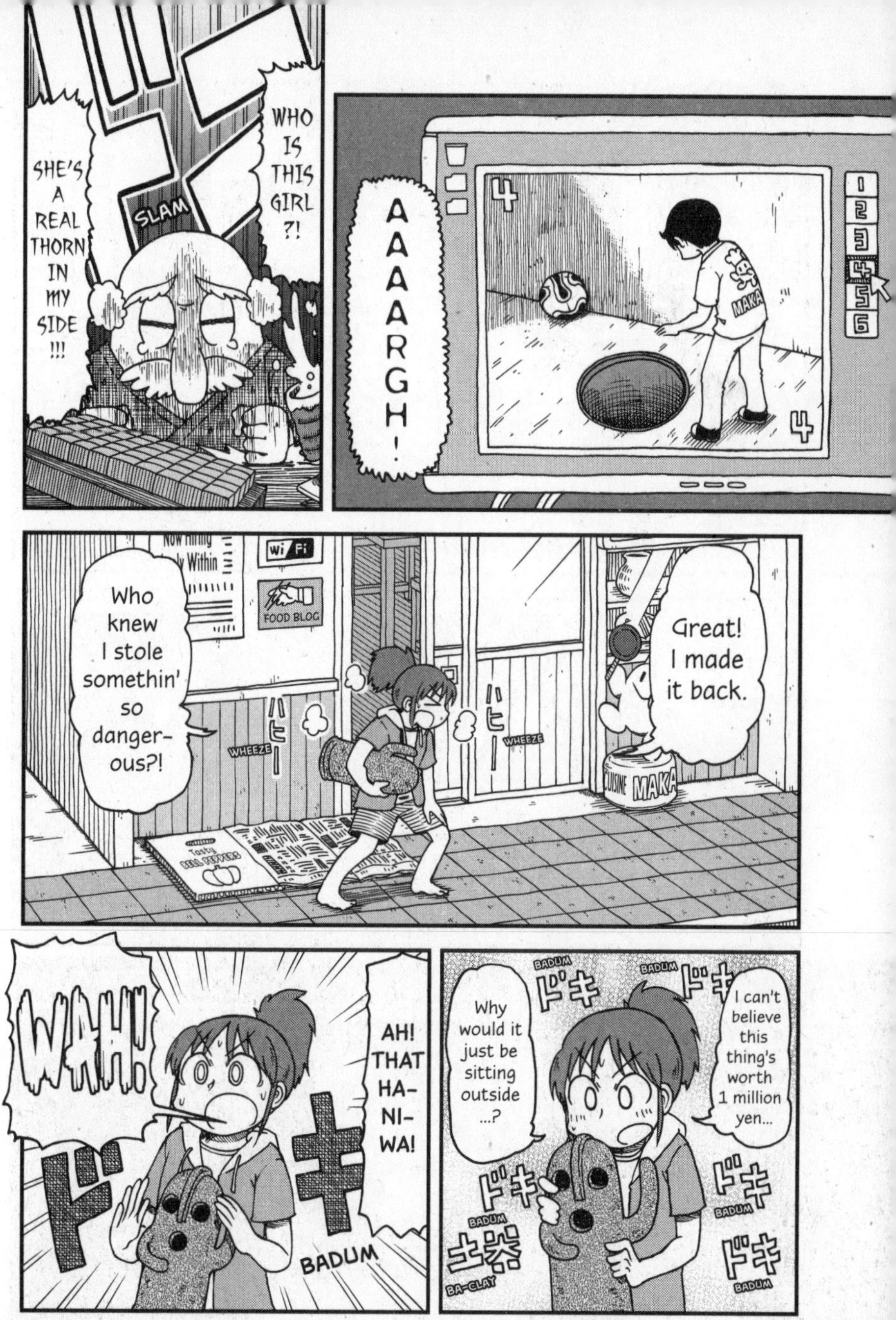
AAAARGH!
WHO IS THIS GIRL?!
SHE'S A REAL THORN IN MY SIDE!!!
SLAM
Great! I made it back.
CUISINE MAKA
WHEEZE
WHEEZE
Who knew I stole somethin' so danger-ous?!
Wi Fi
FOOD BLOG
Tasty BELL PEPPERS
I can't believe this thing's worth 1 million yen...
Why would it just be sitting outside ...?
BADUM
BADUM
BADUM
BADUM
BADUM
BA-CLAY
AH! THAT HA-NI-WA!
WAH!
BADUM

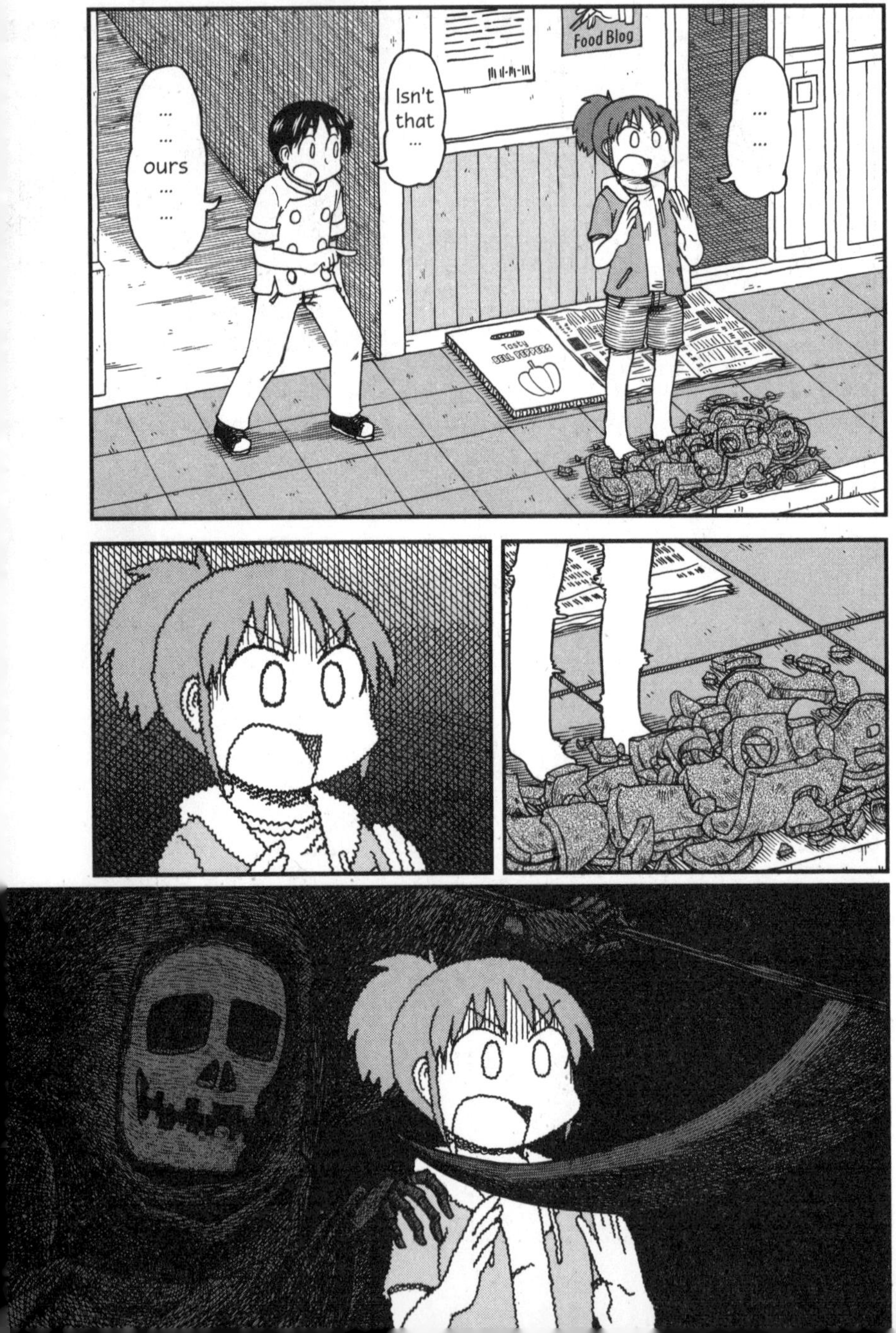
Food Blog
… …
Isn't that …
… … ours … …
Tasty BELL PEPPERS

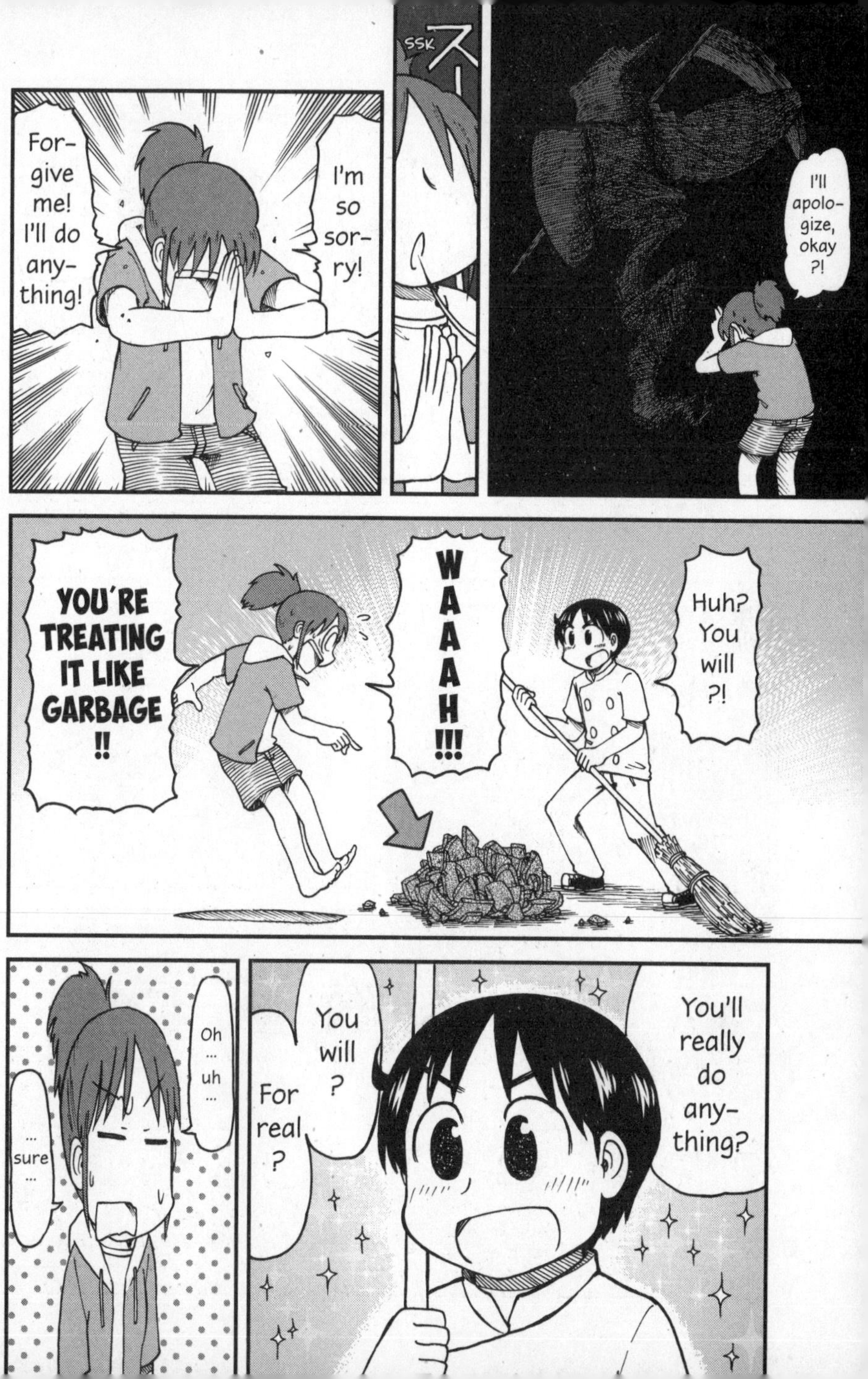
I'll apologize, okay?!
SSK
I'm so sorry!
Forgive me! I'll do anything!
Huh? You will?!
WAAAAH!!!
YOU'RE TREATING IT LIKE GARBAGE!!
You'll really do anything?
You will? For real?
Oh... uh...
...sure...

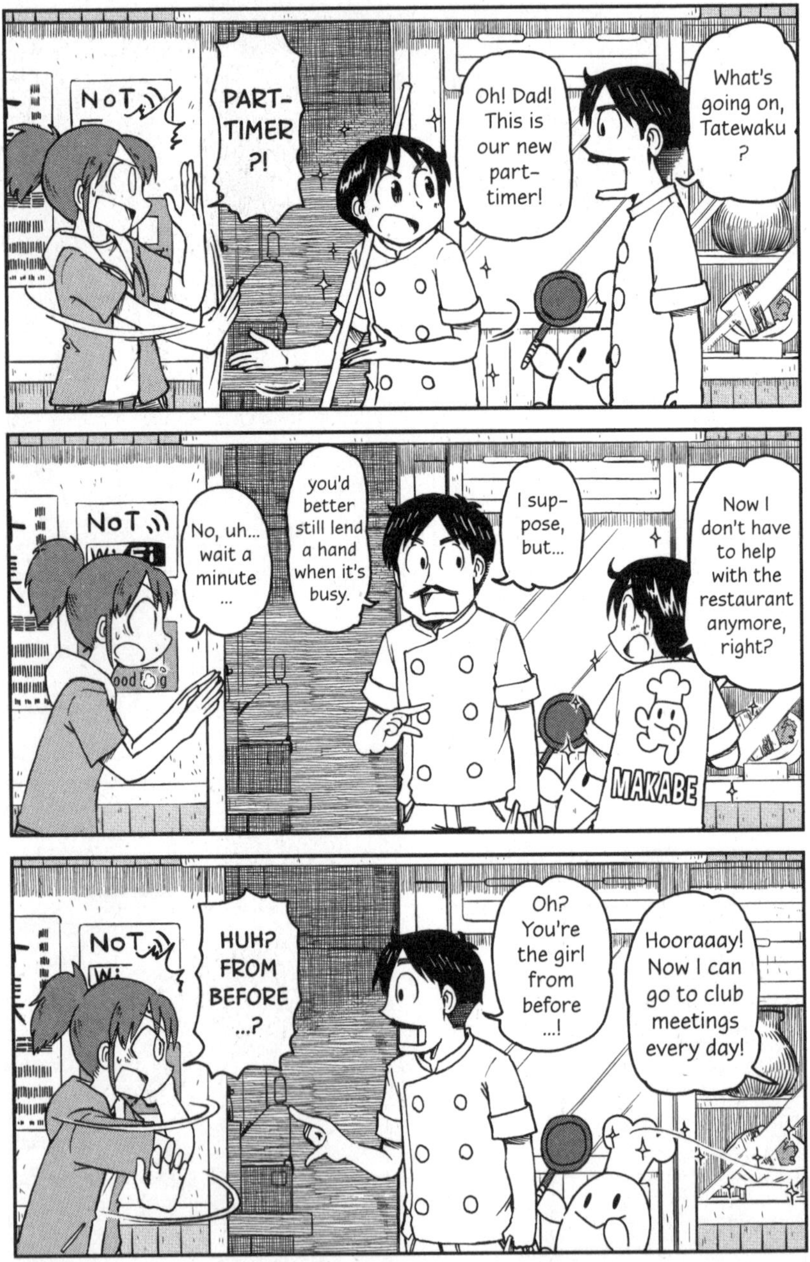
What's going on, Tatewaku?
Oh! Dad! This is our new part-timer!
PART-TIMER?!
NoT
Now I don't have to help with the restaurant anymore, right?
I suppose, but...
you'd better still lend a hand when it's busy.
No, uh... wait a minute ...
NoT
MAKABE
Hooraaay! Now I can go to club meetings every day!
Oh? You're the girl from before ...!
HUH? FROM BEFORE ...?
NoT

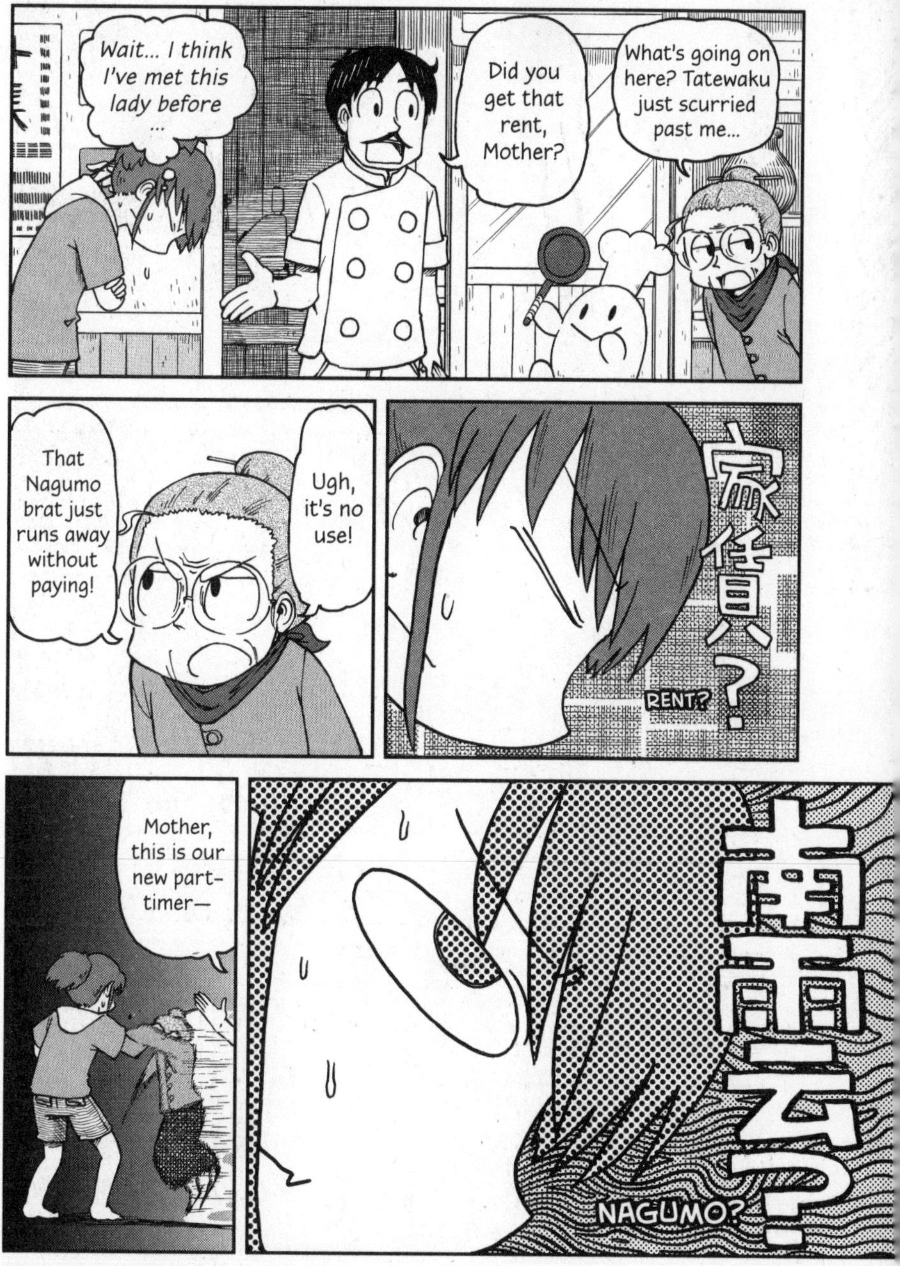
What's going on here? Tatewaku just scurried past me...
Did you get that rent, Mother?
Wait... I think I've met this lady before ...
家賃？
RENT?
Ugh, it's no use!
That Nagumo brat just runs away without paying!
南雲？
NAGUMO?
Mother, this is our new part-timer—

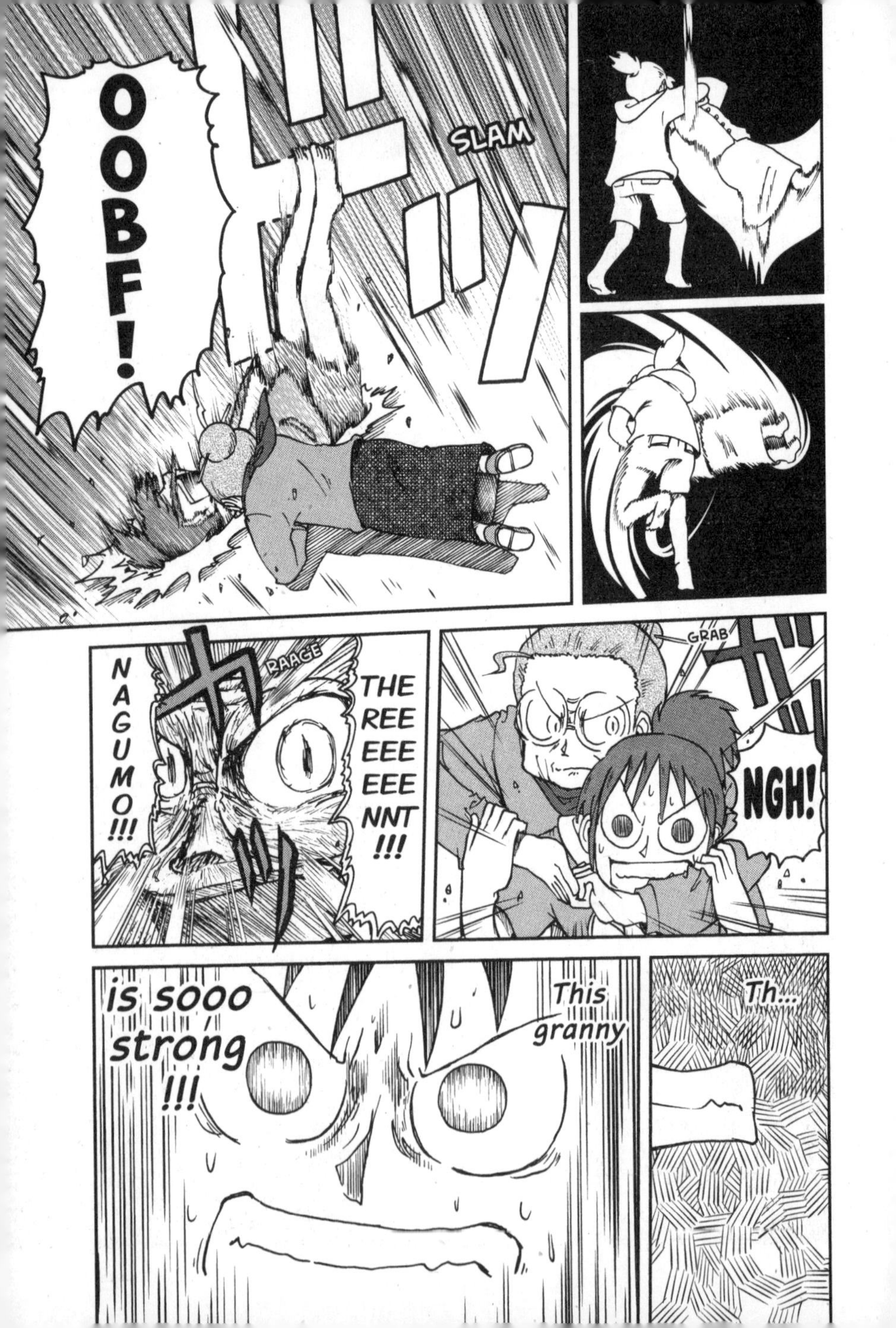
SLAM
OOBF!
GRAB
NGH!
THE REE EEE EEE NNT!!!
RAAGE
NAGUMO!!!
Th...
This granny
is sooo strong!!!

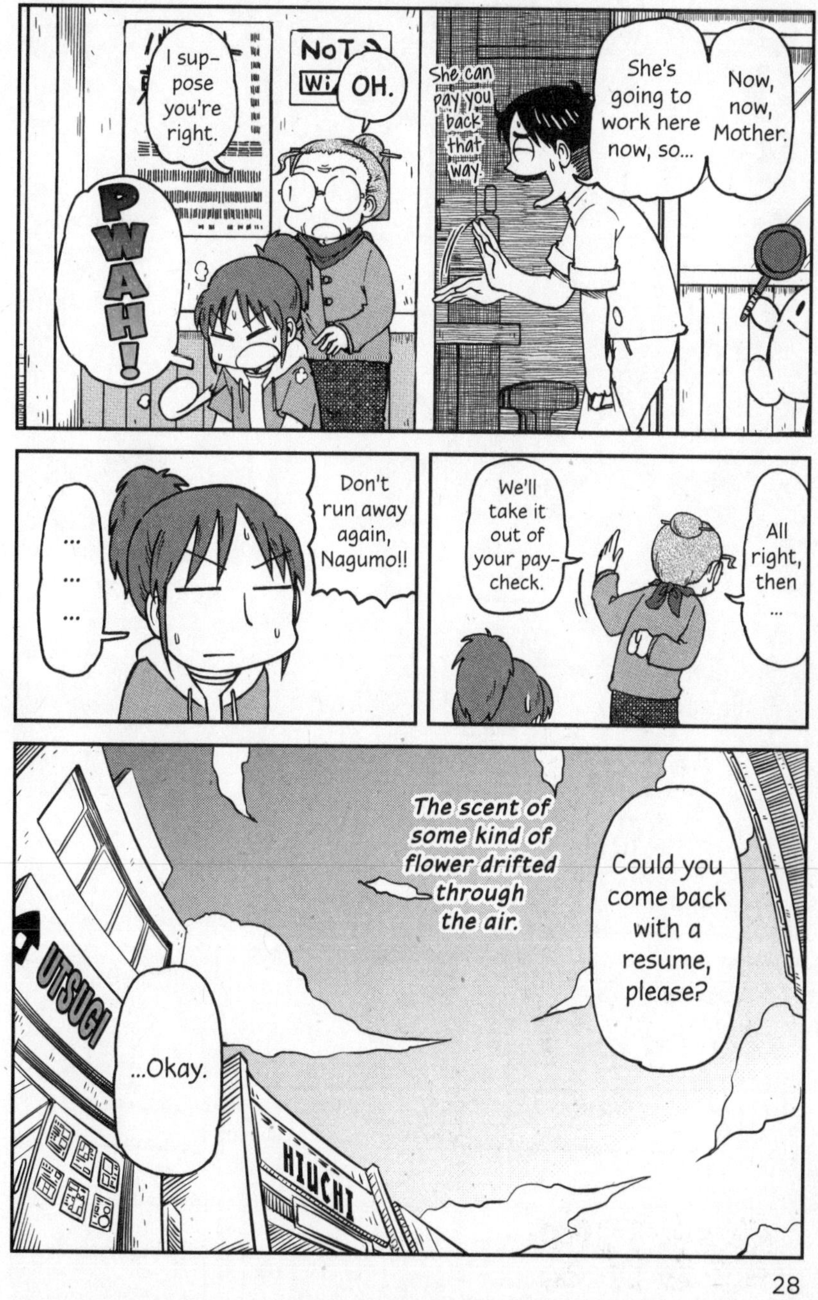
Now, now, Mother.
She's going to work here now, so...
She can pay you back that way.
OH.
I sup-pose you're right.
PWAH!
All right, then ...
We'll take it out of your pay-check.
Don't run away again, Nagumo!!
... ...
Could you come back with a resume, please?
The scent of some kind of flower drifted through the air.
UTSUGI
...Okay.
HIUCHI

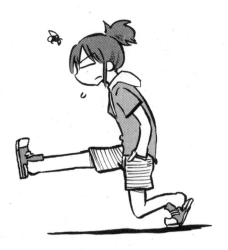

CITY

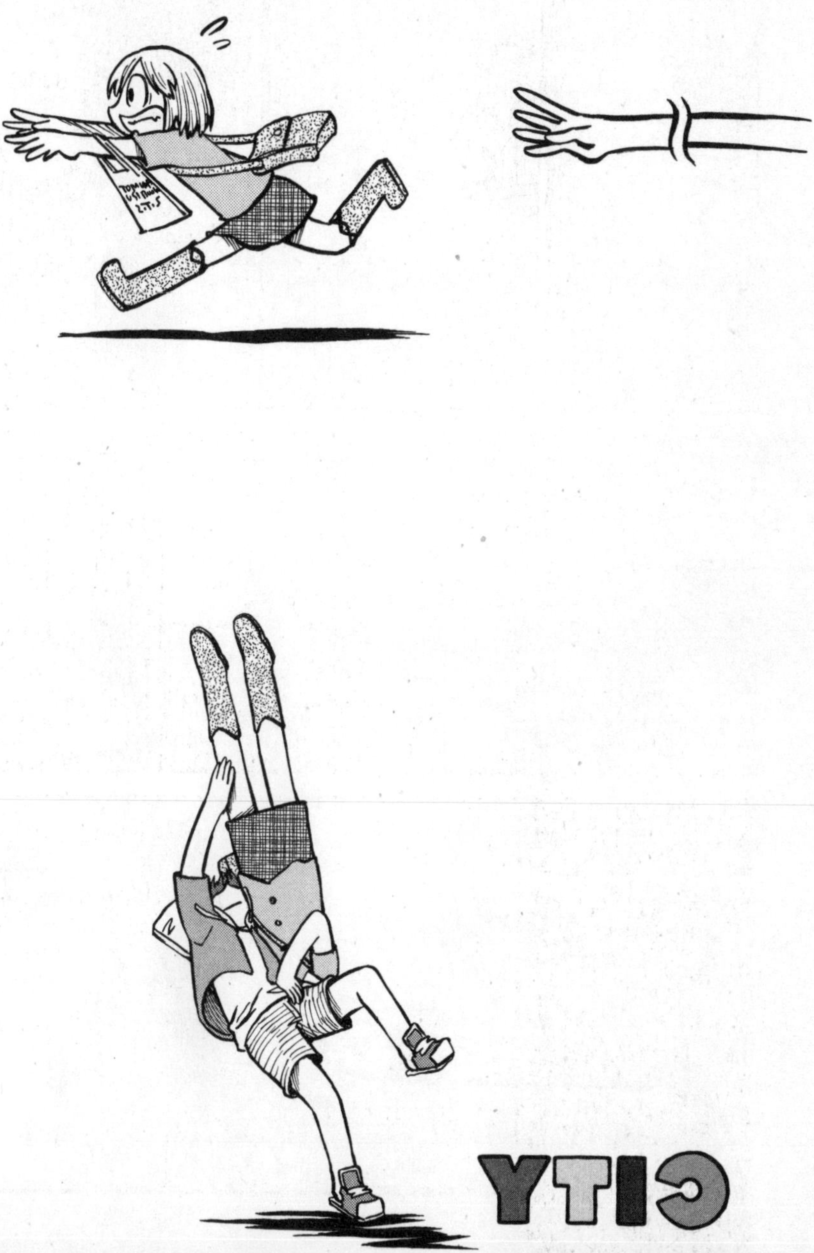

CITY

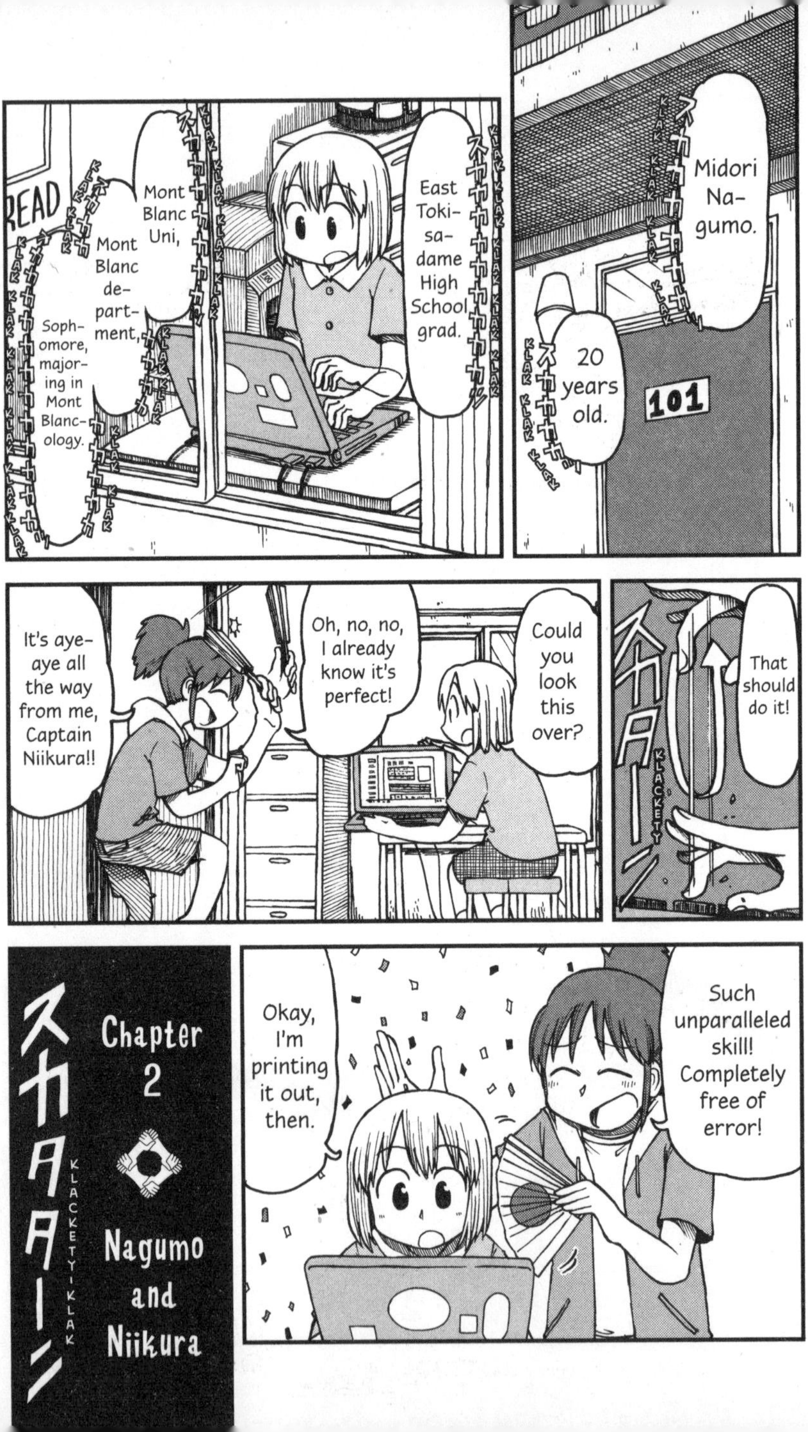
Midori Nagumo.
20 years old.
East Tokisadame High School grad.
Mont Blanc Uni,
Mont Blanc department,
Sophomore, majoring in Mont Blancology.
READ
101
That should do it!
KLACKETY
Could you look this over?
Oh, no, no, I already know it's perfect!
It's aye-aye all the way from me, Captain Niikura!!
Such unparalleled skill! Completely free of error!
Okay, I'm printing it out, then.
KLACKETYIKLAK
Chapter 2
Nagumo and Niikura

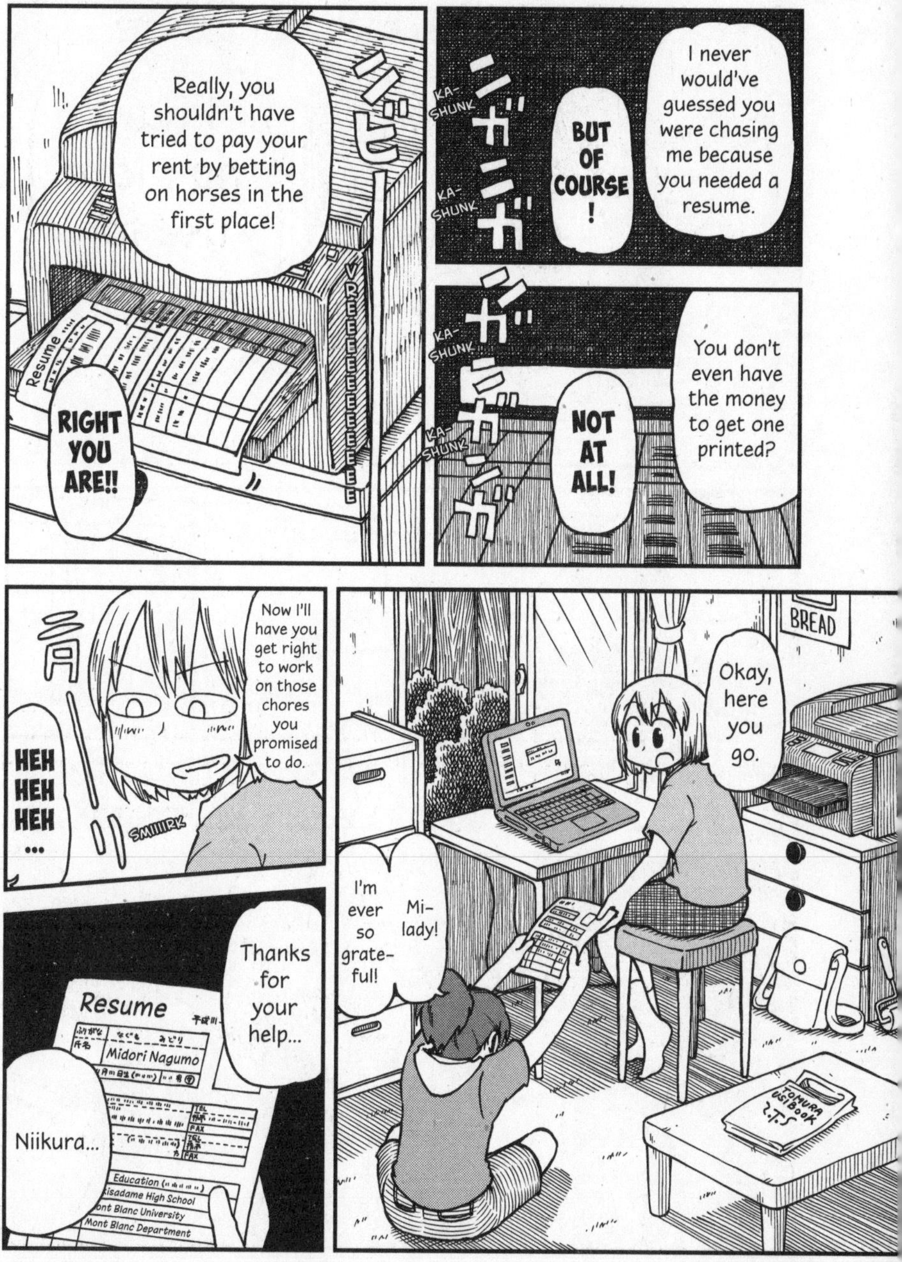

I never would've guessed you were chasing me because you needed a resume.
BUT OF COURSE!
KA-SHUNK
KA-SHUNK
You don't even have the money to get one printed?
NOT AT ALL!
KA-SHUNK
KA-SHUNK
Really, you shouldn't have tried to pay your rent by betting on horses in the first place!
VREEEEEEEEEEEE
Resume
RIGHT YOU ARE!!
BREAD
Okay, here you go.
Mi-lady!
I'm ever so grate-ful!
TOMURA USIBOOK
Now I'll have you get right to work on those chores you promised to do.
SMIIIIRK
HEH HEH HEH...
Thanks for your help...
Niikura...
Resume
Midori Nagumo
Education
Kisadame High School
Mont Blanc University
Mont Blanc Department

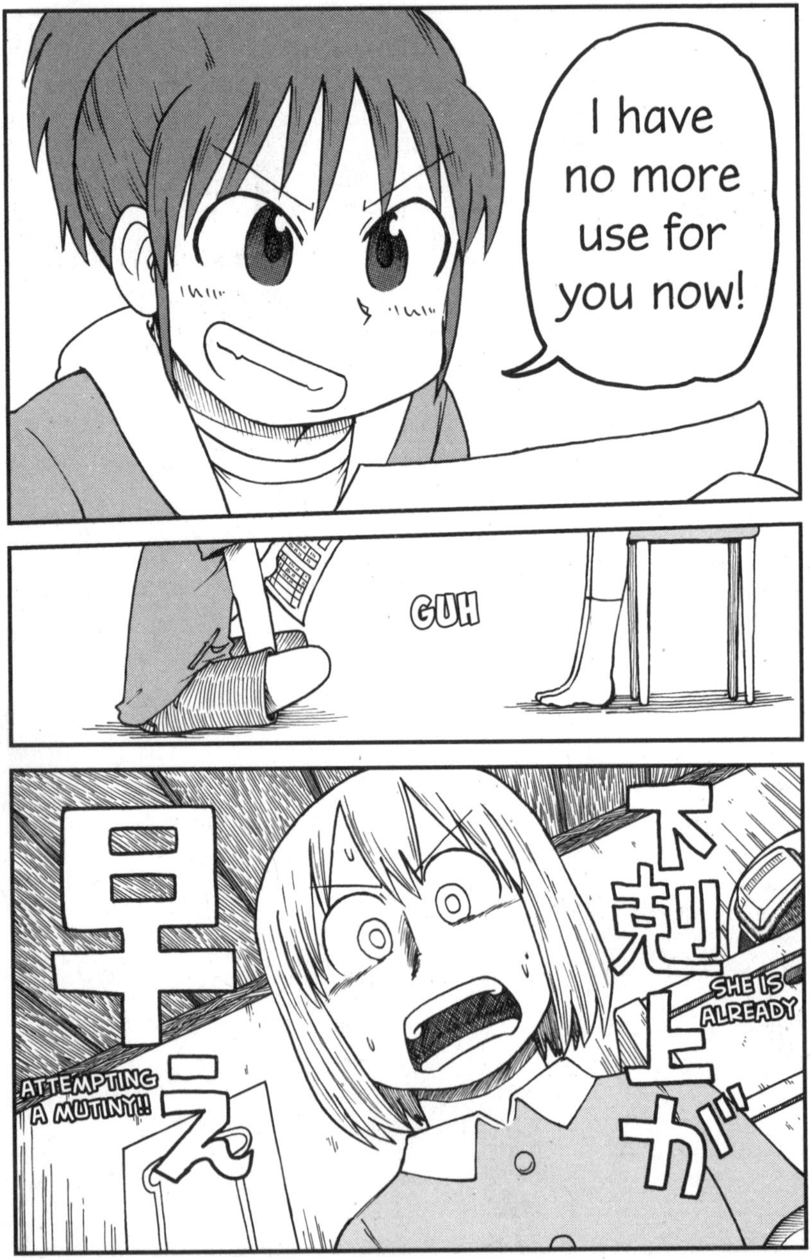
I have no more use for you now!
GUH
下剋上が
SHE IS ALREADY
早え
ATTEMPTING A MUTINY!!

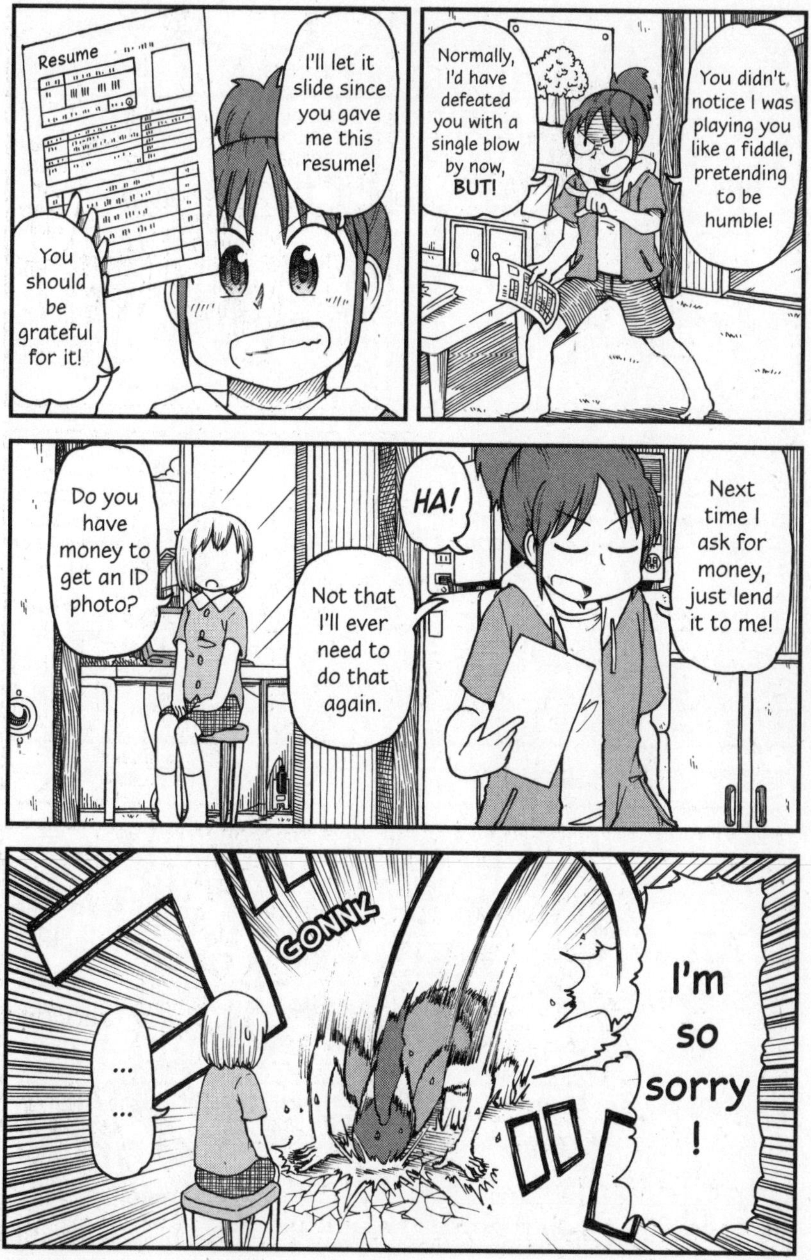

You didn't notice I was playing you like a fiddle, pretending to be humble!
Normally, I'd have defeated you with a single blow by now, **BUT!**
I'll let it slide since you gave me this resume!
Resume
You should be grateful for it!
Next time I ask for money, just lend it to me!
HA!
Not that I'll ever need to do that again.
Do you have money to get an ID photo?
I'm so sorry!
GONNK
...
...

Huh? What was that about never asking for money again?
I'M SO TERRIBLY SORRY !!
JUST THIS ONE TIME! MY LADY PRESIDENT HONORABLE EXCELLENCY!!
FLAIL
FLAIL
FLAIL
FLAIL
You promise to stop both-ering me for money after this?
I do, I do!
You promise not to spend your paychecks on gambling?
Yes !
Of course! I swear! I'll pay you back, with interest!
I
will
CLENCH
NEVER give this back!! You moron !!!
SLAM
HAHAHAHA!
Adios, sucker !!!

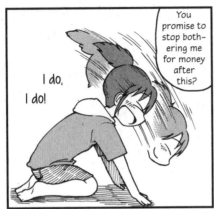

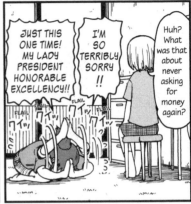

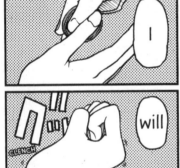

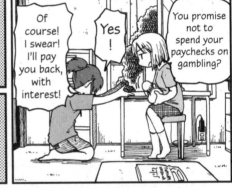

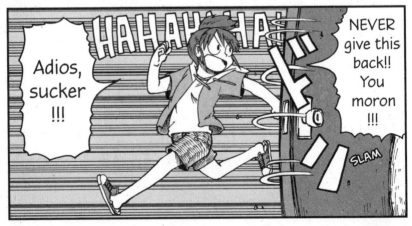

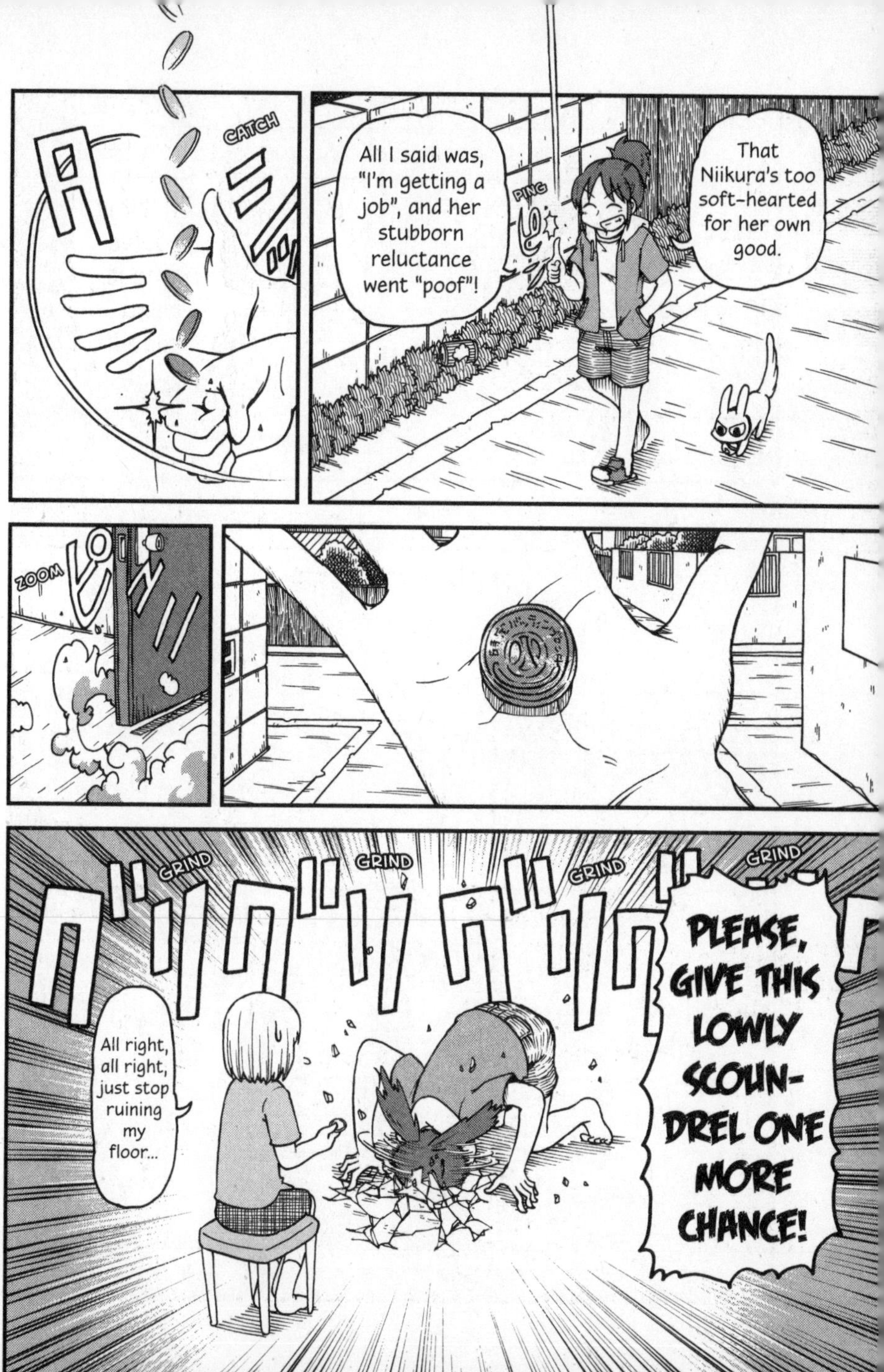
That Niikura's too soft-hearted for her own good.
All I said was, "I'm getting a job", and her stubborn reluctance went "poof"!
PING
CATCH
ZOOM
GRIND
GRIND
GRIND
GRIND
PLEASE, GIVE THIS LOWLY SCOUN-DREL ONE MORE CHANCE!
All right, all right, just stop ruining my floor...

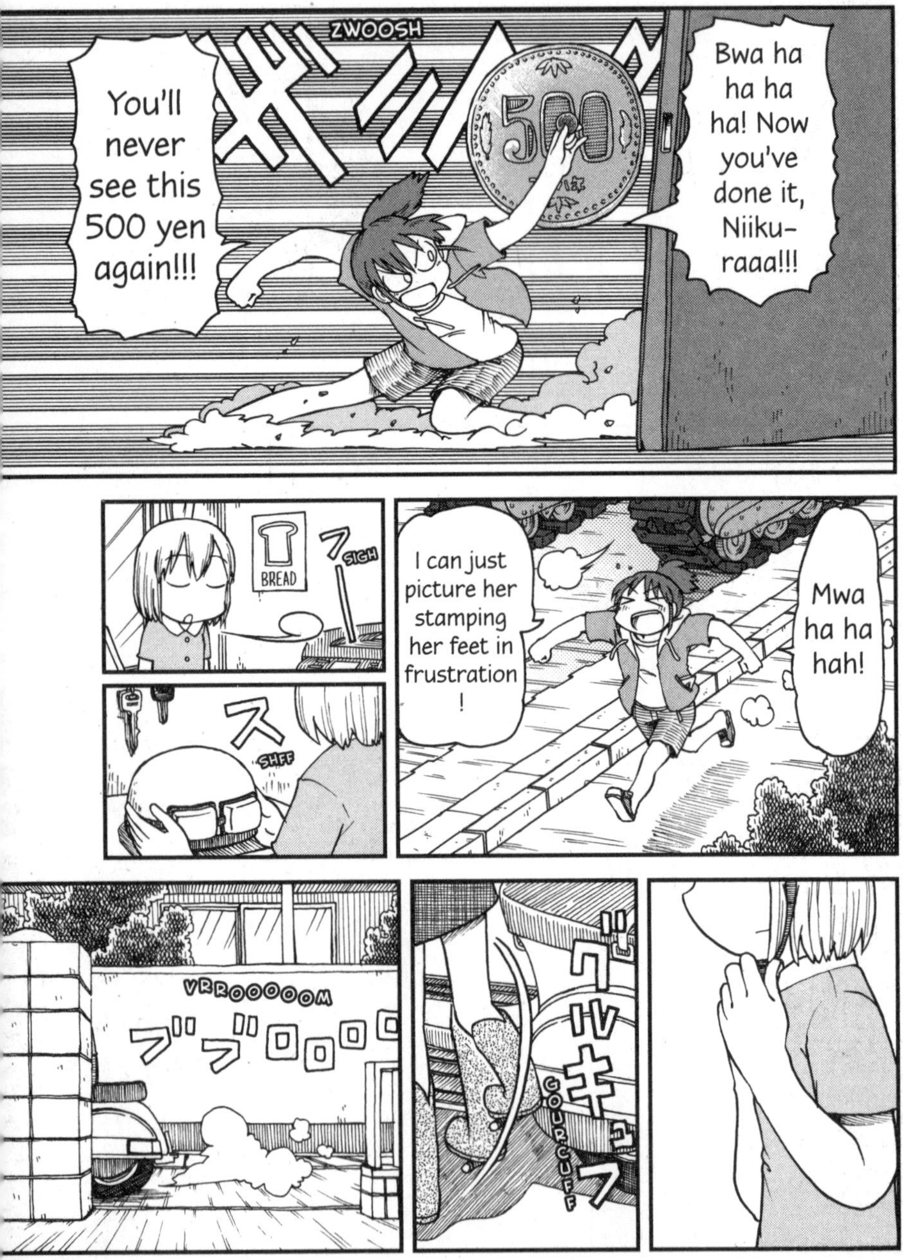
Bwa ha ha ha ha! Now you've done it, Niiku-raaa!!!
ZWOOSH
You'll never see this 500 yen again!!!
Mwa ha ha hah!
I can just picture her stamping her feet in frustration!
SIGH
BREAD
SHFF
GOURCUFF
VRROOOOOOM

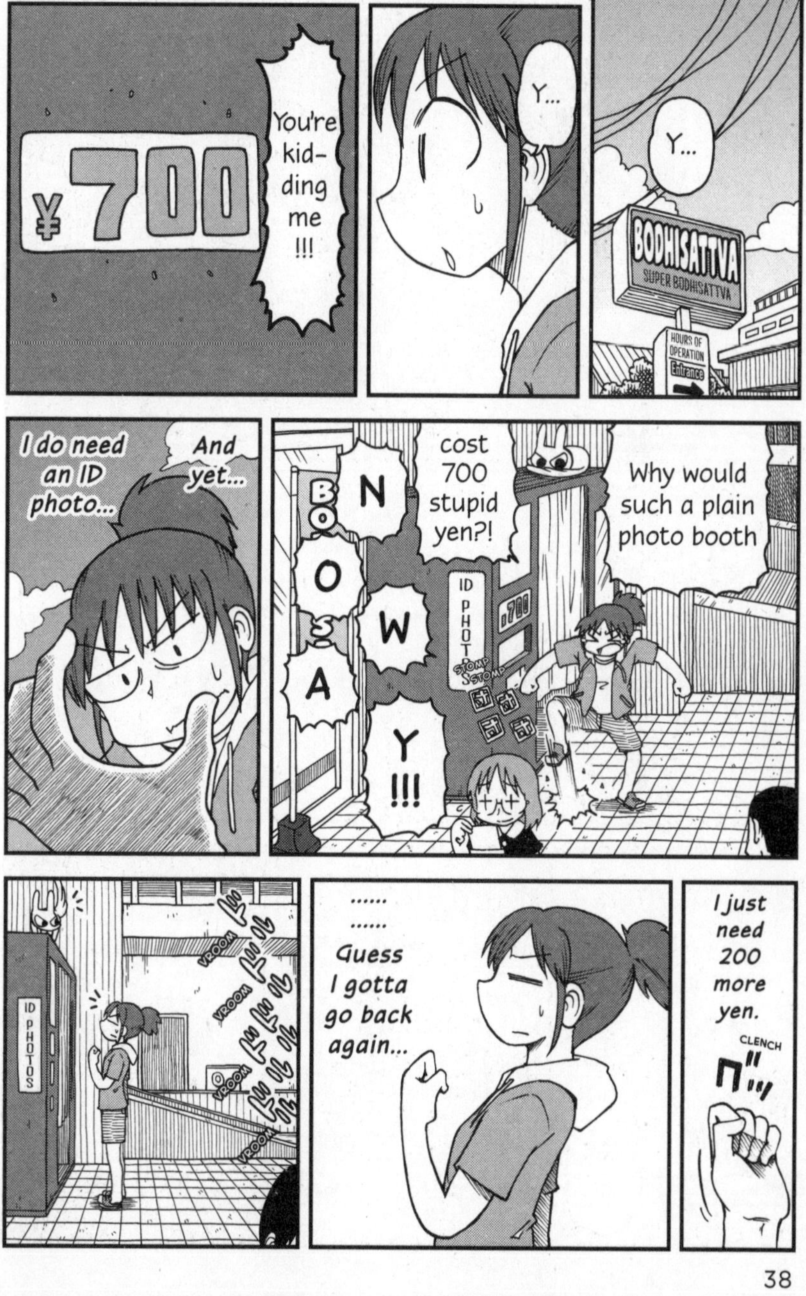
Y...
BODHISATTVA
SUPER BODHISATTVA
HOURS OF OPERATION
Entrance
Y...
You're kid-ding me !!!
¥700
Why would such a plain photo booth
cost 700 stupid yen?!
NOWAY !!!
ID PHOT
¥700
STOMP STOMP
And yet...
I do need an ID photo...
I just need 200 more yen.
CLENCH
.... Guess I gotta go back again...
VROOM
VROOM
VROOM
VROOM
ID PHOTOS

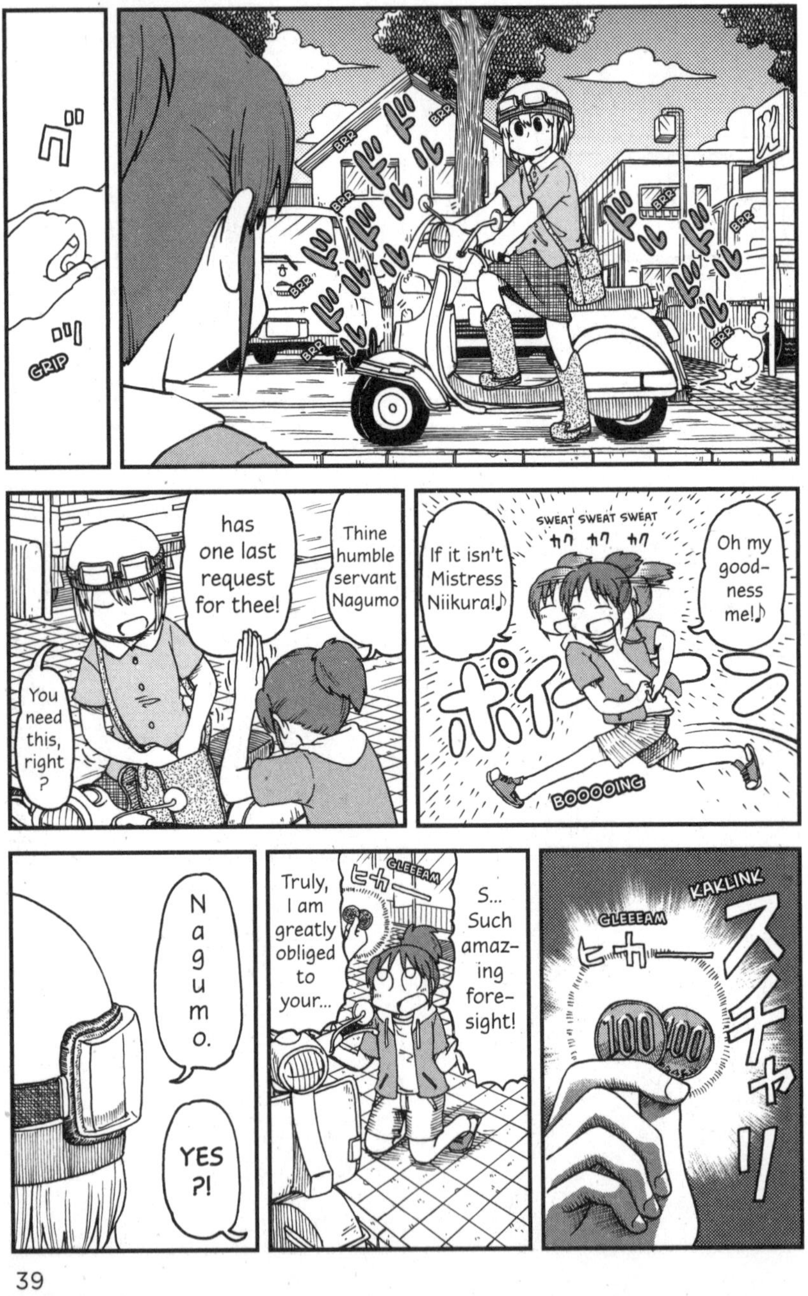
BRR
BRR
BRR
BRR
BRR
BRR
BRR
BRR
グッ
GRIP
Oh my goodness me!♪
SWEAT SWEAT SWEAT
カク カク カク
If it isn't Mistress Niikura!♪
BOOOOING
Thine humble servant Nagumo
has one last request for thee!
You need this, right?
KAKLINK
スチャリ
GLEEEAM
ヒカー
S... Such amazing foresight!
GLEEEAM
ヒカー
Truly, I am greatly obliged to your...
Nagumo.
YES?!

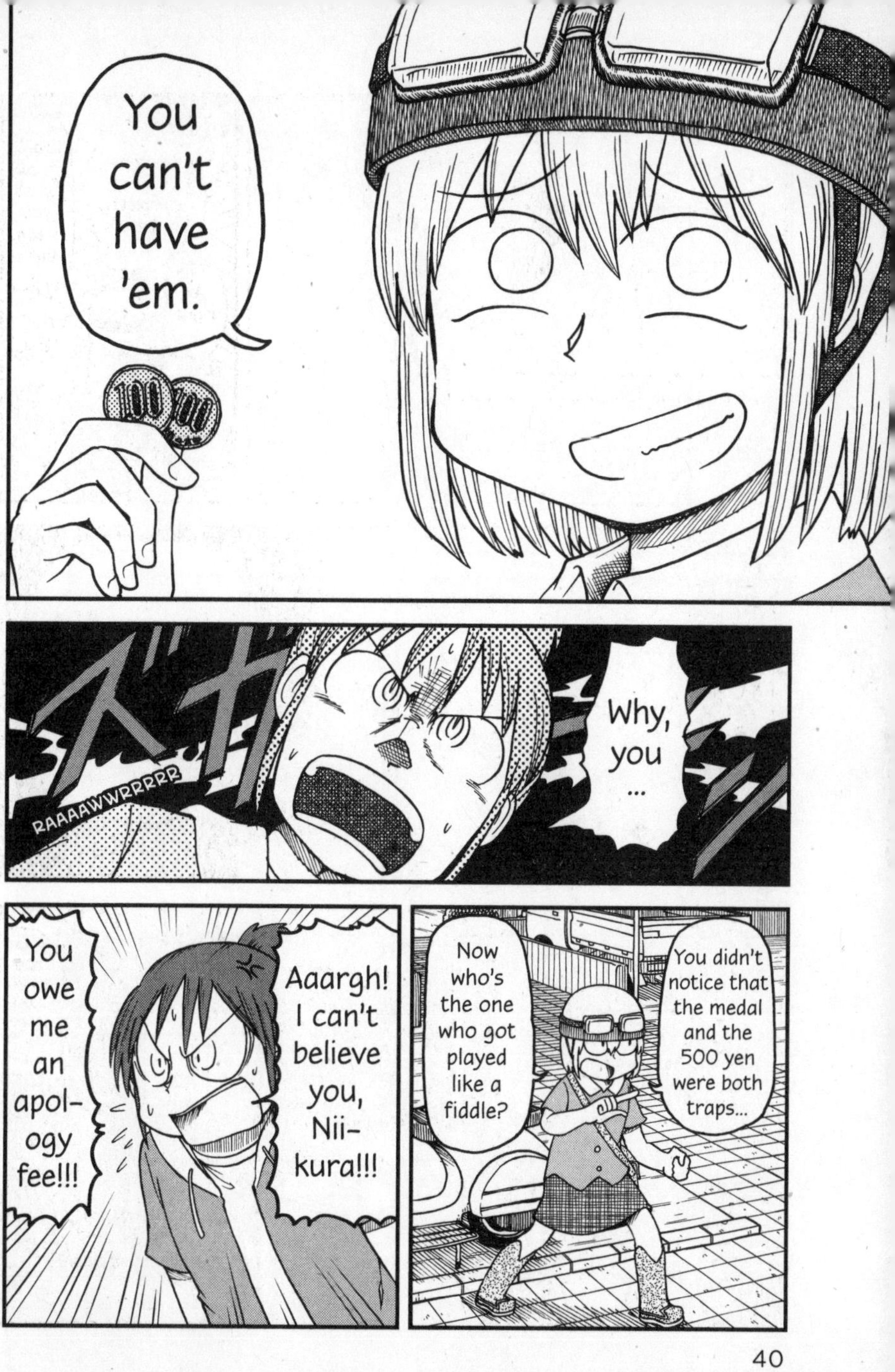
You can't have 'em.
RAAAAWWRRRRR
Why, you ...
You didn't notice that the medal and the 500 yen were both traps...
Now who's the one who got played like a fiddle?
Aaargh! I can't believe you, Nii-kura!!!
You owe me an apology fee!!!

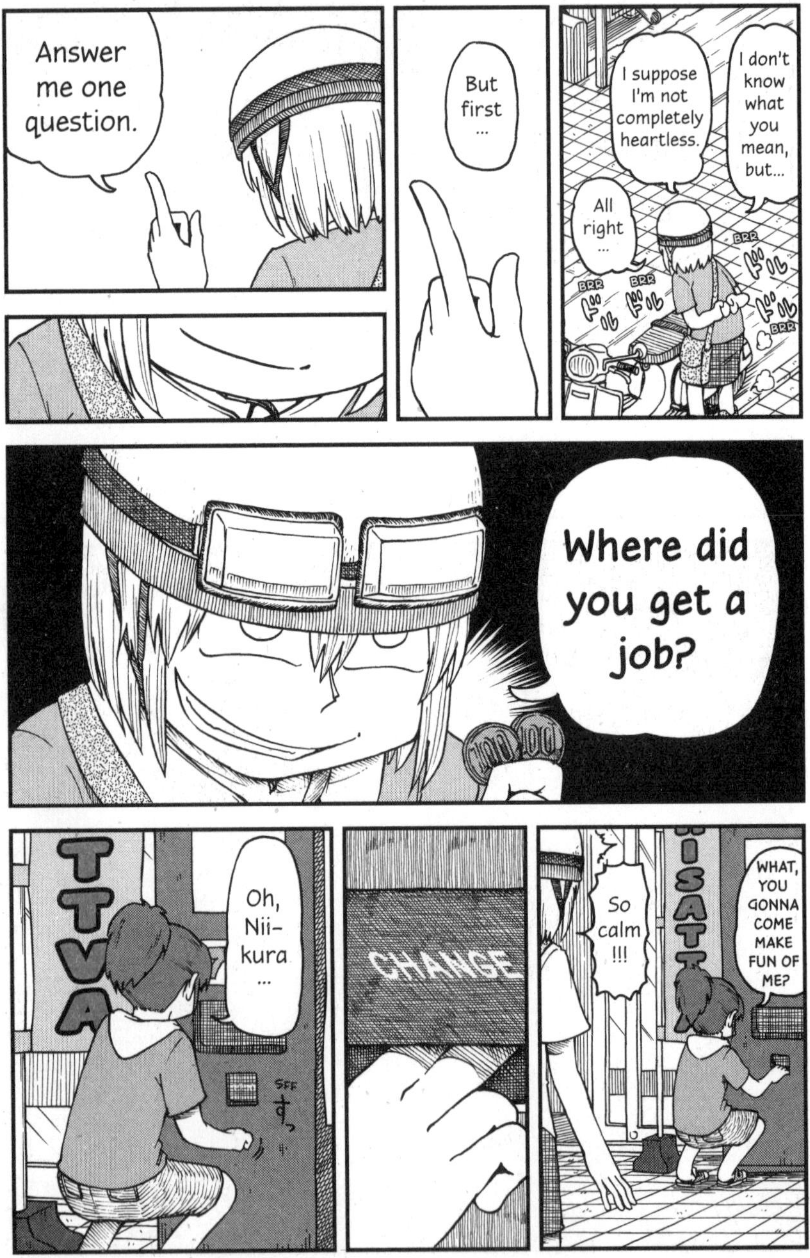
I don't know what you mean, but...
I suppose I'm not completely heartless.
All right ...
BRR ドル
BRR ドル
BRR ドル
BRR ドル
But first ...
Answer me one question.
Where did you get a job?
WHAT, YOU GONNA COME MAKE FUN OF ME?
So calm !!!
CHANGE
Oh, Nii-kura ...
SFF すっ

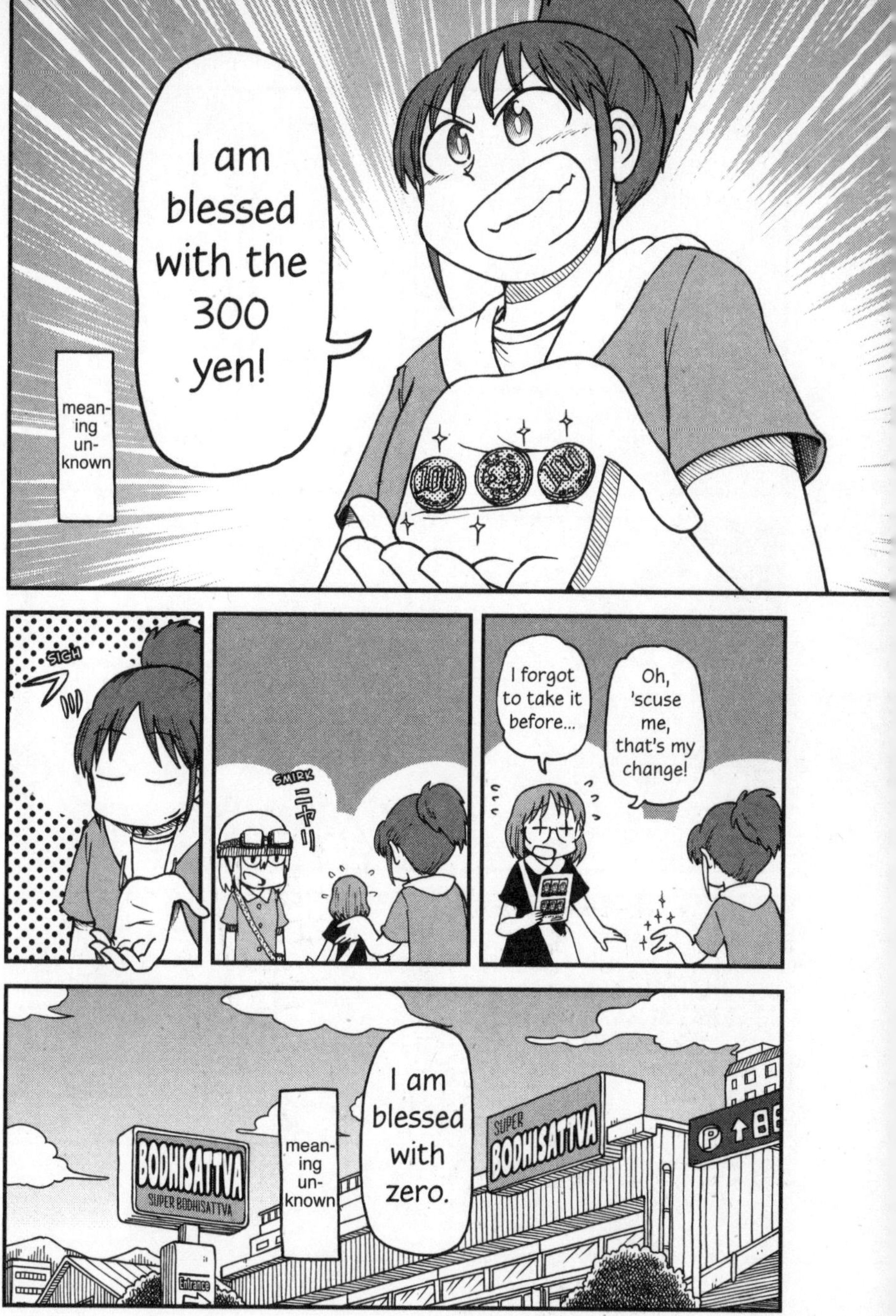
I am blessed with the 300 yen!
meaning unknown
Oh, 'scuse me, that's my change!
I forgot to take it before...
SMIRK
ニヤリ
SIGH
I am blessed with zero.
meaning unknown
SUPER BODHISATTVA
BODHISATTVA
SUPER BODHISATTVA
Entrance

Resume
Now Hiring
Apply Within
Prep in Progress
MAKABE

CITY

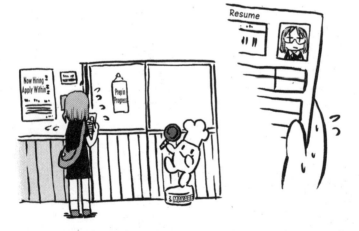

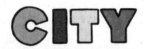

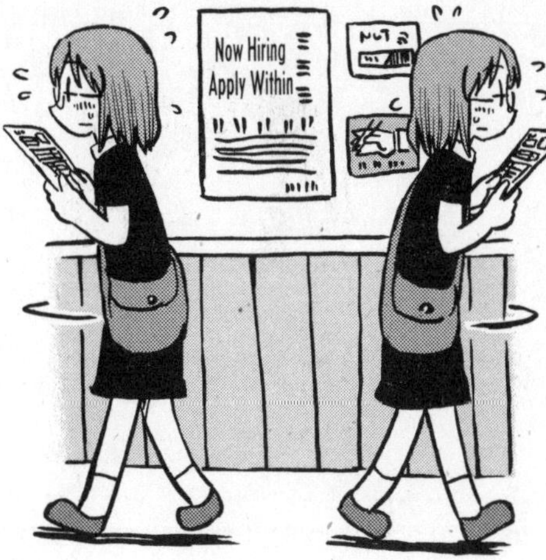
Now Hiring
Apply Within

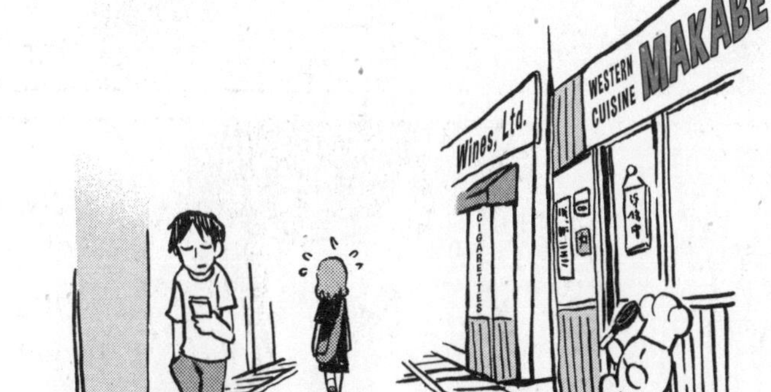
WESTERN CUISINE MAKABE
Wines, Ltd.
CIGARETTES

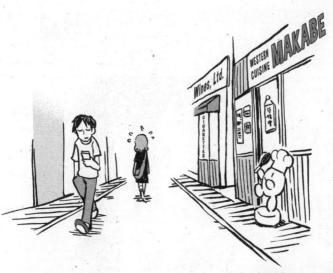

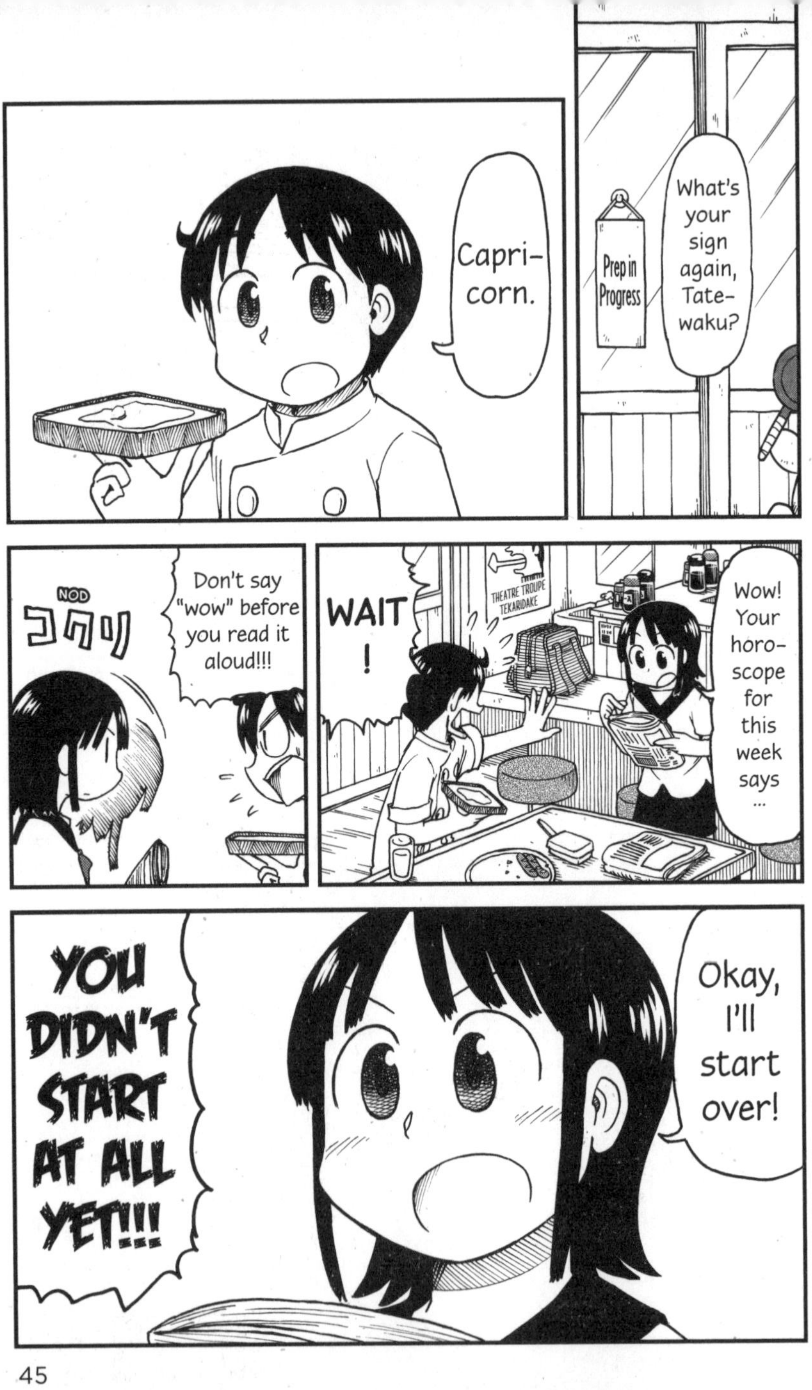
Prep in Progress
What's your sign again, Tate-waku?
Capri-corn.
Wow! Your horo-scope for this week says ...
THEATRE TROUPE TEKARIDAKE
WAIT !
Don't say "wow" before you read it aloud!!!
NOD
コクリ
Okay, I'll start over!
YOU DIDN'T START AT ALL YET!!!

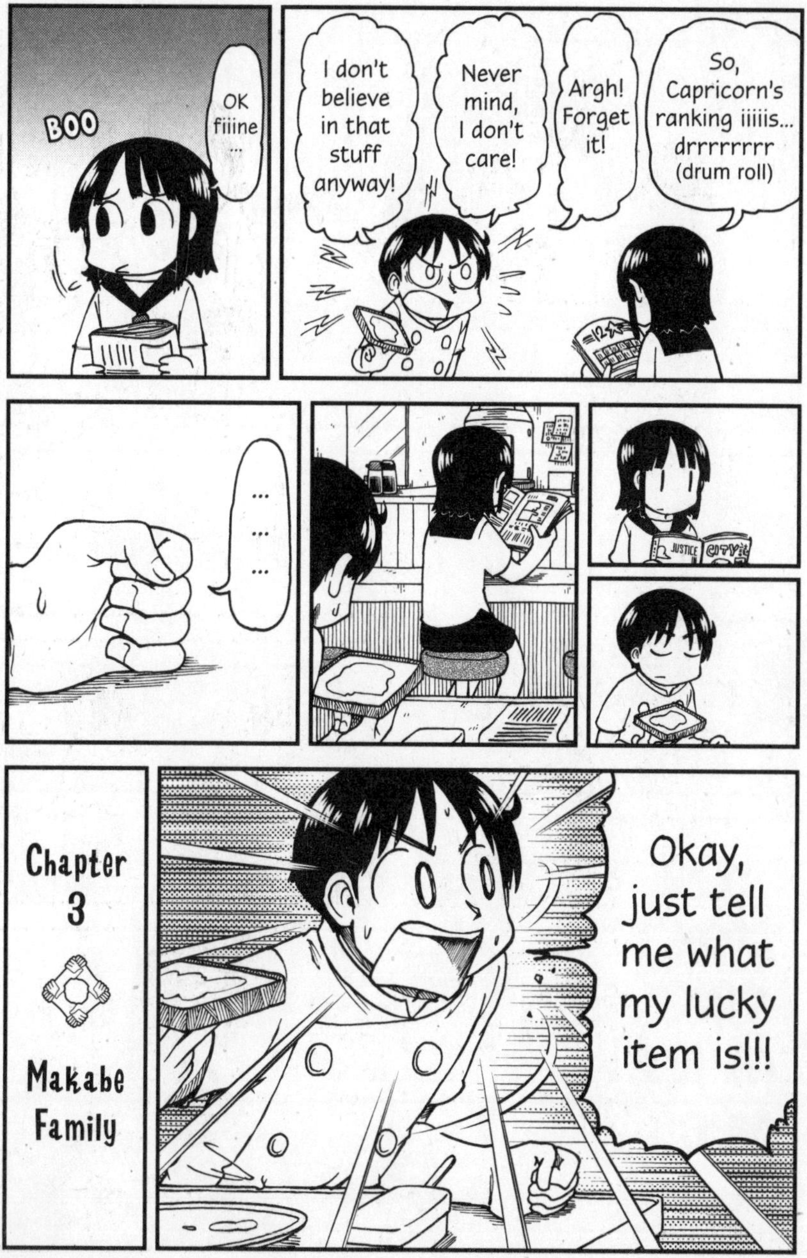
So, Capricorn's ranking iiiiis... drrrrrrrr (drum roll)
Argh! Forget it!
Never mind, I don't care!
I don't believe in that stuff anyway!
OK fiiine ...
BOO
JUSTICE
... ...
Okay, just tell me what my lucky item is!!!
Chapter 3
Makabe Family

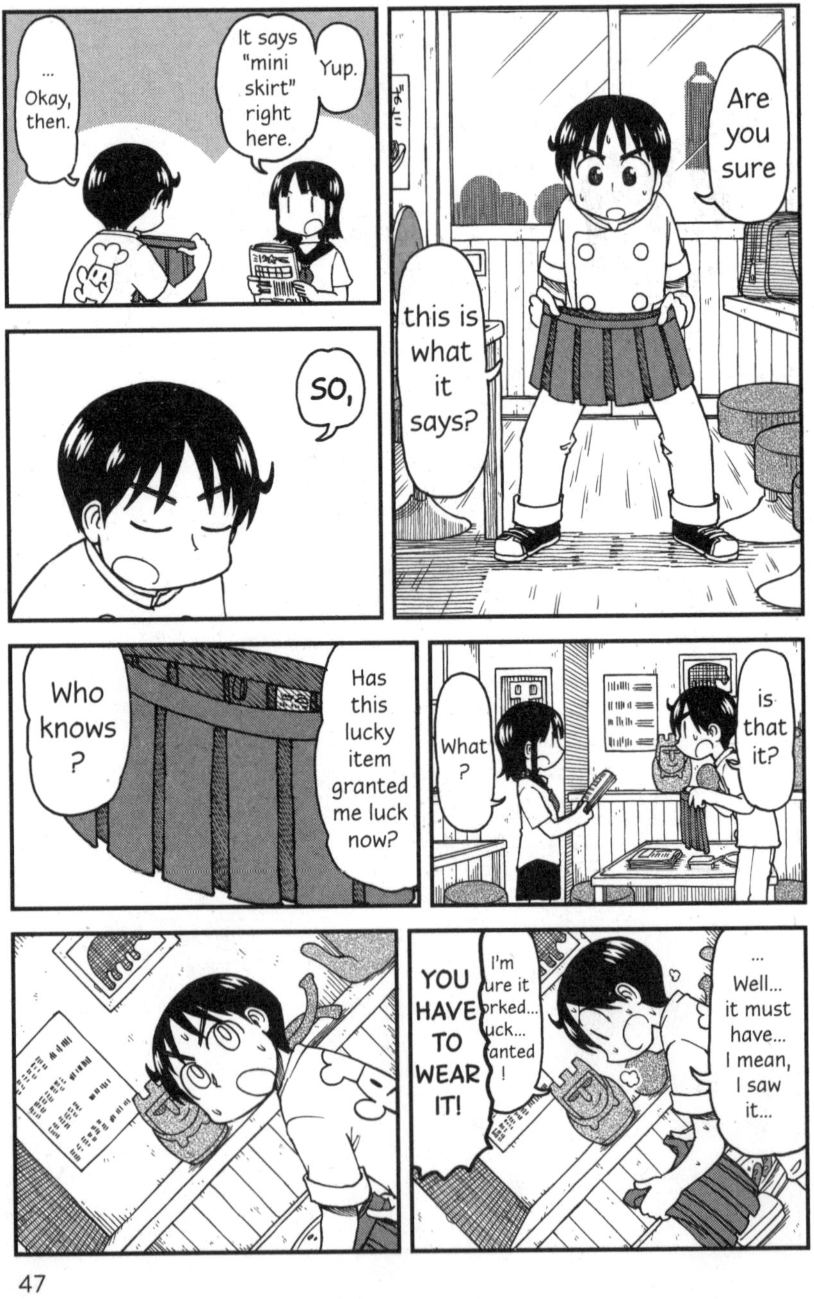

Are you sure
this is what it says?
Yup.
It says "mini skirt" right here.
... Okay, then.
SO,
is that it?
What?
Has this lucky item granted me luck now?
Who knows?
... Well... it must have... I mean, I saw it...
I'm ure it orked... uck... anted !
YOU HAVE TO WEAR IT!

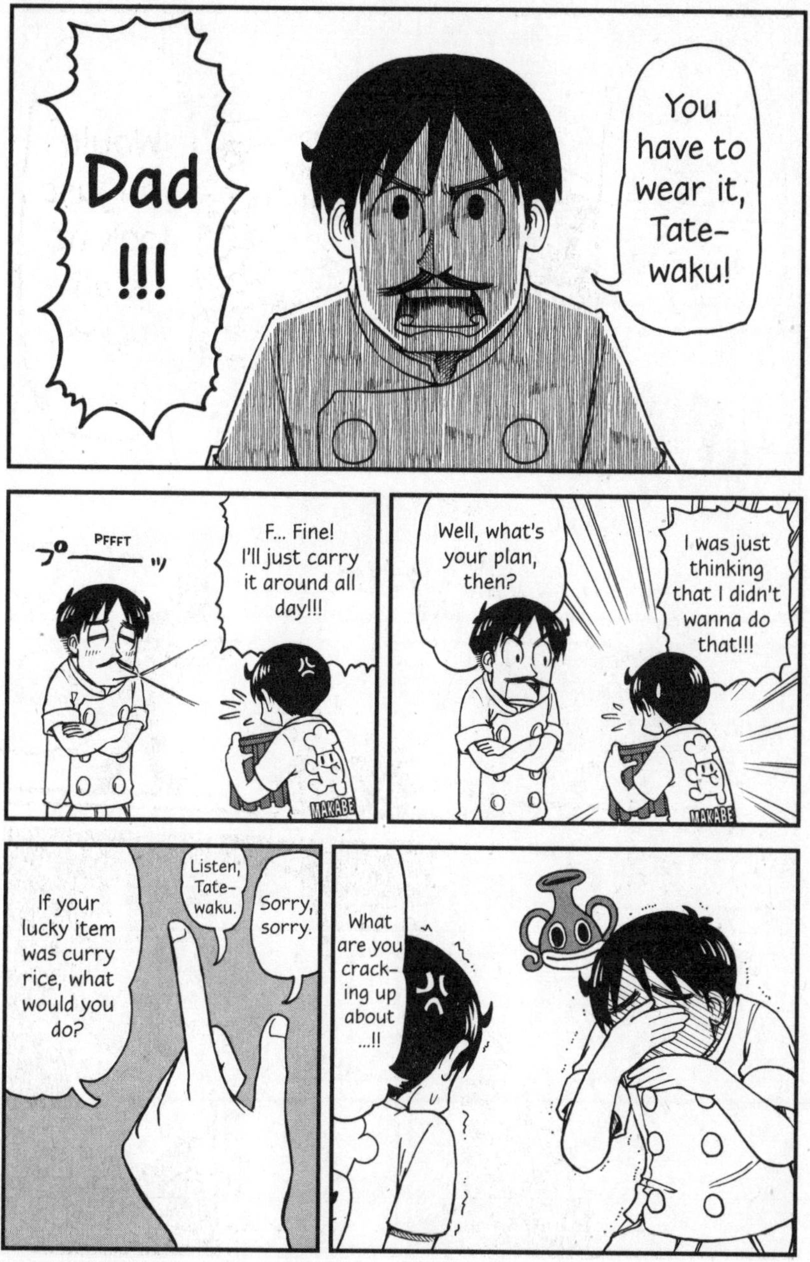
You have to wear it, Tate-waku!
Dad !!!
Well, what's your plan, then?
I was just thinking that I didn't wanna do that!!!
F... Fine! I'll just carry it around all day!!!
プ―――ッ
PFFFT
MAKABE
What are you cracking up about ...!!
Sorry, sorry.
Listen, Tate-waku.
If your lucky item was curry rice, what would you do?

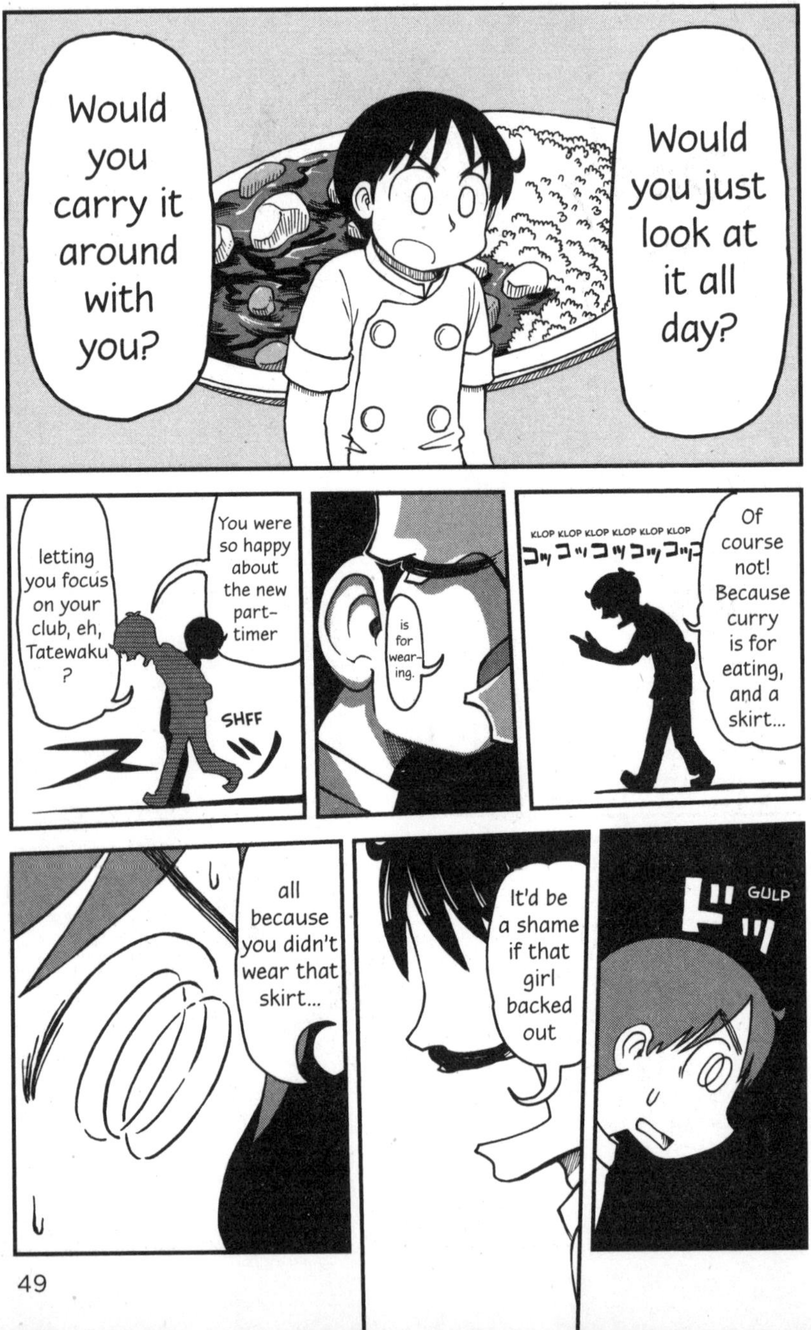

Would you just look at it all day?
Would you carry it around with you?
KLOP KLOP KLOP KLOP KLOP KLOP
Of course not! Because curry is for eating, and a skirt...
is for wear-ing.
You were so happy about the new part-timer
letting you focus on your club, eh, Tatewaku?
SHFF
GULP
It'd be a shame if that girl backed out
all because you didn't wear that skirt...

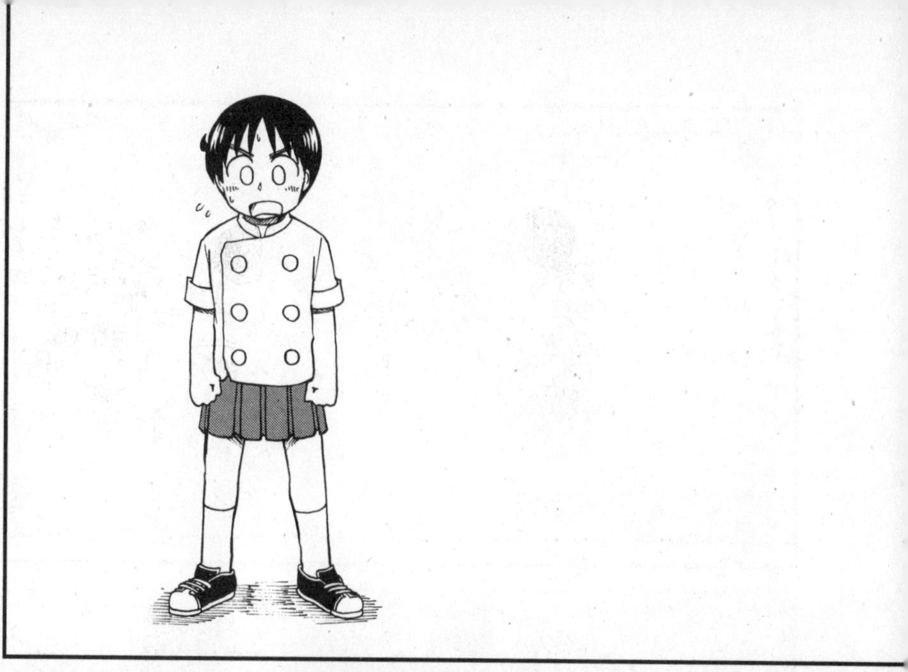

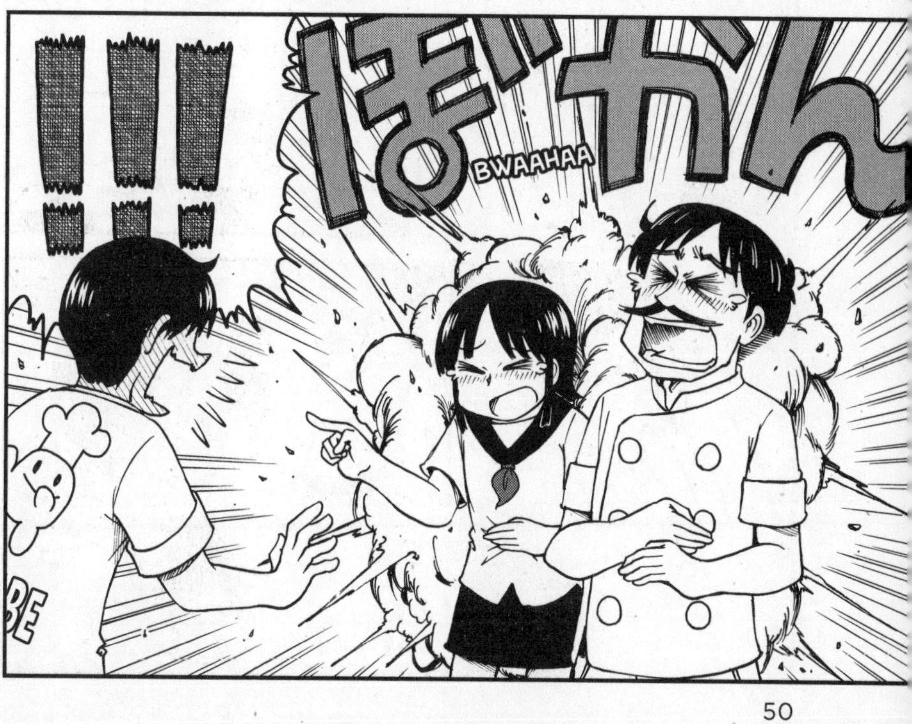
!!!
BWAAHAA

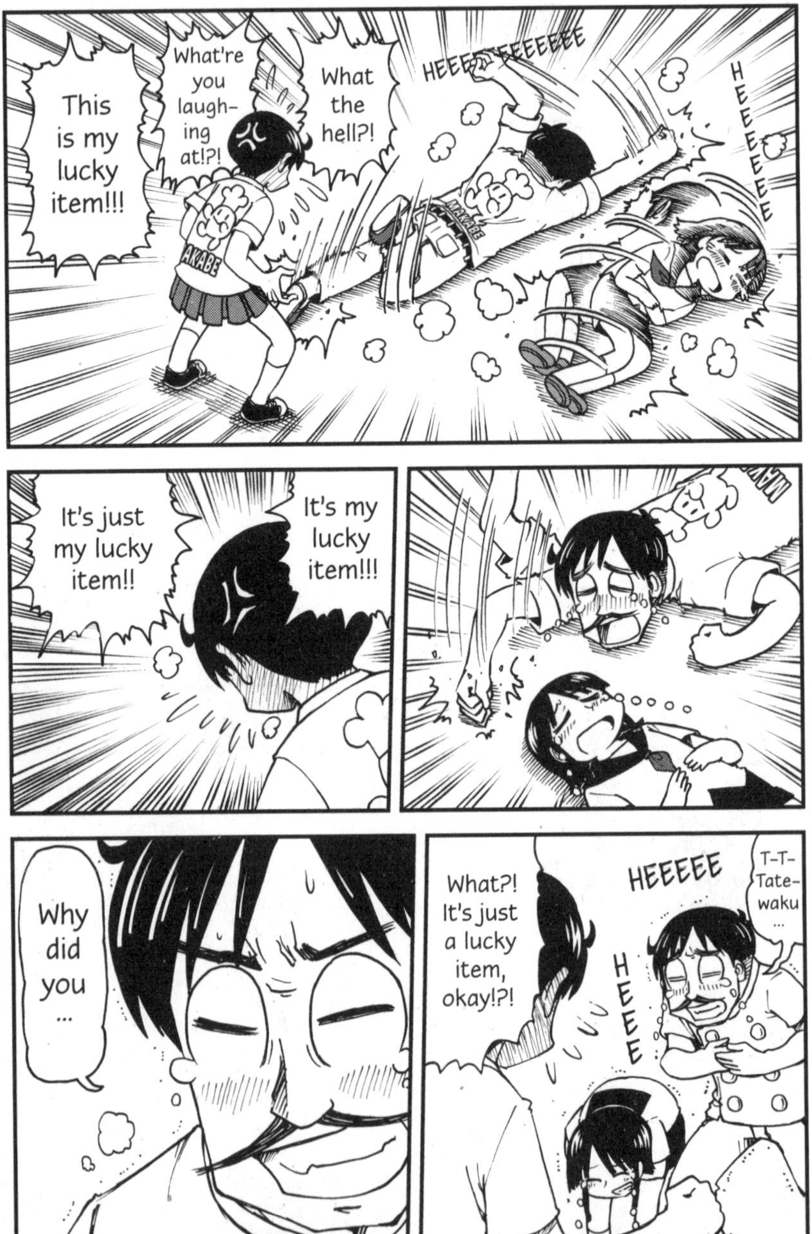
HEEEEEEE
HEEEEEEEEEEE
What the hell?!
What're you laugh-ing at!?!
This is my lucky item!!!
It's my lucky item!!!
It's just my lucky item!!
T-T-Tate-waku ...
HEEEEE
What?! It's just a lucky item, okay!?!
HEEE
Why did you ...

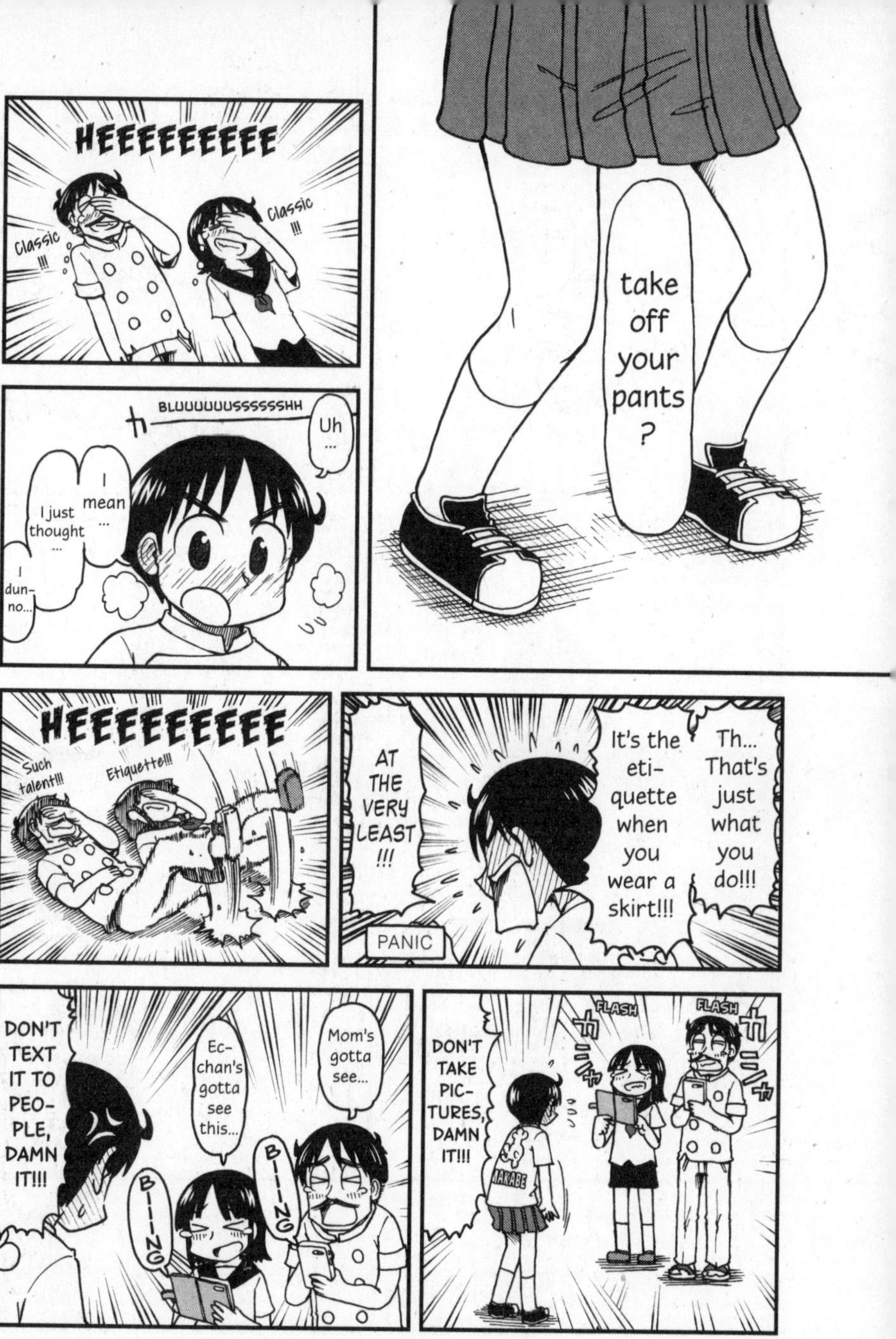
take off your pants ?
HEEEEEEEEE
Classic !!!
Classic !!!
BLUUUUUUSSSSSSHH
Uh ...
I mean ...
I just thought ...
I dun-no...
Th... That's just what you do!!!
It's the eti-quette when you wear a skirt!!!
AT THE VERY LEAST !!!
PANIC
HEEEEEEEEE
Etiquette!!!
Such talent!!!
FLASH
FLASH
DON'T TAKE PIC-TURES, DAMN IT!!!
MAKABE
Mom's gotta see...
Ec-chan's gotta see this...
BIING
BIING
DON'T TEXT IT TO PEO-PLE, DAMN IT!!!

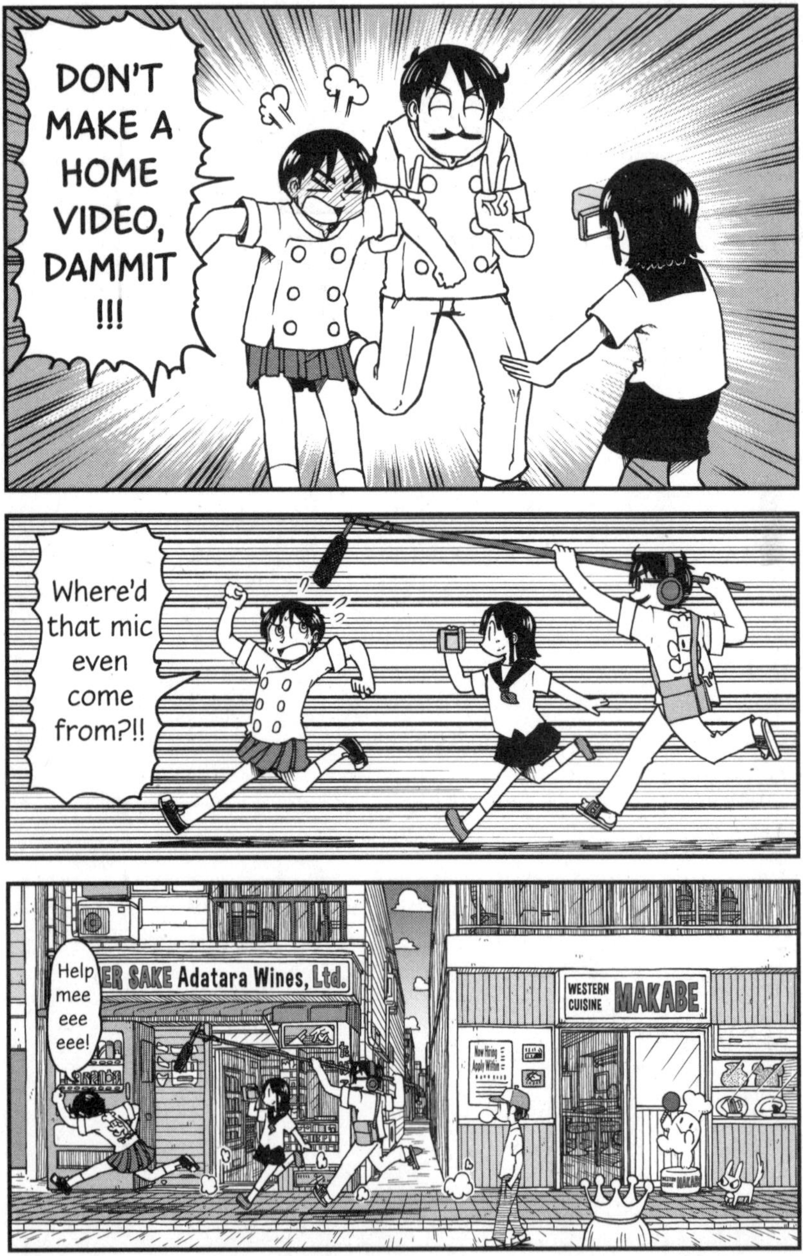
DON'T MAKE A HOME VIDEO, DAMMIT!!!
Where'd that mic even come from?!!
ER SAKE Adatara Wines, Ltd.
Help mee eee eee!
WESTERN CUISINE MAKABE
Now Hiring Apply Within

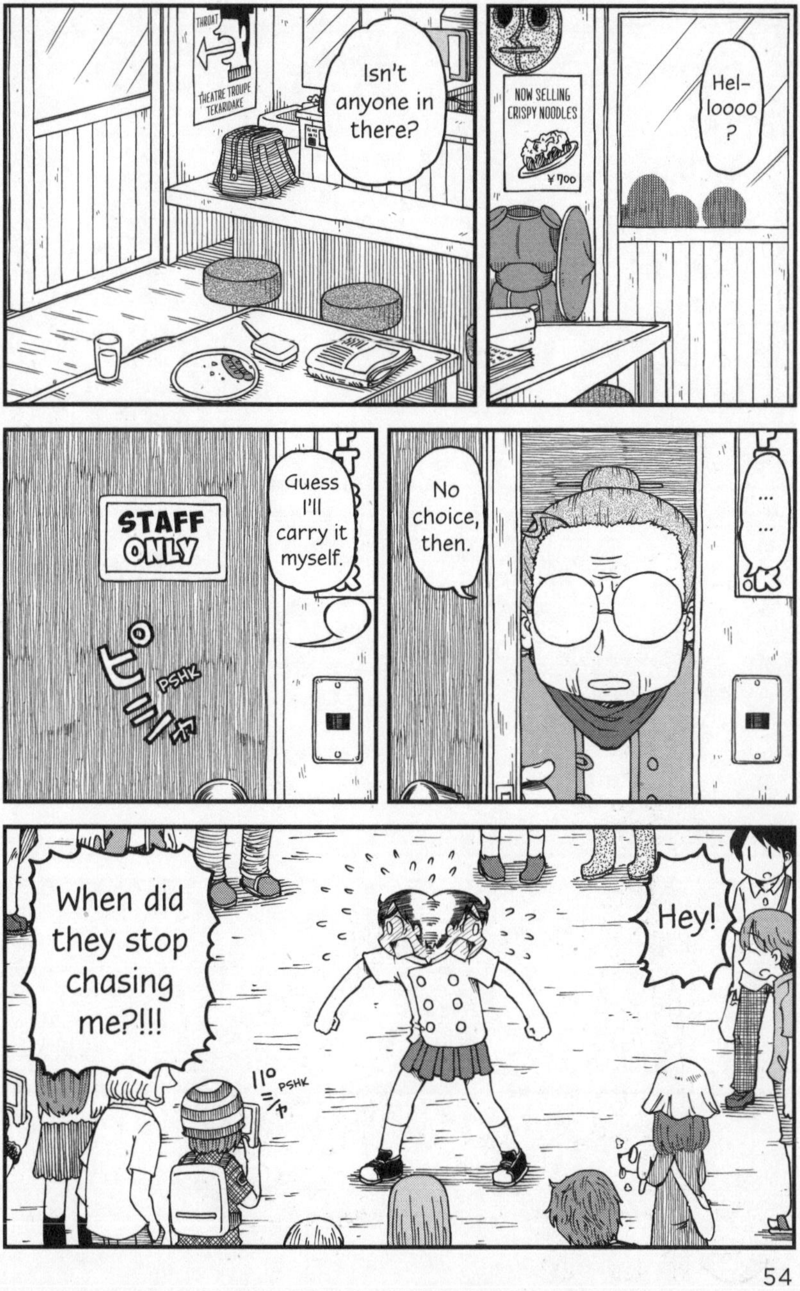
Hel-loooo?
NOW SELLING CRISPY NOODLES
¥700
THROAT
THEATRE TROUPE TEKARIDAKE
Isn't anyone in there?
……
……
No choice, then.
Guess I'll carry it myself.
STAFF ONLY
PSHK
Hey!
When did they stop chasing me?!!!
PSHK

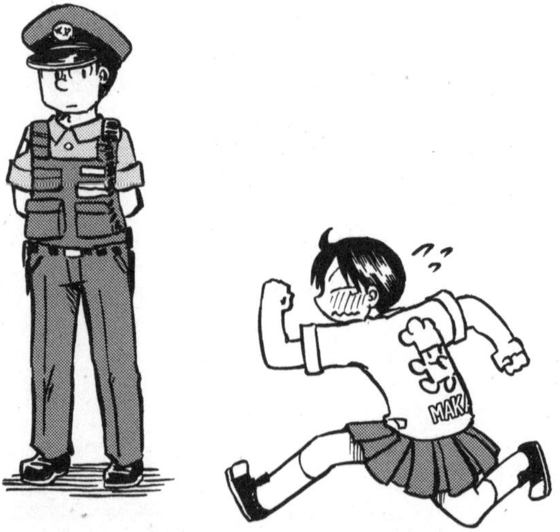
MAKA

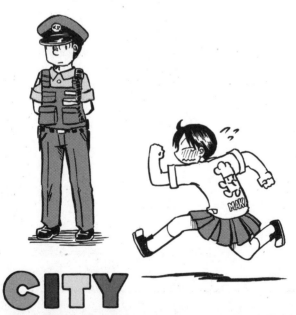

CITY

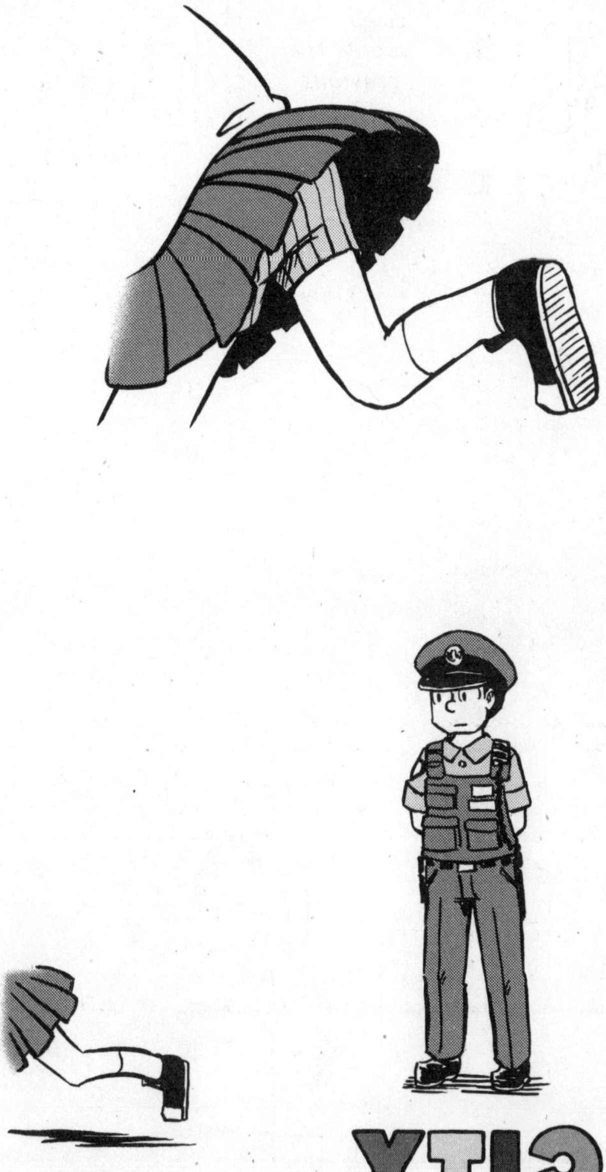
CITY

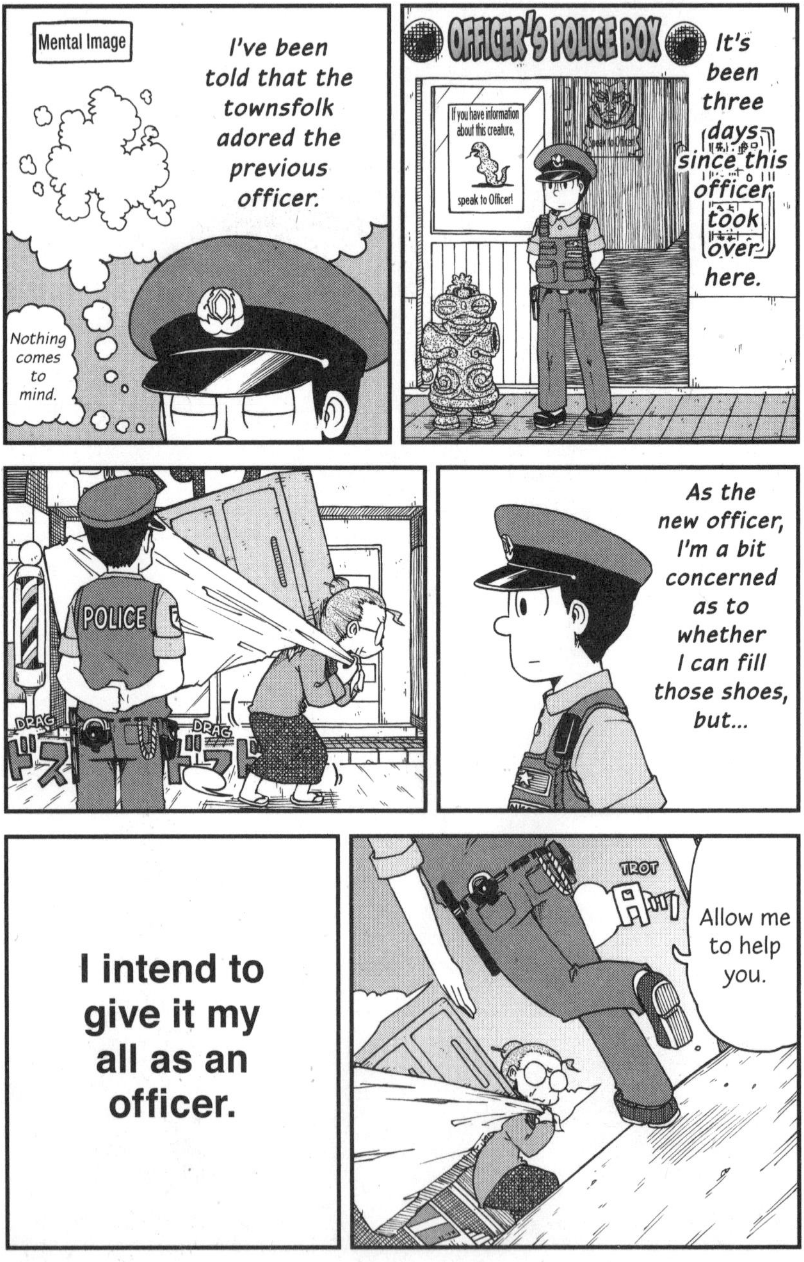
OFFICER'S POLICE BOX
If you have information about this creature,
speak to Officer!
It's been three days since this officer took over here.
Mental Image
I've been told that the townsfolk adored the previous officer.
Nothing comes to mind.
As the new officer, I'm a bit concerned as to whether I can fill those shoes, but...
POLICE
DRAG
DRAG
TROT
Allow me to help you.
I intend to give it my all as an officer.

POLICE
KRAK

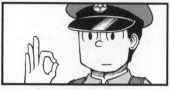

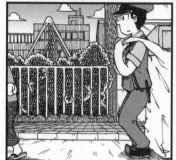

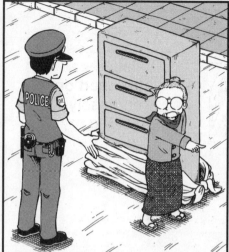

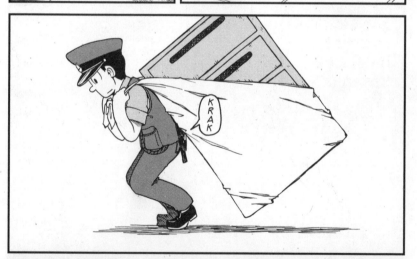

Chapter 4 Officer

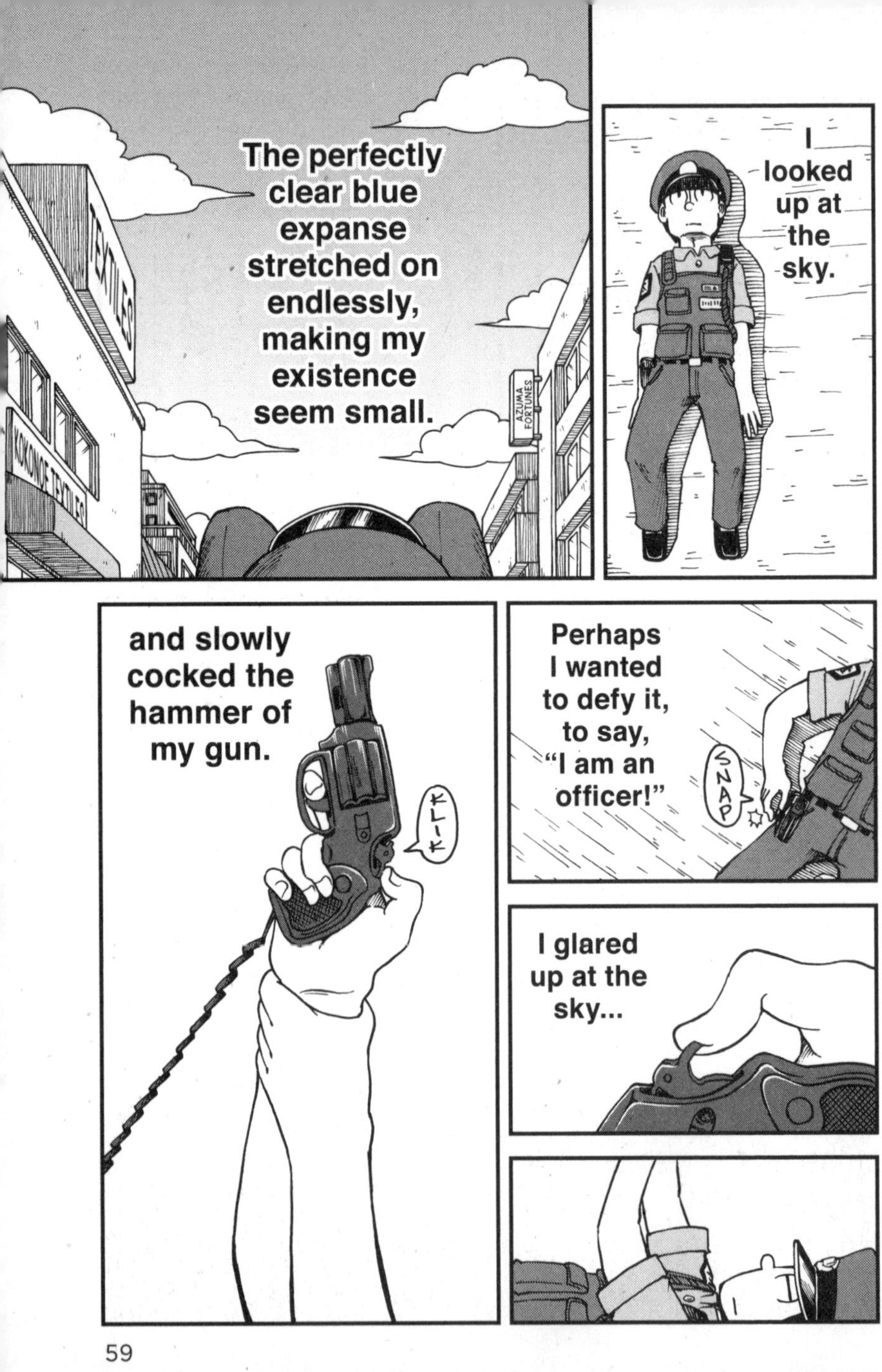
I looked up at the sky.
The perfectly clear blue expanse stretched on endlessly, making my existence seem small.
TEXTILES
KOKONOE TEXTILES
AZUMA FORTUNES
Perhaps I wanted to defy it, to say, "I am an officer!"
SNAP
I glared up at the sky...
and slowly cocked the hammer of my gun.
KLIK

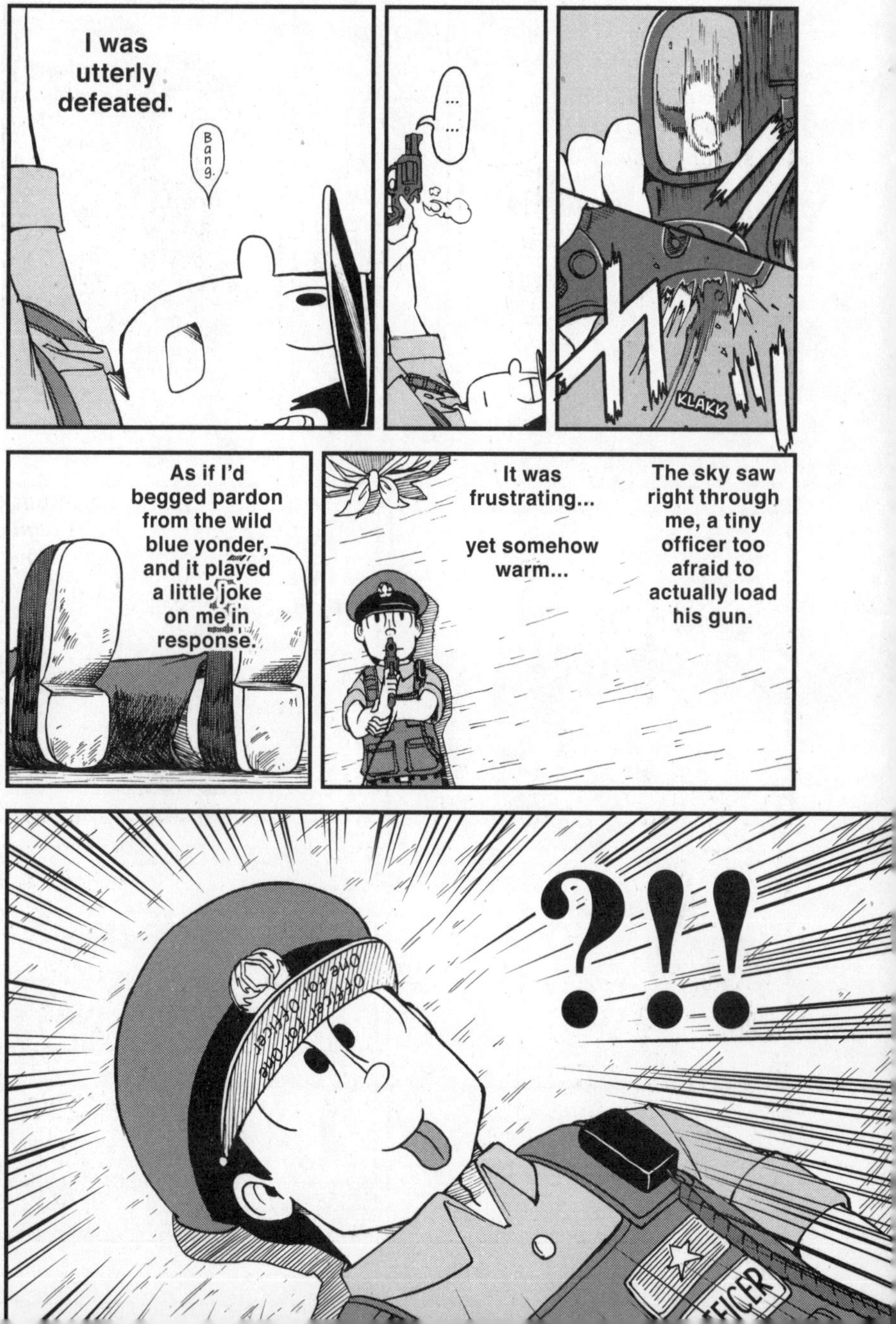
KLAKK
...
...
I was utterly defeated.
Bang.
The sky saw right through me, a tiny officer too afraid to actually load his gun.
It was frustrating...
yet somehow warm...
As if I'd begged pardon from the wild blue yonder, and it played a little joke on me in response.
?!!
Officer for One
One for Officer

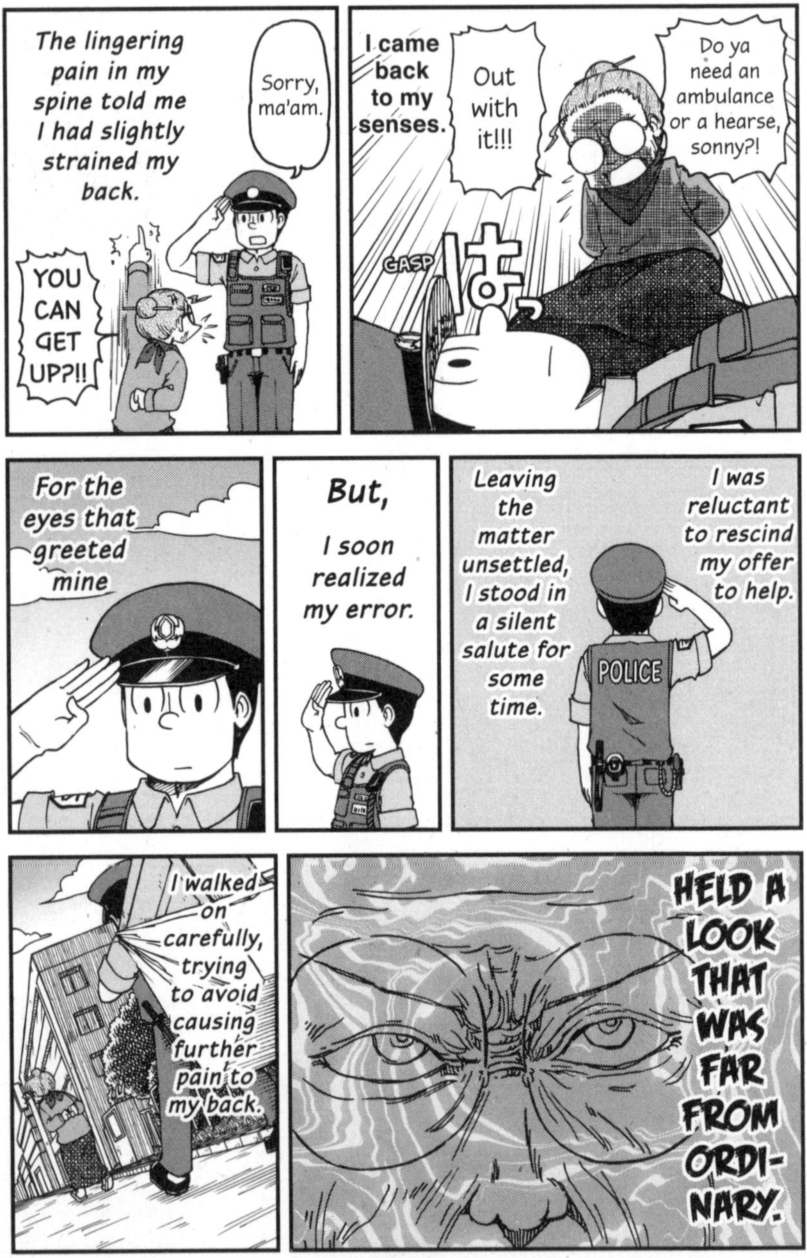
Do ya need an ambulance or a hearse, sonny?!
Out with it!!!
I came back to my senses.
GASP
はっ
Sorry, ma'am.
The lingering pain in my spine told me I had slightly strained my back.
YOU CAN GET UP?!!
I was reluctant to rescind my offer to help.
Leaving the matter unsettled, I stood in a silent salute for some time.
POLICE
But,
I soon realized my error.
For the eyes that greeted mine
HELD A LOOK THAT WAS FAR FROM ORDI-NARY.
I walked on carefully, trying to avoid causing further pain to my back.

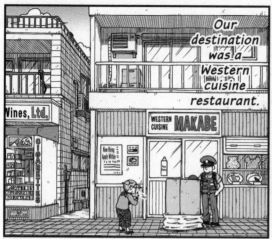

WHUMP
Our destination was a Western cuisine restaurant.
Wines, Ltd.
WESTERN CUISINE MAKABE
Now Hiring Apply Within
CIGARETTES
Apparently, this was the restaurant of the chef I'd met earlier.
OFFICER
Well then,
if you'll excuse this officer...
JUST A MIN-UTE.
OFFICER
Go to this ad-dress
and bring me all these items, y'hear?

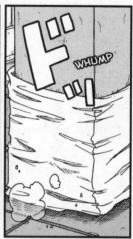

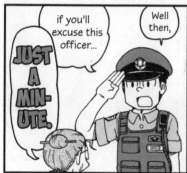

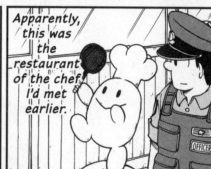

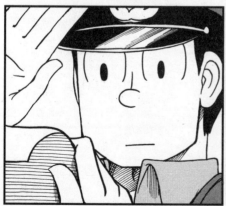

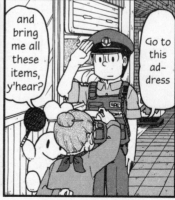

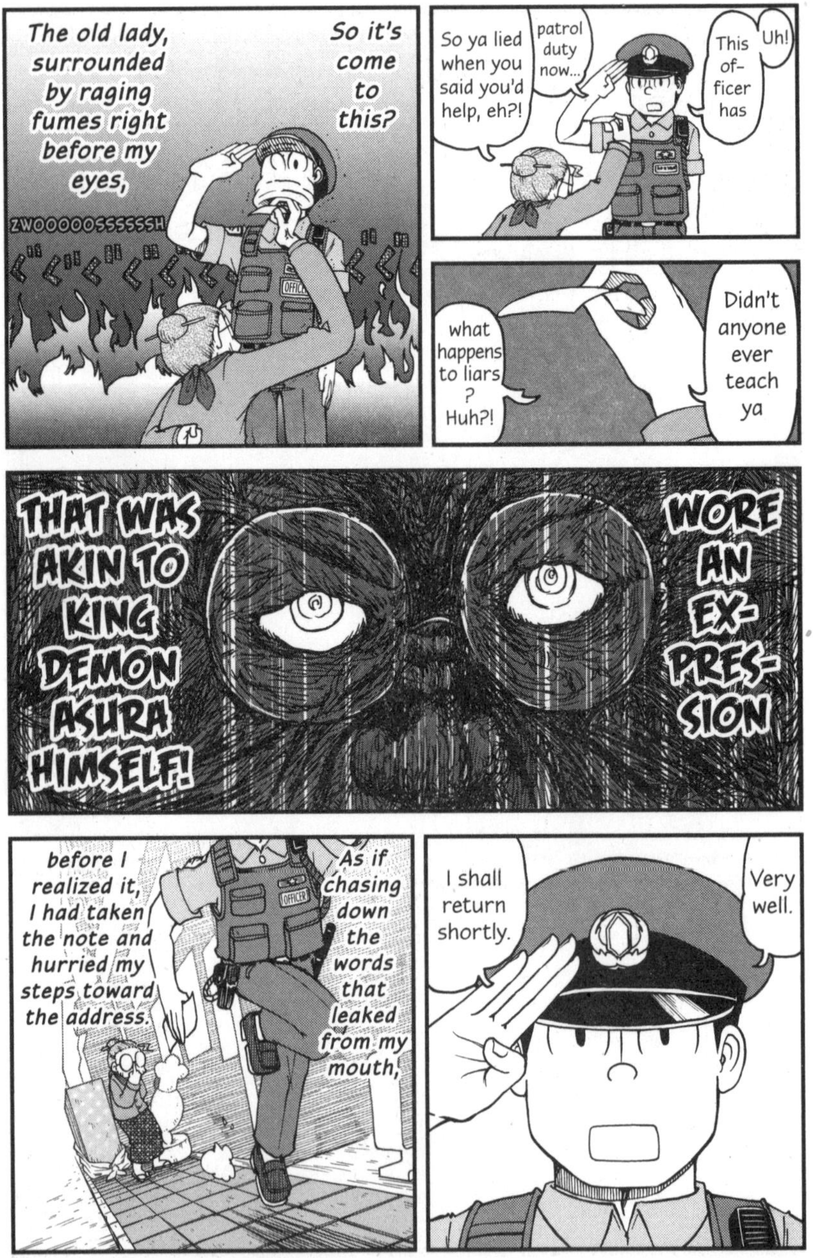
Uh!
This officer has
patrol duty now...
So ya lied when you said you'd help, eh?!
Didn't anyone ever teach ya
what happens to liars? Huh?!
So it's come to this?
The old lady, surrounded by raging fumes right before my eyes,
ZWOOOOOSSSSSSH
WORE AN EX-PRES-SION
THAT WAS AKIN TO KING DEMON ASURA HIMSELF!
Very well.
I shall return shortly.
As if chasing down the words that leaked from my mouth,
before I realized it, I had taken the note and hurried my steps toward the address.

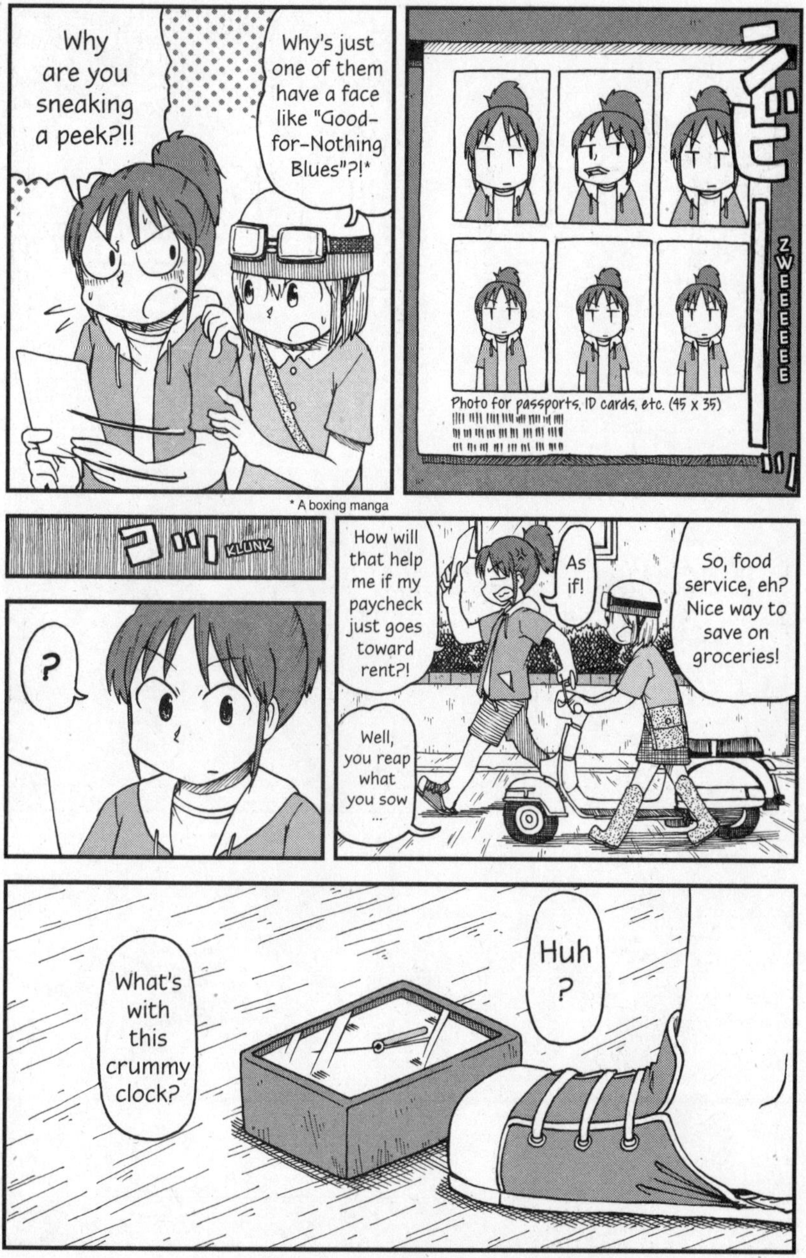
Photo for passports, ID cards, etc. (45 x 35)
ZWEEEEEEE
Why's just one of them have a face like "Good-for-Nothing Blues"?!*
Why are you sneaking a peek?!!
So, food service, eh? Nice way to save on groceries!
As if!
How will that help me if my paycheck just goes toward rent?!
Well, you reap what you sow ...
KLUNK
?
Huh ?
What's with this crummy clock?
* A boxing manga

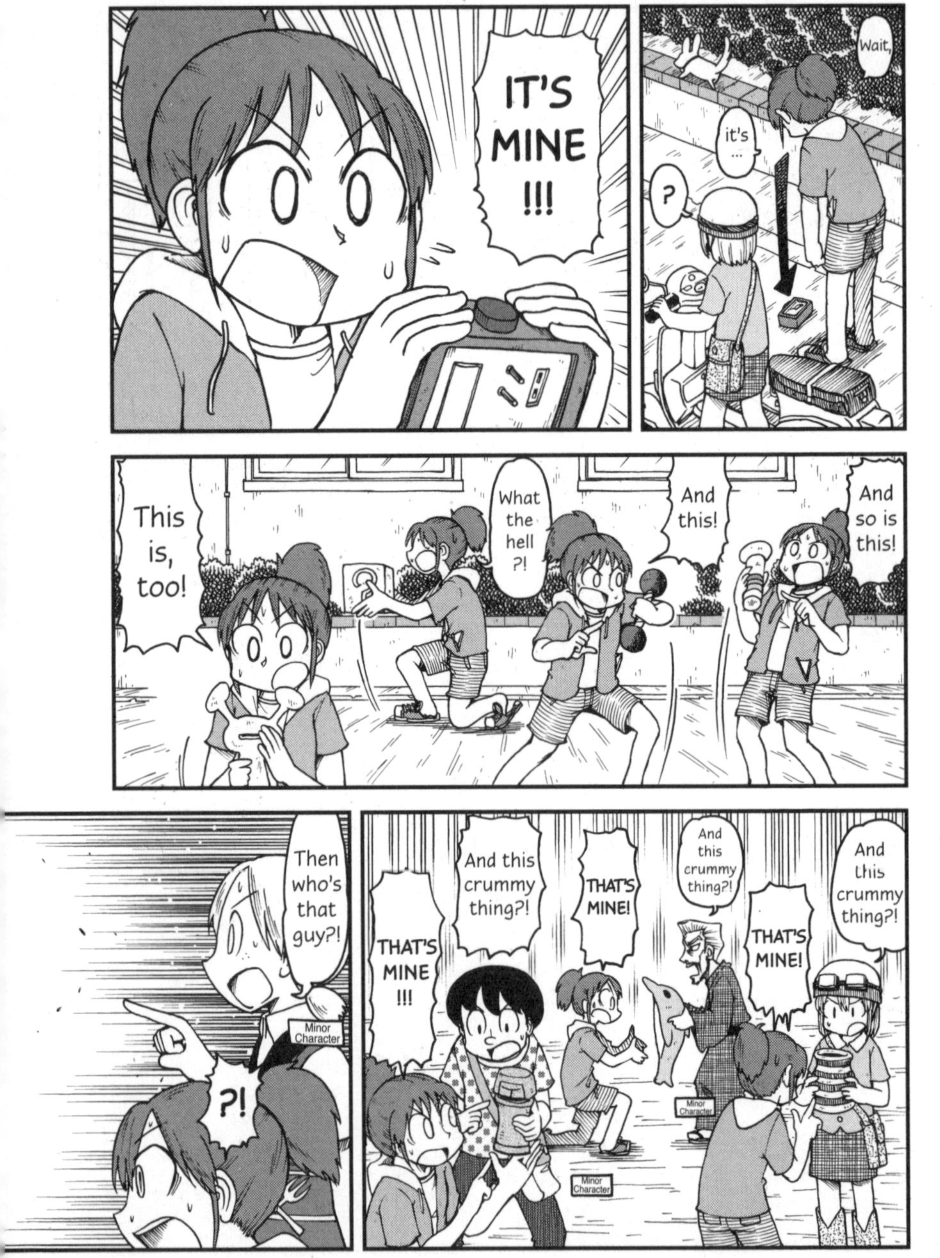

Wait,
it's ...
?
IT'S MINE !!!
And so is this!
And this!
What the hell ?!
This is, too!
And this crummy thing?!
And this crummy thing?!
THAT'S MINE!
THAT'S MINE!
Minor Character
And this crummy thing?!
THAT'S MINE !!!
Minor Character
Then who's that guy?!
Minor Character
?!

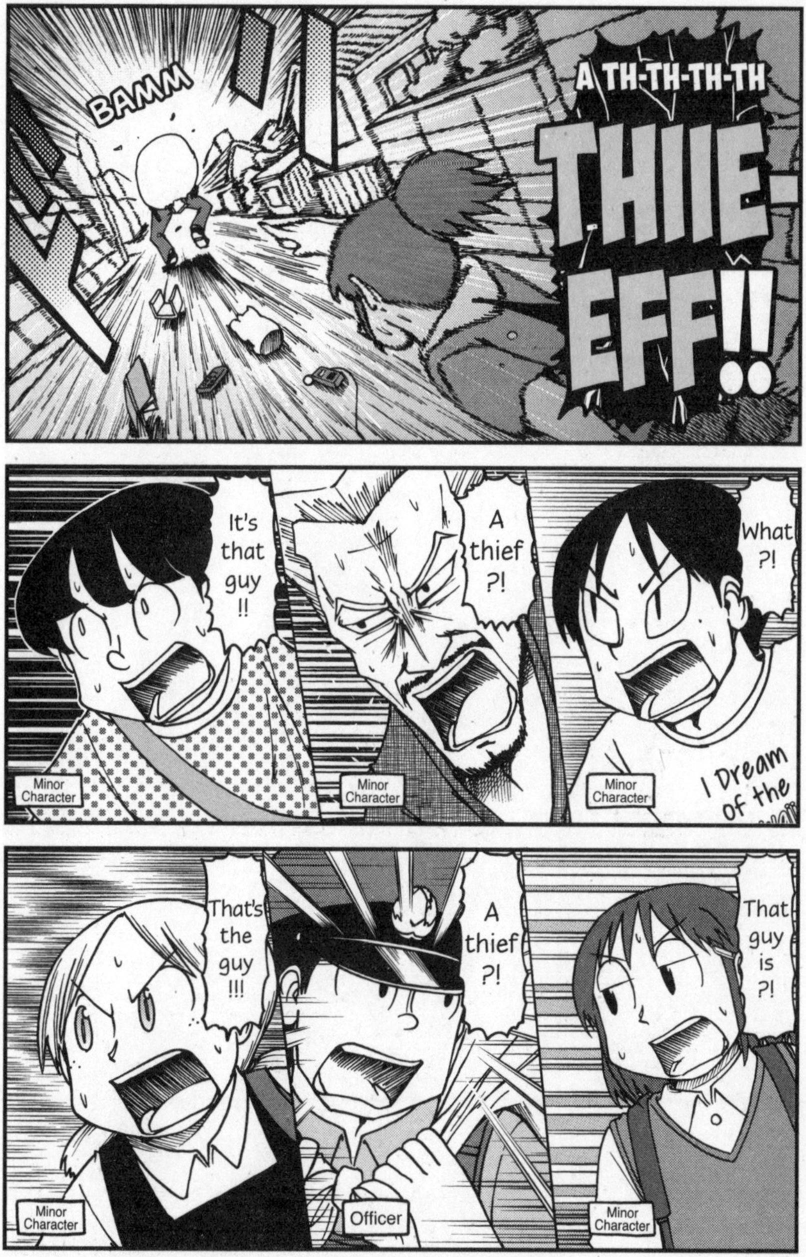
A TH-TH-TH-TH
THIIE-EFF!!
BAMM
What ?!
Minor Character
I Dream of the
A thief ?!
Minor Character
It's that guy !!
Minor Character
That guy is ?!
Minor Character
A thief ?!
Officer
That's the guy !!!
Minor Character

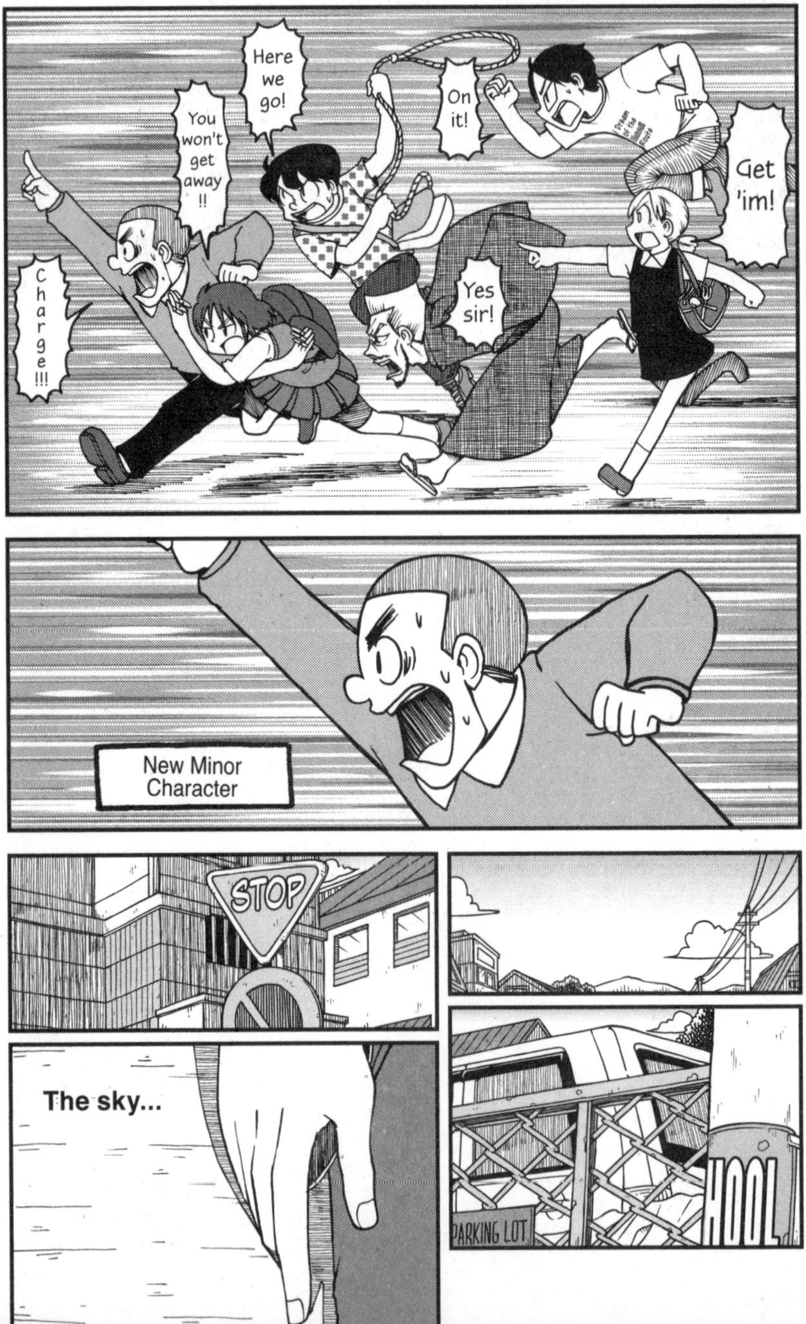
Get 'im!
On it!
Yes sir!
Here we go!
You won't get away!!
Charge!!!
New Minor Character
STOP
HOOL
PARKING LOT
The sky...

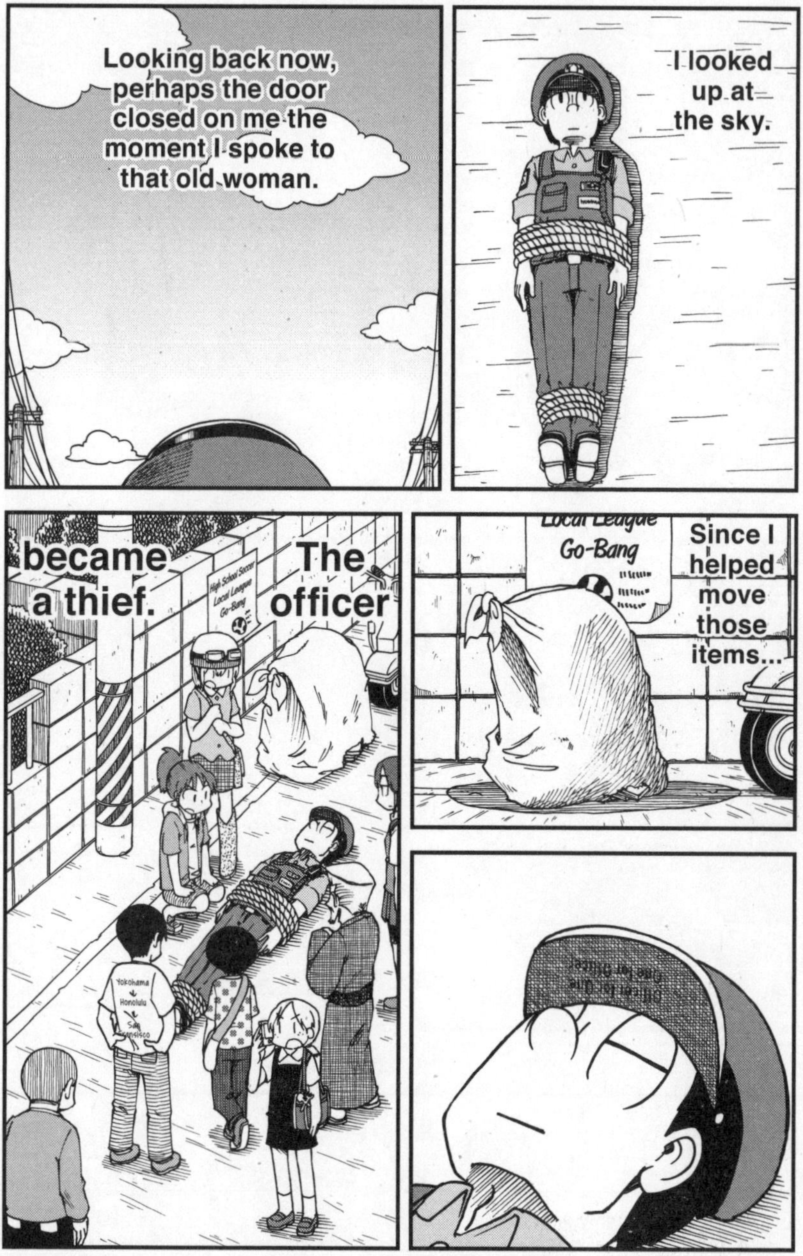
I looked up at the sky.
Looking back now, perhaps the door closed on me the moment I spoke to that old woman.
Go-Bang
Since I helped move those items...
The officer became a thief.
High School Soccer Local League Go-Bang
Yokohama
Honolulu

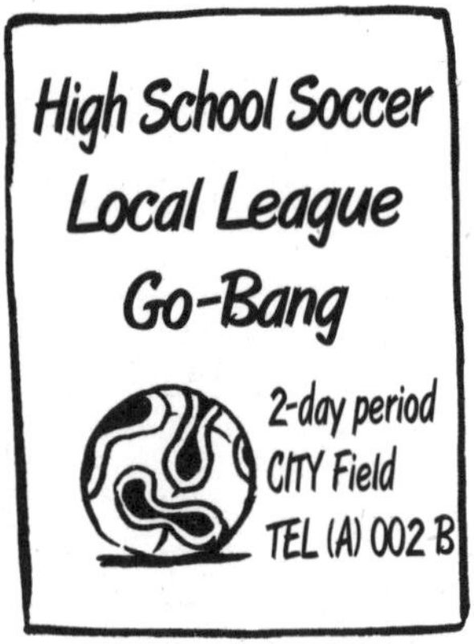

High School Soccer
Local League
Go-Bang

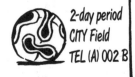

2-day period
CITY Field
TEL (A) 002 B

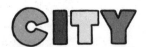

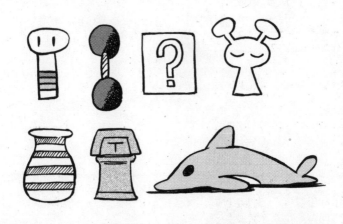

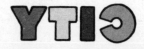

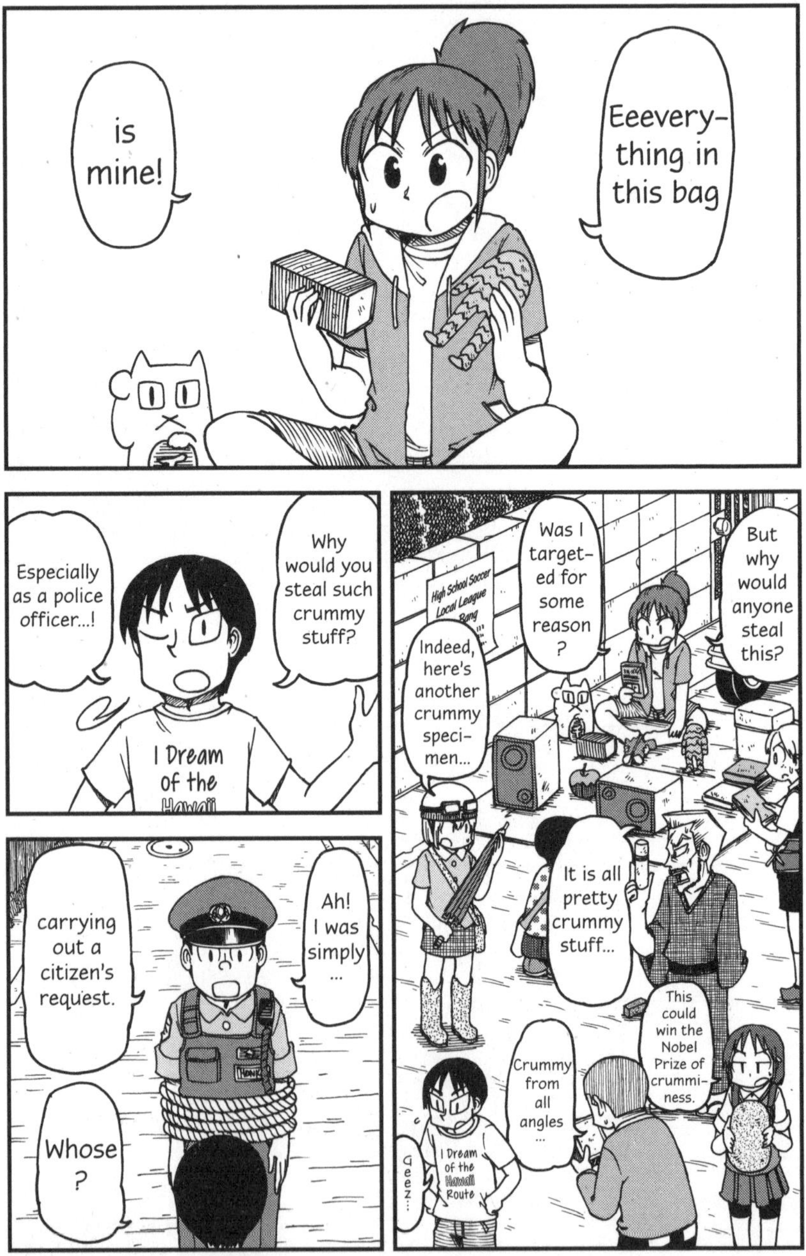
Eeevery-thing in this bag
is mine!
But why would anyone steal this?
Was I target-ed for some reason?
High School Soccer Local League Bang
Indeed, here's another crummy speci-men...
It is all pretty crummy stuff...
This could win the Nobel Prize of crummi-ness.
Crummy from all angles...
Geez...
I Dream of the Hawaii Route
Why would you steal such crummy stuff?
Especially as a police officer...!
I Dream of the
Ah! I was simply ...
carrying out a citizen's request.
Whose?

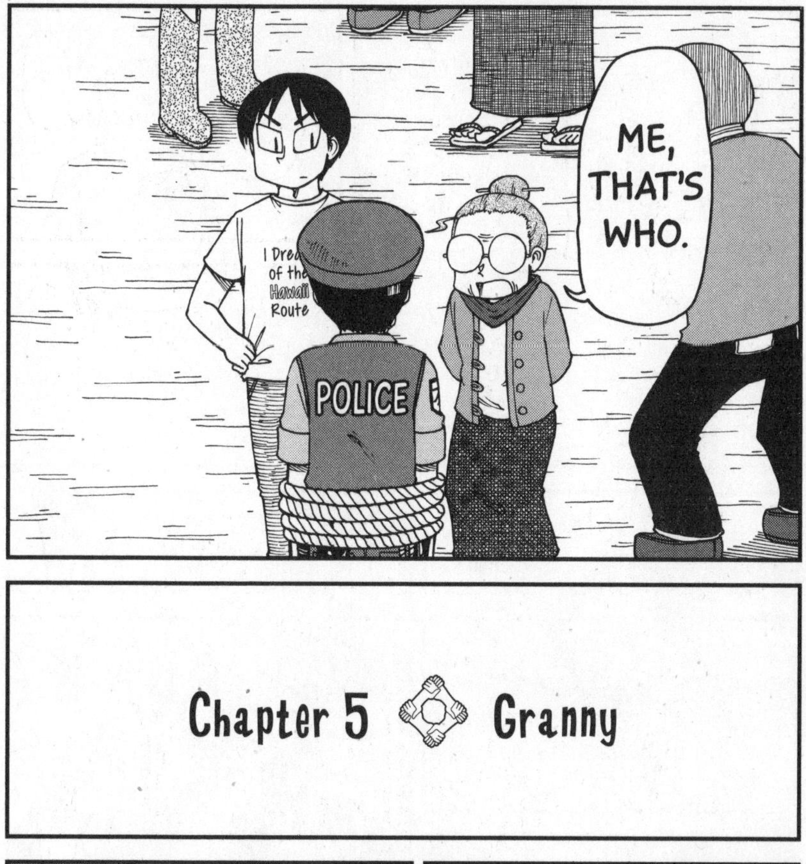
ME, THAT'S WHO.
POLICE

Chapter 5 Granny

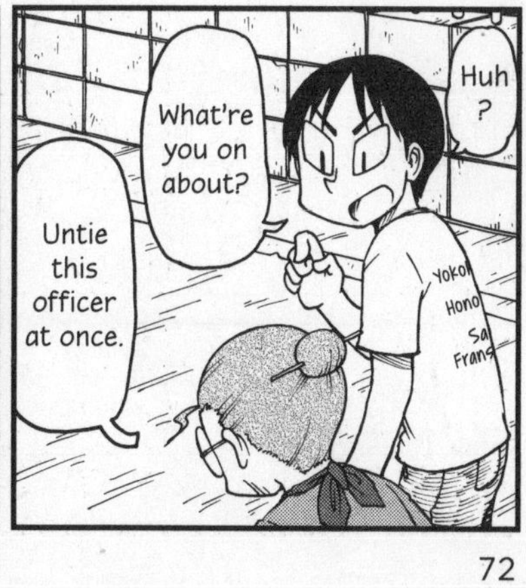
Huh?
What're you on about?
Untie this officer at once.

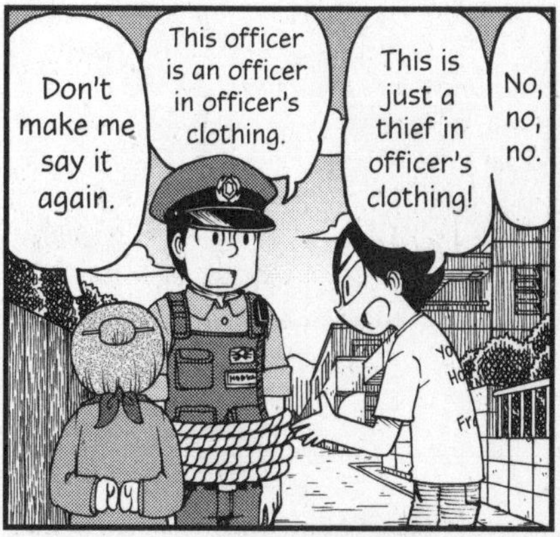
No, no, no.
This is just a thief in officer's clothing!
This officer is an officer in officer's clothing.
Don't make me say it again.

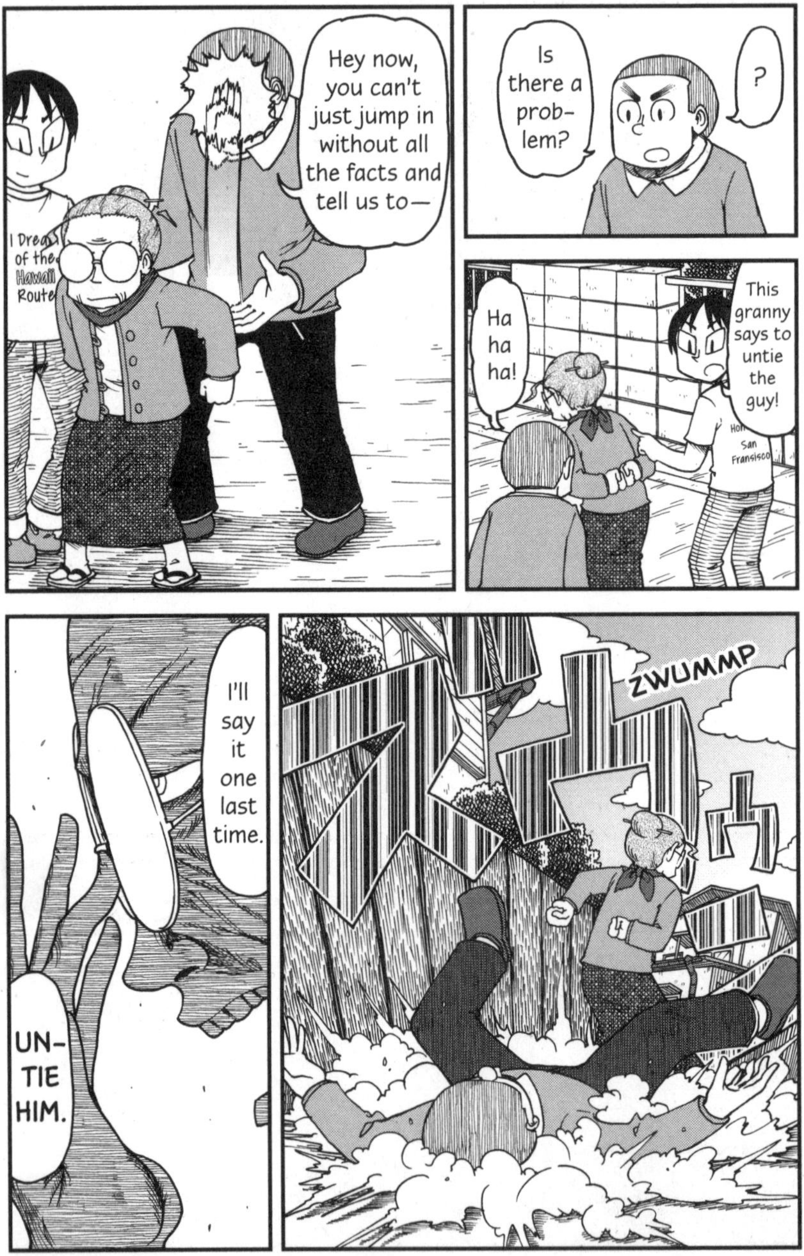
?
Is there a prob-lem?
This granny says to untie the guy!
San Fransisco
Ha ha ha!
Hey now, you can't just jump in without all the facts and tell us to—
of the Hawaii Route
ZWUMMP
I'll say it one last time.
UN-TIE HIM.

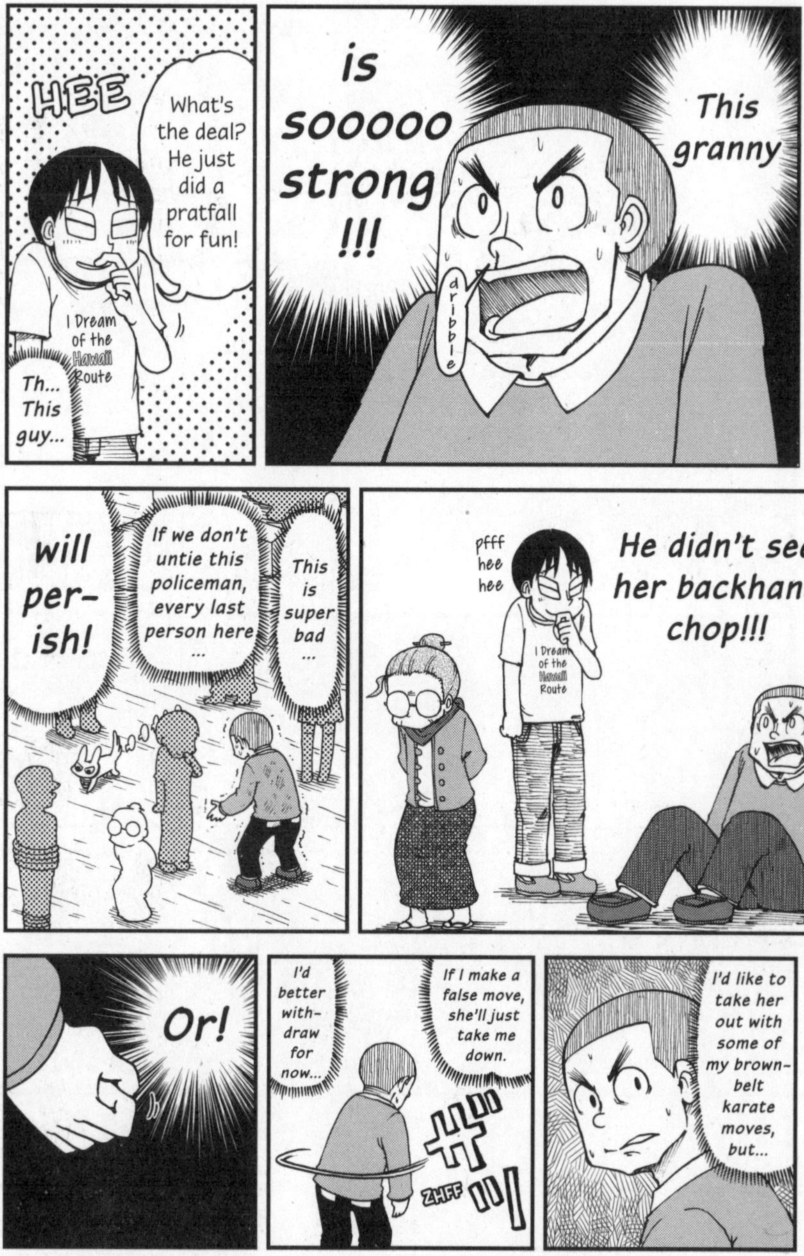
This granny
is sooooo strong!!!
dribble
What's the deal? He just did a pratfall for fun!
HEE
I Dream of the Hawaii Route
Th... This guy...
He didn't see her backhand chop!!!
pfff hee hee
I Dream of the Hawaii Route
This is super bad...
If we don't untie this policeman, every last person here...
will per-ish!
I'd like to take her out with some of my brown-belt karate moves, but...
If I make a false move, she'll just take me down.
I'd better with-draw for now...
ZHFF
Or!

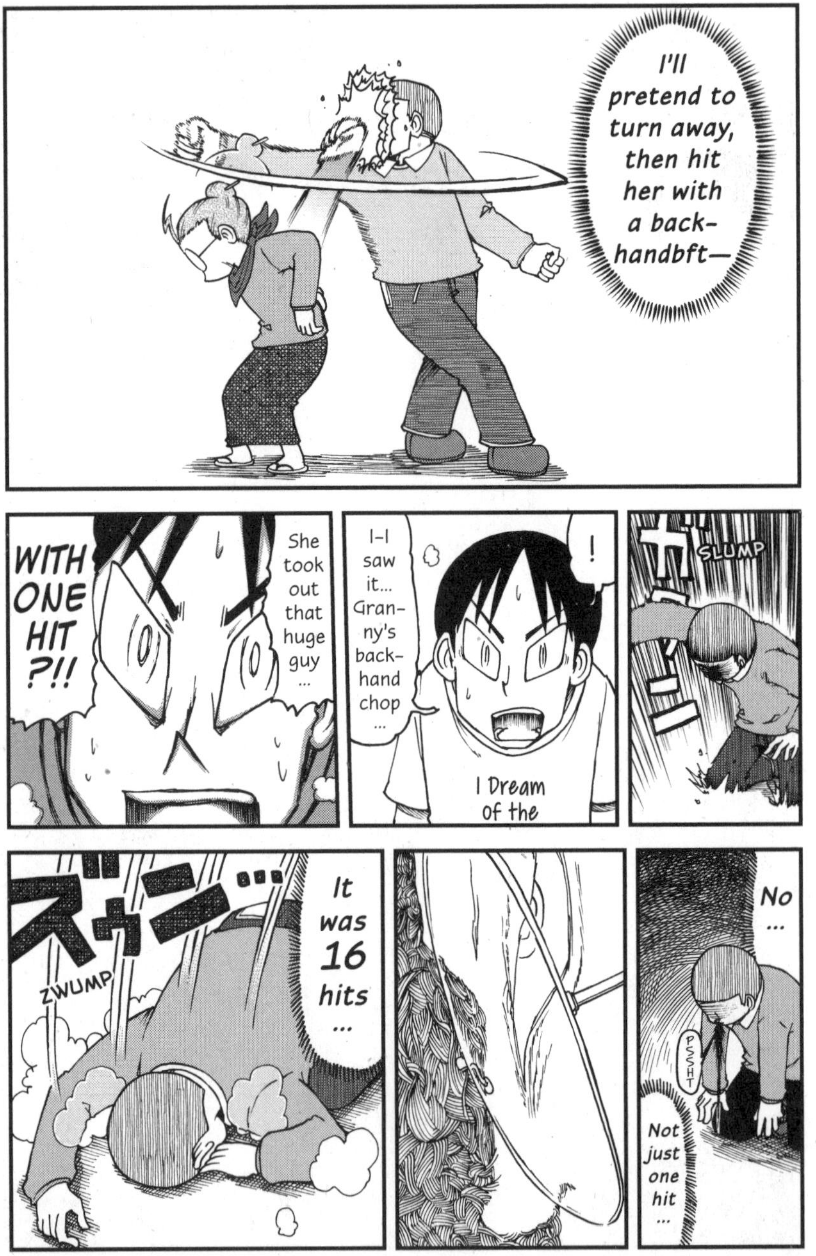
I'll pretend to turn away, then hit her with a back-handbft—
SLUMP
!
I-I saw it... Gran-ny's back-hand chop ...
I Dream of the
She took out that huge guy ...
WITH ONE HIT ?!!
No ...
PSSHT
Not just one hit ...
ズゥン…
ZWUMP
It was 16 hits ...

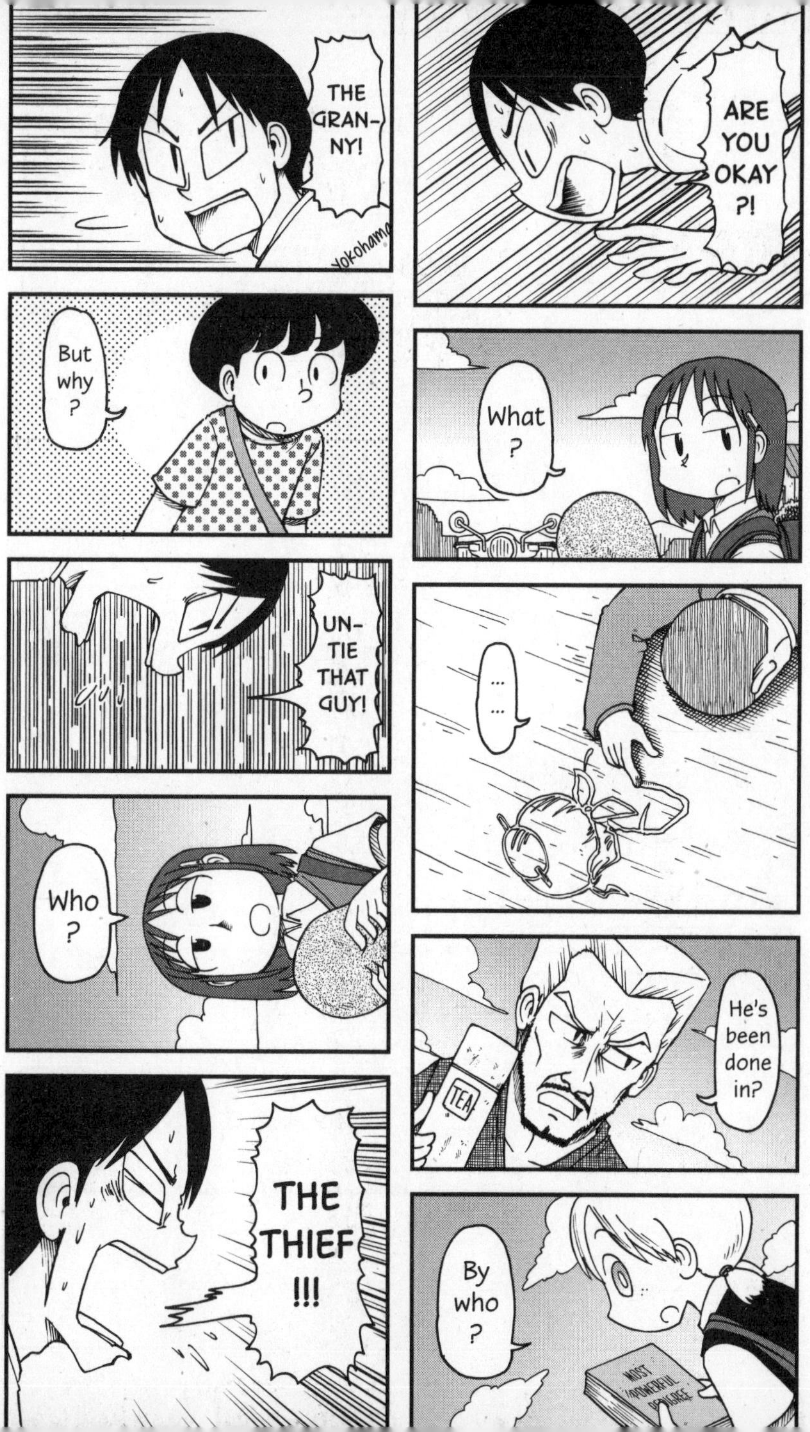
ARE YOU OKAY ?!
What ?
… …
He's been done in?
TEA
By who ?
MOST POWERFUL
THE GRAN-NY!
Yokohama
But why ?
UN-TIE THAT GUY!
Who ?
THE THIEF !!!

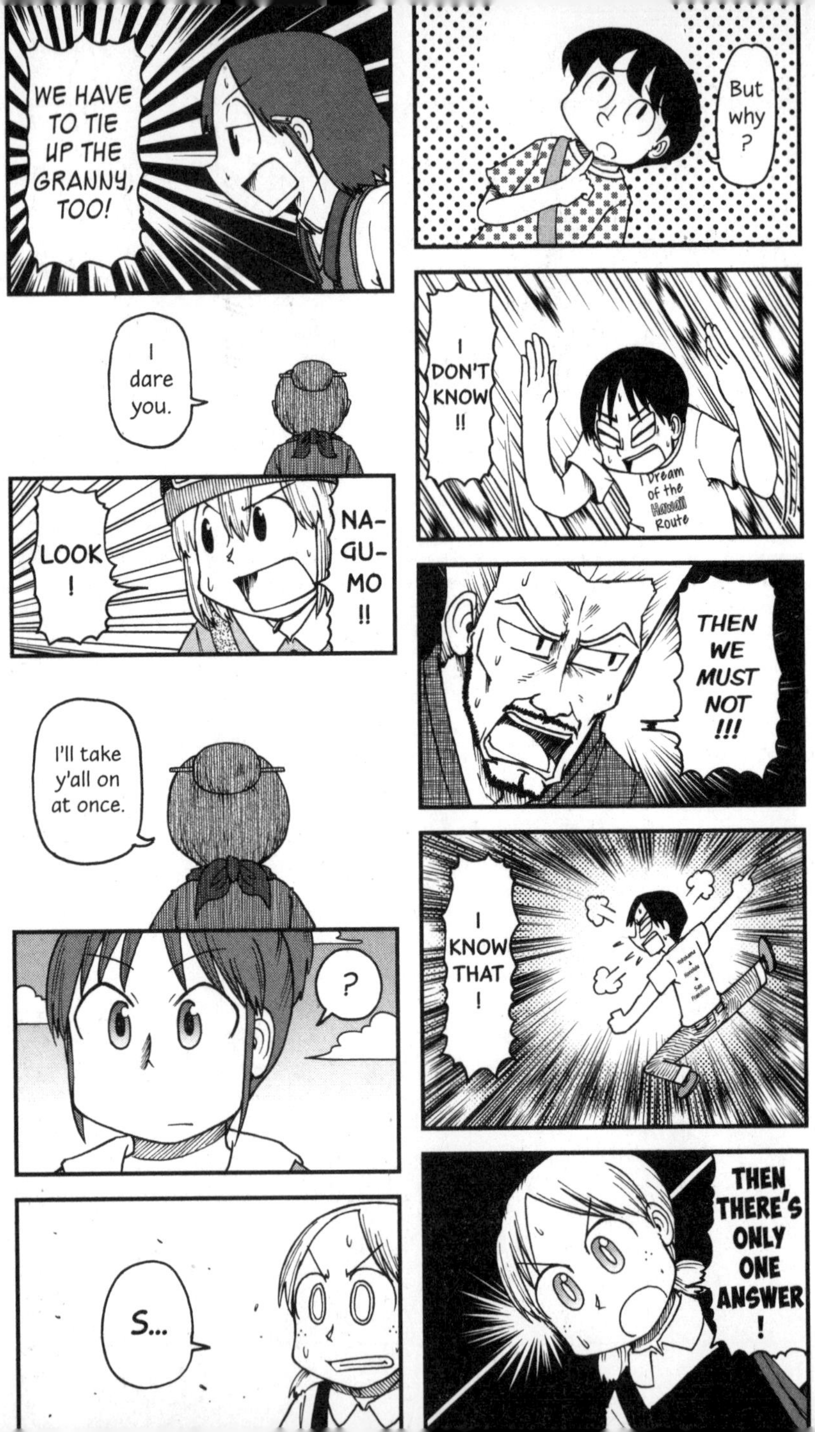
But why ?
I DON'T KNOW !!
I Dream of the Hawaii Route
THEN WE MUST NOT !!!
I KNOW THAT !
THEN THERE'S ONLY ONE ANSWER !
WE HAVE TO TIE UP THE GRANNY, TOO!
I dare you.
NA-GU-MO !!
LOOK !
I'll take y'all on at once.
?
S...

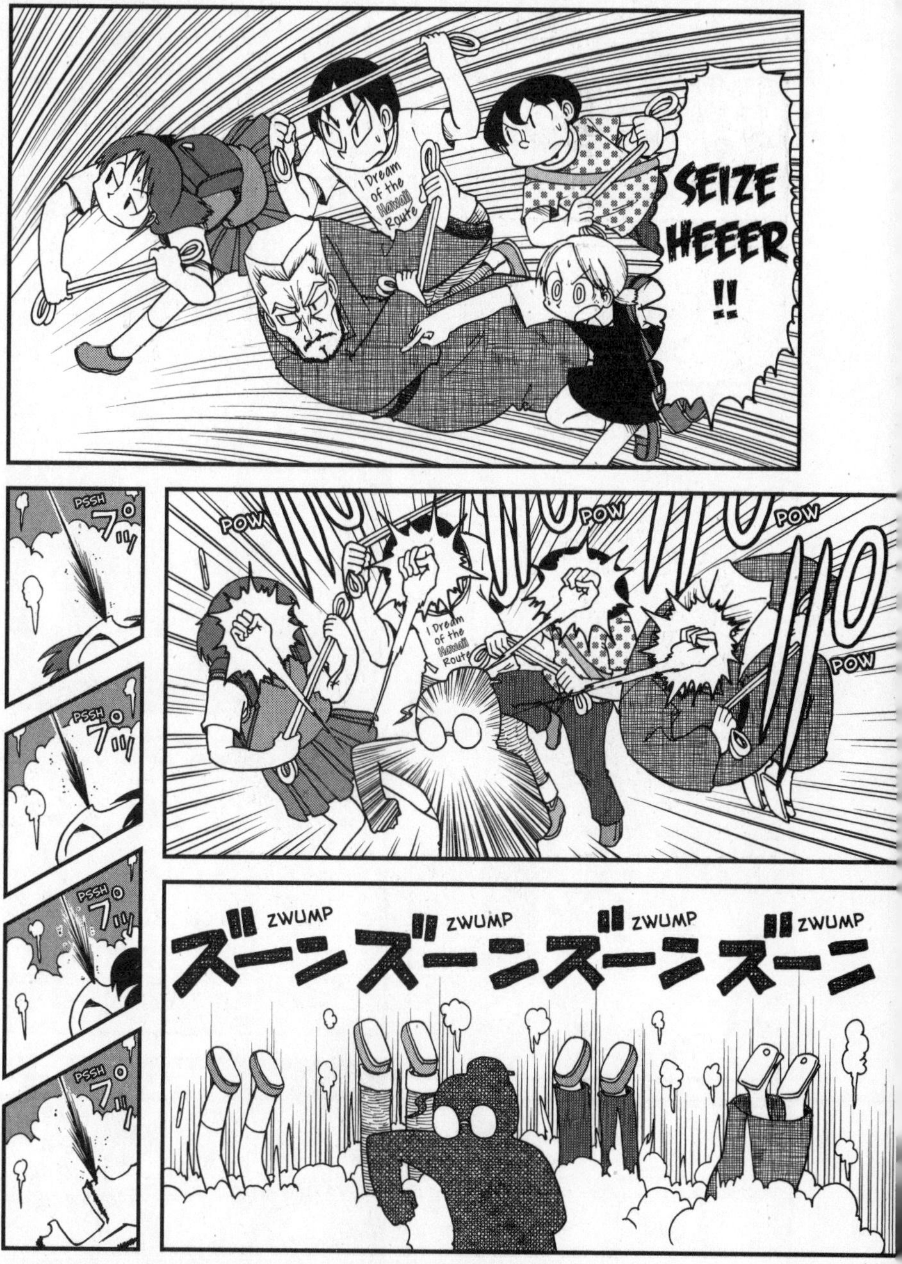
SEIZE HEEER !!
I Dream of the Hawaii Route
POW
POW
POW
POW
I Dream of the Hawaii Route
ZWUMP
ZWUMP
ZWUMP
ZWUMP
ズーンズーンズーン
PSSH
プッ
PSSH
プッ
PSSH
プッ
PSSH
プッ

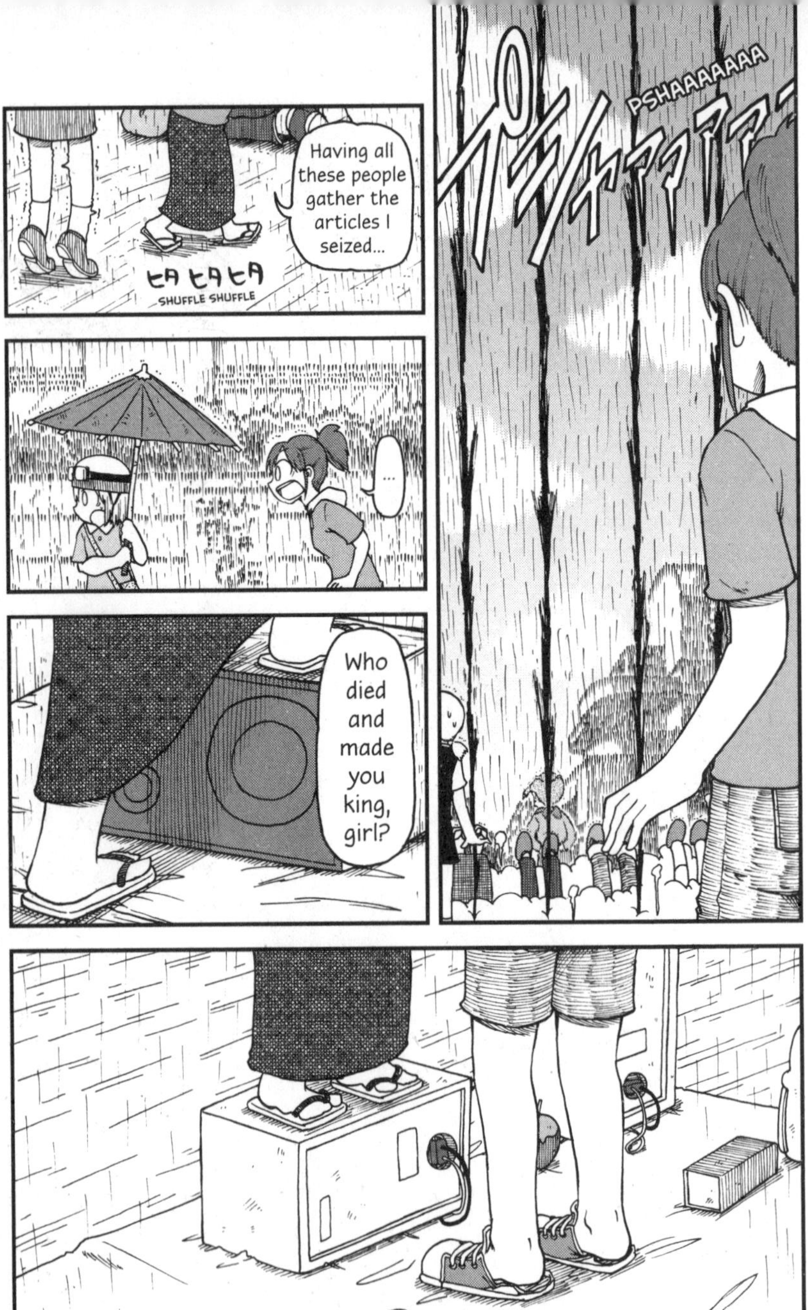
PSHAAAAAAA
Having all these people gather the articles I seized...
ヒタ ヒタ ヒタ
SHUFFLE SHUFFLE
...
Who died and made you king, girl?

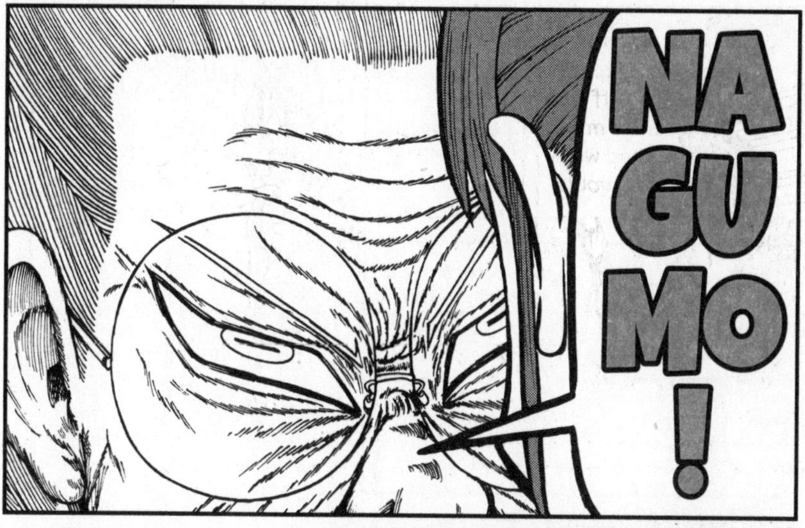
NAGUMO!
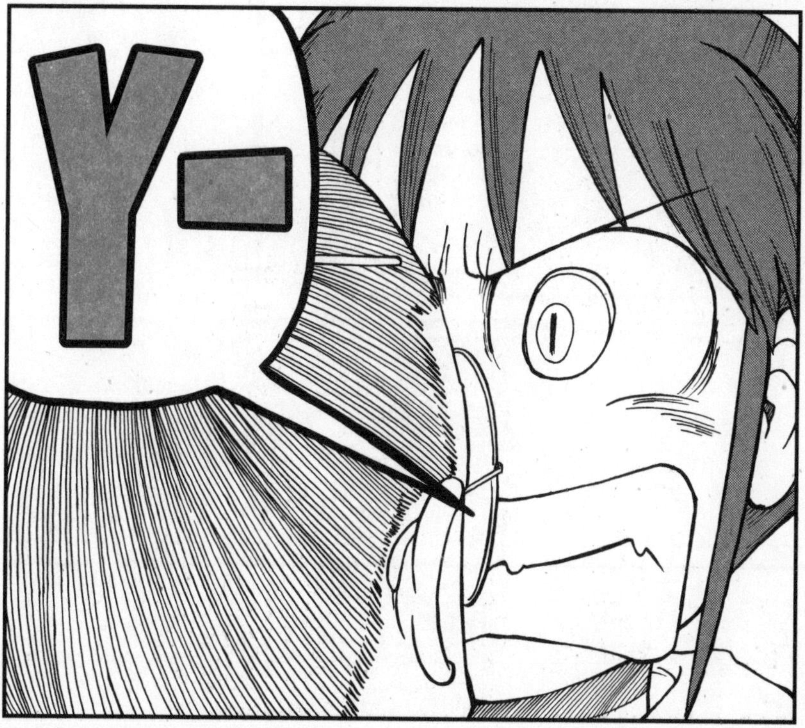
Y-

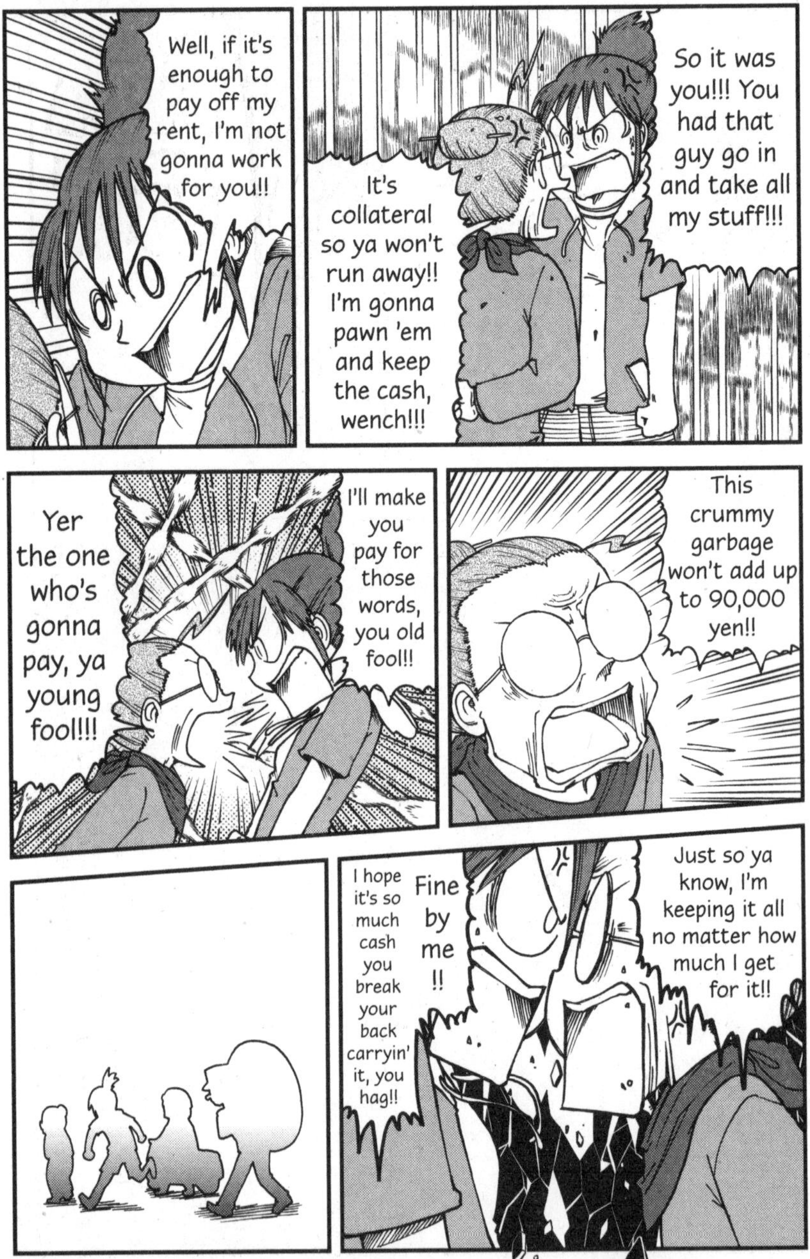
So it was you!!! You had that guy go in and take all my stuff!!!
It's collateral so ya won't run away!! I'm gonna pawn 'em and keep the cash, wench!!!
Well, if it's enough to pay off my rent, I'm not gonna work for you!!
This crummy garbage won't add up to 90,000 yen!!
I'll make you pay for those words, you old fool!!
Yer the one who's gonna pay, ya young fool!!!
Just so ya know, I'm keeping it all no matter how much I get for it!!
Fine by me !!
I hope it's so much cash you break your back carryin' it, you hag!!

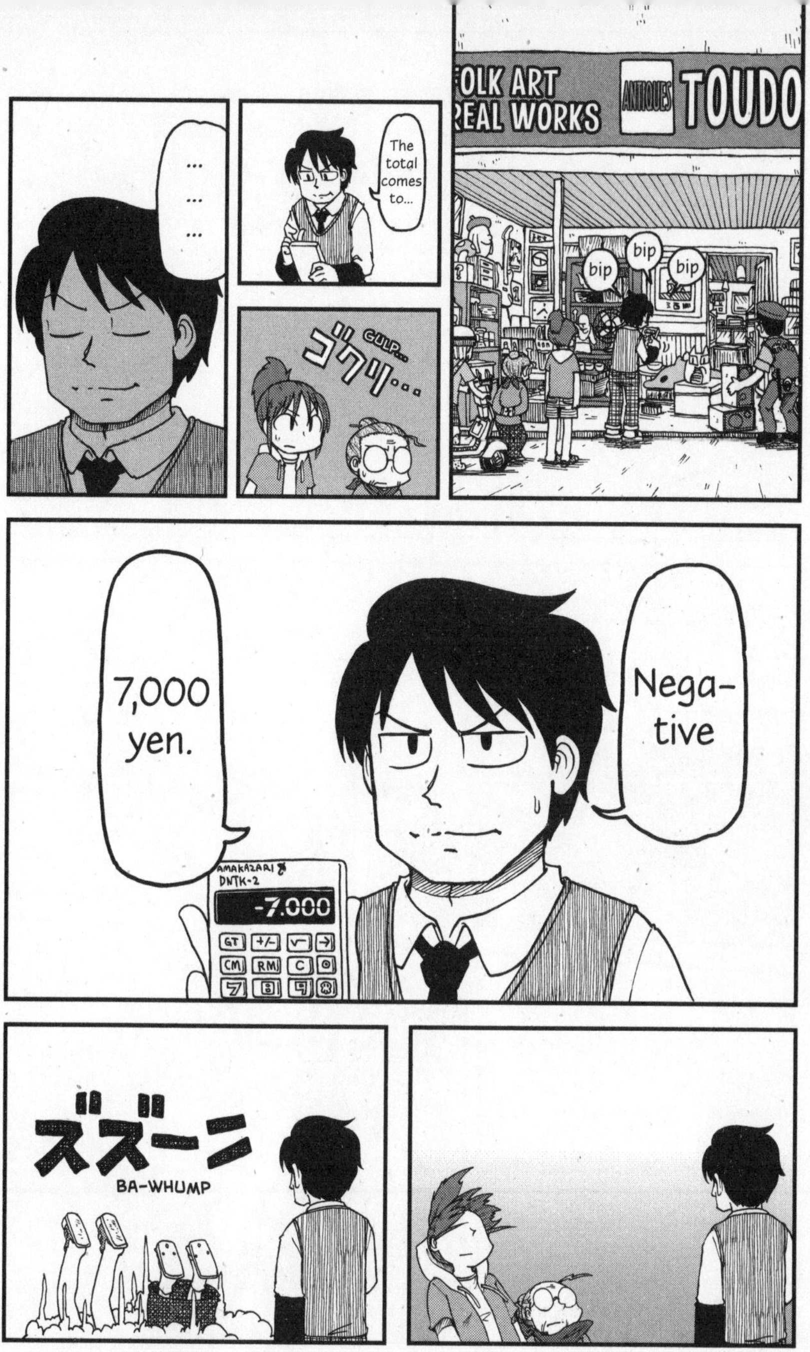
FOLK ART
REAL WORKS
ANTIQUES
TOUDO
bip
bip
bip
The total comes to...
ゴクリ...
GULP...
...
...
...
Nega-tive
7,000 yen.
AMAKAZARI
DNTK-2
-7.000
ズズーン
BA-WHUMP

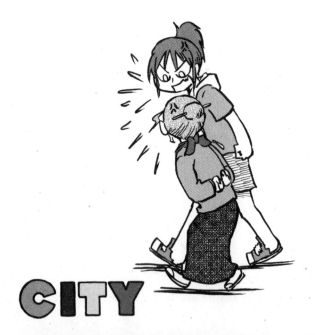

CITY

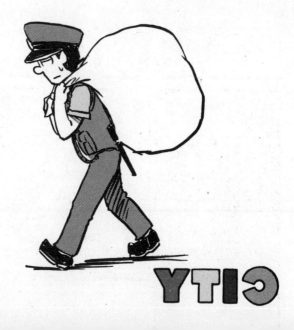

CITY

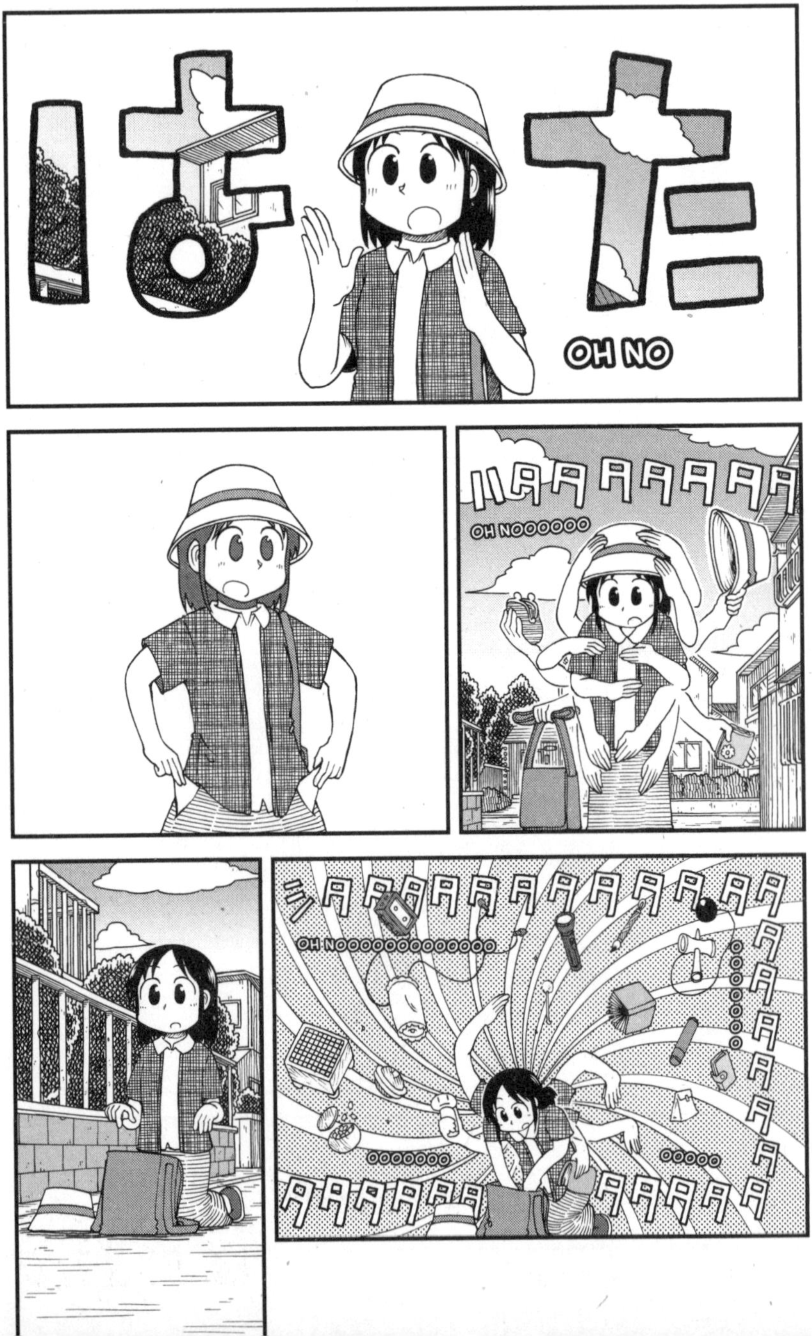
OH NO
OH NOOOOOO
OH NOOOOOOOOOOOOO
OOOOOOO
OOOOO
OOOOOOO

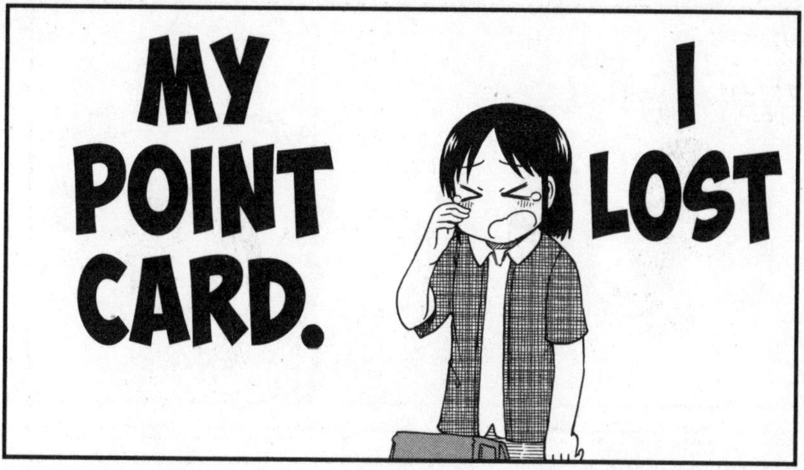
I LOST
MY POINT CARD.

Chapter 6

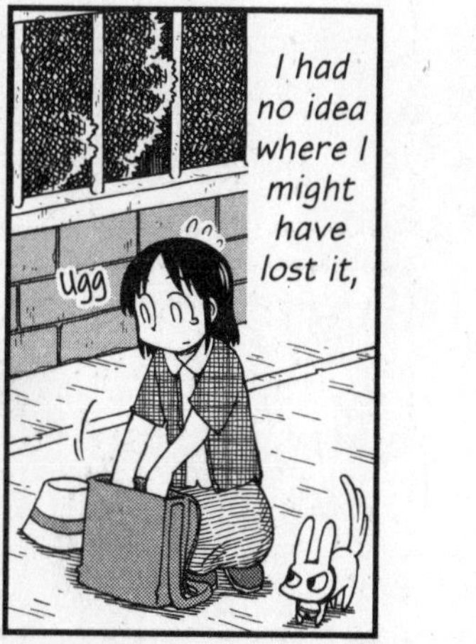
I had no idea where I might have lost it,
Ugg

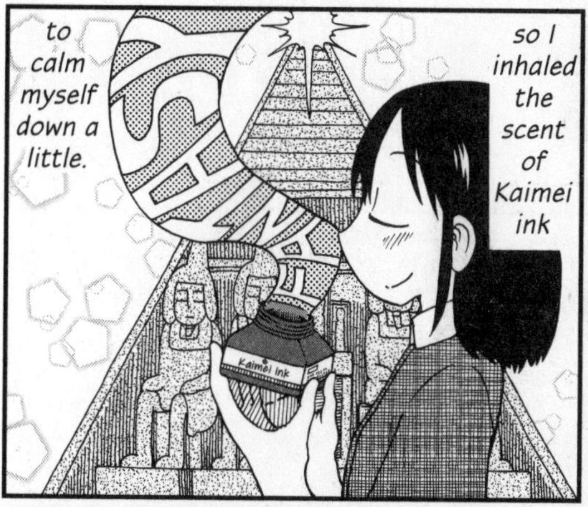
so I inhaled the scent of Kaimei ink
to calm myself down a little.
Kaimei Ink

Wako Izumi

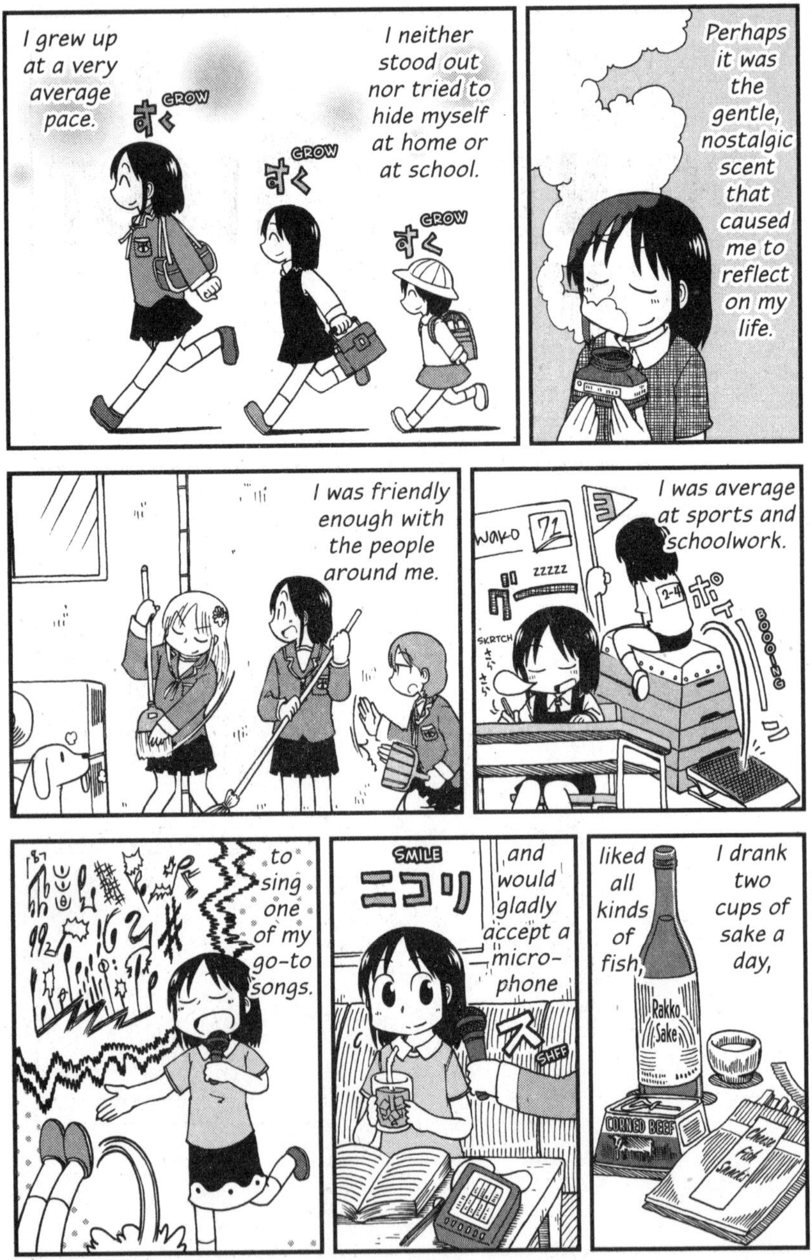
Perhaps it was the gentle, nostalgic scent that caused me to reflect on my life.
I grew up at a very average pace.
I neither stood out nor tried to hide myself at home or at school.
すく GROW
すく GROW
すく GROW
I was average at sports and schoolwork.
WAKO
71
ZZZZZ
SKRTCH
2-4
BOOOING
I was friendly enough with the people around me.
I drank two cups of sake a day,
liked all kinds of fish,
Rakko Sake
CORNED BEEF
Cheese Fish Snacks
and would gladly accept a microphone
SMILE
ニコリ
SHFF
to sing one of my go-to songs.

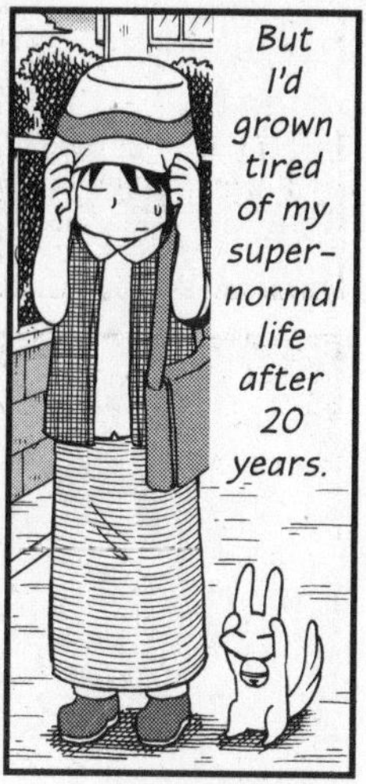
But I'd grown tired of my super-normal life after 20 years.

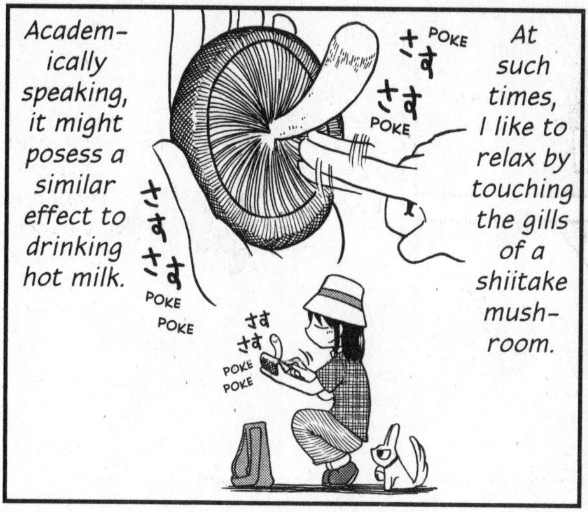
At such times, I like to relax by touching the gills of a shiitake mush-room.
さす
POKE
さす
POKE
さす さす
POKE
POKE
さす さす
POKE
POKE
Academ-ically speaking, it might posess a similar effect to drinking hot milk.

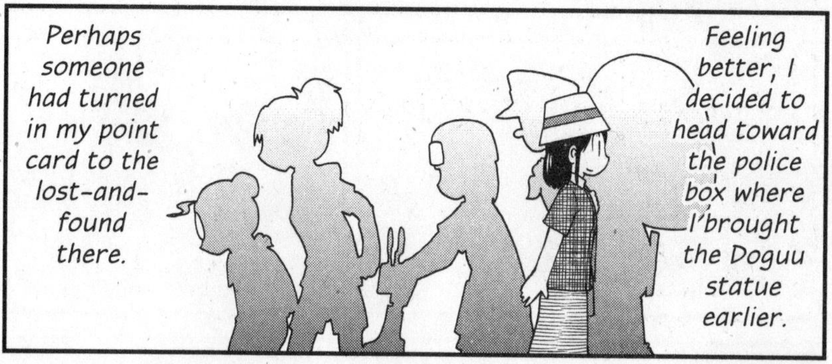
Feeling better, I decided to head toward the police box where I brought the Doguu statue earlier.
Perhaps someone had turned in my point card to the lost-and-found there.

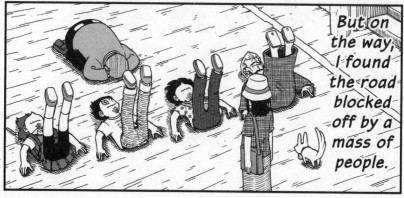

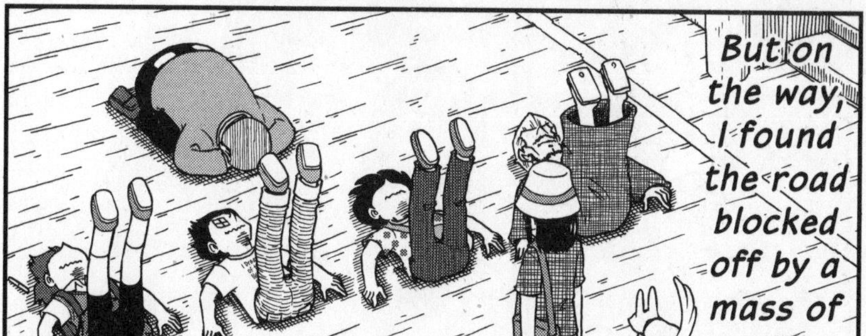
But on the way, I found the road blocked off by a mass of people.

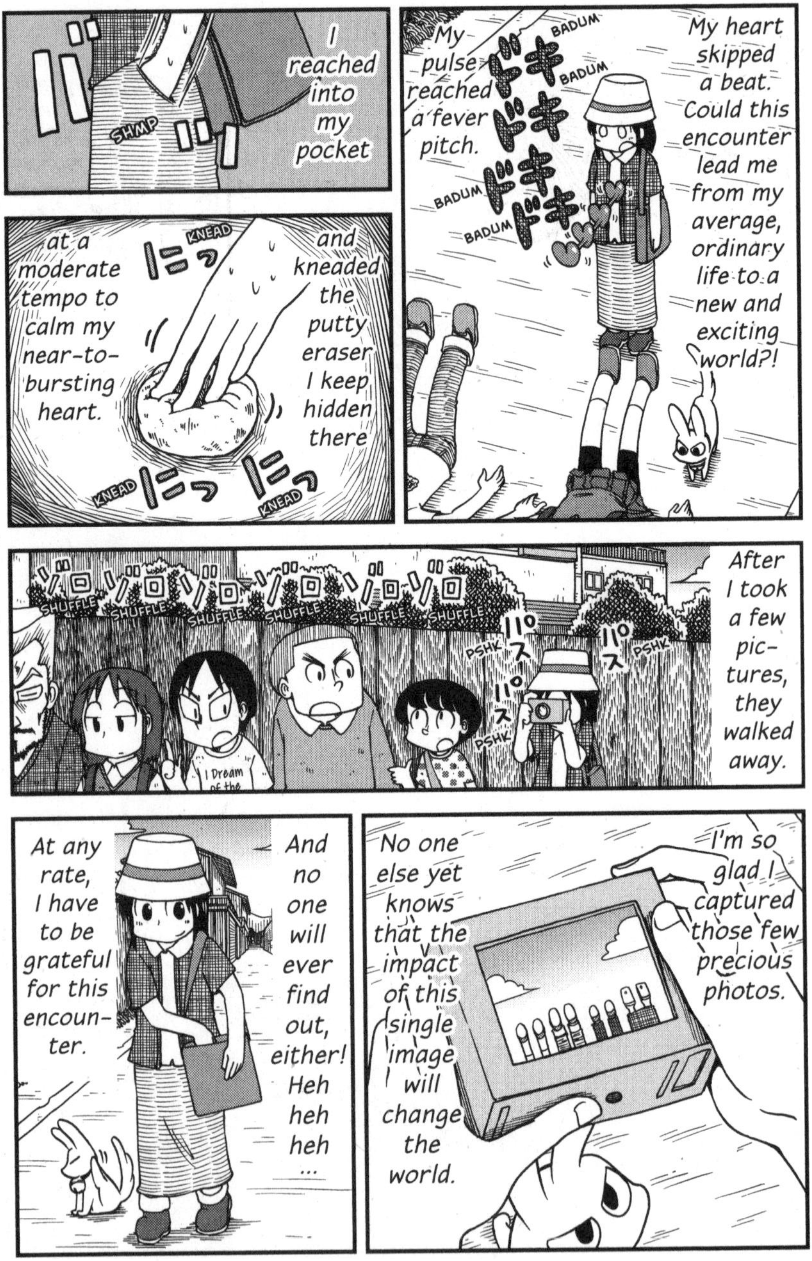
My heart skipped a beat. Could this encounter lead me from my average, ordinary life to a new and exciting world?!
BADUM
BADUM
ドキドキドキドキ
BADUM
BADUM
My pulse reached a fever pitch.
I reached into my pocket
バッ
SHMP
and kneaded the putty eraser I keep hidden there
にっ
KNEAD
at a moderate tempo to calm my near-to-bursting heart.
にっ
KNEAD
にっ
KNEAD
After I took a few pictures, they walked away.
パス
PSHK
パス
PSHK
パス
PSHK
ゾロゾロゾロゾロゾロゾロ
SHUFFLE
SHUFFLE
SHUFFLE
SHUFFLE
SHUFFLE
SHUFFLE
I'm so glad I captured those few precious photos.
No one else yet knows that the impact of this single image will change the world.
And no one will ever find out, either! Heh heh heh ...
At any rate, I have to be grateful for this encounter.

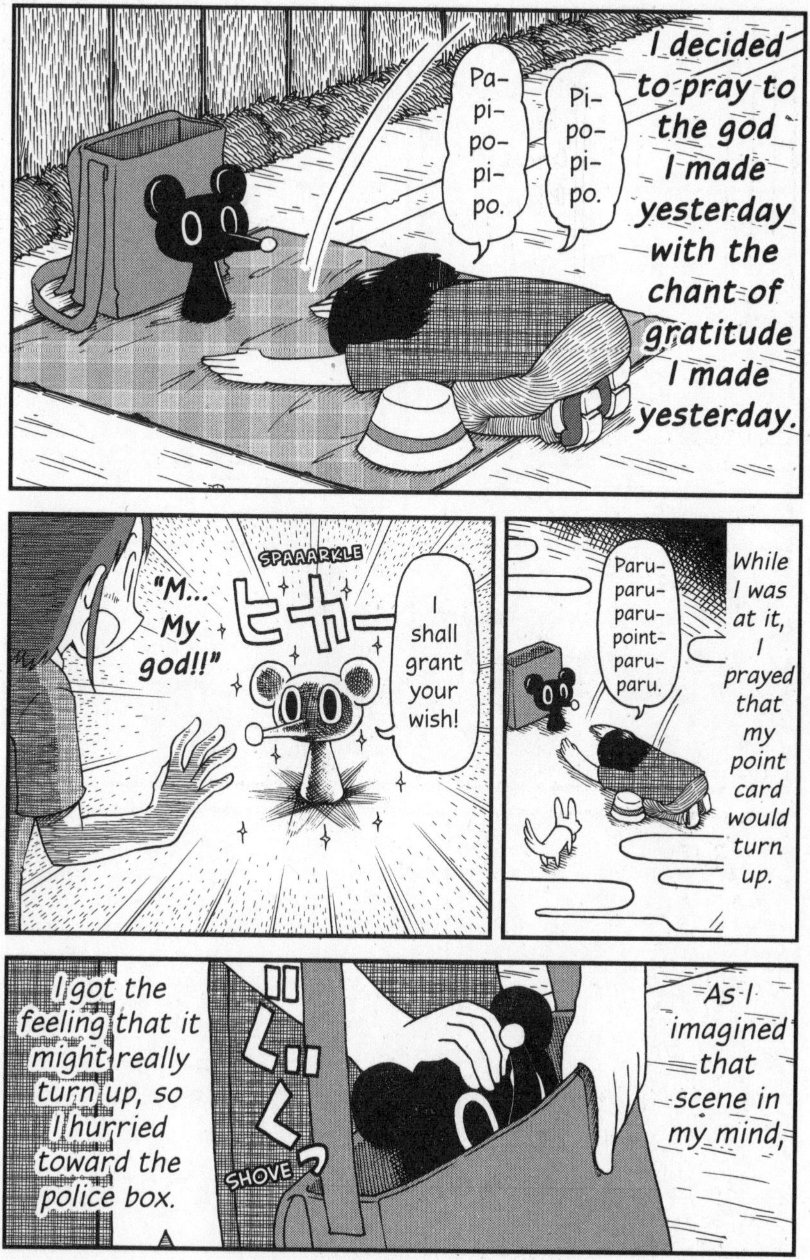
I decided to pray to the god I made yesterday with the chant of gratitude I made yesterday.
Pi-po-pi-po.
Pa-pi-po-pi-po.
While I was at it, I prayed that my point card would turn up.
Paru-paru-paru-point-paru-paru.
I shall grant your wish!
SPAAARKLE
ヒカー
"M... My god!!"
As I imagined that scene in my mind,
SHOVE
I got the feeling that it might really turn up, so I hurried toward the police box.

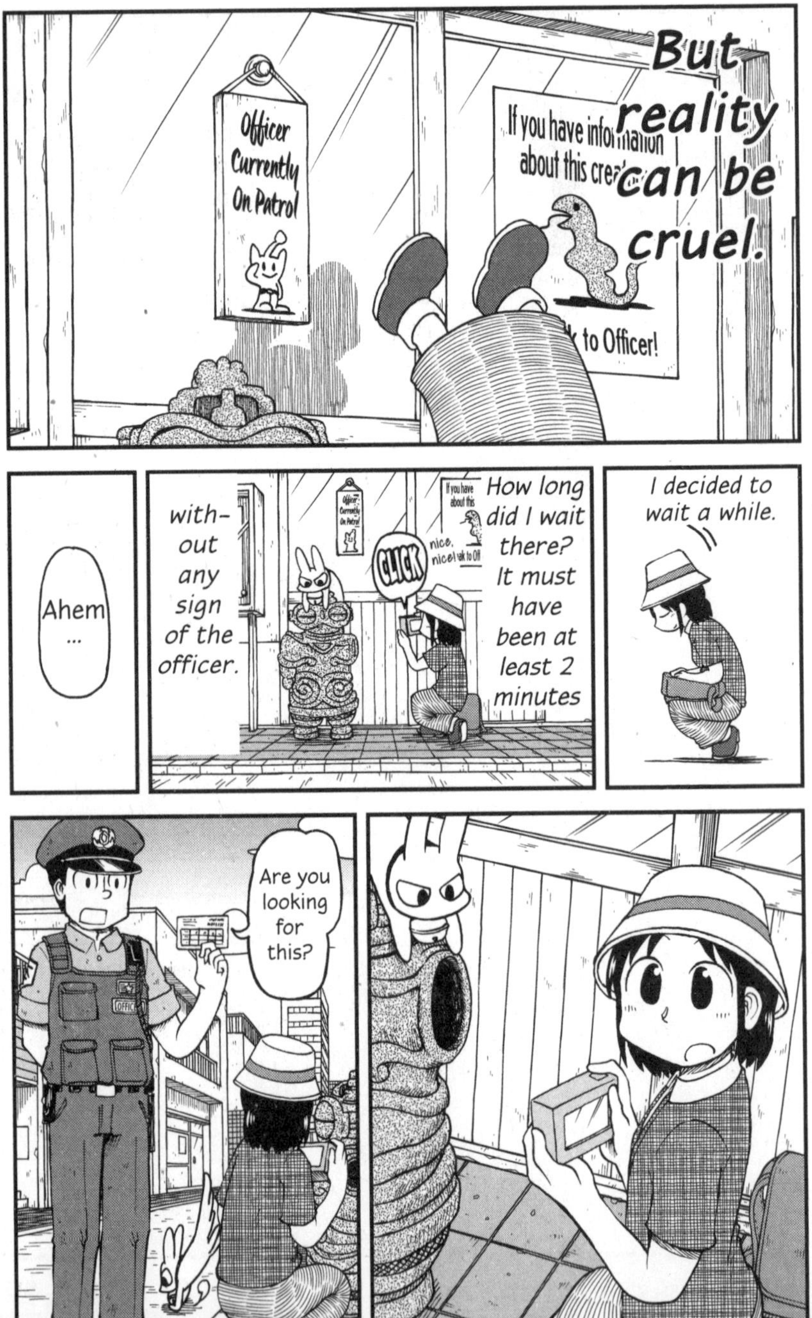
Officer Currently On Patrol
But reality can be cruel.
I decided to wait a while.
How long did I wait there? It must have been at least 2 minutes
CLICK
nice, nice!
with-out any sign of the officer.
Ahem ...
Are you looking for this?

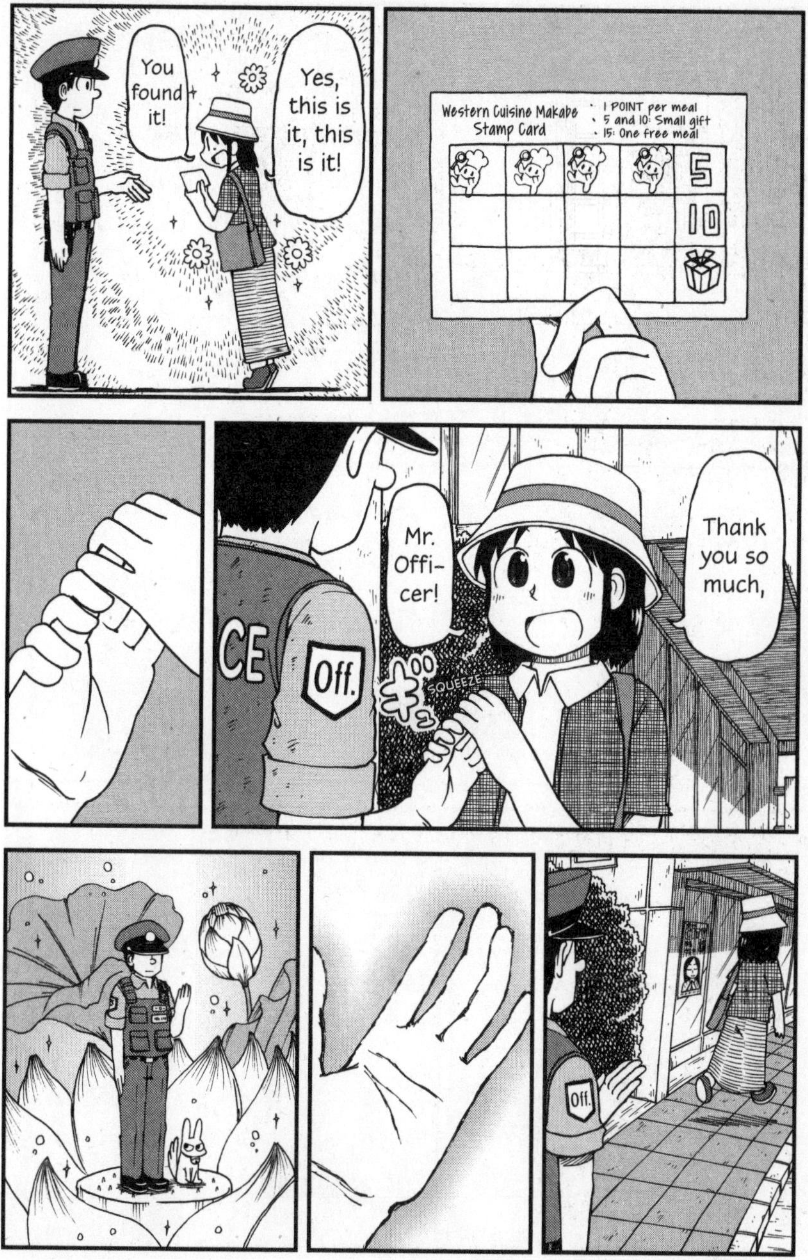
Western Cuisine Makabe Stamp Card
• 1 POINT per meal
• 5 and 10: Small gift
• 15: One free meal
5
10
Yes, this is it, this is it!
You found it!
Thank you so much,
Mr. Officer!
SQUEEZE
CE
Off.
Off.

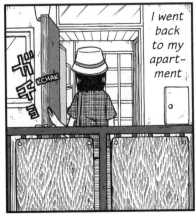

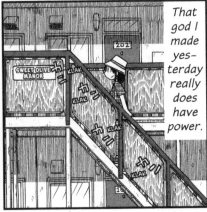

That god I made yesterday really does have power.
SWEET OLIVE MANOR
KLAK
KLAK
KLAK
KLAK
I went back to my apartment
KCHAK
and took out the container
that contained the freebies from my Papico ice cream, as an offering.
Papico freebie
Eating that Papico right before it melted was especially delicious.
Perhaps if I kept stacking up such happy moments, I'd have a crazy amount of happiness!

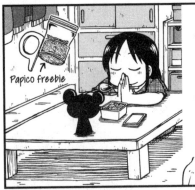

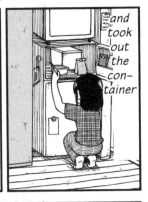

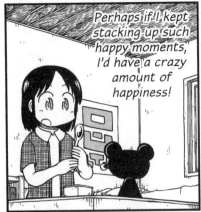

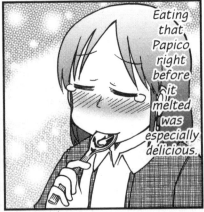

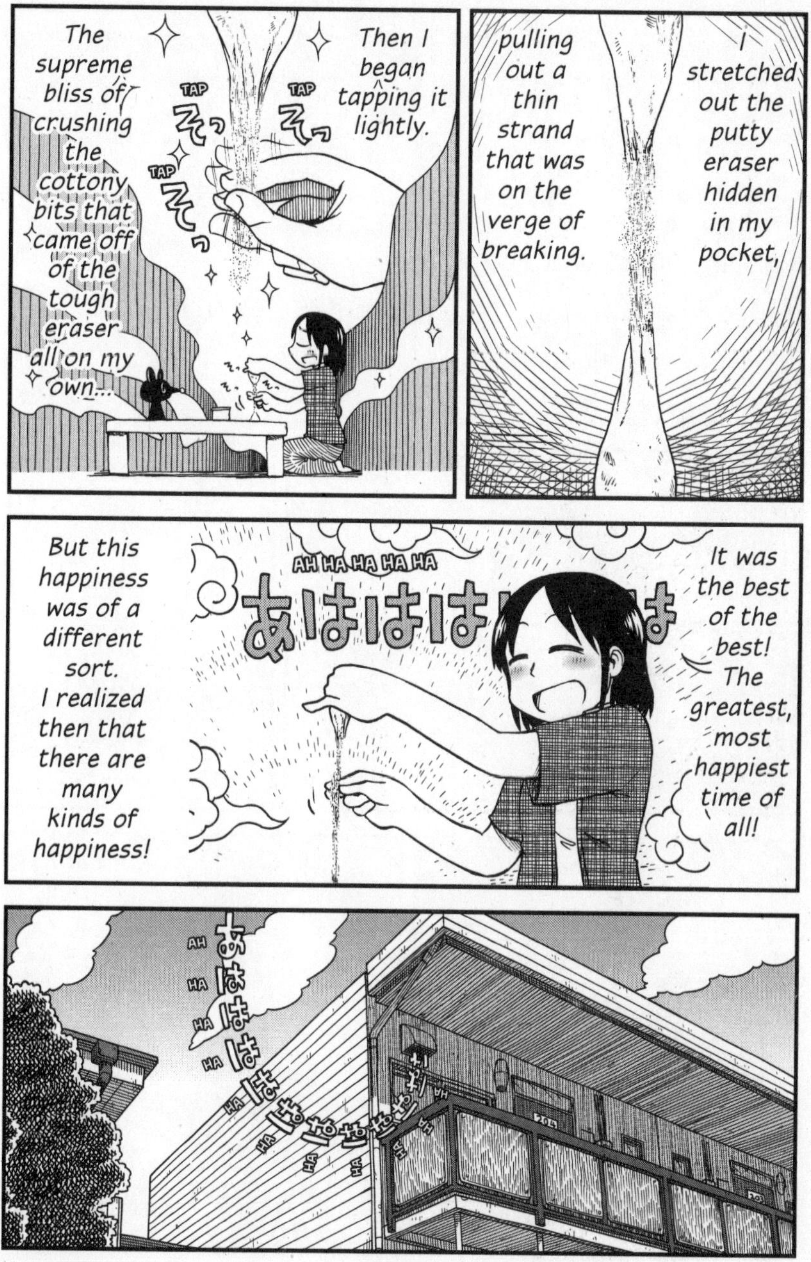

I stretched out the putty eraser hidden in my pocket,
pulling out a thin strand that was on the verge of breaking.
Then I began tapping it lightly.
TAP
TAP
TAP
The supreme bliss of crushing the cottony bits that came off of the tough eraser all on my own...
It was the best of the best! The greatest, most happiest time of all!
AH HA HA HA HA
But this happiness was of a different sort. I realized then that there are many kinds of happiness!
AH
HA
HA
HA
HA
HA
HA
HA
HA
HA

AH HA HA HA HA

CITY

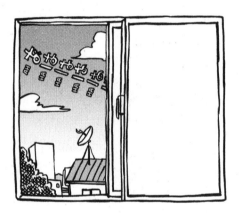

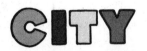

ボロボロ
SOB SOB
はー
HA

CITY

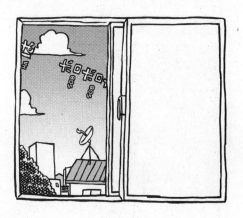

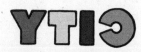

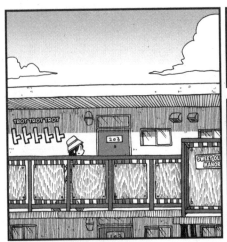

TROT TROT TROT

SWEET OLIVE MANOR

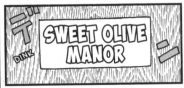

DINK

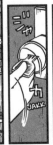

JAKK

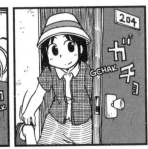

204

G-CHAK

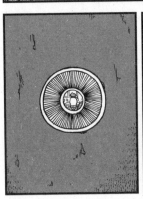

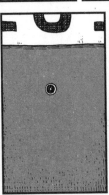

Chapter 7 ◈ #203

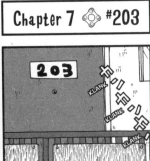

203

KLANK
KLANK
KLANK

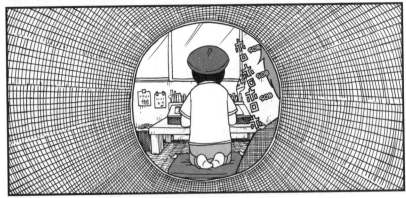

SOB
SOB
SOB

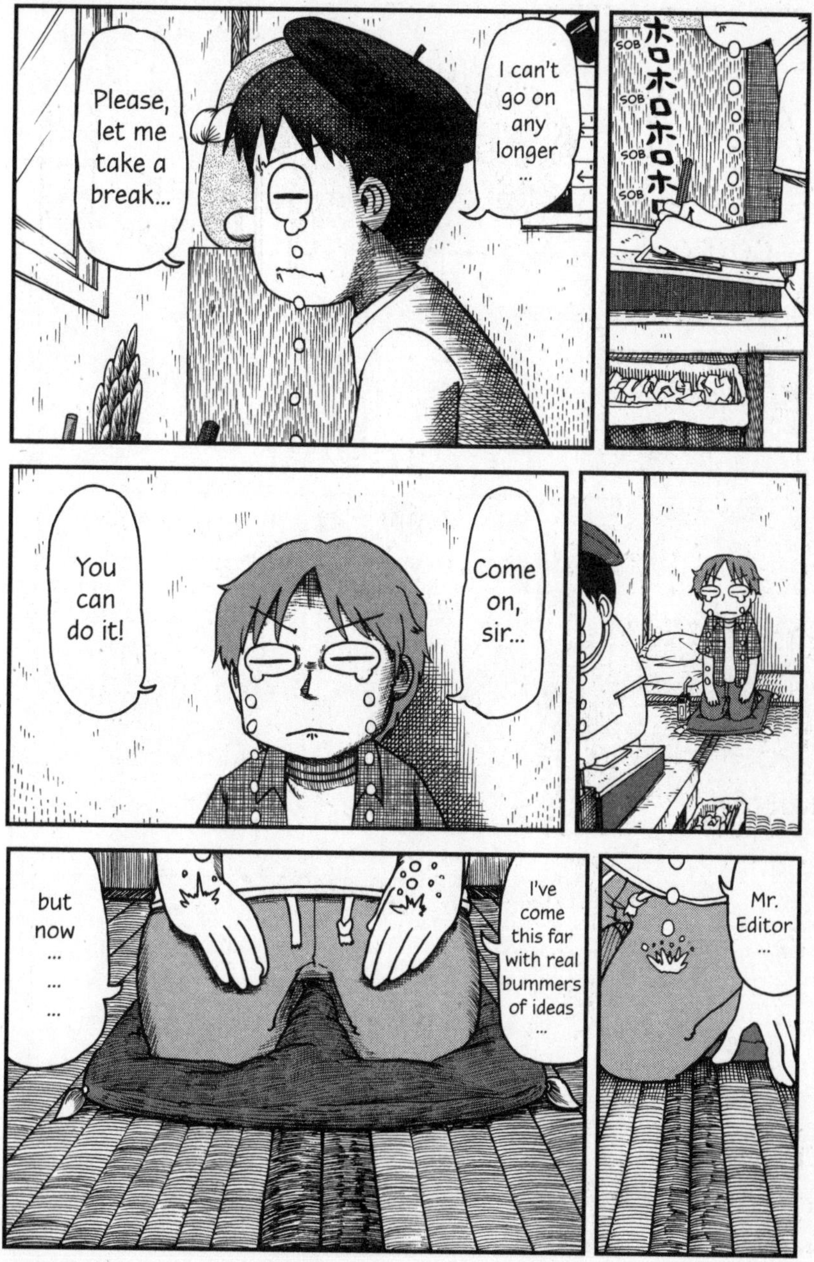
ホロホロホロ
SOB SOB SOB SOB
I can't go on any longer ...
Please, let me take a break...
Come on, sir...
You can do it!
Mr. Editor ...
I've come this far with real bummers of ideas ...
but now ... ...

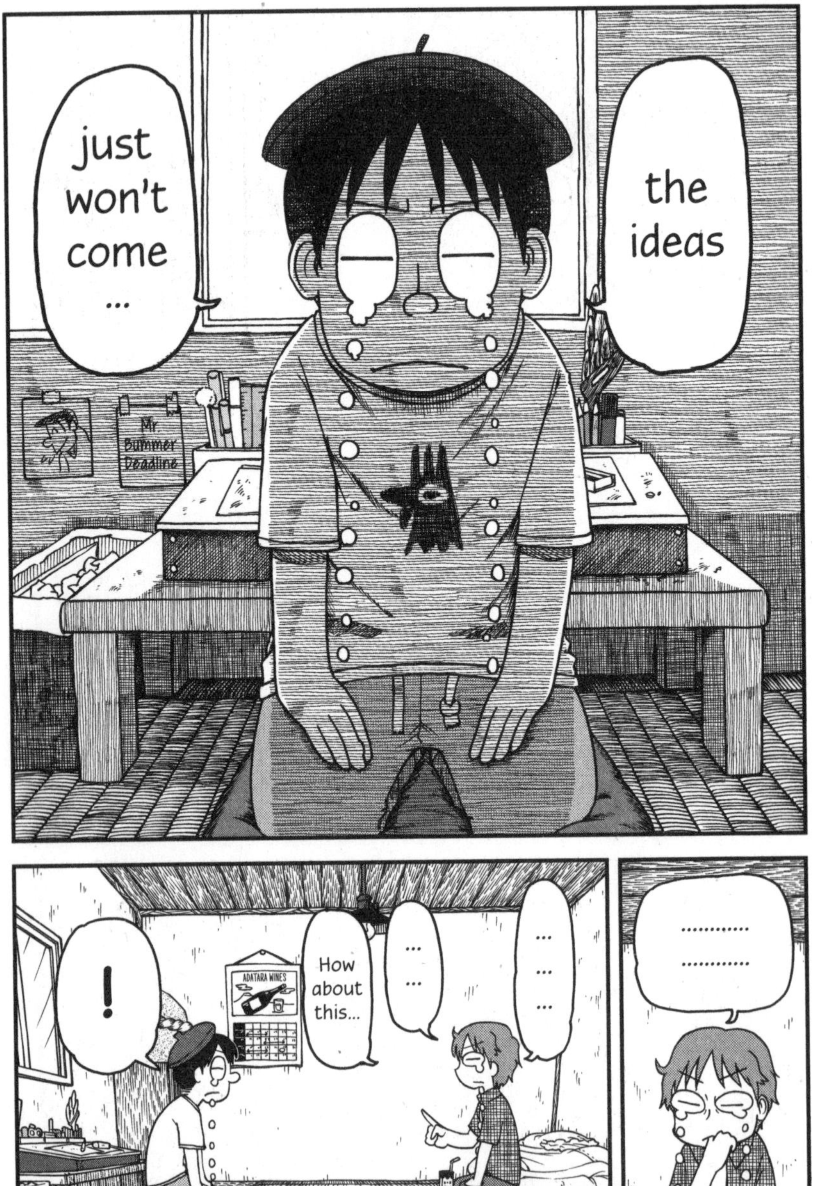
the ideas
just won't come ...
Mr. Bummer Deadline
....
... ...
... ...
How about this...
ADATARA WINES
!

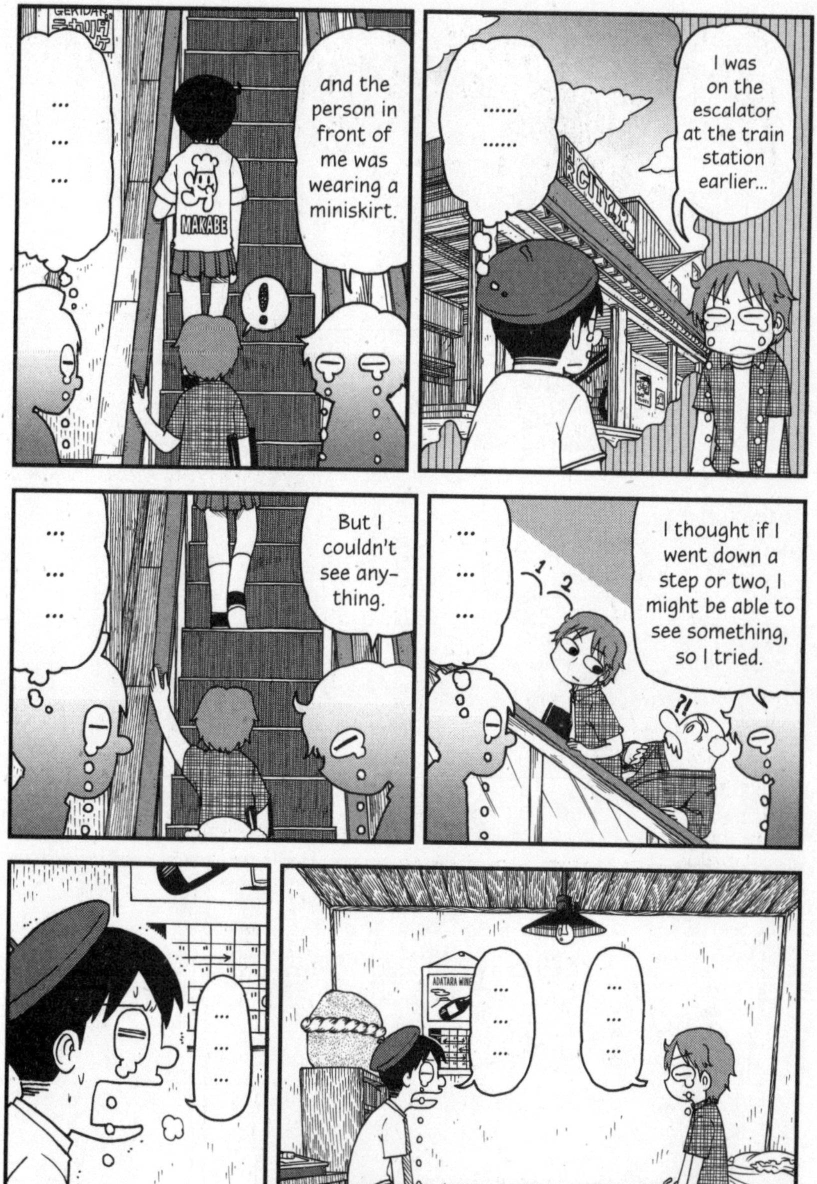
I was on the escalator at the train station earlier...
....
and the person in front of me was wearing a miniskirt.
MAKABE
!
... ...
I thought if I went down a step or two, I might be able to see something, so I tried.
1 2
?!
... ...
But I couldn't see any-thing.
... ...
... ...
ADATARA WINE
... ...
... ...

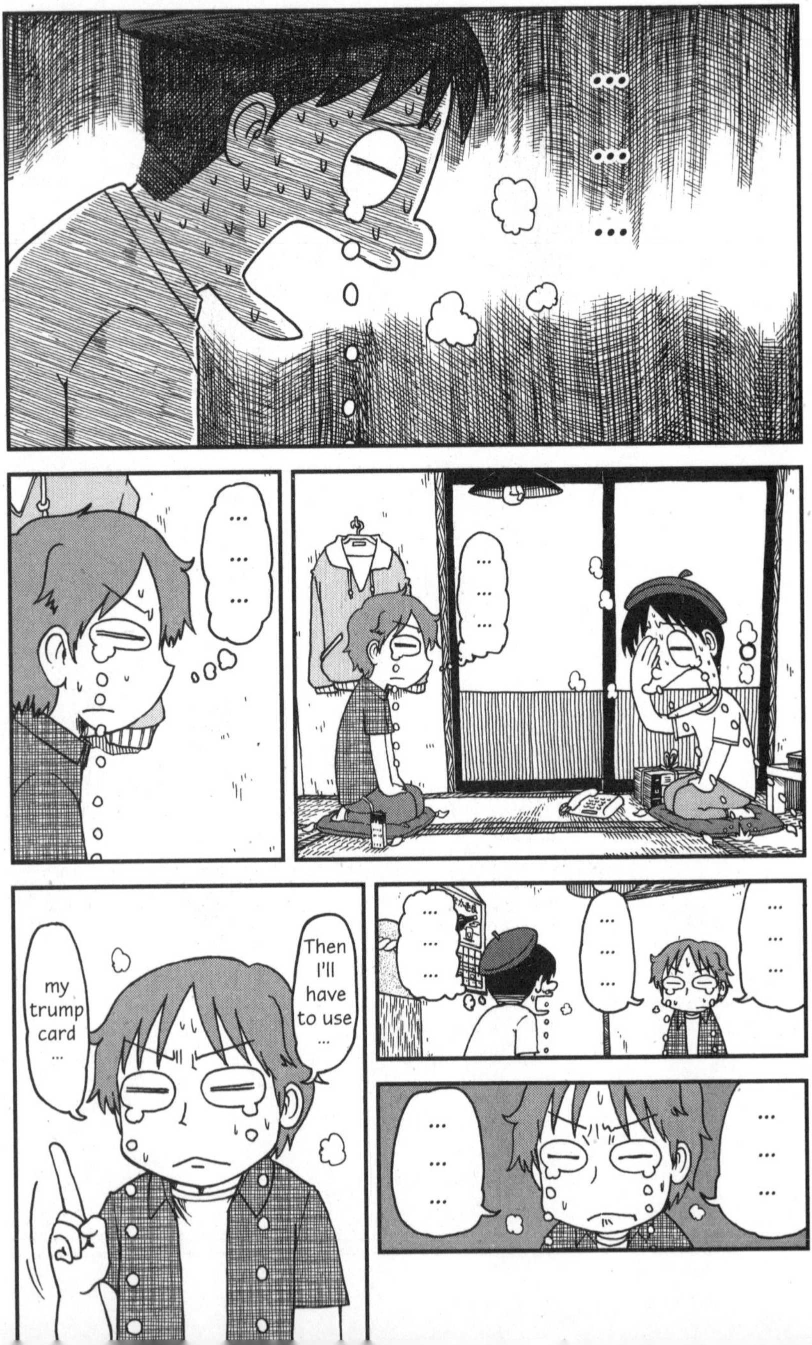
...
...
...
... ...
... ...
... ...
... ...
... ...
... ...
... ...
Then I'll have to use ...
my trump card ...

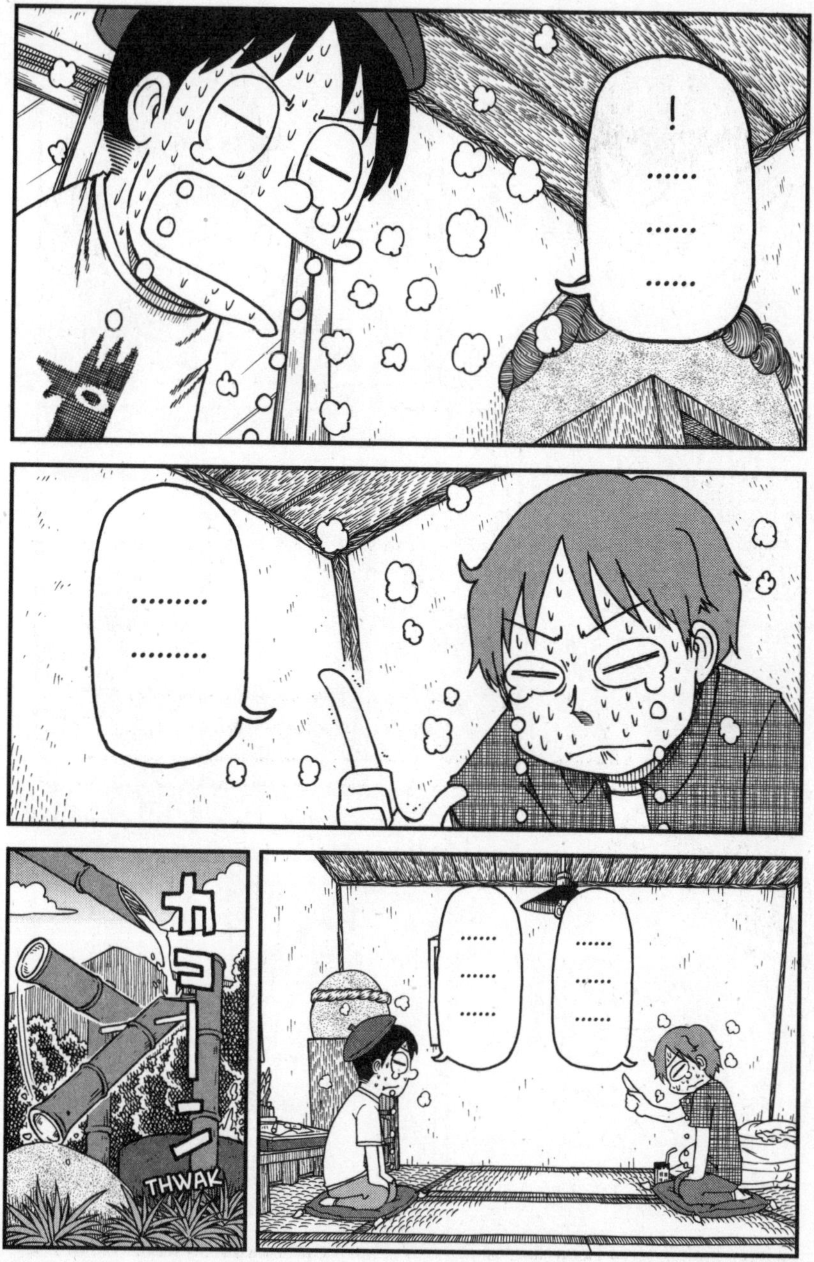
!
......
......
......
....
....
......
......
......
......
......
......
カコーン
THWAK

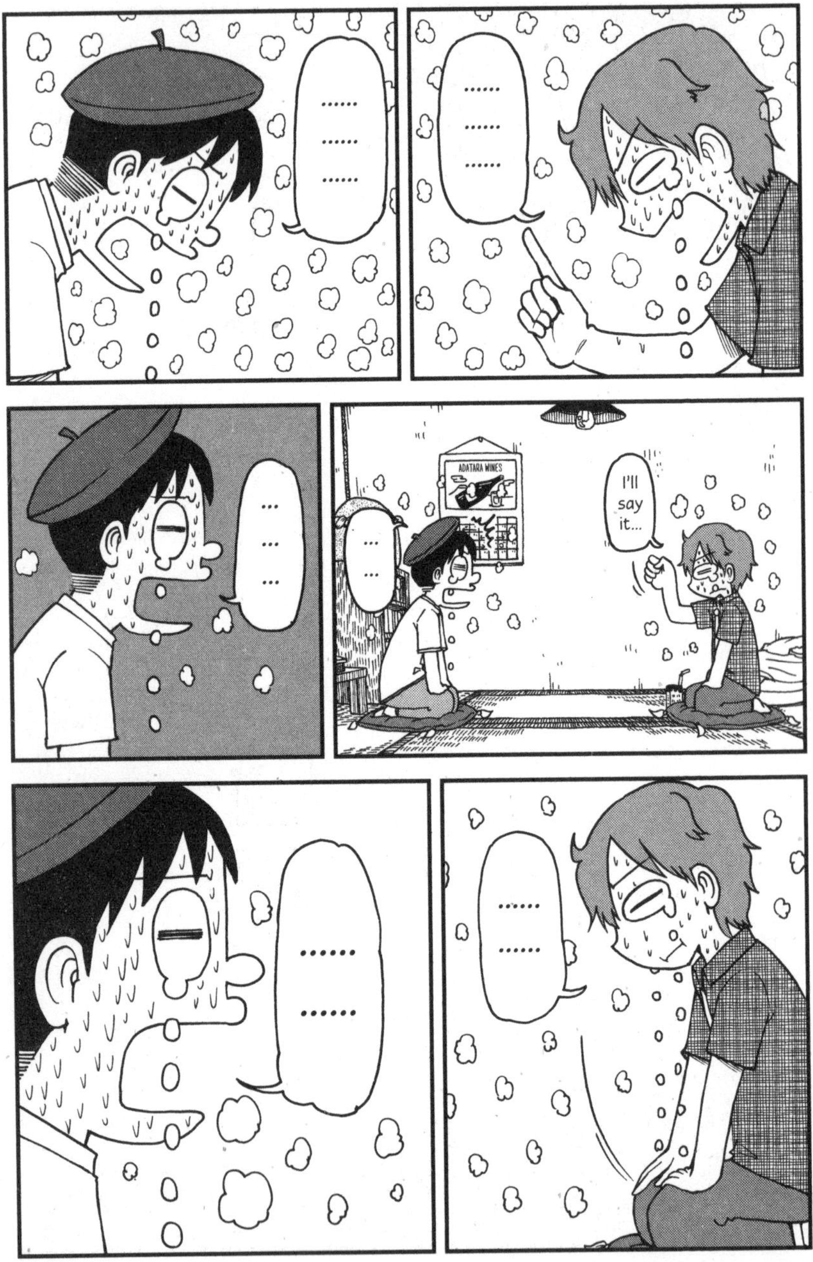
……
……
……
……
……
……
I'll say it…
…
…
…
…
…
……
……
……
……

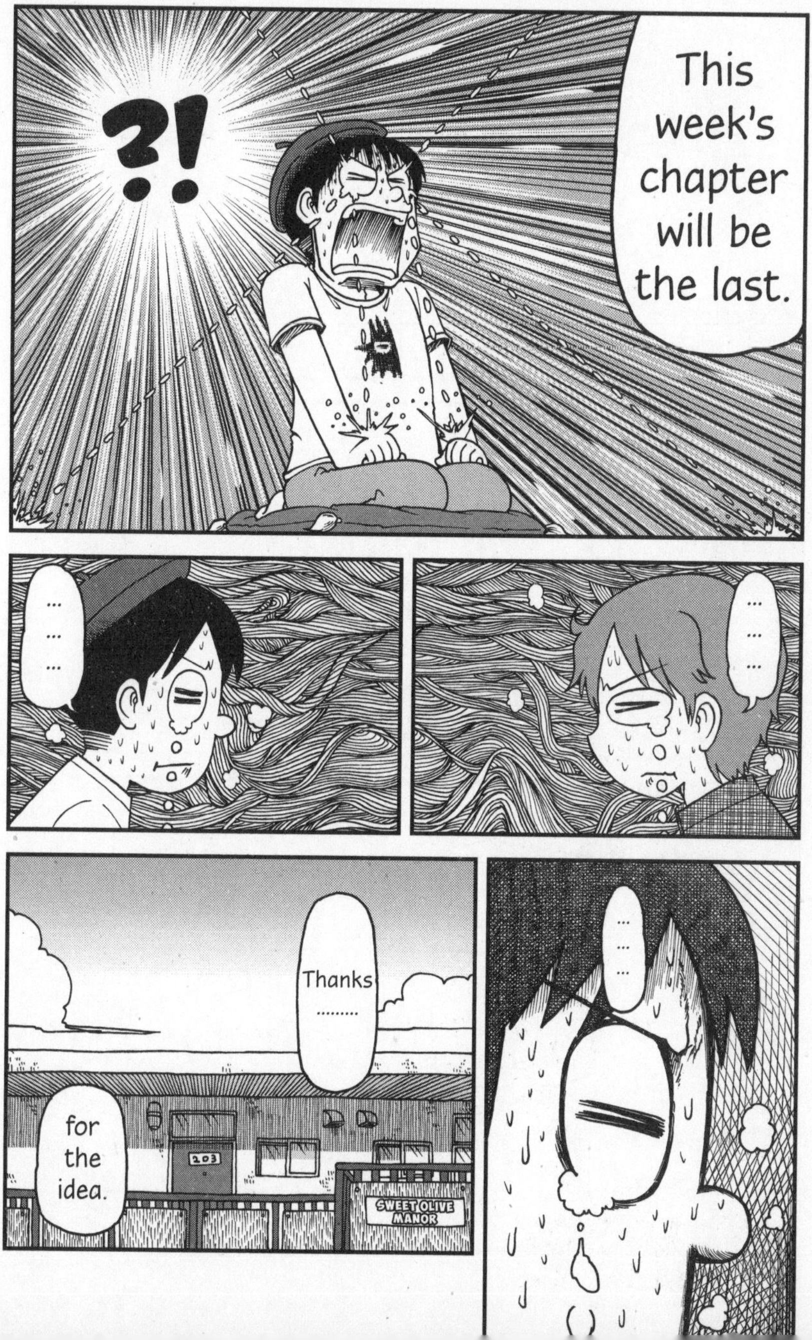
This week's chapter will be the last.
?!
………
………
………
Thanks ………
203
SWEET OLIVE MANOR
for the idea.

CITY

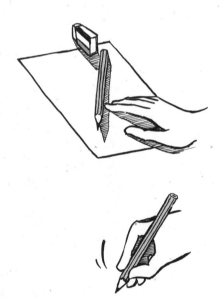

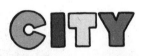

Resume
Reading
Nagumo Midori
Name
南雲美鳥
place photo here

Resume
Reading
Nagumo Midori
Name
南雲美鳥

CITY

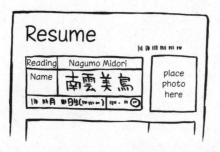

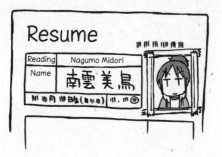

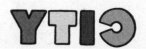

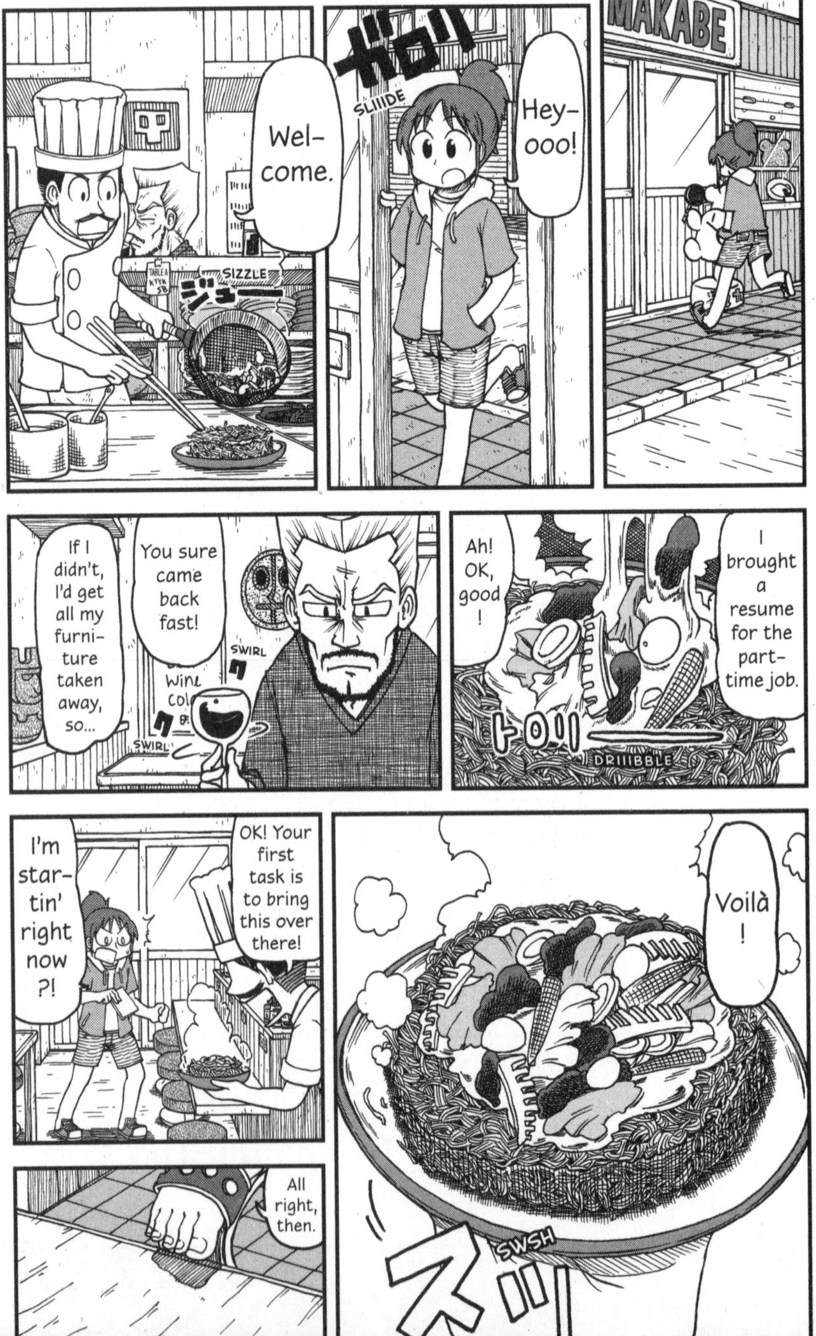
MAKABE
SLIIIDE
Hey-ooo!
Wel-come.
SIZZLE
I brought a resume for the part-time job.
Ah! OK, good!
DRIIIBBLE
You sure came back fast!
SWIRL
SWIRL
If I didn't, I'd get all my furniture taken away, so...
Voilà!
SWSH
OK! Your first task is to bring this over there!
I'm startin' right now?!
All right, then.

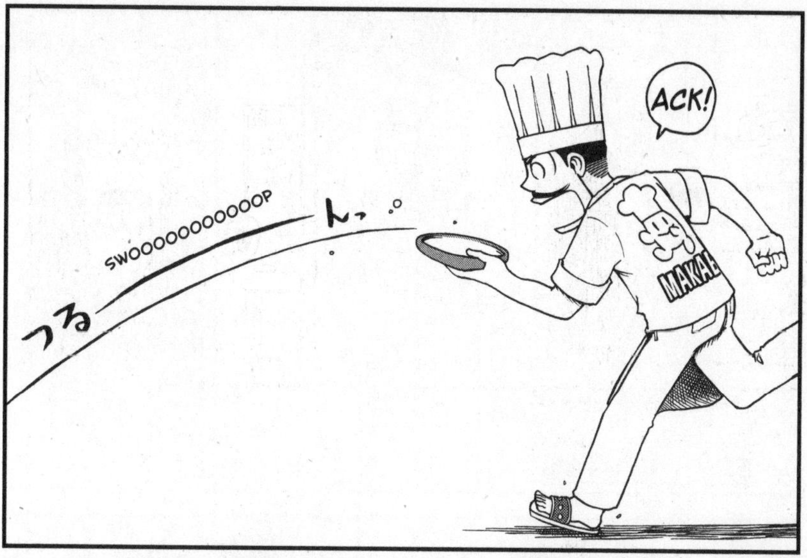
ACK!
MAKAE
SWOOOOOOOOOOOP
んっ
つる

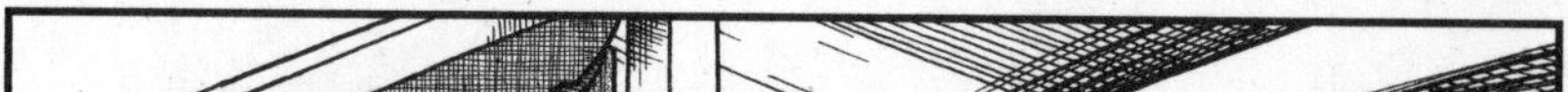
SPLOP
スポッ

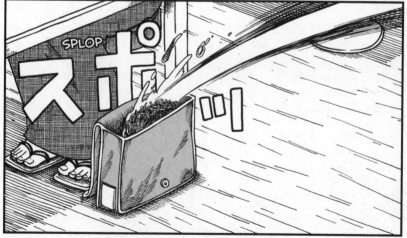

Chapter 8 Crispy Noodles

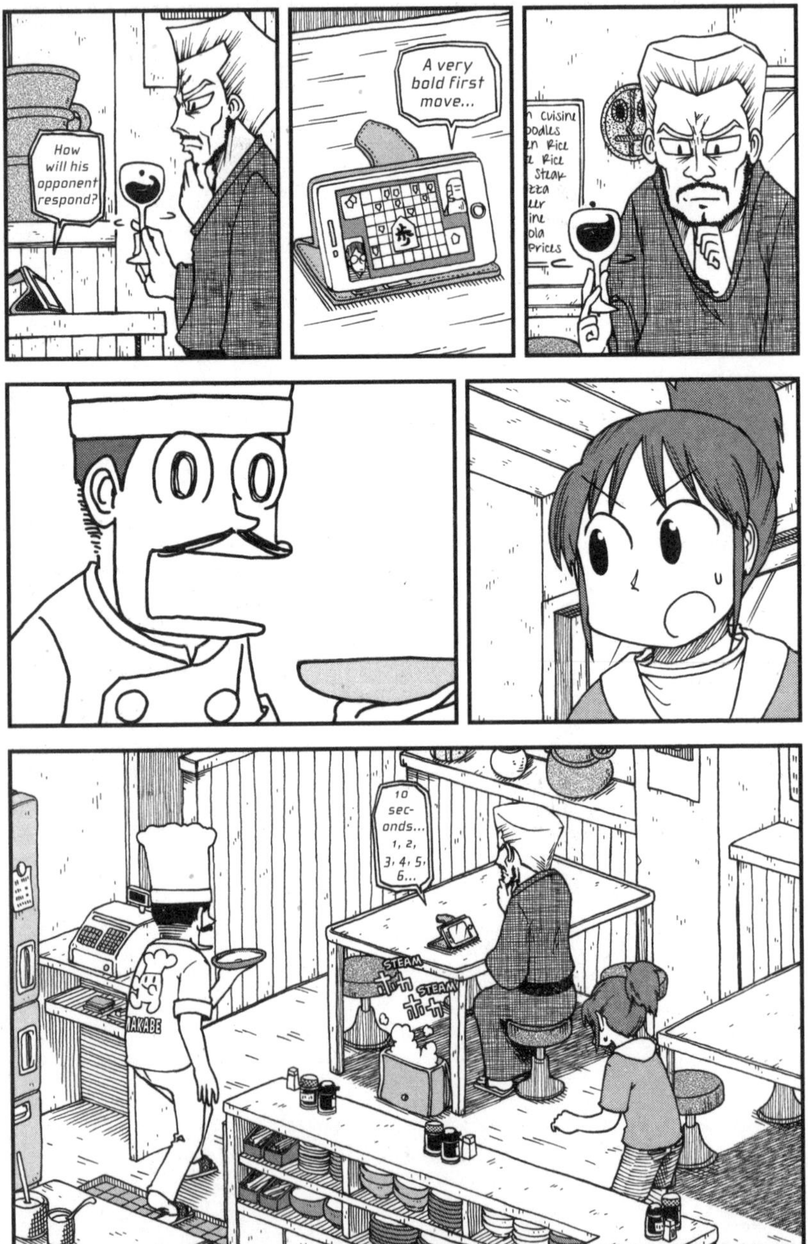
A very bold first move...
How will his opponent respond?
10 seconds... 1, 2, 3, 4, 5, 6...
STEAM
STEAM

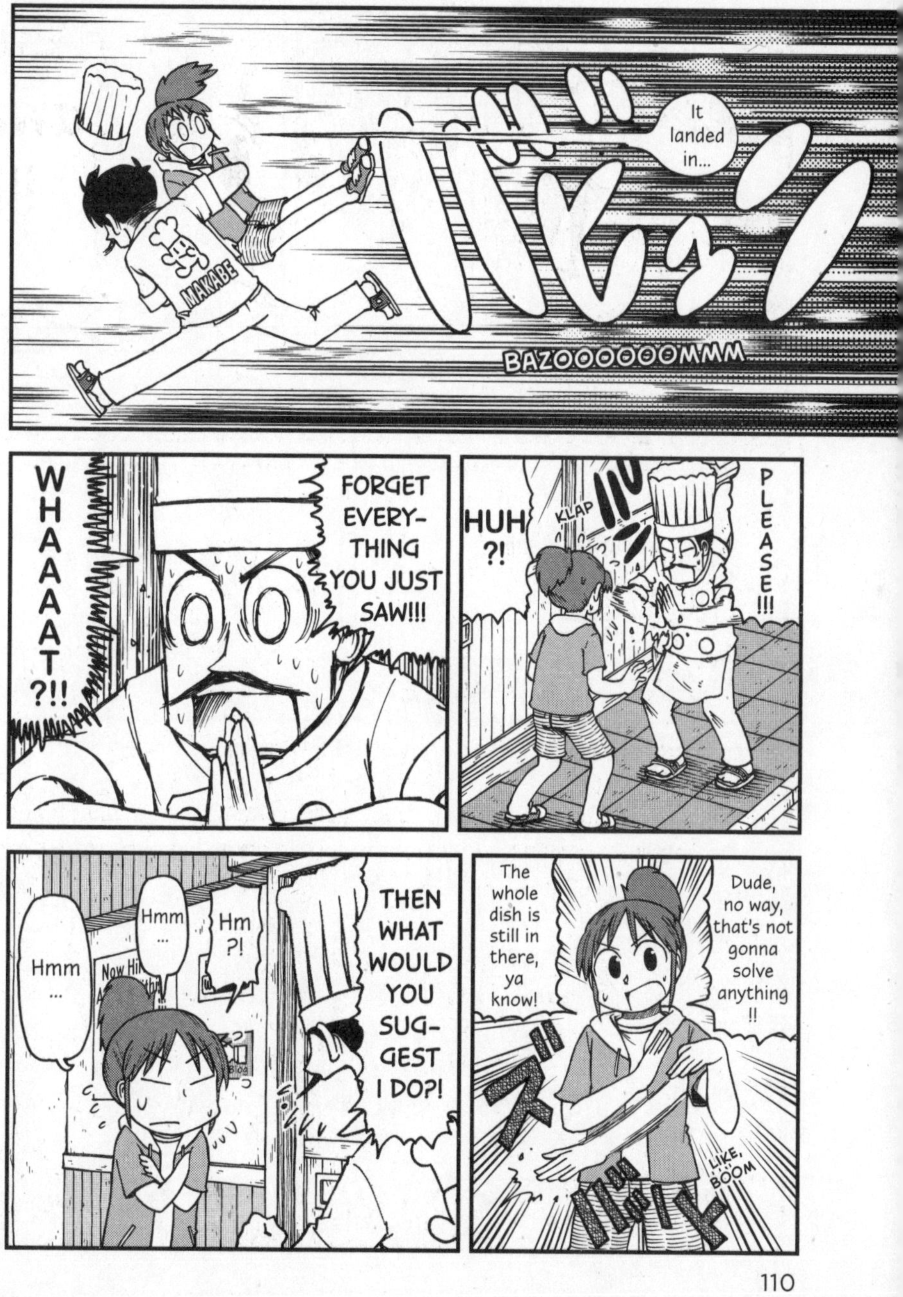
It landed in...
BAZOOOOOOMMM
PLEASE!!!
KLAP
HUH ?!
FORGET EVERY-THING YOU JUST SAW!!!
WHAAAAAT ?!!
Dude, no way, that's not gonna solve anything !!
The whole dish is still in there, ya know!
LIKE, BOOM
THEN WHAT WOULD YOU SUG-GEST I DO?!
Hm ?!
Hmm ...
Hmm ...

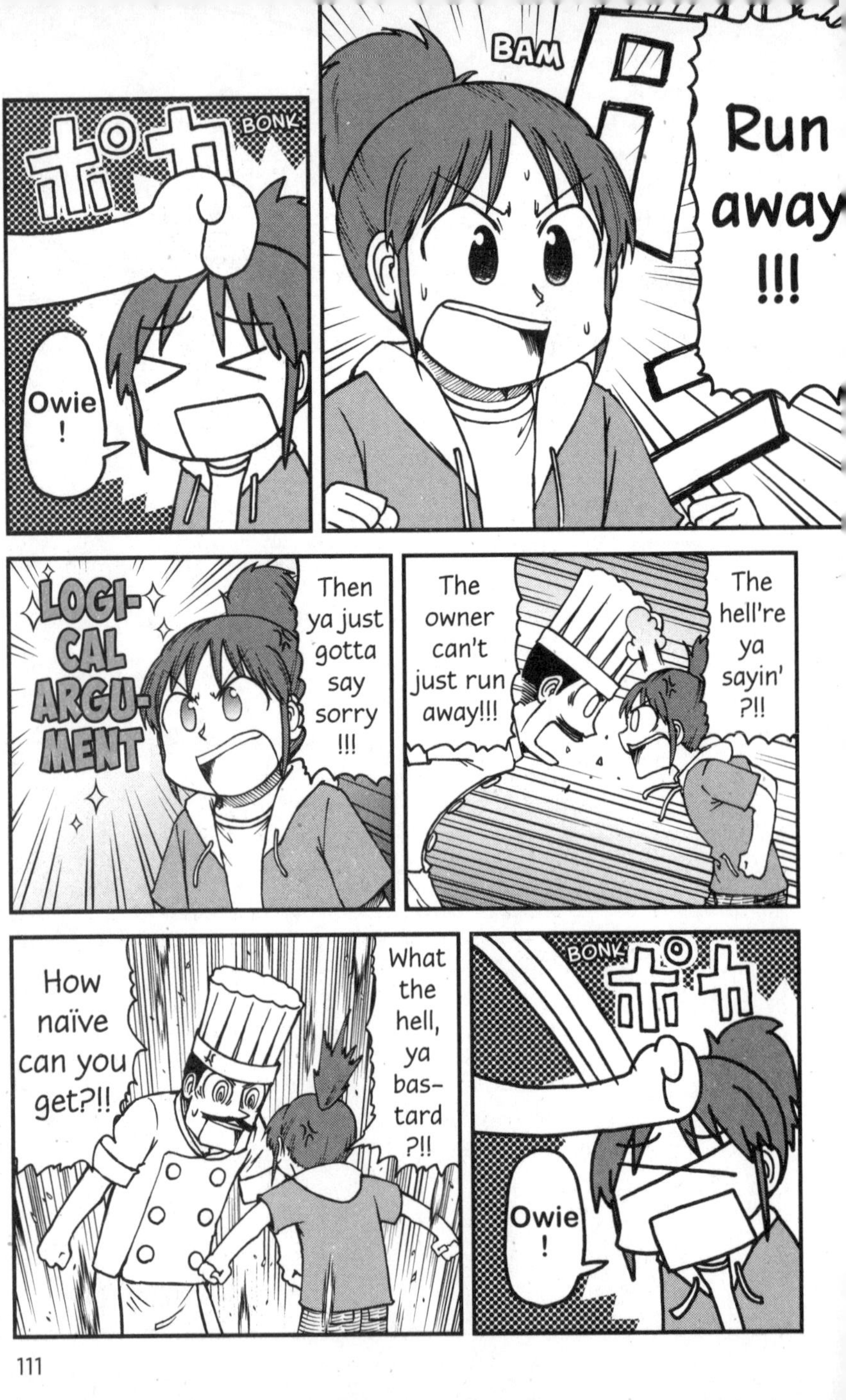
BAM
Run away!!!
ポカ
BONK
Owie!
The hell're ya sayin'?!!
The owner can't just run away!!!
Then ya just gotta say sorry!!!
LOGICAL ARGUMENT
ポカ
BONK
Owie!
What the hell, ya bastard?!!
How naïve can you get?!!

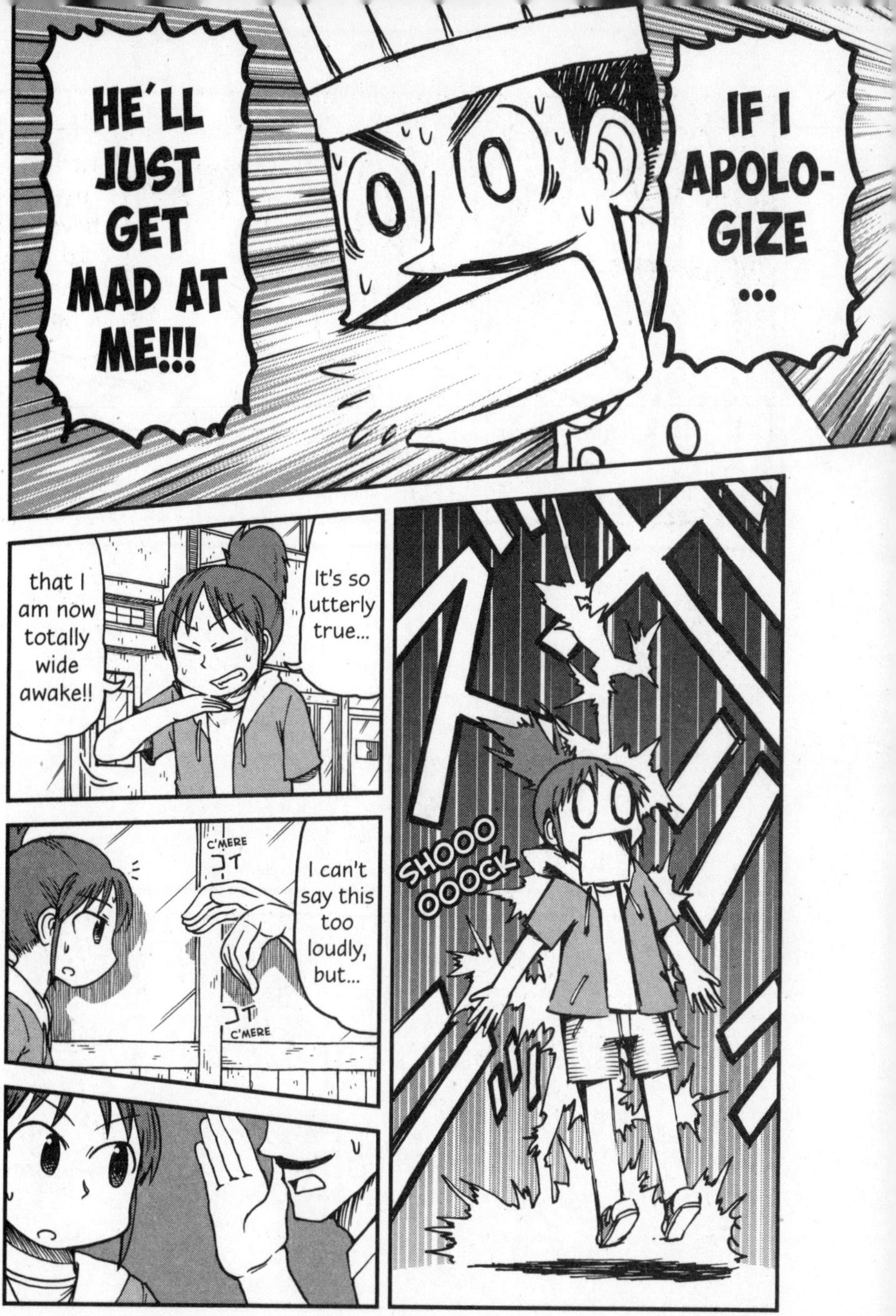
IF I APOLO-GIZE...
HE'LL JUST GET MAD AT ME!!!
SHOOOOOOCK
It's so utterly true...
that I am now totally wide awake!!
C'MERE
I can't say this too loudly, but...
C'MERE

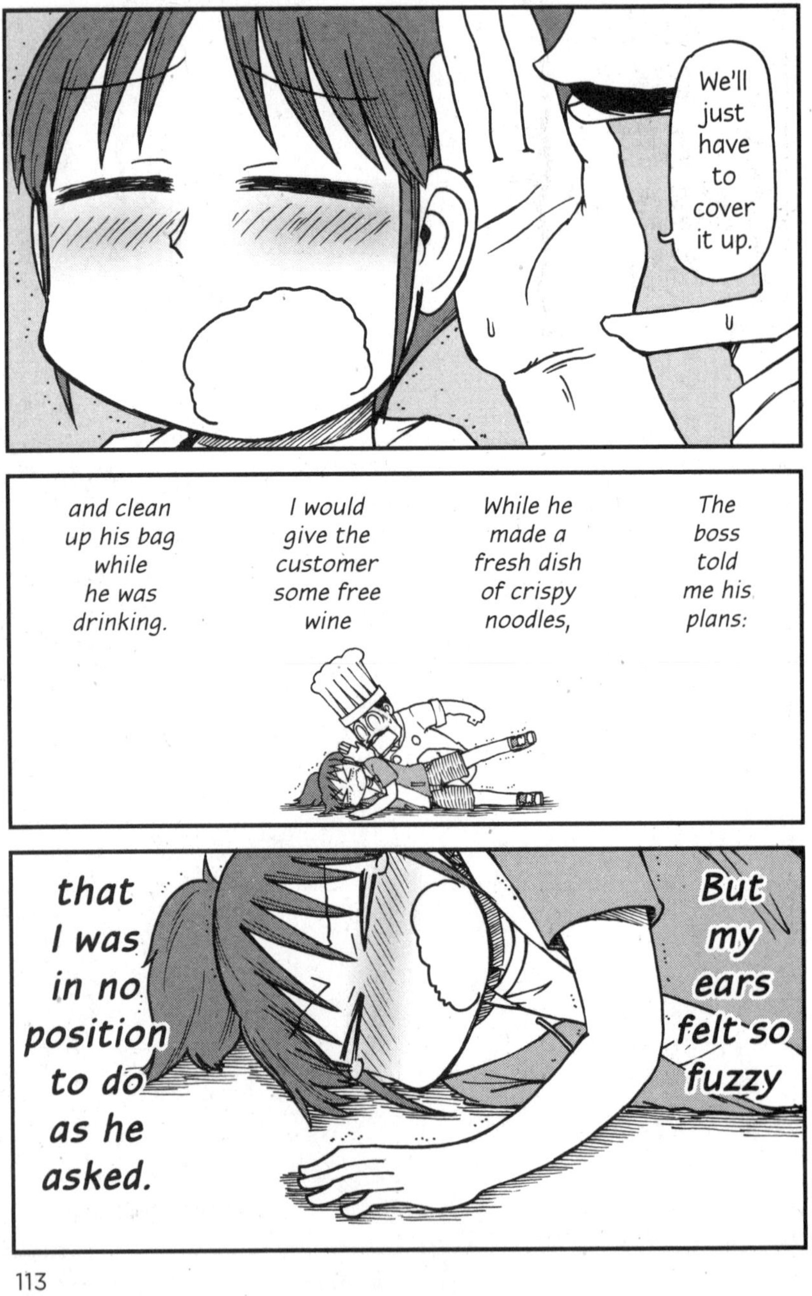
We'll just have to cover it up.
The boss told me his plans:
While he made a fresh dish of crispy noodles,
I would give the customer some free wine
and clean up his bag while he was drinking.
But my ears felt so fuzzy
that I was in no position to do as he asked.

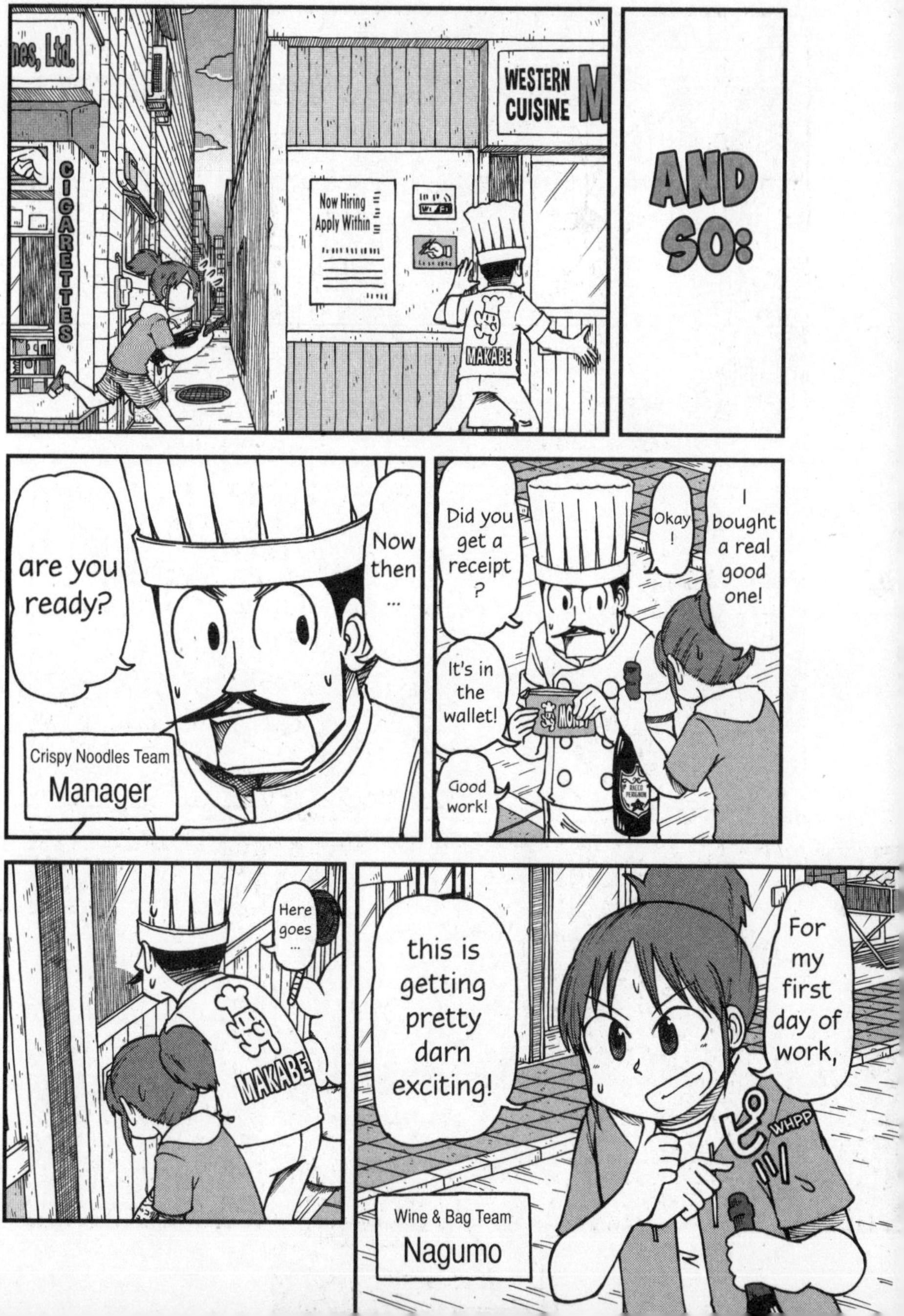
AND SO:
WESTERN CUISINE M
Now Hiring Apply Within
MAKABE
nes, Ltd.
CIGARETTES
I bought a real good one!
Okay!
Did you get a receipt?
It's in the wallet!
Good work!
Now then...
are you ready?
Crispy Noodles Team
Manager
For my first day of work,
this is getting pretty darn exciting!
WHPP
Wine & Bag Team
Nagumo
Here goes...
MAKABE

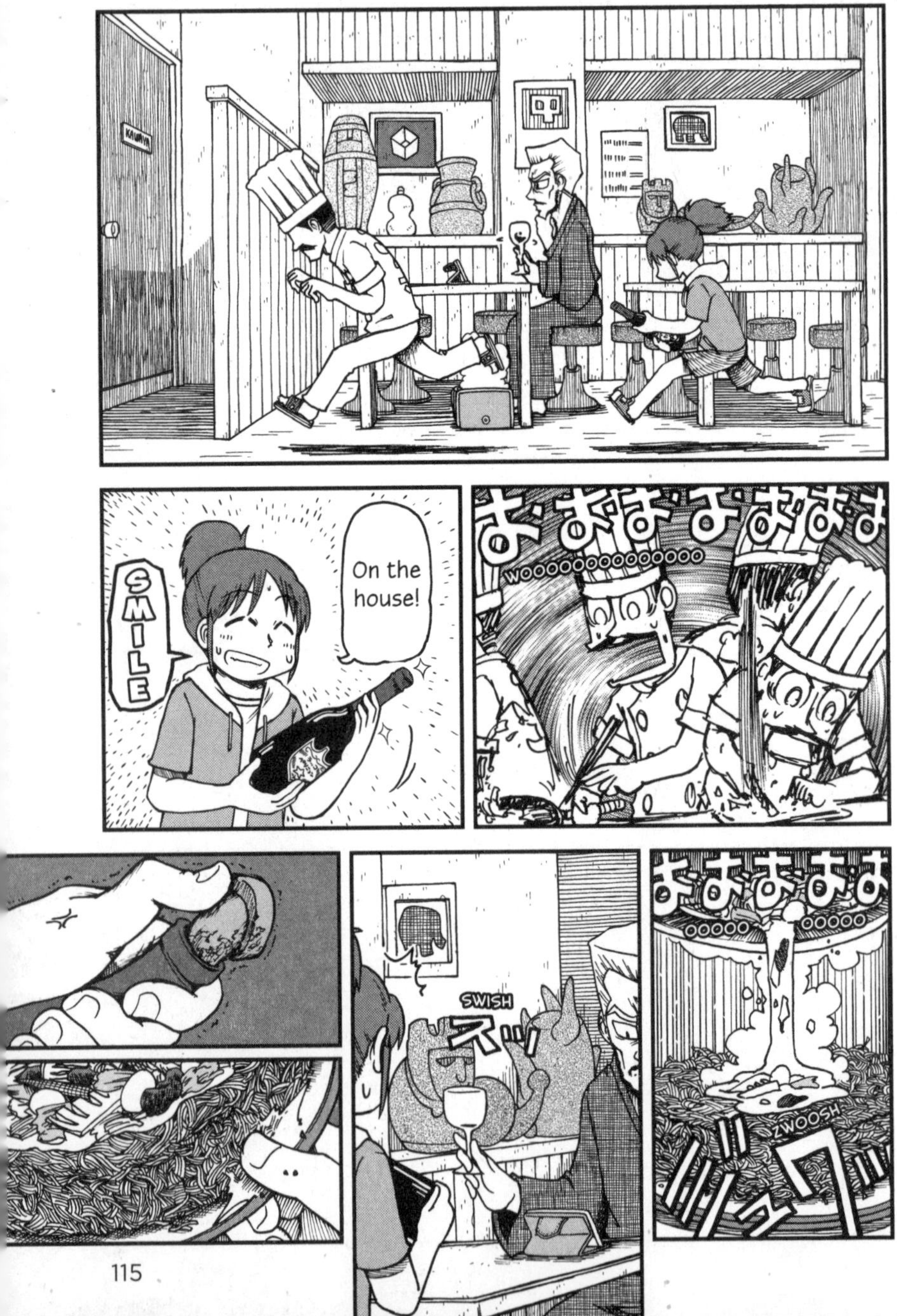
WOOOOOOOOOOOOO
On the house!
SMILE
OOOOO OOOOO
ZWOOSH
SWISH

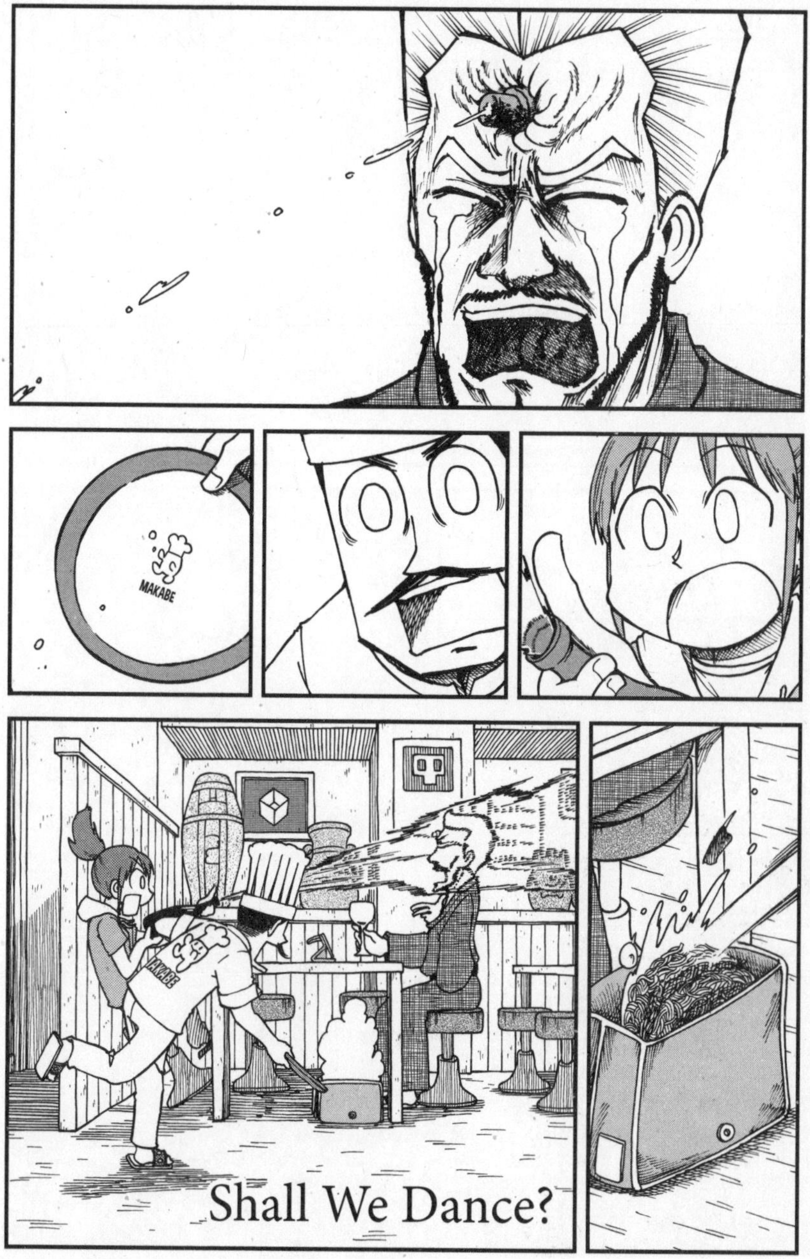
MAKABE
MAKABE
Shall We Dance?

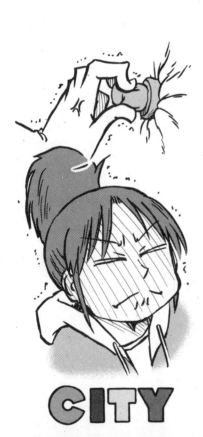

CITY

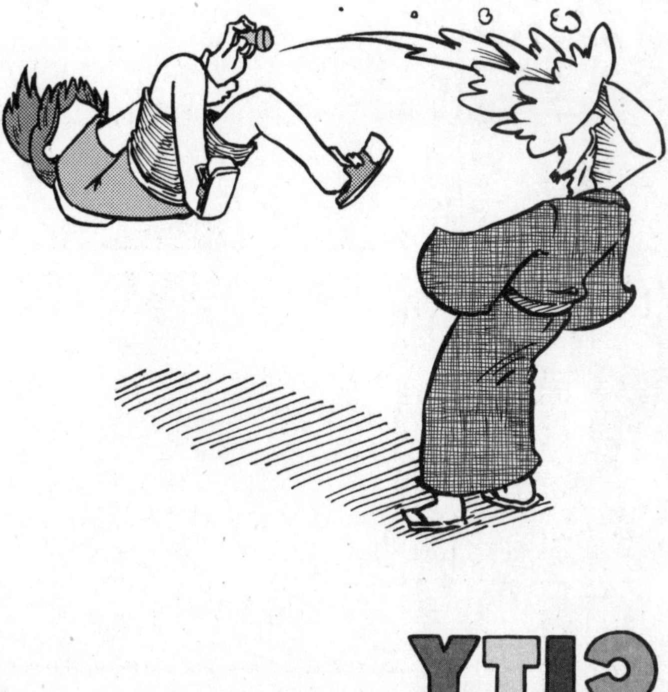
CITY

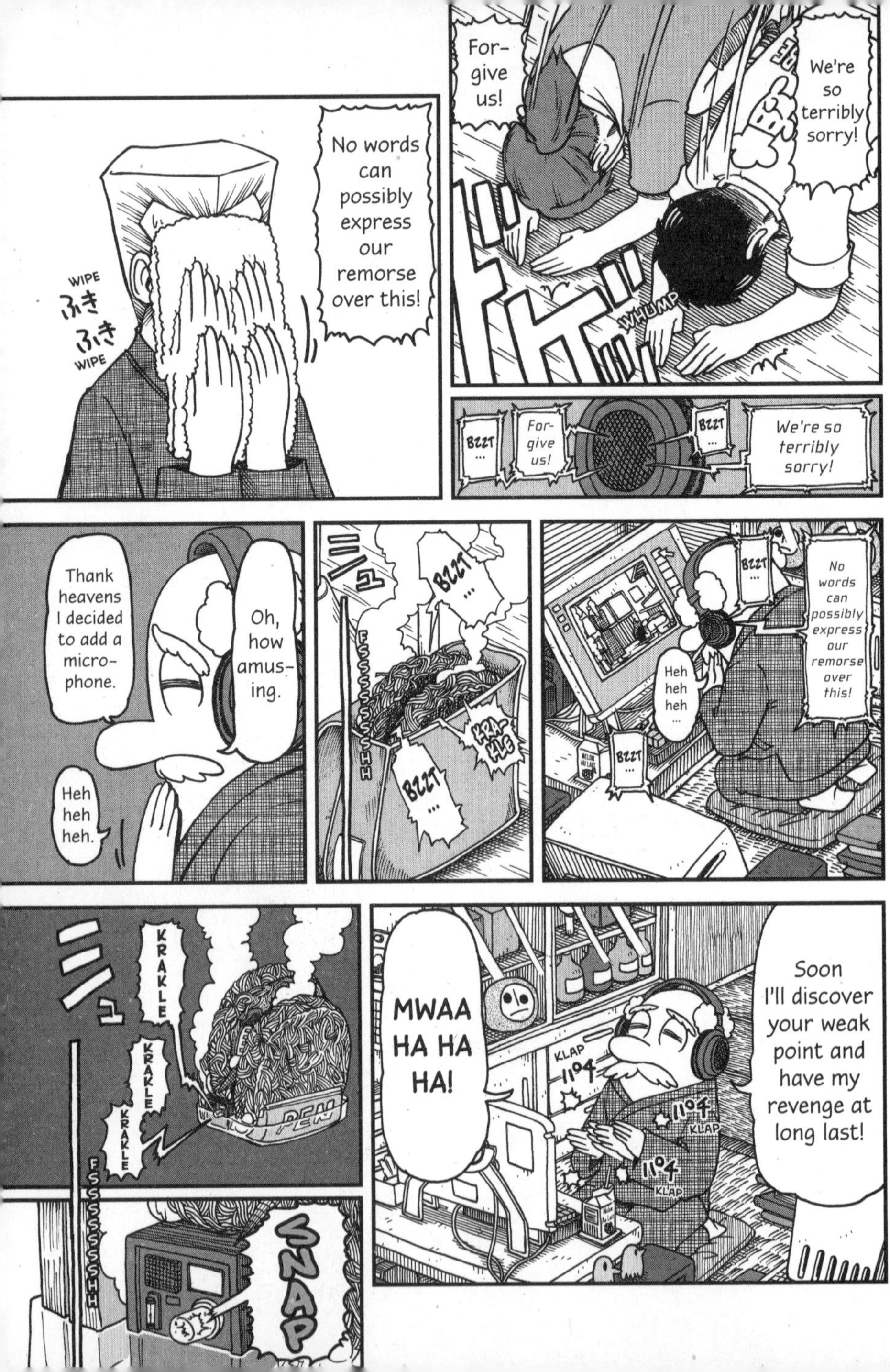

We're so terribly sorry!
For-give us!
WHUMP
We're so terribly sorry!
BZZT ...
For-give us!
BZZT ...
No words can possibly express our remorse over this!
WIPE
ふき
ふき
WIPE
No words can possibly express our remorse over this!
BZZT ...
Heh heh heh ...
BZZT ...
BZZT ...
KRAKLE
BZZT ...
FSSSSSSHH
Oh, how amus-ing.
Thank heavens I decided to add a micro-phone.
Heh heh heh.
Soon I'll discover your weak point and have my revenge at long last!
MWAA HA HA HA!
KLAP
KLAP
KLAP
KRAKLE
KRAKLE
KRAKLE
FSSSSSSHH
SNAP

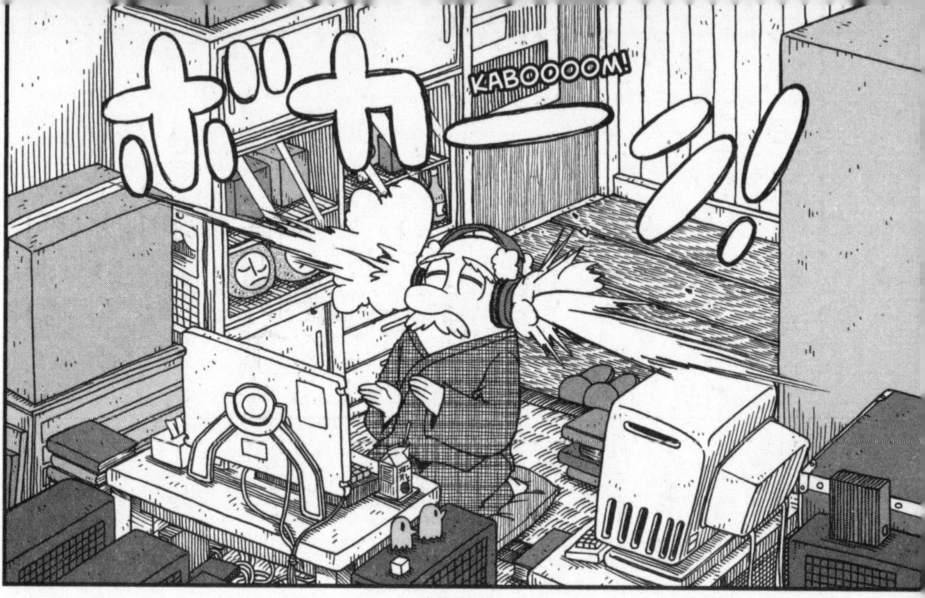
ボカーン!
KABOOOOM!

Chapter 9 ◇ Dr. Adatara

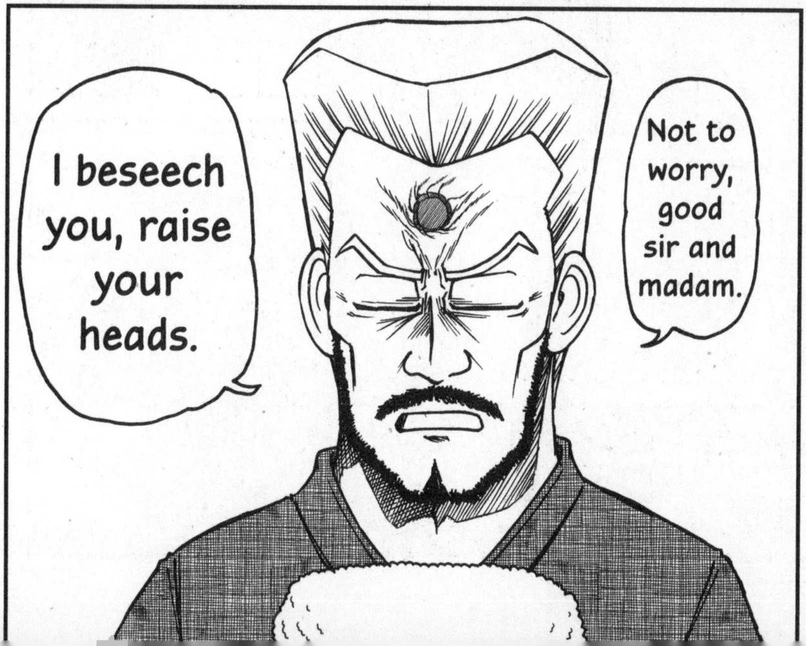
Not to worry, good sir and madam.
I beseech you, raise your heads.

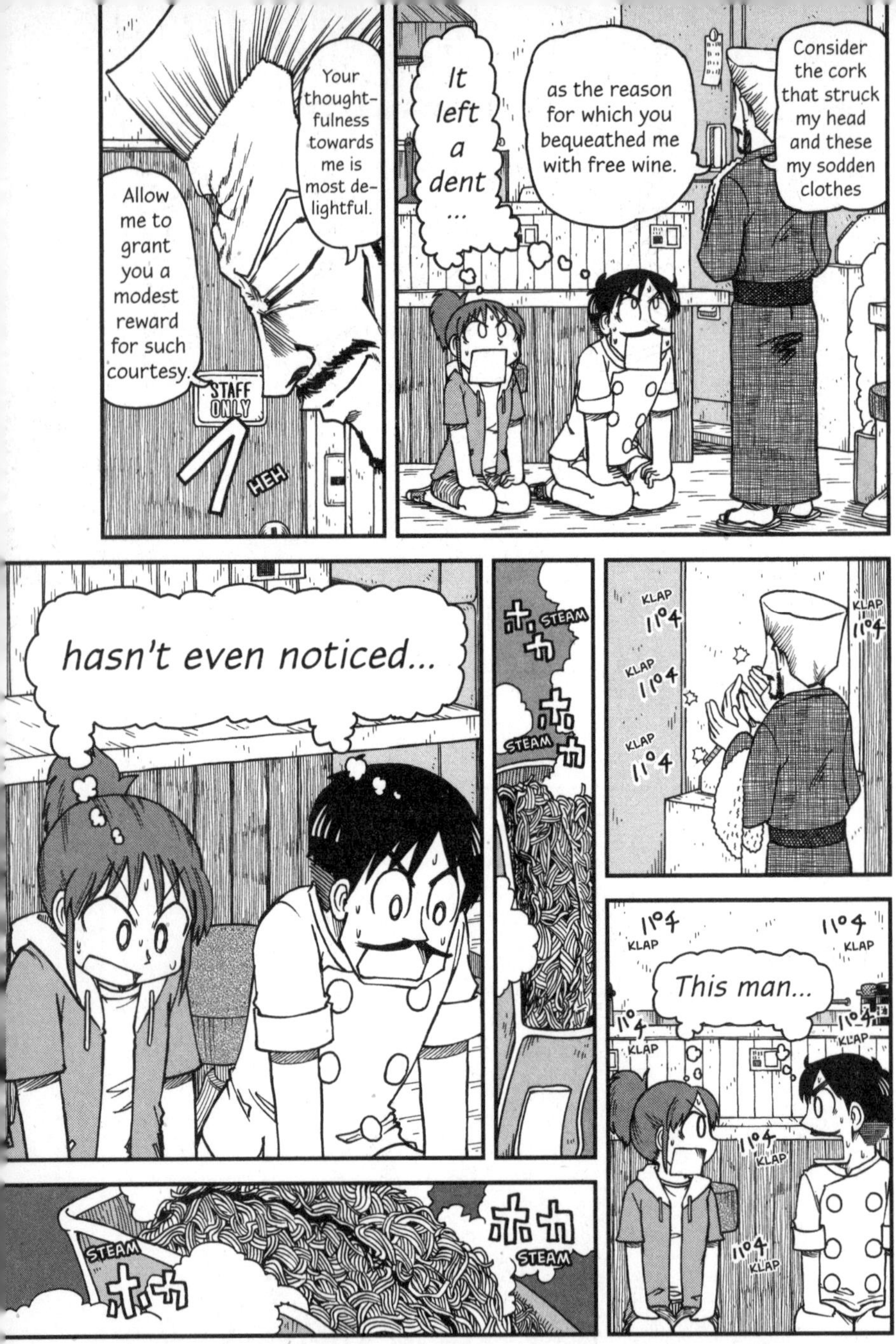
Consider the cork that struck my head and these my sodden clothes
as the reason for which you bequeathed me with free wine.
It left a dent ...
Your thoughtfulness towards me is most delightful.
Allow me to grant you a modest reward for such courtesy.
STAFF ONLY
HEH
KLAP
KLAP
KLAP
KLAP
KLAP
KLAP
This man...
KLAP
KLAP
KLAP
KLAP
STEAM
STEAM
hasn't even noticed...
STEAM
STEAM

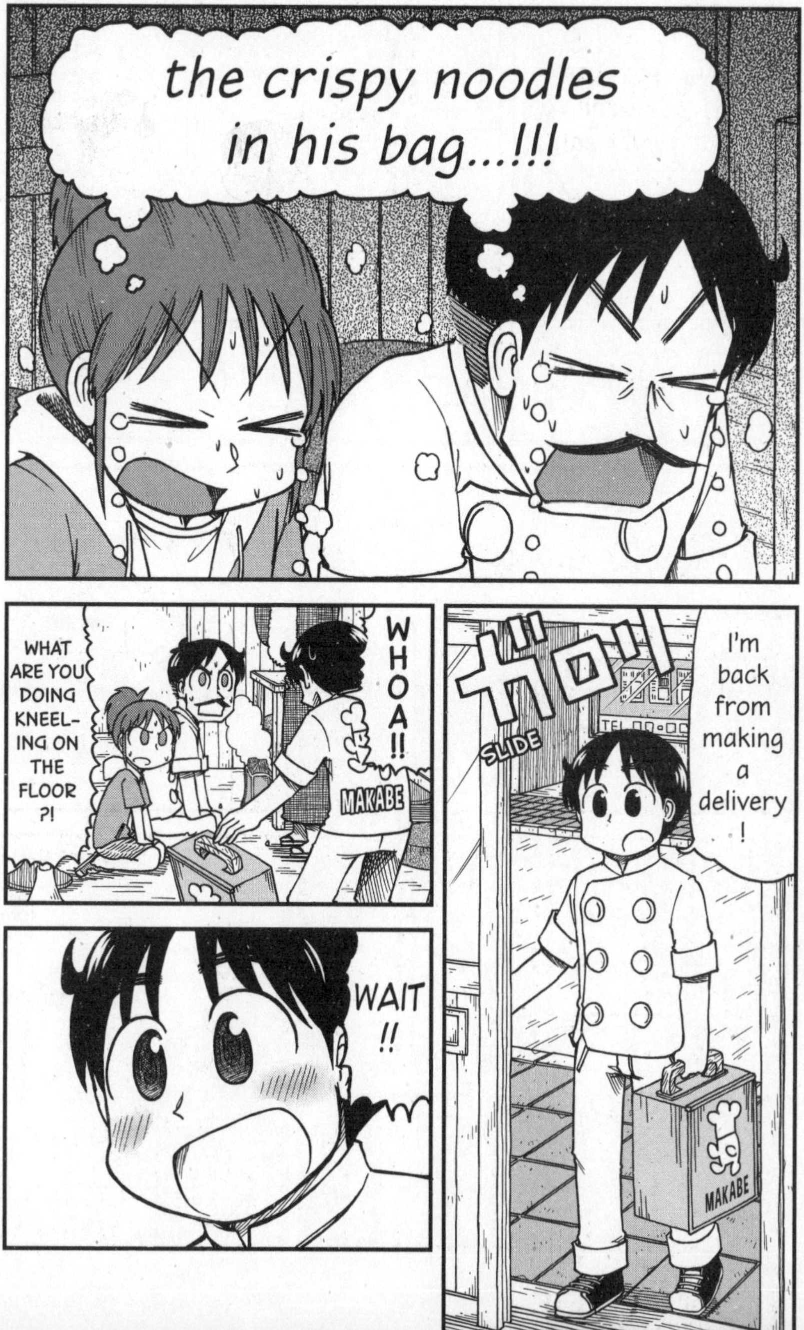
the crispy noodles in his bag...!!!
I'm back from making a delivery!
ガロッ
SLIDE
MAKABE
WHOA!!
MAKABE
WHAT ARE YOU DOING KNEEL-ING ON THE FLOOR?!
WAIT!!

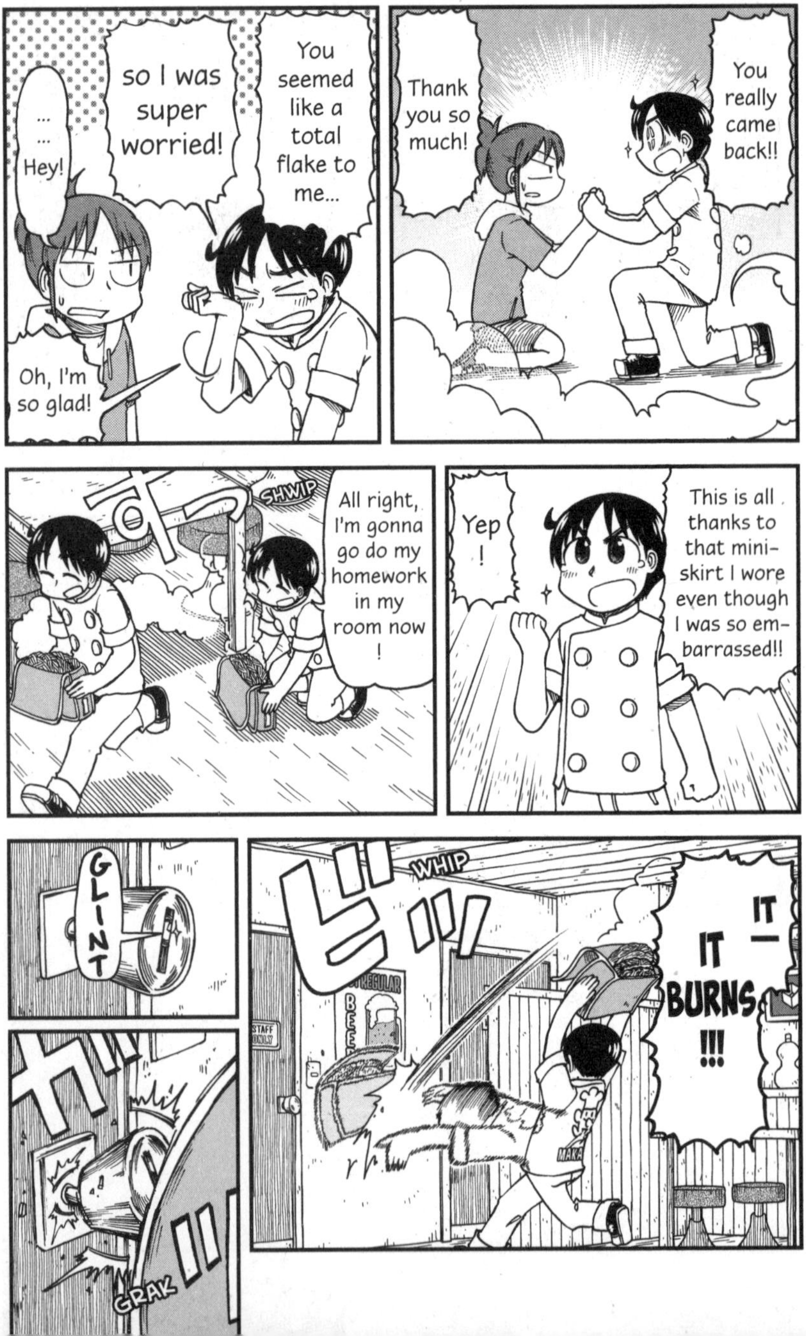
You really came back!!
Thank you so much!
You seemed like a total flake to me...
so I was super worried!
... ... Hey!
Oh, I'm so glad!
This is all thanks to that mini-skirt I wore even though I was so embarrassed!!
Yep!
All right, I'm gonna go do my homework in my room now!
SHWIP
IT— IT BURNS!!!
WHIP
REGULAR BEER
STAFF ONLY
GLINT
GRAK

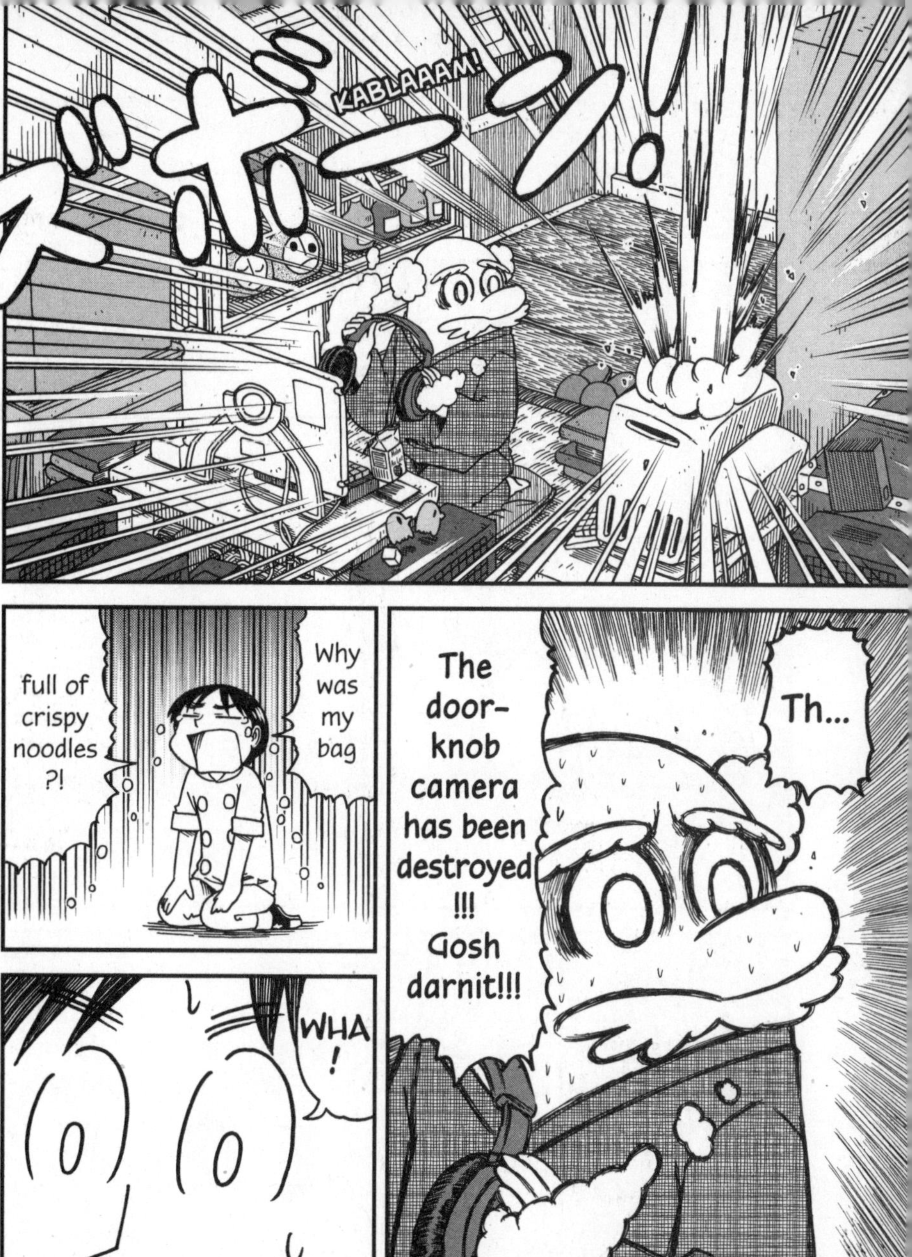
ズボーン!
KABLAAAM!
Th...
The door-knob camera has been destroyed!!! Gosh darnit!!!
Why was my bag full of crispy noodles?!
WHA!

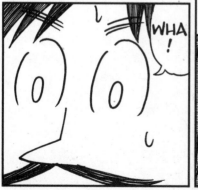

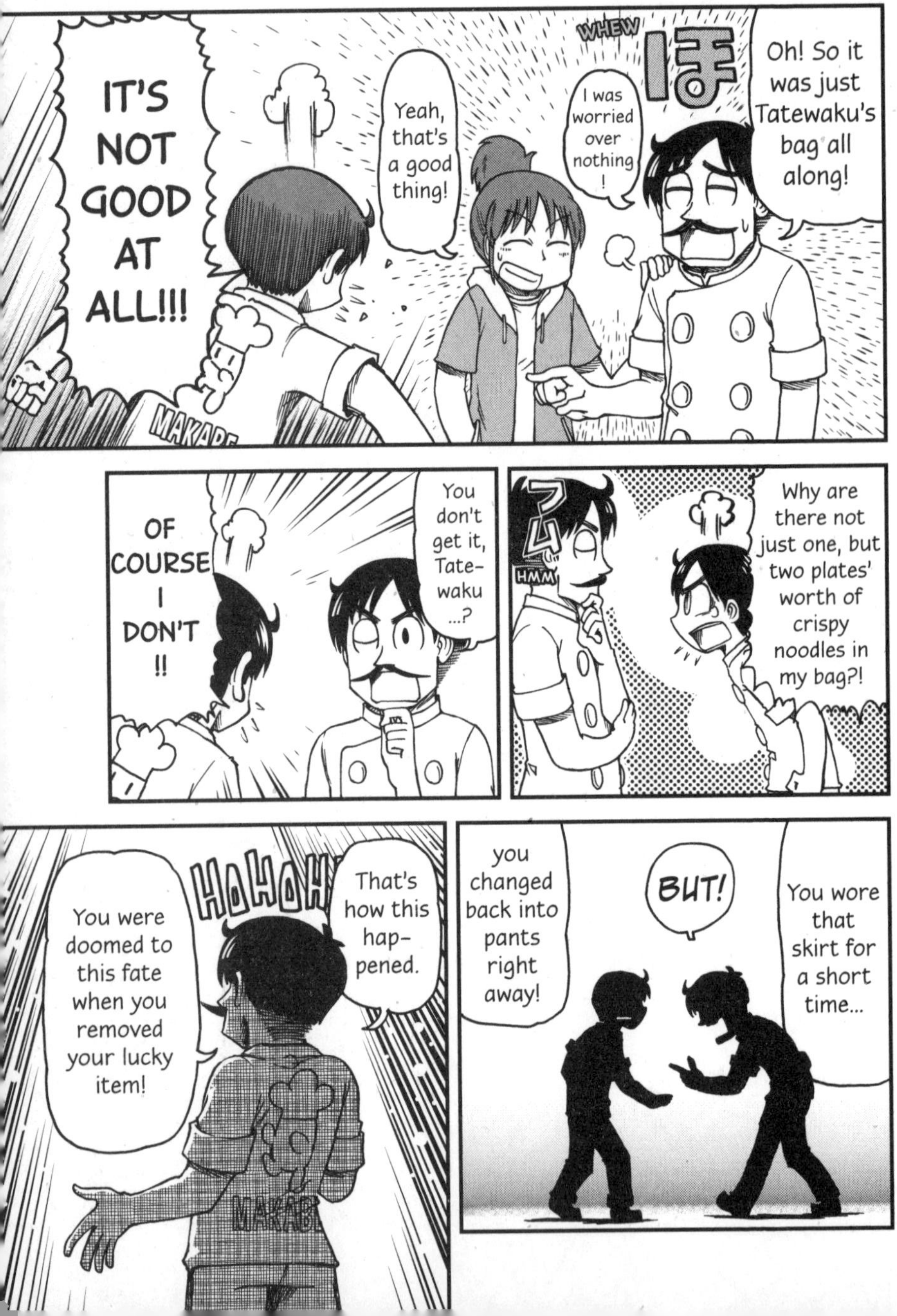
Oh! So it was just Tatewaku's bag all along!
WHEW
ほ
I was worried over nothing!
Yeah, that's a good thing!
IT'S NOT GOOD AT ALL!!!
MAKABE
Why are there not just one, but two plates' worth of crispy noodles in my bag?!
ム
HMM
You don't get it, Tatewaku...?
OF COURSE I DON'T!!
You wore that skirt for a short time...
BUT!
you changed back into pants right away!
That's how this happened.
HOHOHO
You were doomed to this fate when you removed your lucky item!
MAKABE

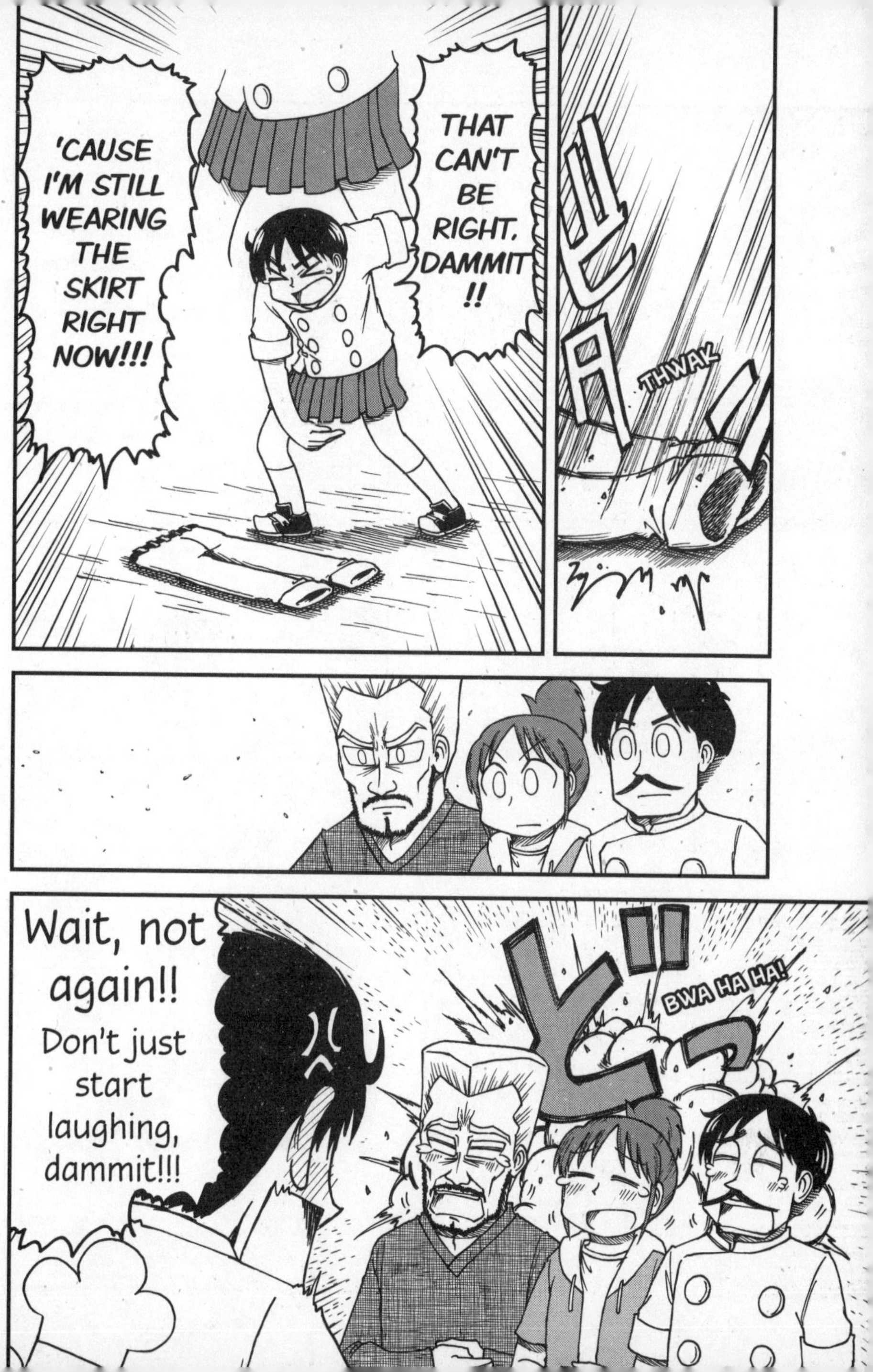
THWAK
THAT CAN'T BE RIGHT, DAMMIT!!
'CAUSE I'M STILL WEARING THE SKIRT RIGHT NOW!!!
BWA HA HA!
Wait, not again!!
Don't just start laughing, dammit!!!

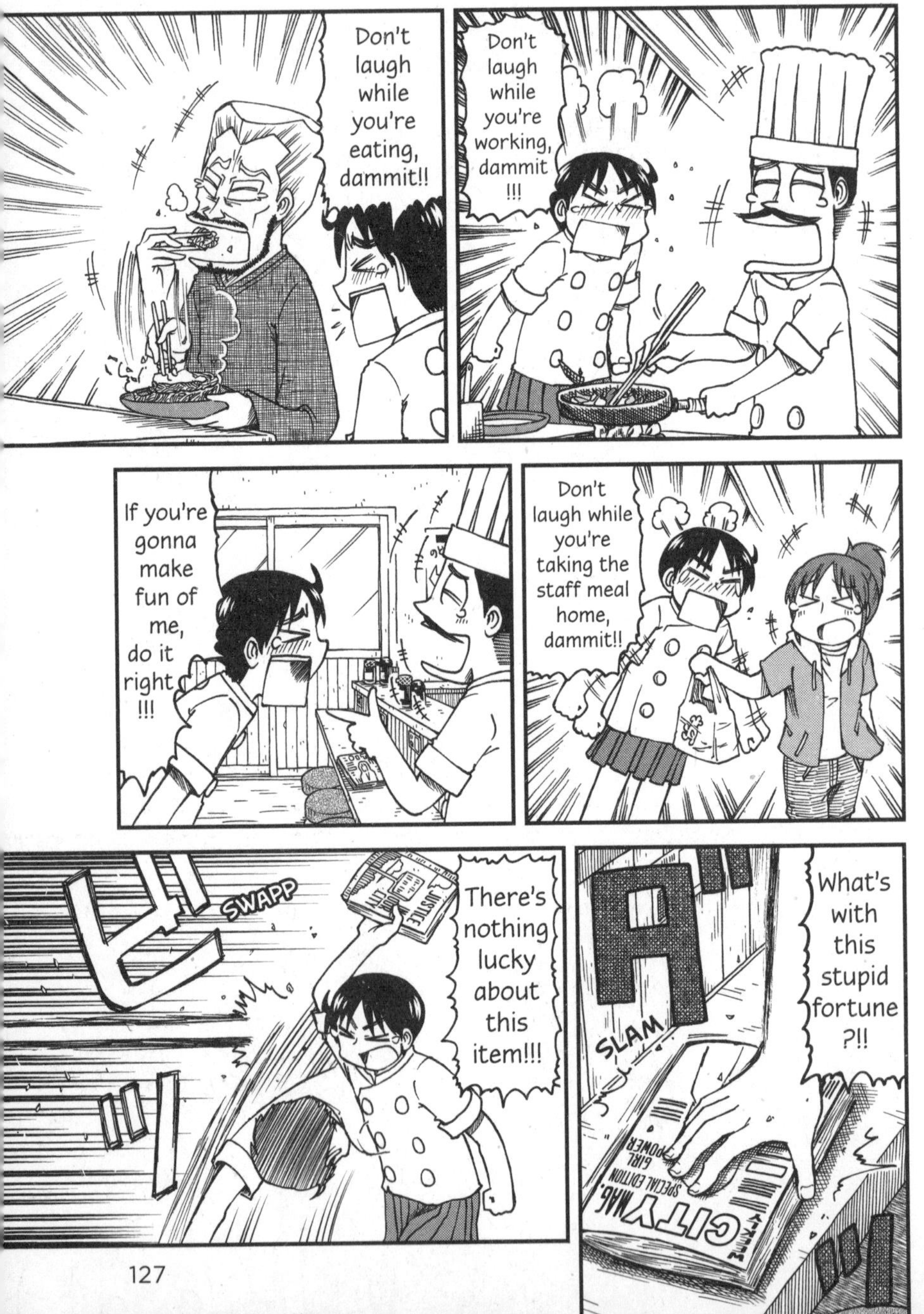
Don't laugh while you're working, dammit !!!
Don't laugh while you're eating, dammit!!
Don't laugh while you're taking the staff meal home, dammit!!
If you're gonna make fun of me, do it right !!!
What's with this stupid fortune ?!!
SLAM
CITY MAG.
SPECIAL EDITION
GIRL POWER
SWAPP
JUSTICE
CITY
There's nothing lucky about this item!!!

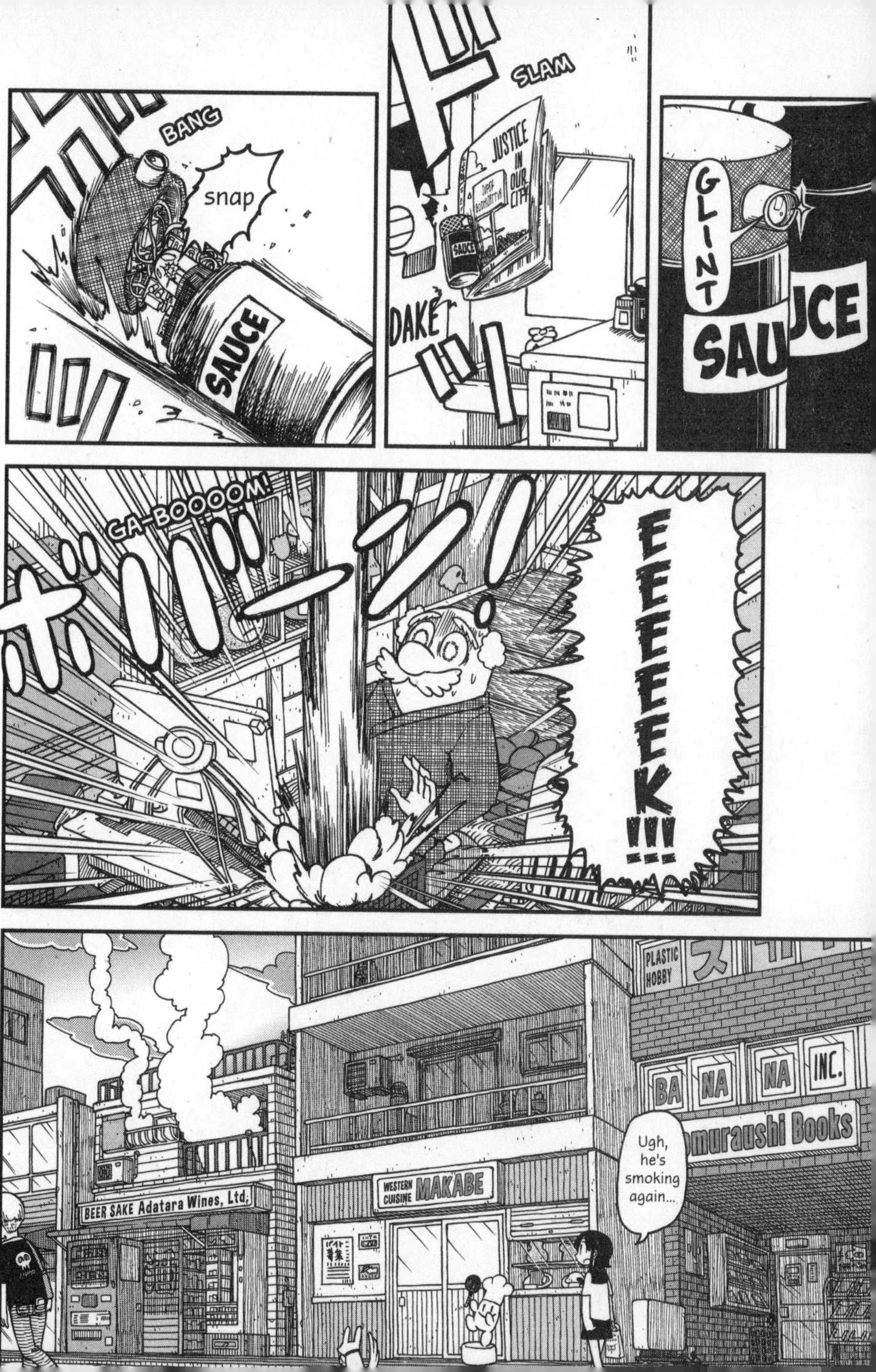

GLINT
SAUCE
SLAM
JUSTICE IN OUR CITY
SAUCE
DAKE
BANG
snap
SAUCE
GA-BOOOOM!
EEEEEEEK!!!
PLASTIC HOBBY
BA NA NA INC.
omuraushi Books
WESTERN CUISINE MAKABE
BEER SAKE Adatara Wines, Ltd.
Ugh, he's smoking again...

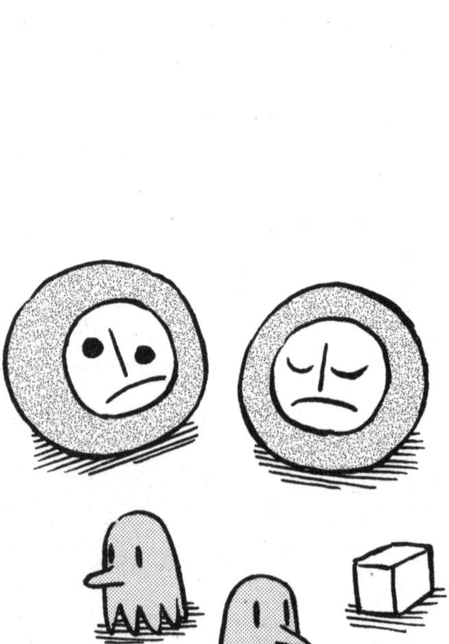

CITY

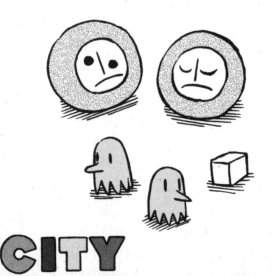

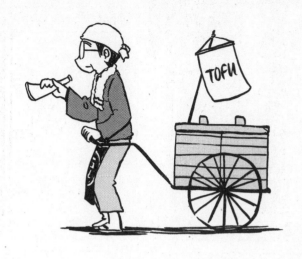

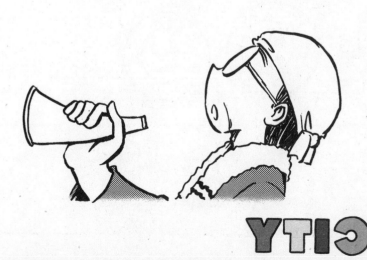

CITY

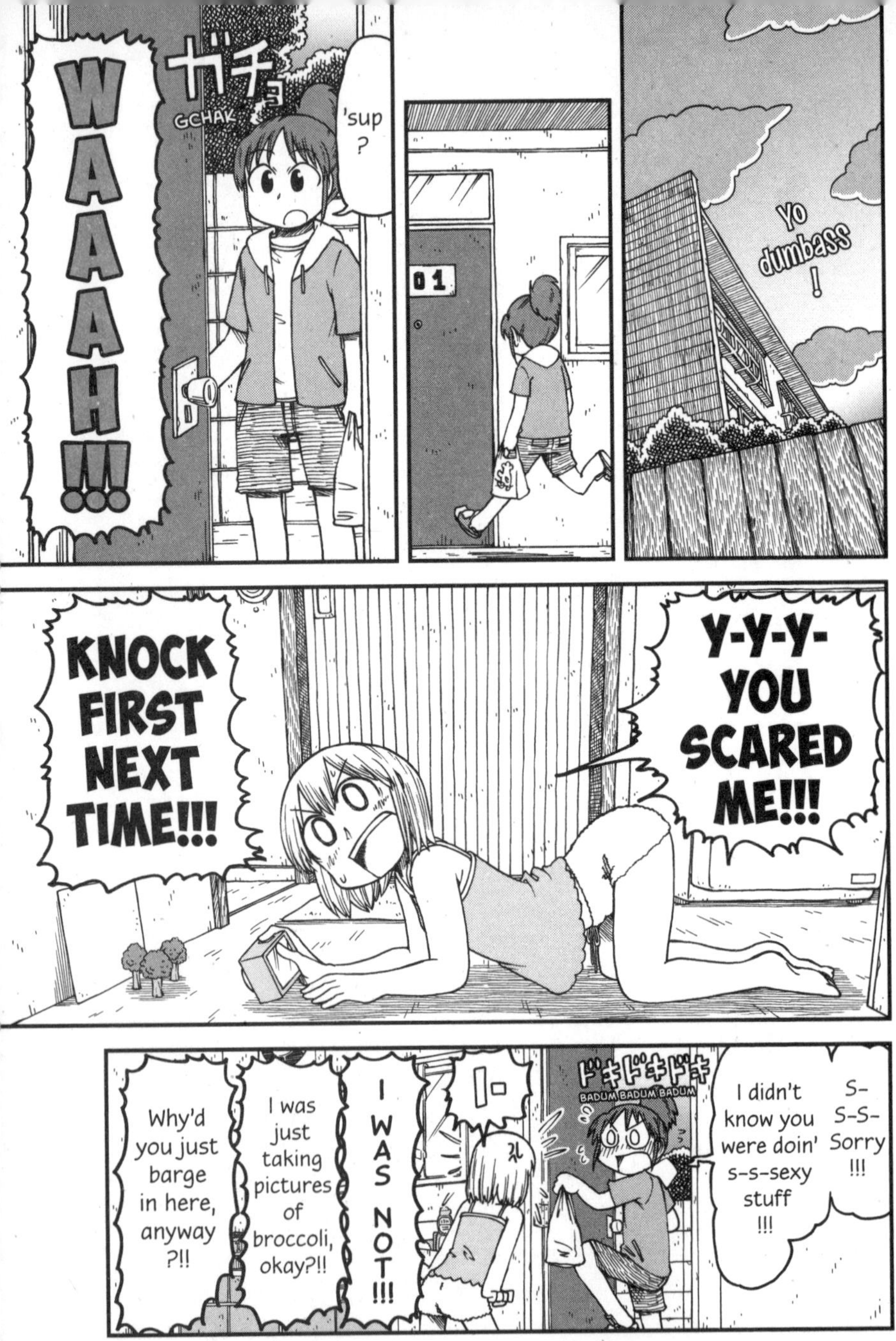
Yo dumbass!
'sup?
ガチョ
GCHAK
WAAAAH!!!
Y-Y-Y-YOU SCARED ME!!!
KNOCK FIRST NEXT TIME!!!
S-S-S-Sorry!!!
I didn't know you were doin' s-s-sexy stuff!!!
ドキドキドキ
BADUM BADUM BADUM
I-
I WAS NOT!!!
I was just taking pictures of broccoli, okay?!!
Why'd you just barge in here, anyway?!!

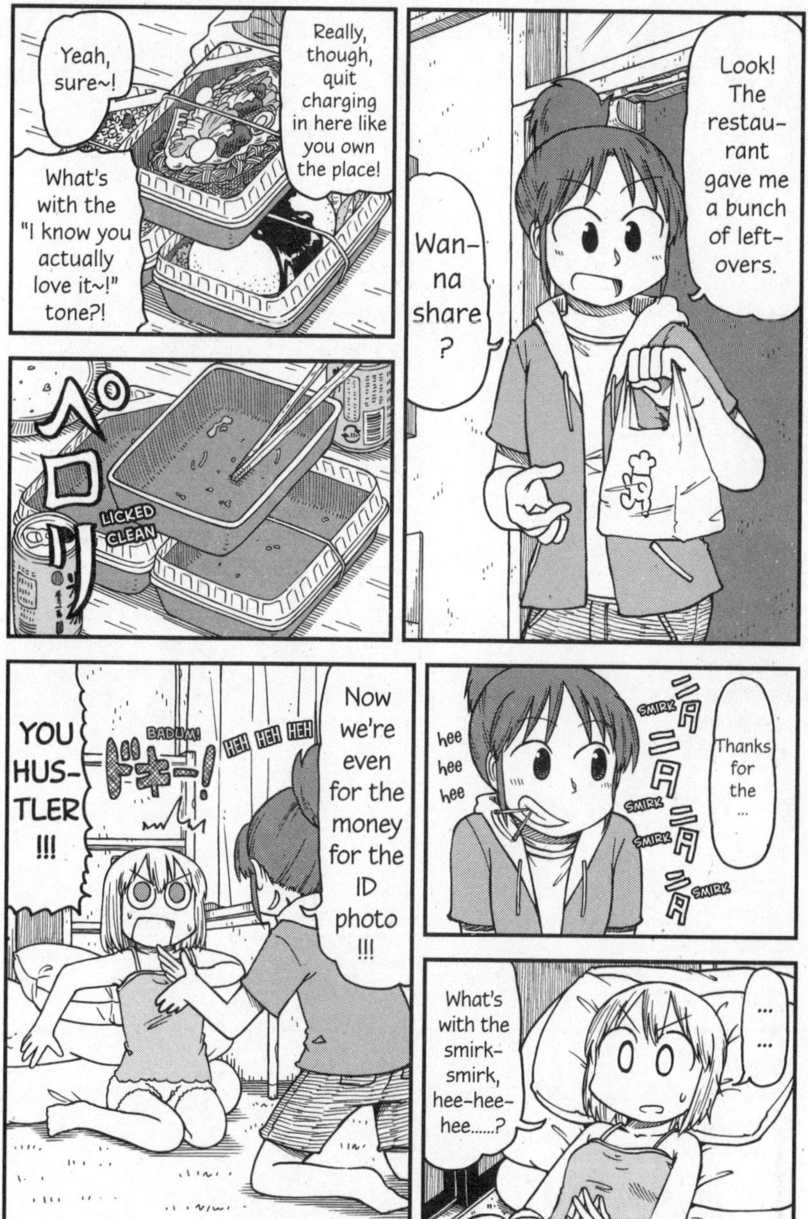

Look! The restaurant gave me a bunch of leftovers.
Wanna share?
Really, though, quit charging in here like you own the place!
Yeah, sure~!
What's with the "I know you actually love it~!" tone?!
ペロリ
LICKED CLEAN
Thanks for the ...
ニタ ニタ ニタ ニタ
SMIRK SMIRK SMIRK SMIRK
hee hee hee
......
What's with the smirk-smirk, hee-hee-hee......?
Now we're even for the money for the ID photo!!!
HEH HEH HEH
BADUM!
ドキー!
YOU HUSTLER!!!

Chapter 10 Dream

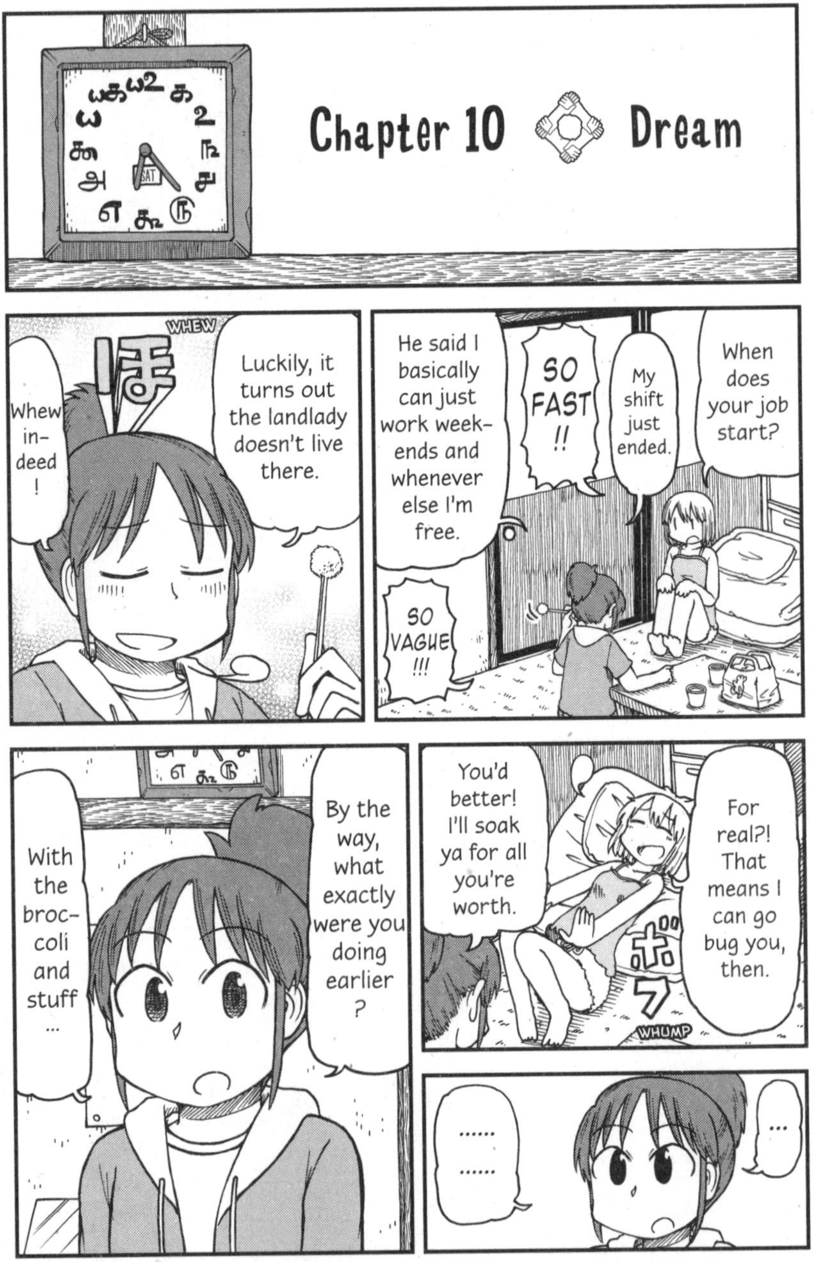

When does your job start?
My shift just ended.
SO FAST!!
He said I basically can just work weekends and whenever else I'm free.
SO VAGUE!!!
Luckily, it turns out the landlady doesn't live there.
WHEW
Whew indeed!
For real?! That means I can go bug you, then.
WHUMP
You'd better! I'll soak ya for all you're worth.
...
....
By the way, what exactly were you doing earlier?
With the broccoli and stuff...

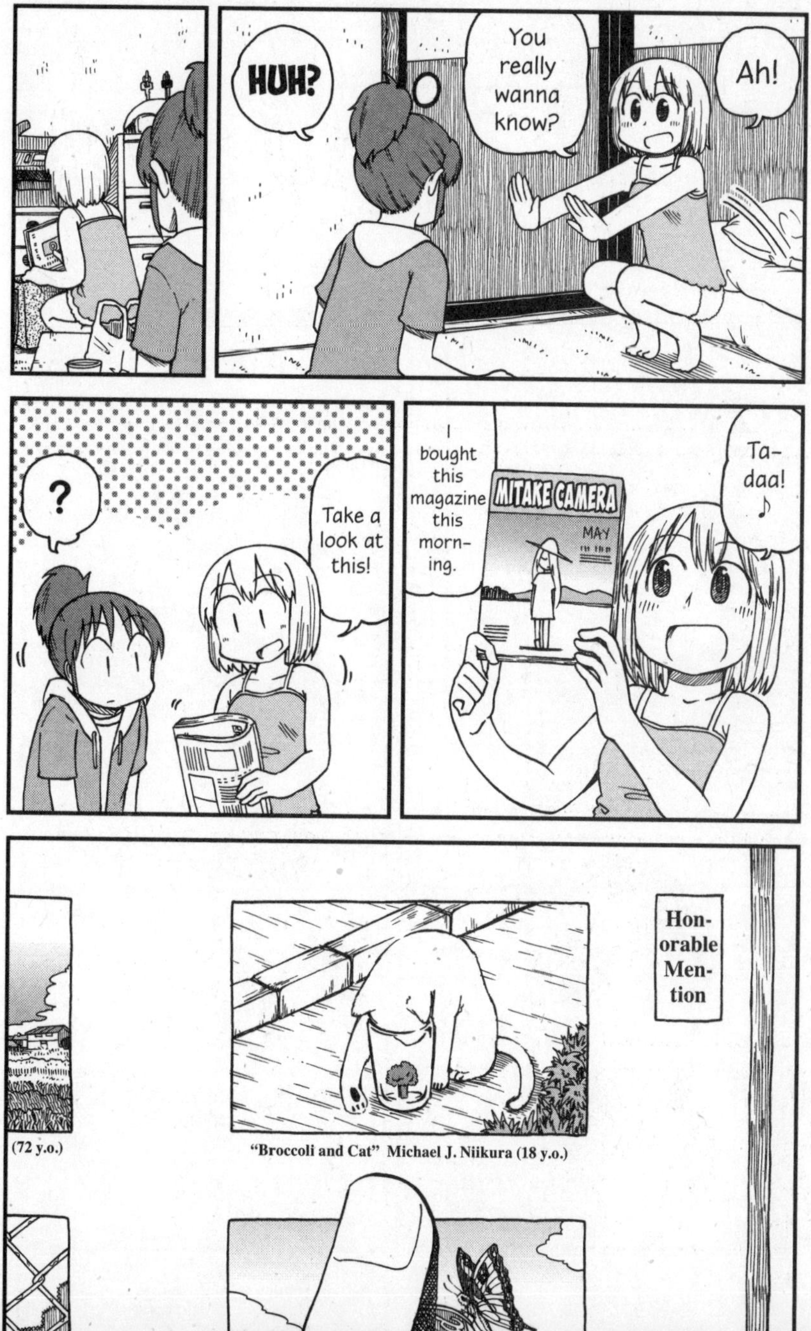
Ah!
You really wanna know?
HUH?
Ta-daa! ♪
I bought this magazine this morning.
MITAKE CAMERA
MAY
Take a look at this!
?
Hon-orable Men-tion
"Broccoli and Cat" Michael J. Niikura (18 y.o.)
(72 y.o.)

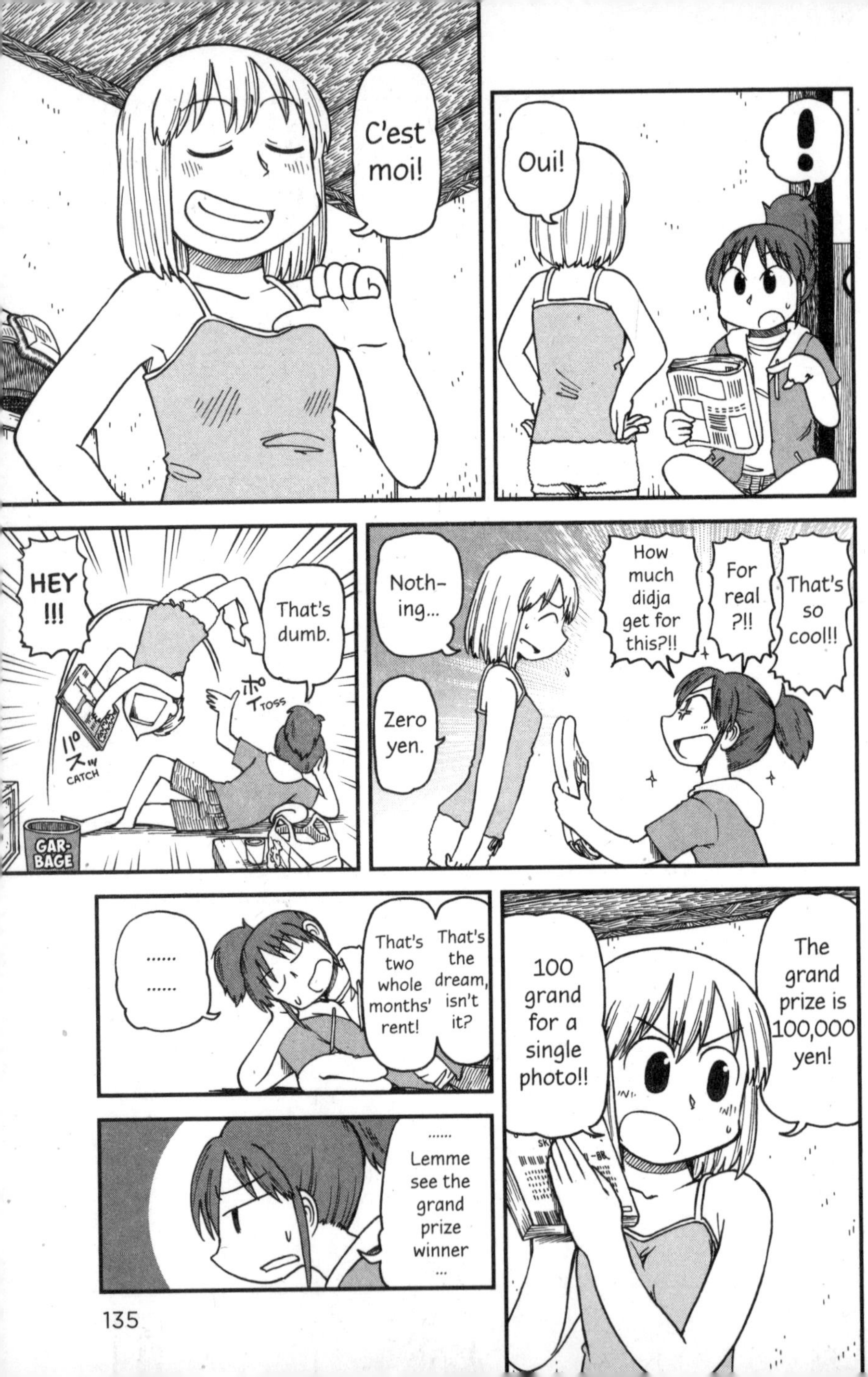
!
Oui!
C'est moi!
That's so cool!!
For real ?!!
How much didja get for this?!!
Noth- ing...
Zero yen.
That's dumb.
HEY !!!
TOSS
CATCH
GAR- BAGE
The grand prize is 100,000 yen!
100 grand for a single photo!!
That's the dream, isn't it?
That's two whole months' rent!
....
...... Lemme see the grand prize winner ...

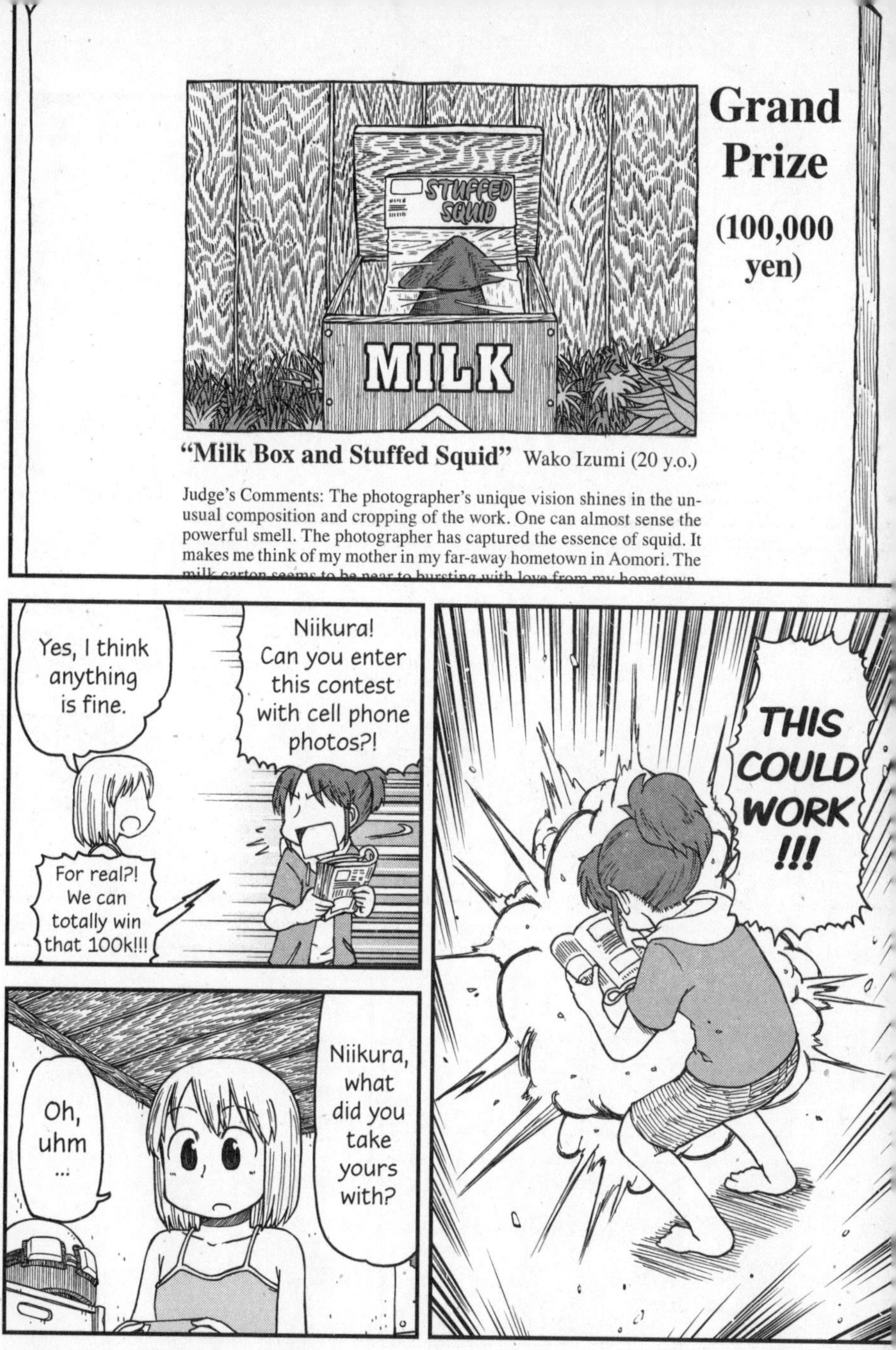

Grand Prize
(100,000 yen)
STUFFED SQUID
MILK
"Milk Box and Stuffed Squid" Wako Izumi (20 y.o.)
Judge's Comments: The photographer's unique vision shines in the unusual composition and cropping of the work. One can almost sense the powerful smell. The photographer has captured the essence of squid. It makes me think of my mother in my far-away hometown in Aomori. The milk carton seems to be near to bursting with love from my hometown
THIS COULD WORK !!!
Niikura! Can you enter this contest with cell phone photos?!
Yes, I think anything is fine.
For real?! We can totally win that 100k!!!
Niikura, what did you take yours with?
Oh, uhm ...

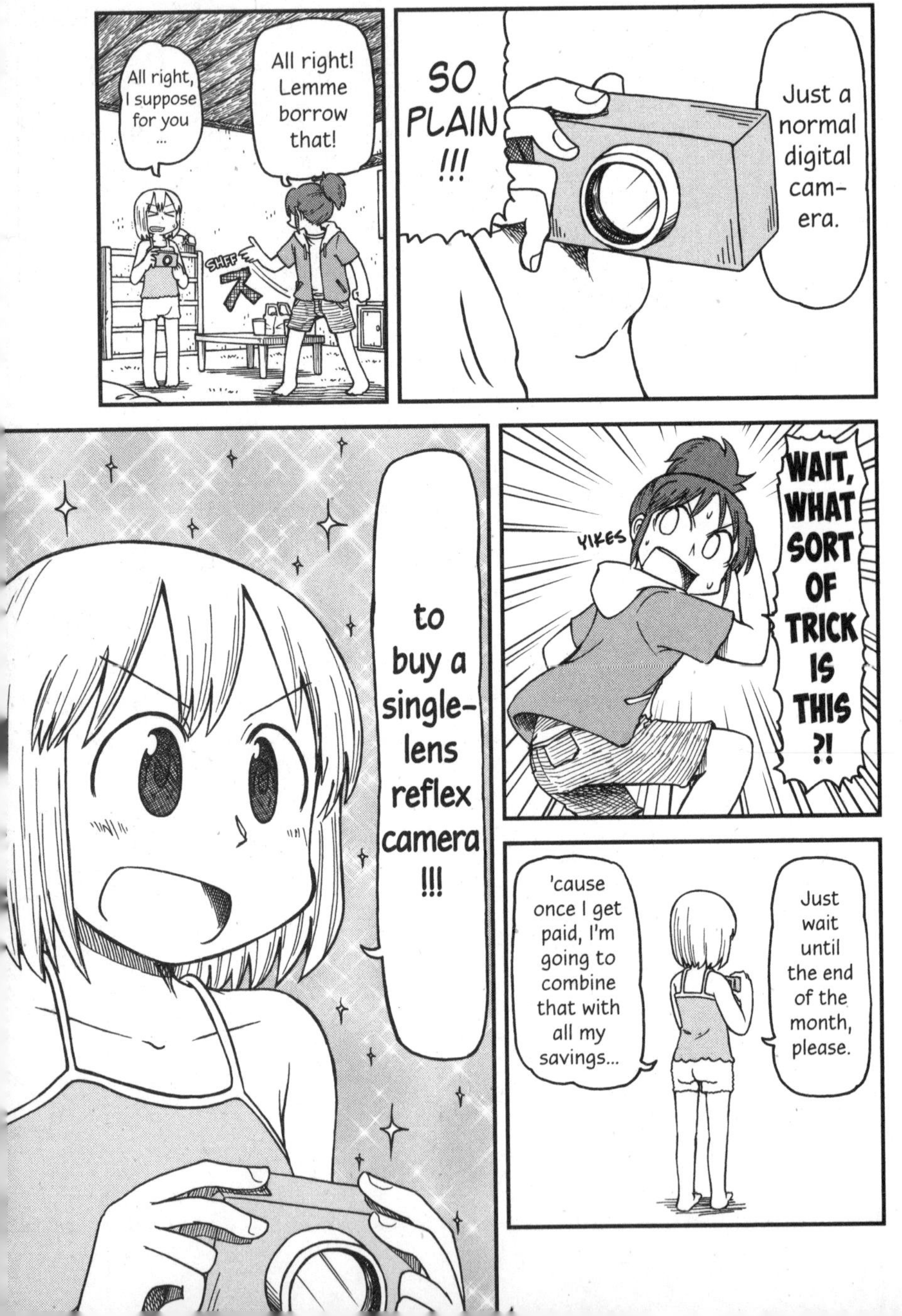

Just a normal digital cam-era.
SO PLAIN!!!
All right! Lemme borrow that!
All right, I suppose for you ...
SHFF
WAIT, WHAT SORT OF TRICK IS THIS?!
YIKES
Just wait until the end of the month, please.
'cause once I get paid, I'm going to combine that with all my savings...
to buy a single-lens reflex camera!!!

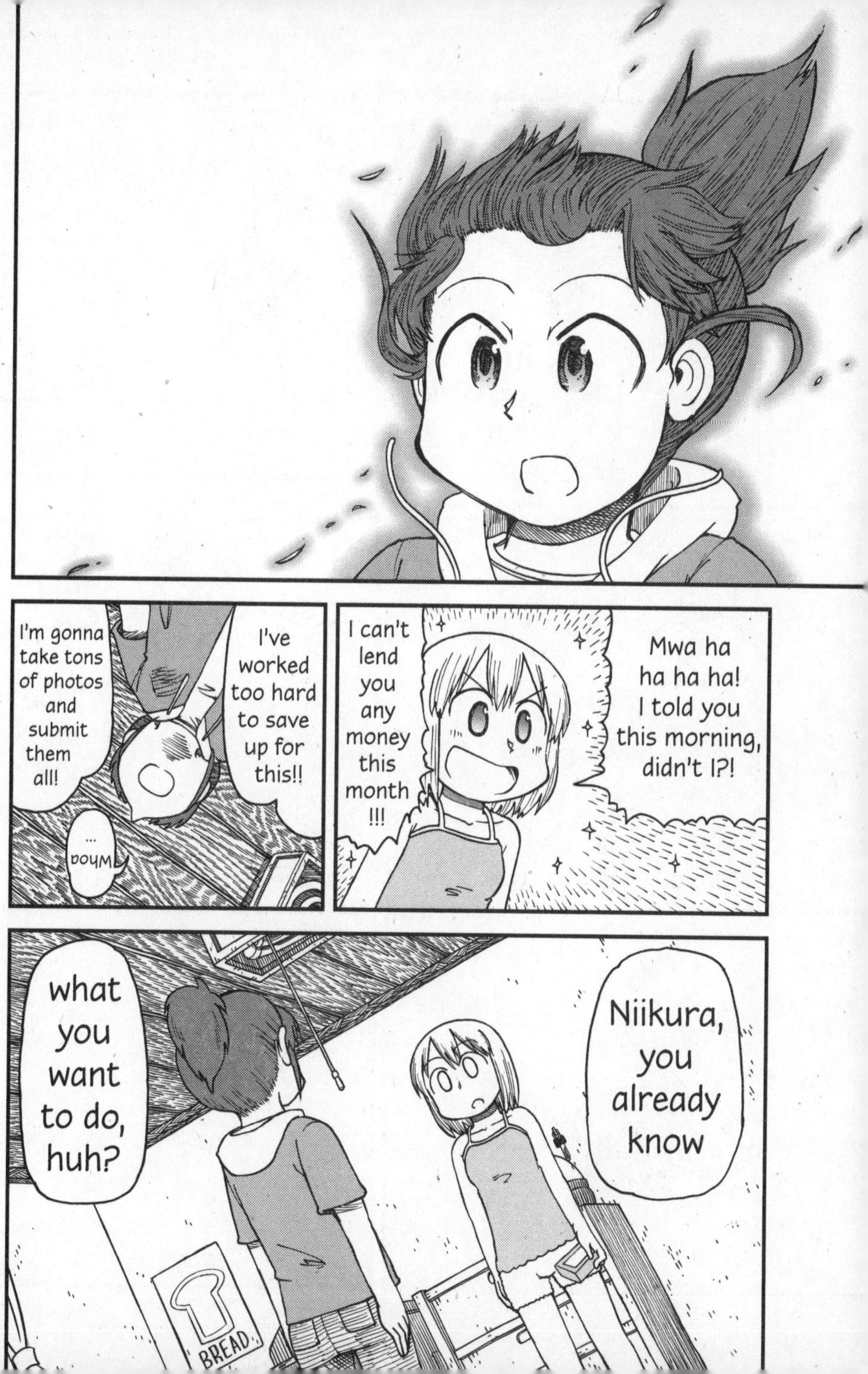
Mwa ha ha ha ha! I told you this morning, didn't I?!
I can't lend you any money this month!!!
I've worked too hard to save up for this!!
I'm gonna take tons of photos and submit them all!
Whoa ...
Niikura, you already know
what you want to do, huh?

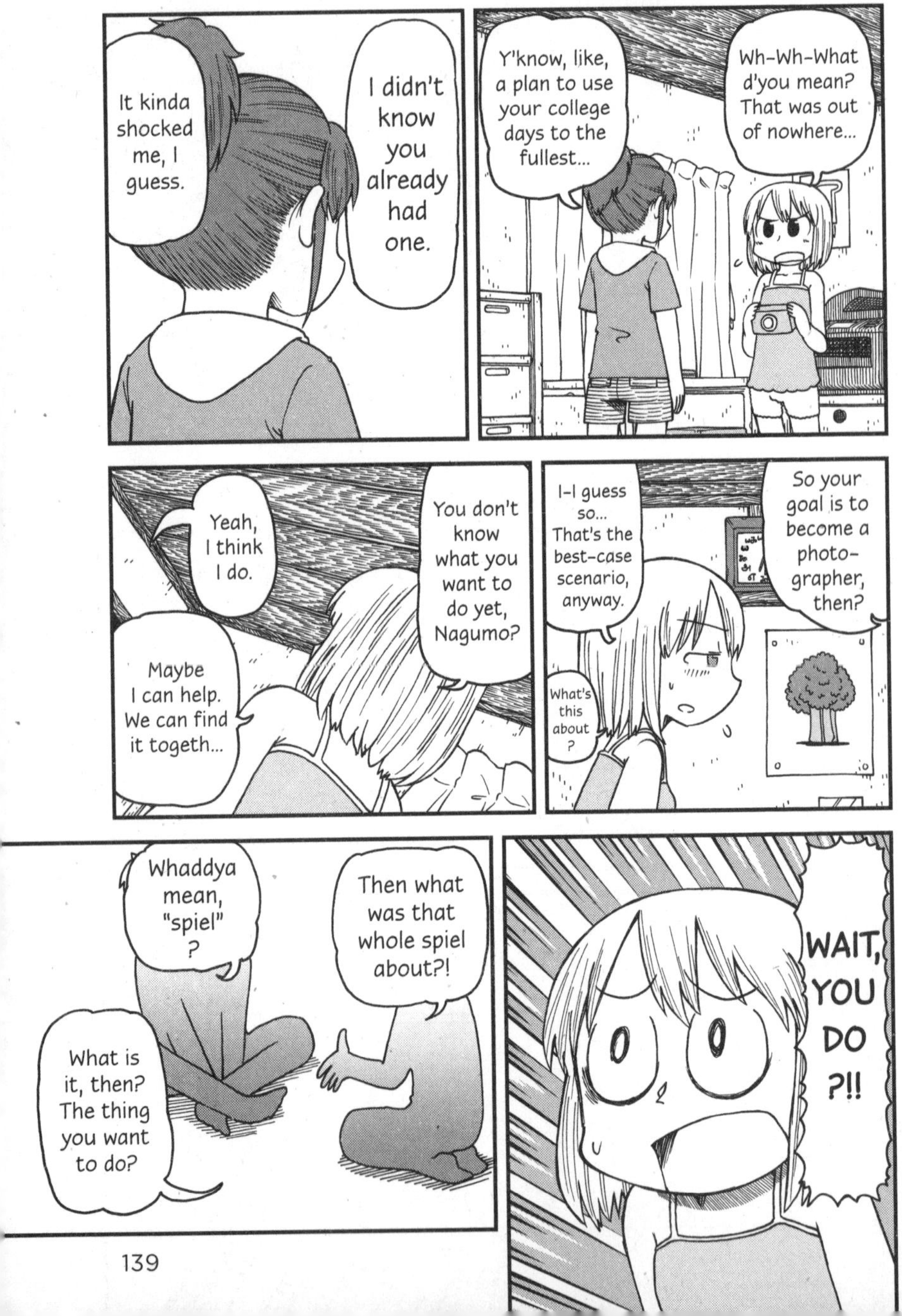

Wh-Wh-What d'you mean? That was out of nowhere...
Y'know, like, a plan to use your college days to the fullest...
I didn't know you already had one.
It kinda shocked me, I guess.
So your goal is to become a photographer, then?
I-I guess so... That's the best-case scenario, anyway.
What's this about?
You don't know what you want to do yet, Nagumo?
Yeah, I think I do.
Maybe I can help. We can find it togeth...
WAIT, YOU DO?!!
Then what was that whole spiel about?!
Whaddya mean, "spiel"?
What is it, then? The thing you want to do?

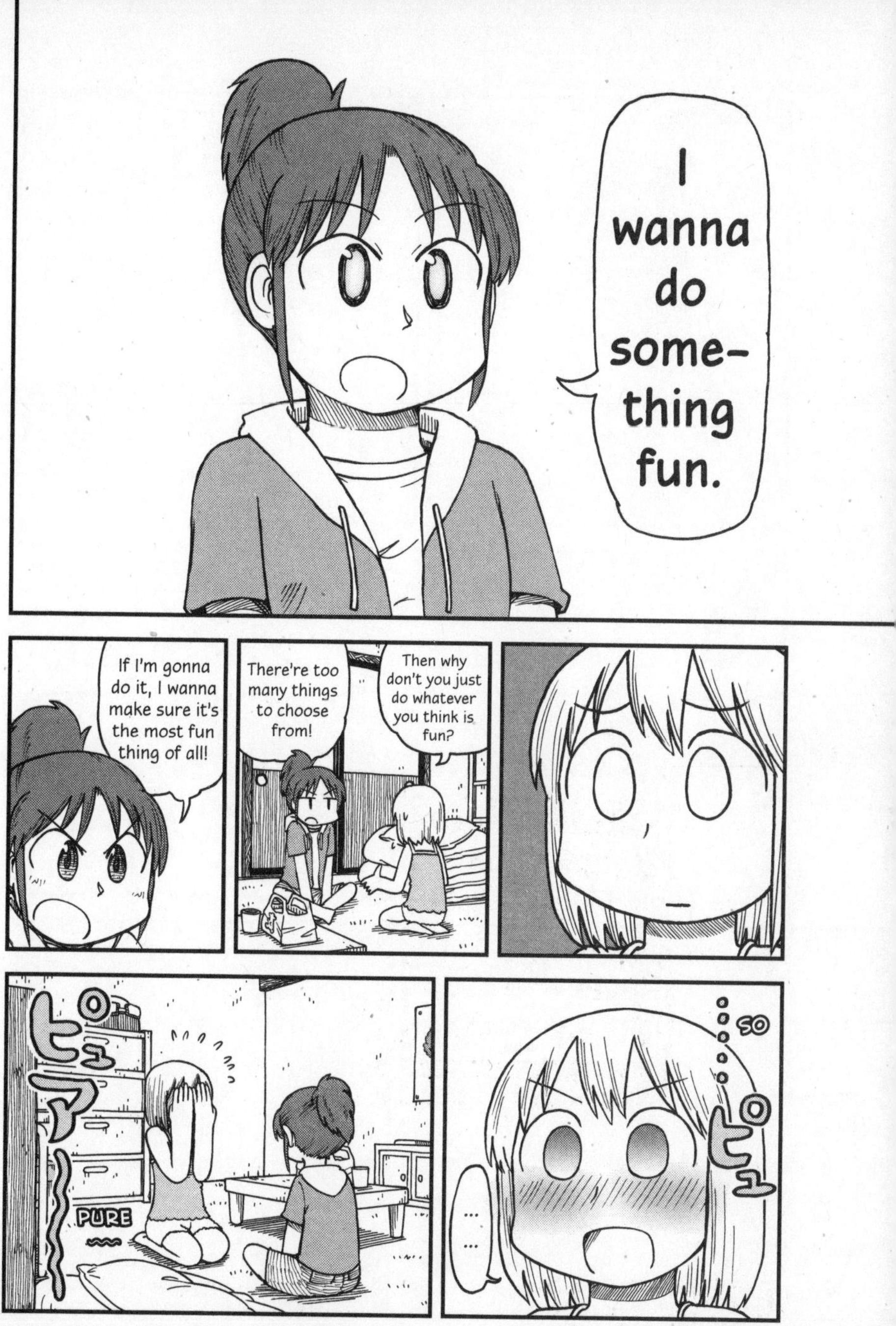

I wanna do some-thing fun.
Then why don't you just do whatever you think is fun?
There're too many things to choose from!
If I'm gonna do it, I wanna make sure it's the most fun thing of all!
......so
ピュ
...
...
ピュア〜〜
PURE
〜〜

SAT

CITY

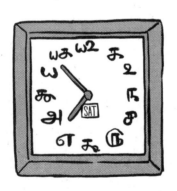

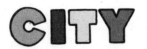

SAT

CITY

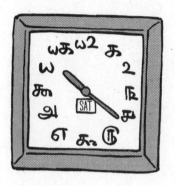

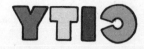

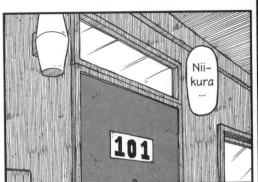

Nii-kura...

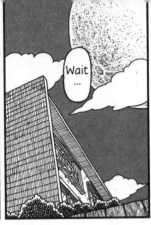

Wait...

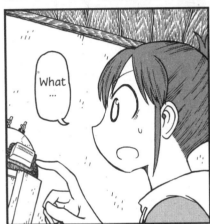

What...

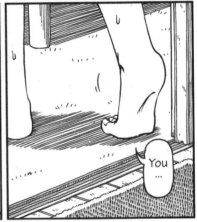

You...

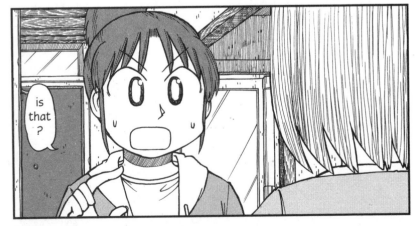

is that?

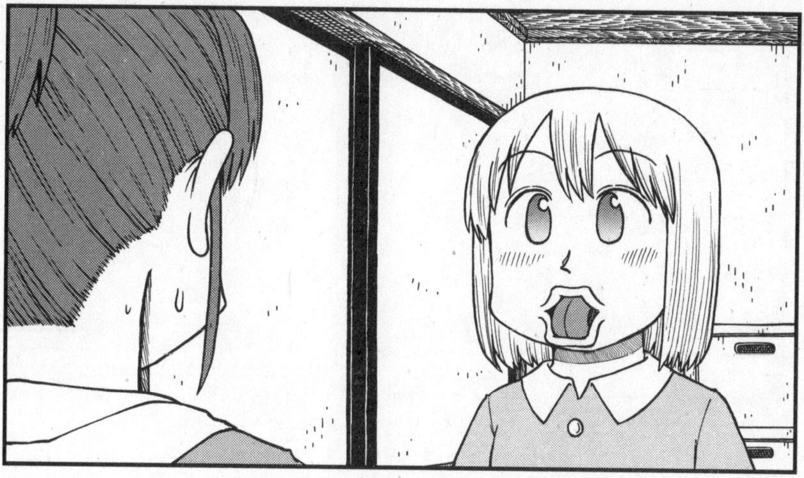

Chapter 11 Indication

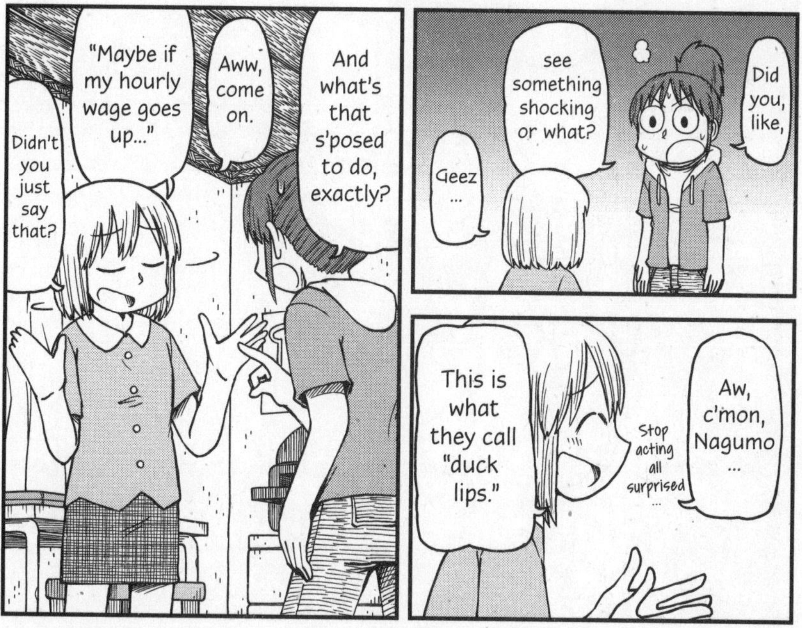

Did you, like,
see something shocking or what?
Geez ...
Aw, c'mon, Nagumo ...
Stop acting all surprised ...
This is what they call "duck lips."
And what's that s'posed to do, exactly?
Aww, come on.
"Maybe if my hourly wage goes up..."
Didn't you just say that?

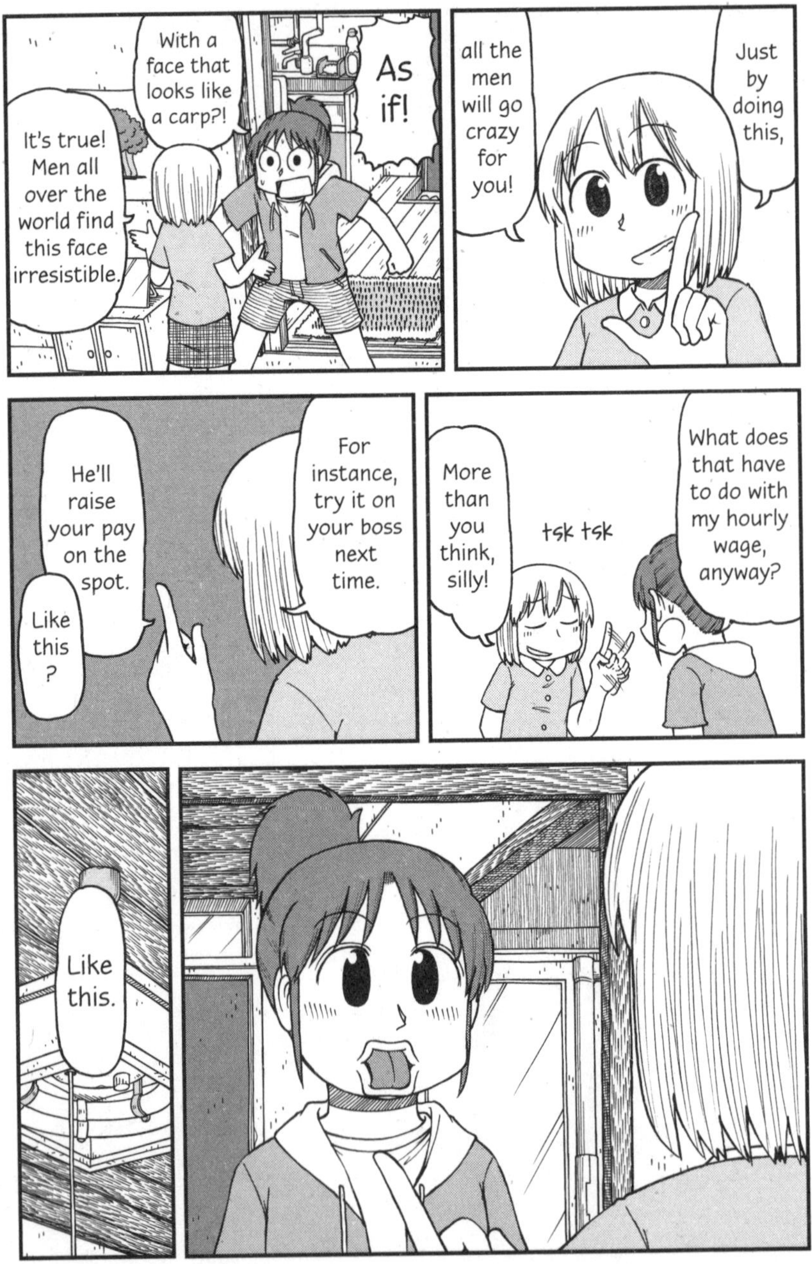
Just by doing this,
all the men will go crazy for you!
As if!
With a face that looks like a carp?!
It's true! Men all over the world find this face irresistible.
What does that have to do with my hourly wage, anyway?
tsk tsk
More than you think, silly!
For instance, try it on your boss next time.
He'll raise your pay on the spot.
Like this?
Like this.

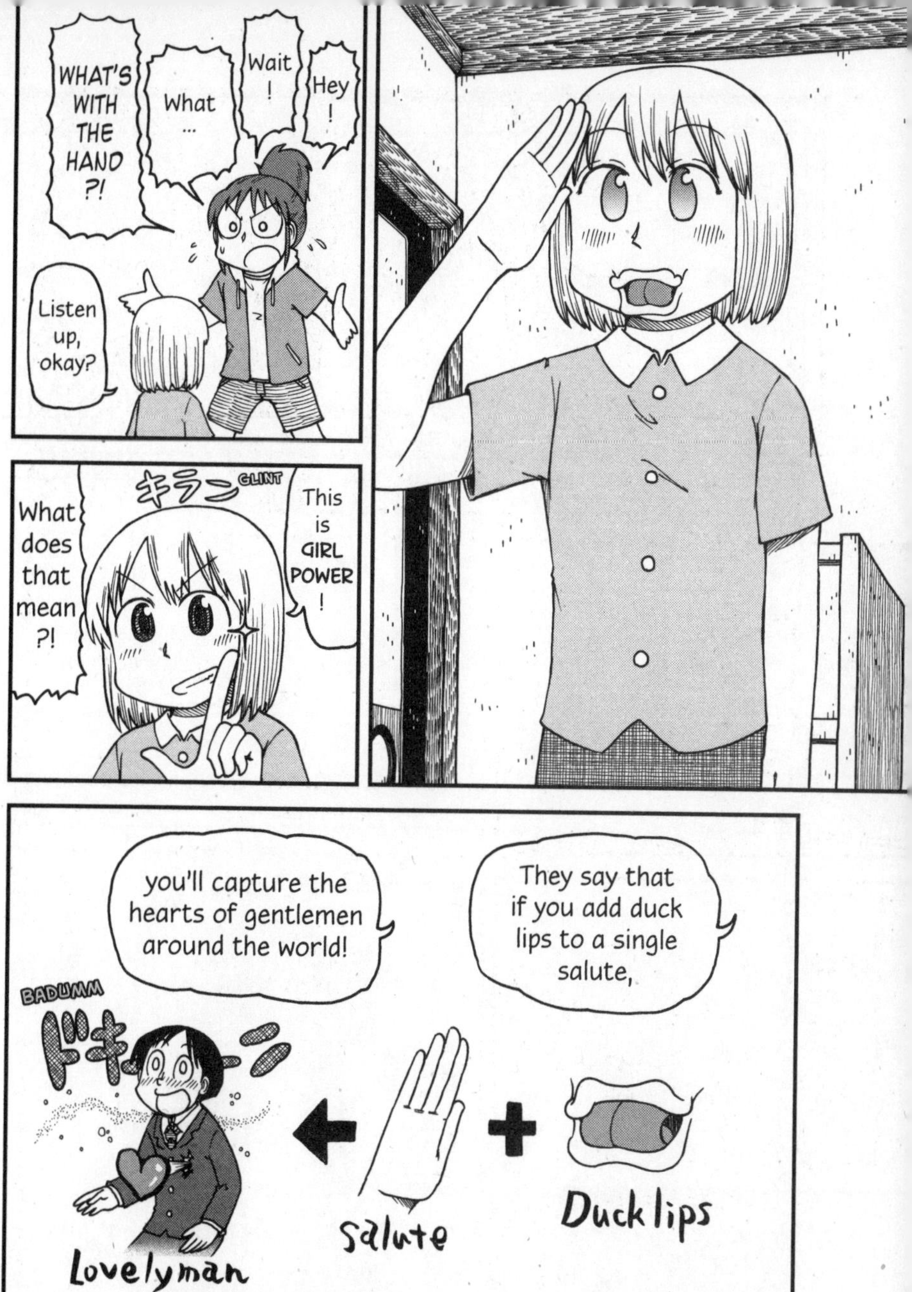
Hey!
Wait!
What...
WHAT'S WITH THE HAND?!
Listen up, okay?
キラン GLINT
This is GIRL POWER!
What does that mean?!
They say that if you add duck lips to a single salute,
you'll capture the hearts of gentlemen around the world!
Duck lips
Salute
BADUMM
Lovelyman

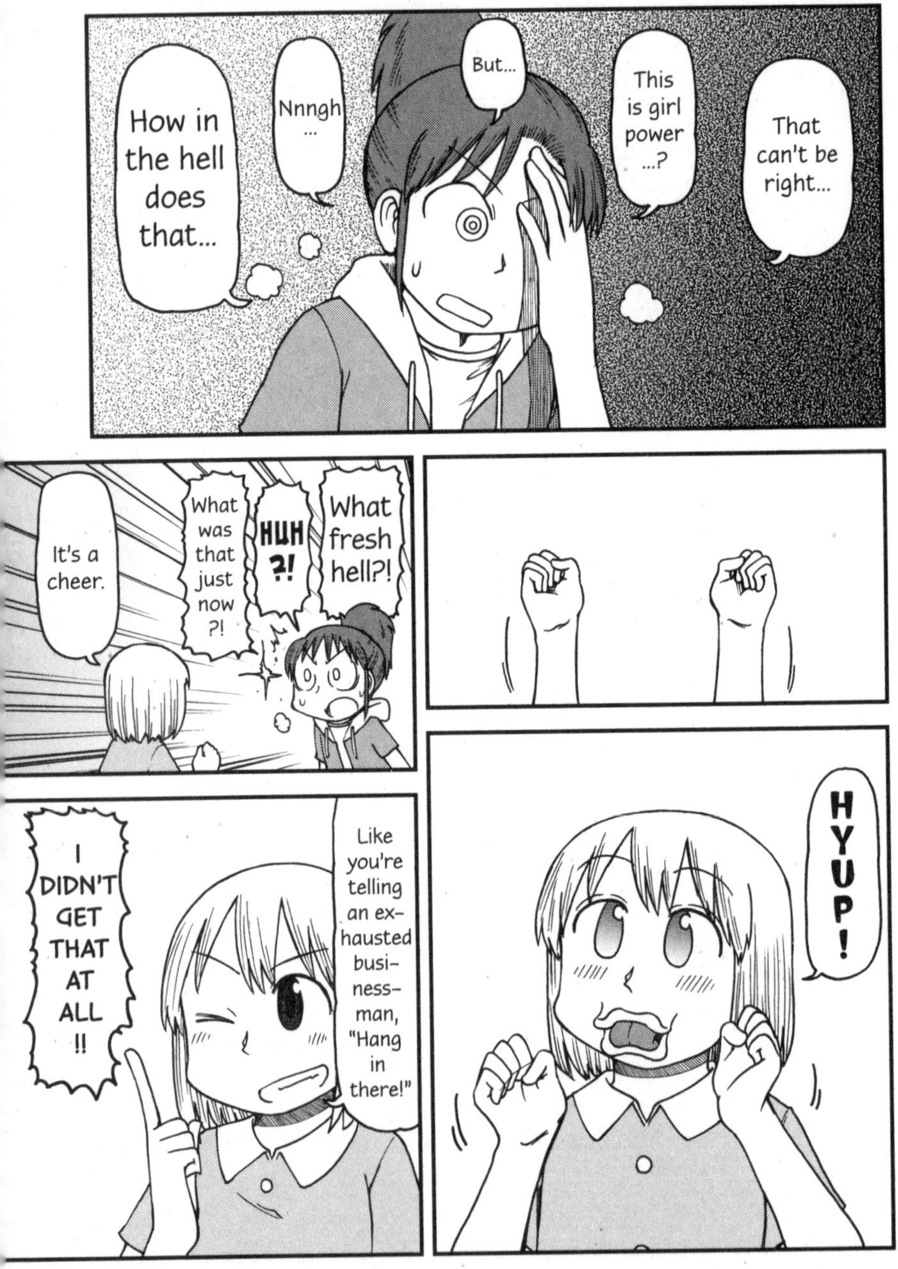
That can't be right...
This is girl power ...?
But...
Nnngh ...
How in the hell does that...
What fresh hell?!
HUH ?!
What was that just now ?!
It's a cheer.
HYUP!
Like you're telling an exhausted businessman, "Hang in there!"
I DIDN'T GET THAT AT ALL !!

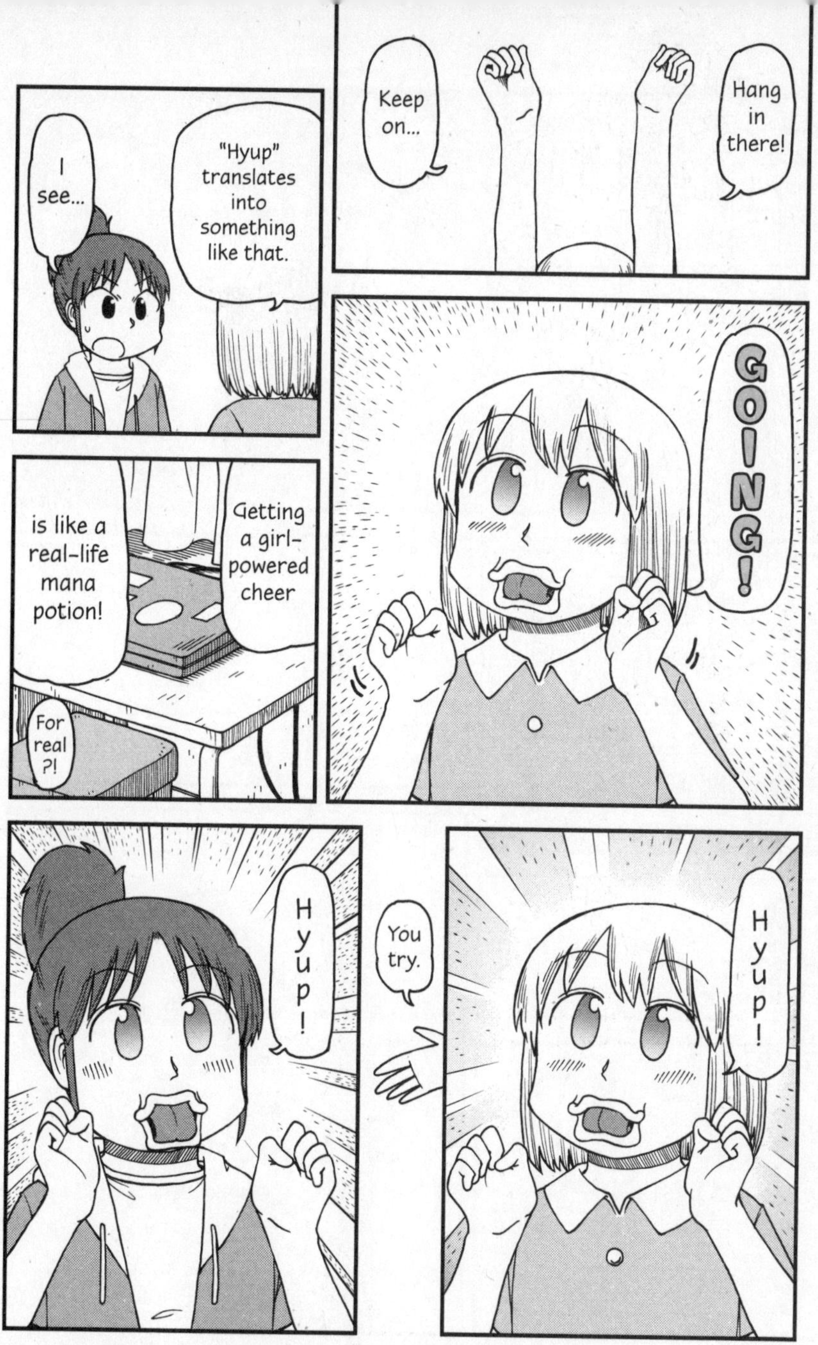

Hang in there!
Keep on...
"Hyup" translates into something like that.
I see...
GOING!
Getting a girl-powered cheer
is like a real-life mana potion!
For real?!
Hyup!
You try.
Hyup!

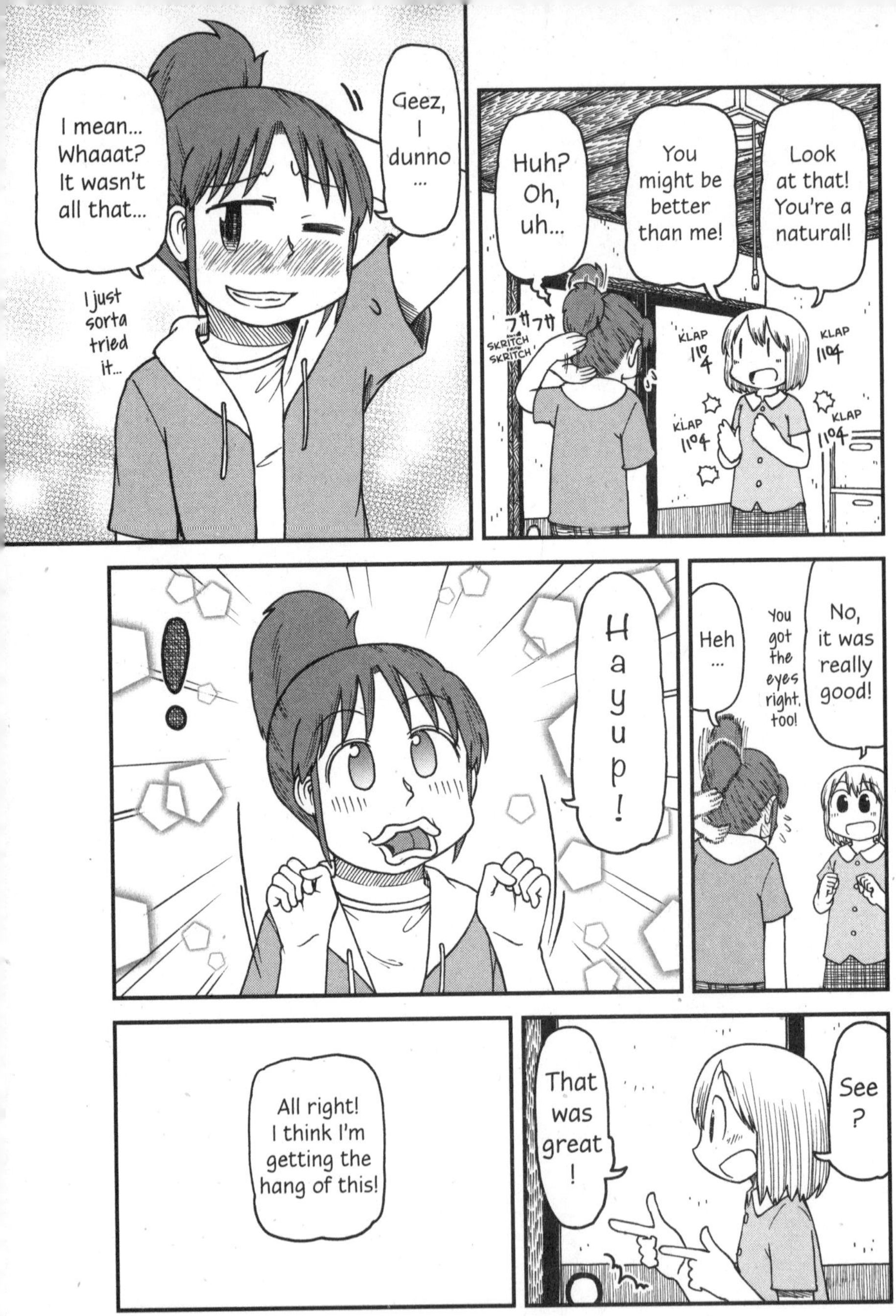
Look at that! You're a natural!
You might be better than me!
KLAP
KLAP
KLAP
Huh? Oh, uh...
SKRITCH SKRITCH
Geez, I dunno ...
I mean... Whaaat? It wasn't all that...
I just sorta tried it...
No, it was really good!
You got the eyes right, too!
Heh ...
Hayup!
See?
That was great!
All right! I think I'm getting the hang of this!

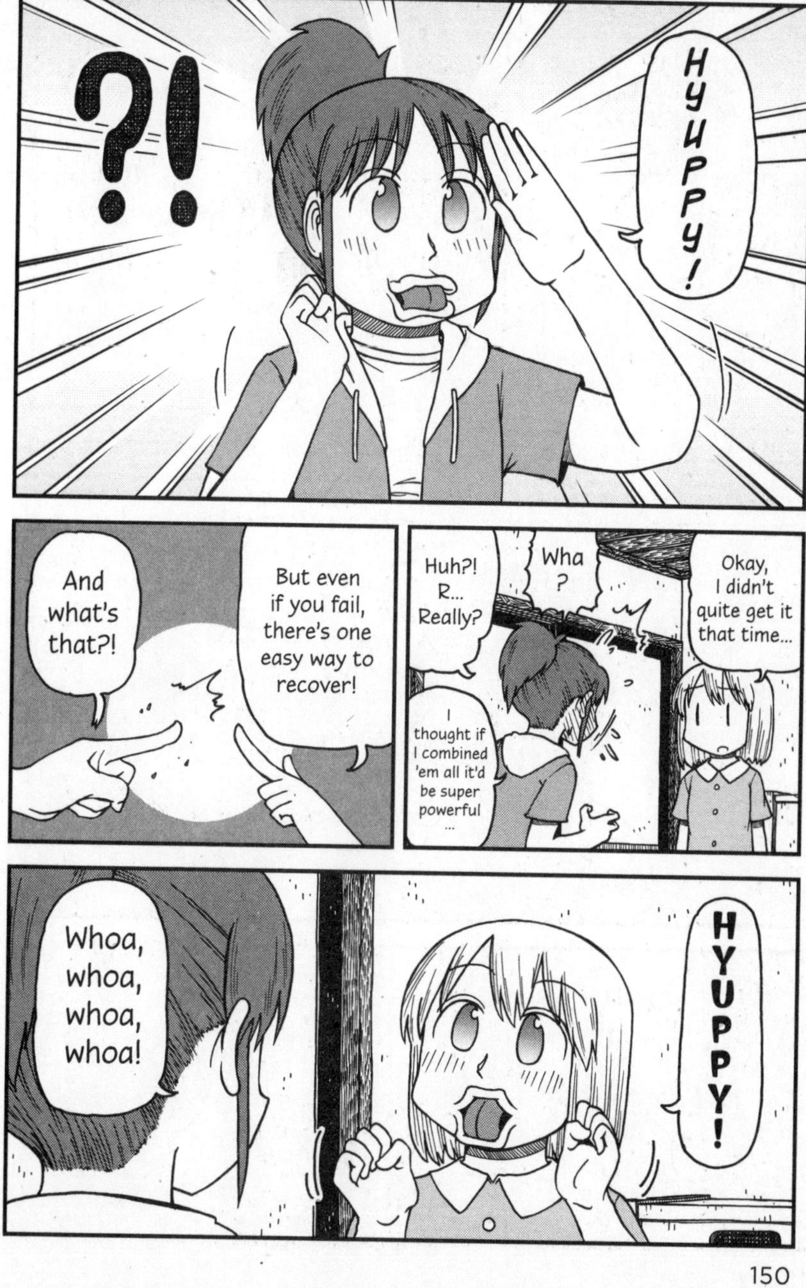
HYUPPY!
?!
Okay, I didn't quite get it that time...
Wha?
Huh?! R... Really?
I thought if I combined 'em all it'd be super powerful ...
But even if you fail, there's one easy way to recover!
And what's that?!
HYUPPY!
Whoa, whoa, whoa, whoa!

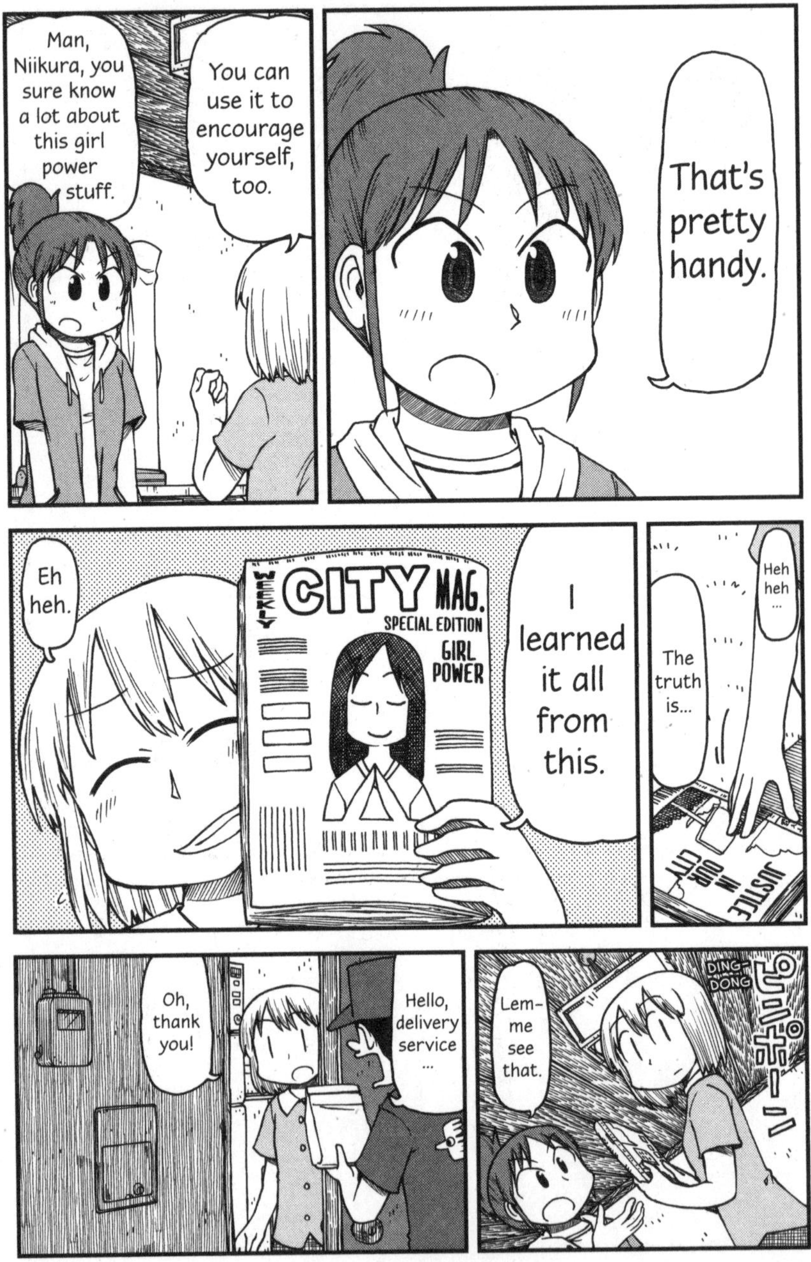

That's pretty handy.
You can use it to encourage yourself, too.
Man, Niikura, you sure know a lot about this girl power stuff.
Heh heh...
The truth is...
JUSTICE IN OUR CITY
I learned it all from this.
WEEKLY CITY MAG.
SPECIAL EDITION
GIRL POWER
Eh heh.
DING-DONG
ピンポーン
Lem-me see that.
Hello, delivery service...
Oh, thank you!

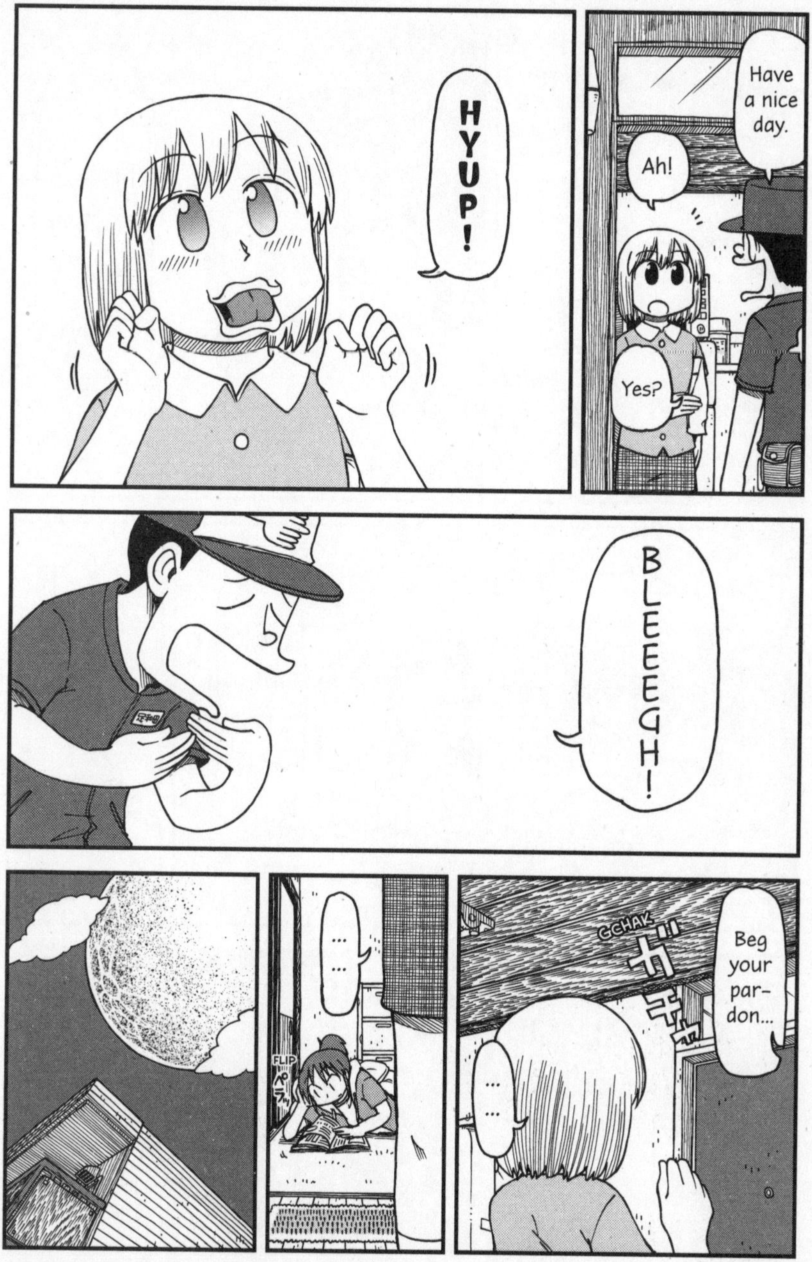
Have a nice day.
Ah!
Yes?
HYUP!
BLEEEGH!
Beg your par-don...
GCHAK
... ...
... ...
FLIP

Acorn Express Delivery

CITY

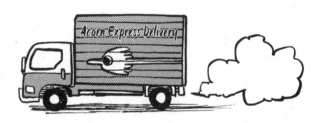

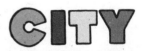

キュ
SCREECH
Acorn Express Delivery
バタン
SLAM
Acorn Express Delivery
オエー
HOOOORK
Acorn Express Delivery

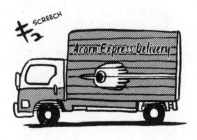

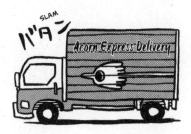

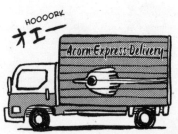

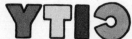

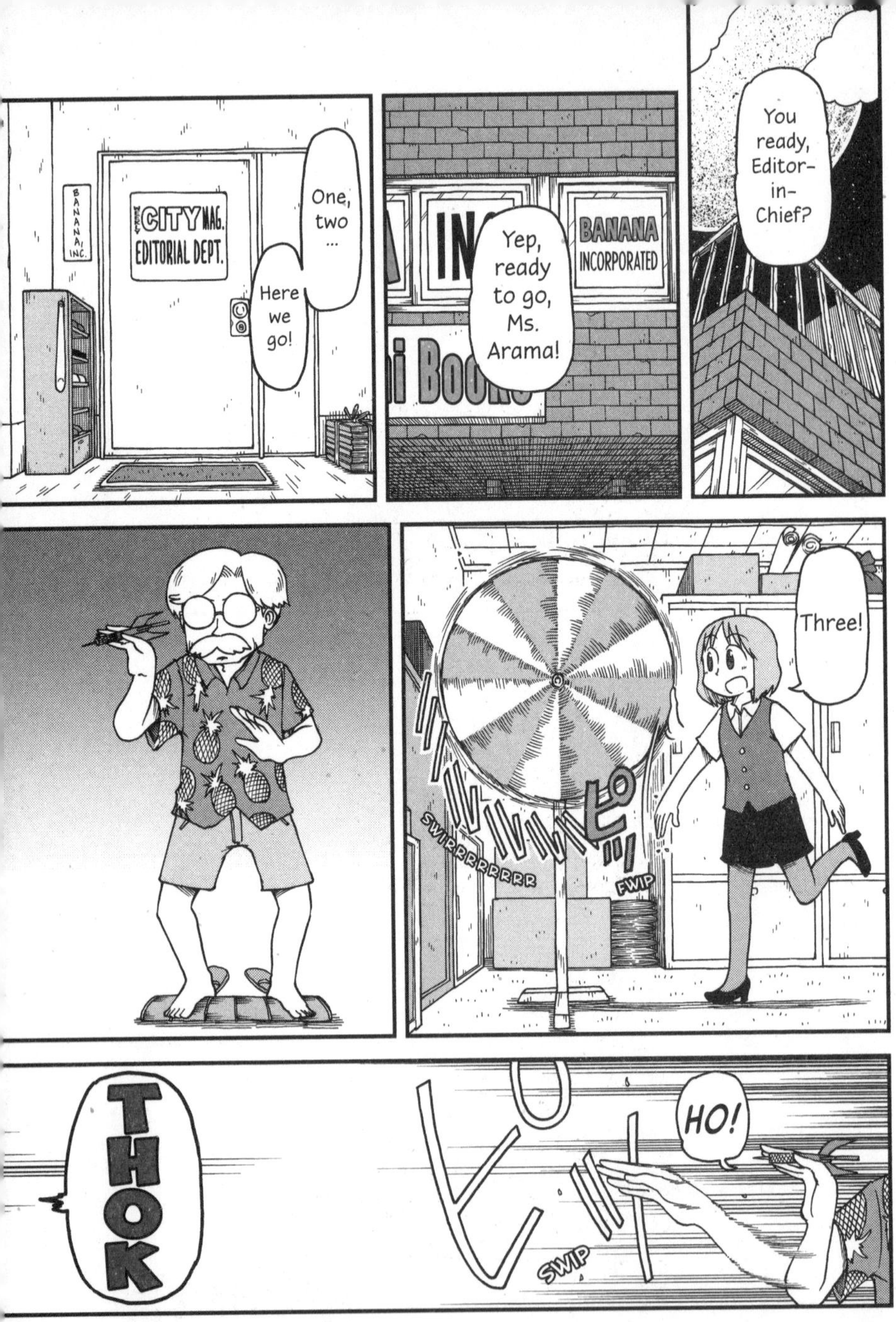
You ready, Editor-in-Chief?
BANANA INCORPORATED
Yep, ready to go, Ms. Arama!
CITY MAG. EDITORIAL DEPT.
BANANA, INC.
One, two ...
Here we go!
Three!
SWIRRRRRRRRR
FWIP
HO!
SWIP
THOK

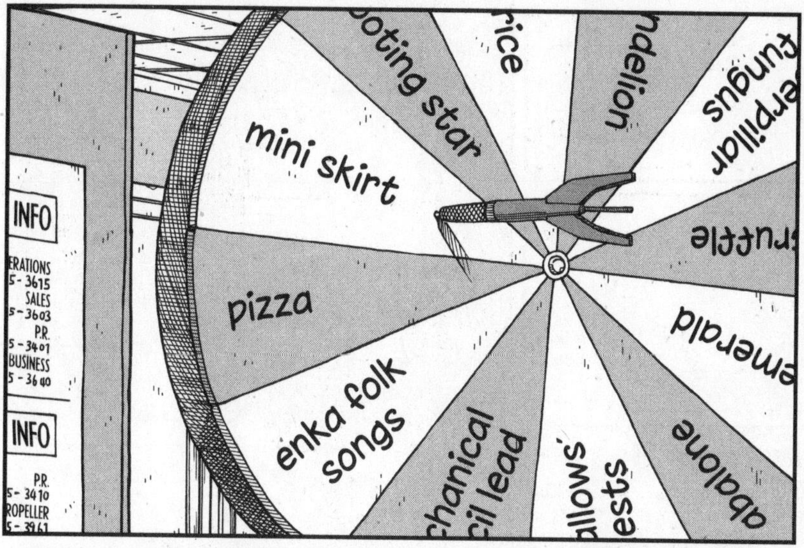
ooting star
rice
ndelion
terpillar fungus
mini skirt
truffle
pizza
emerald
enka folk songs
chanical cil lead
allows' ests
abalone
INFO
ERATIONS 5-3615
SALES 5-3603
P.R. 5-3407
BUSINESS 5-3640
INFO
P.R. 5-3410
ROPELLER 5-3961

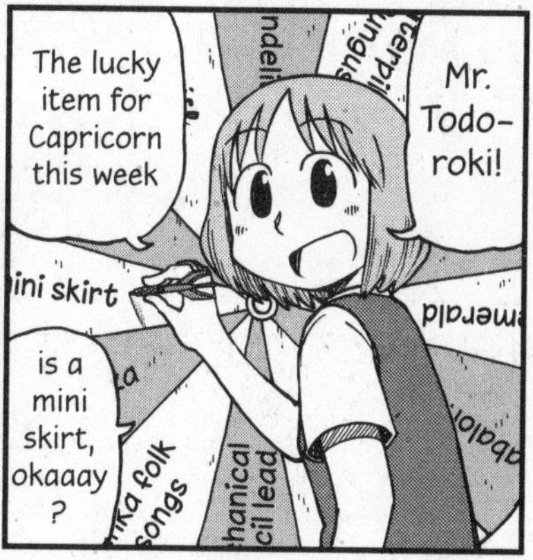
Mr. Todo-roki!
The lucky item for Capricorn this week
is a mini skirt, okaaay?

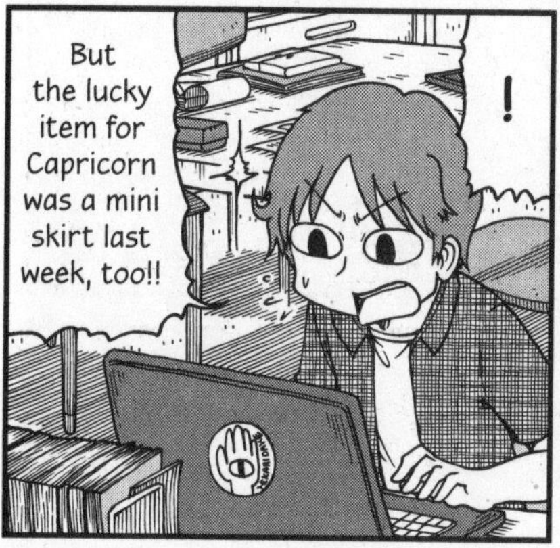
!
But the lucky item for Capricorn was a mini skirt last week, too!!

Chapter 12 Editorial Trio

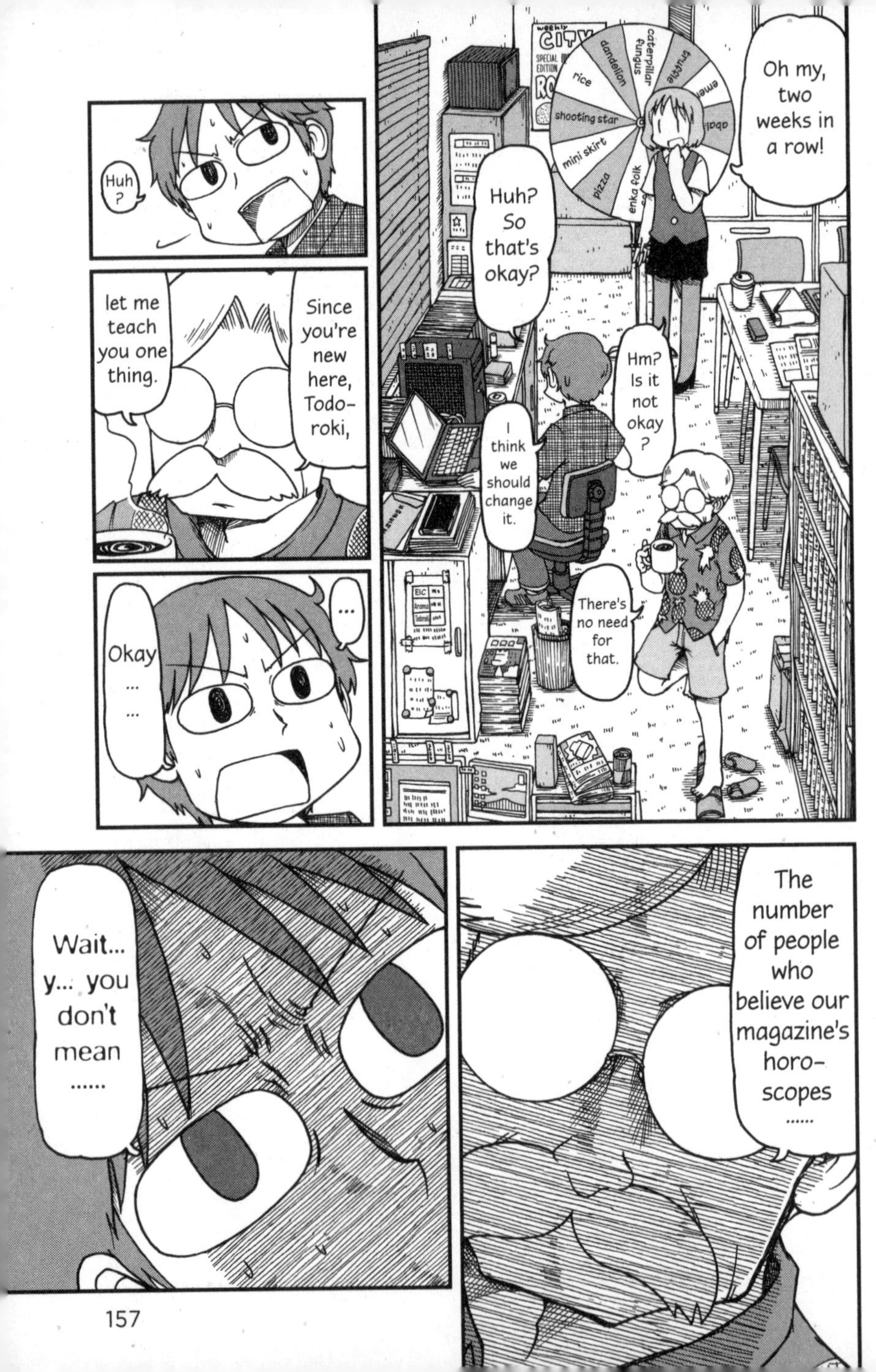
weekly CITY SPECIAL EDITION
caterpillar fungus
dandelion
rice
shooting star
mini skirt
pizza
enka folk
opal
Oh my, two weeks in a row!
Huh? So that's okay?
Hm? Is it not okay?
I think we should change it.
There's no need for that.
Huh?
Since you're new here, Todoroki,
let me teach you one thing.
...
Okay... ...
The number of people who believe our magazine's horoscopes ......
Wait... y... you don't mean ......

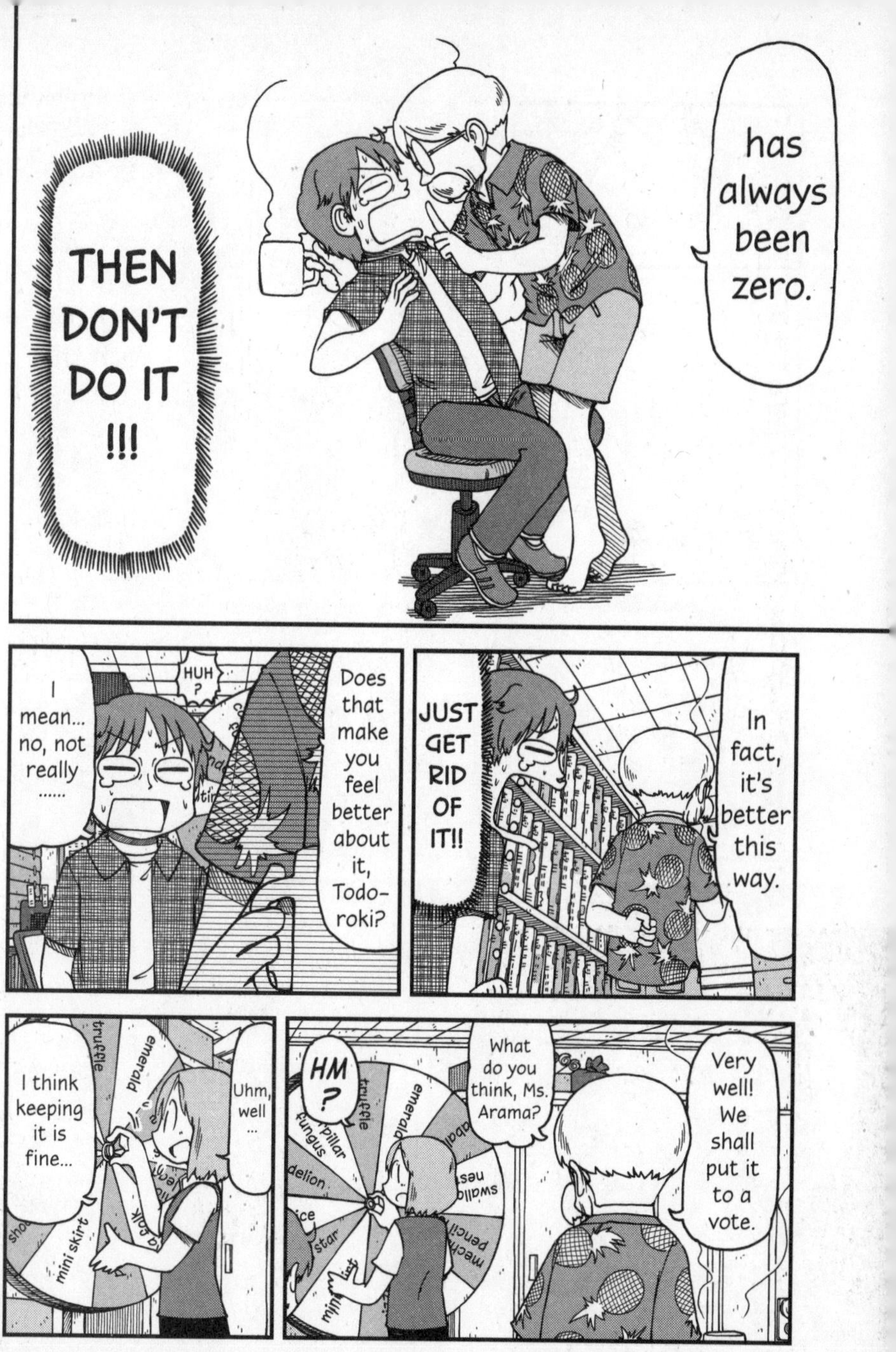
has always been zero.
THEN DON'T DO IT !!!
In fact, it's better this way.
JUST GET RID OF IT!!
Does that make you feel better about it, Todoroki?
HUH ?
I mean... no, not really ......
Very well! We shall put it to a vote.
What do you think, Ms. Arama?
HM ?
truffle
emerald
fungus
star
Uhm, well ...
I think keeping it is fine...
truffle
emerald
mini skirt

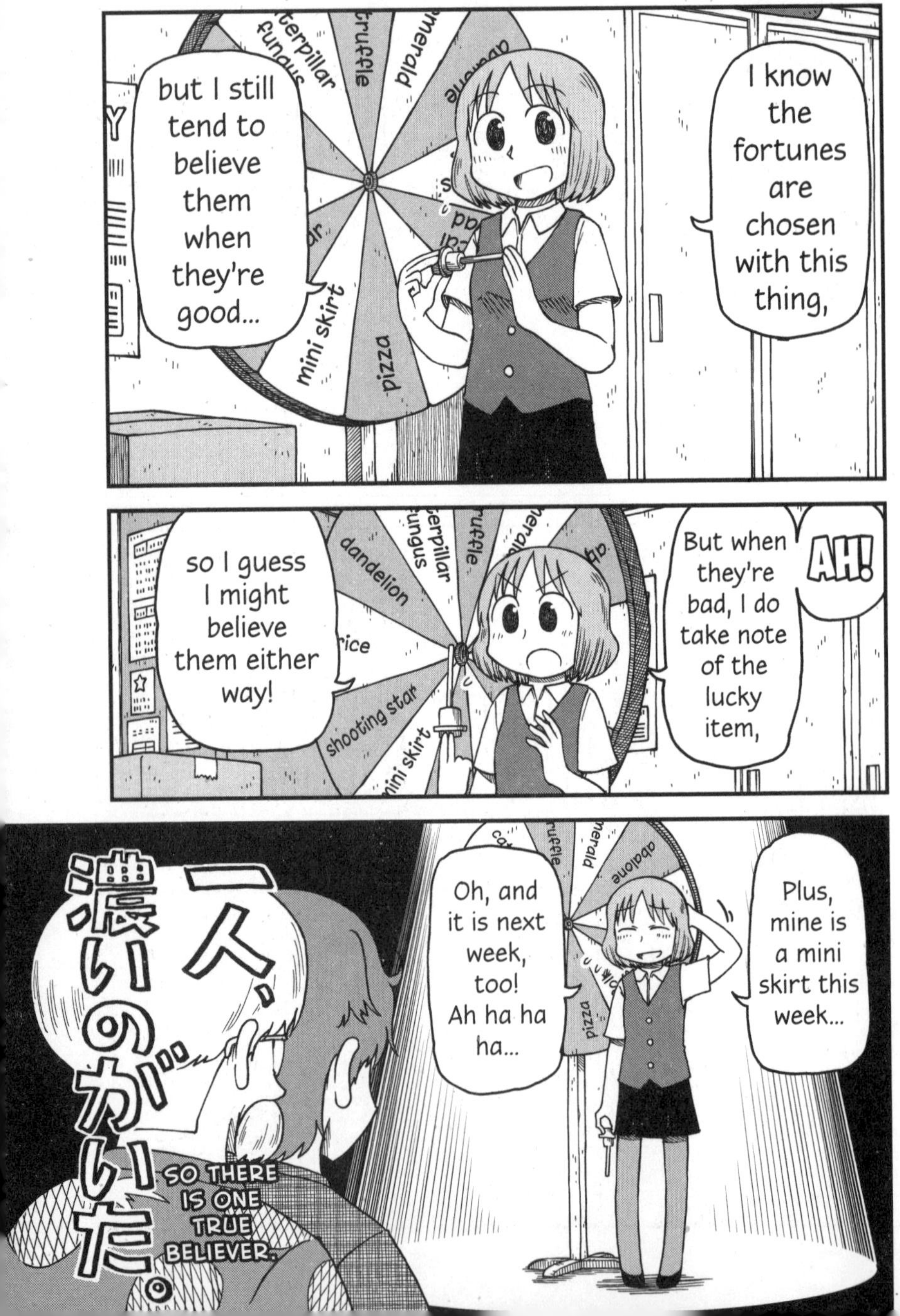

I know the fortunes are chosen with this thing,
but I still tend to believe them when they're good...
truffle
fungus
mini skirt
pizza
AH!
But when they're bad, I do take note of the lucky item,
so I guess I might believe them either way!
truffle
dandelion
rice
shooting star
Plus, mine is a mini skirt this week...
Oh, and it is next week, too! Ah ha ha ha...
abalone
truffle
pizza
一人、濃いのがいた。
SO THERE IS ONE TRUE BELIEVER.

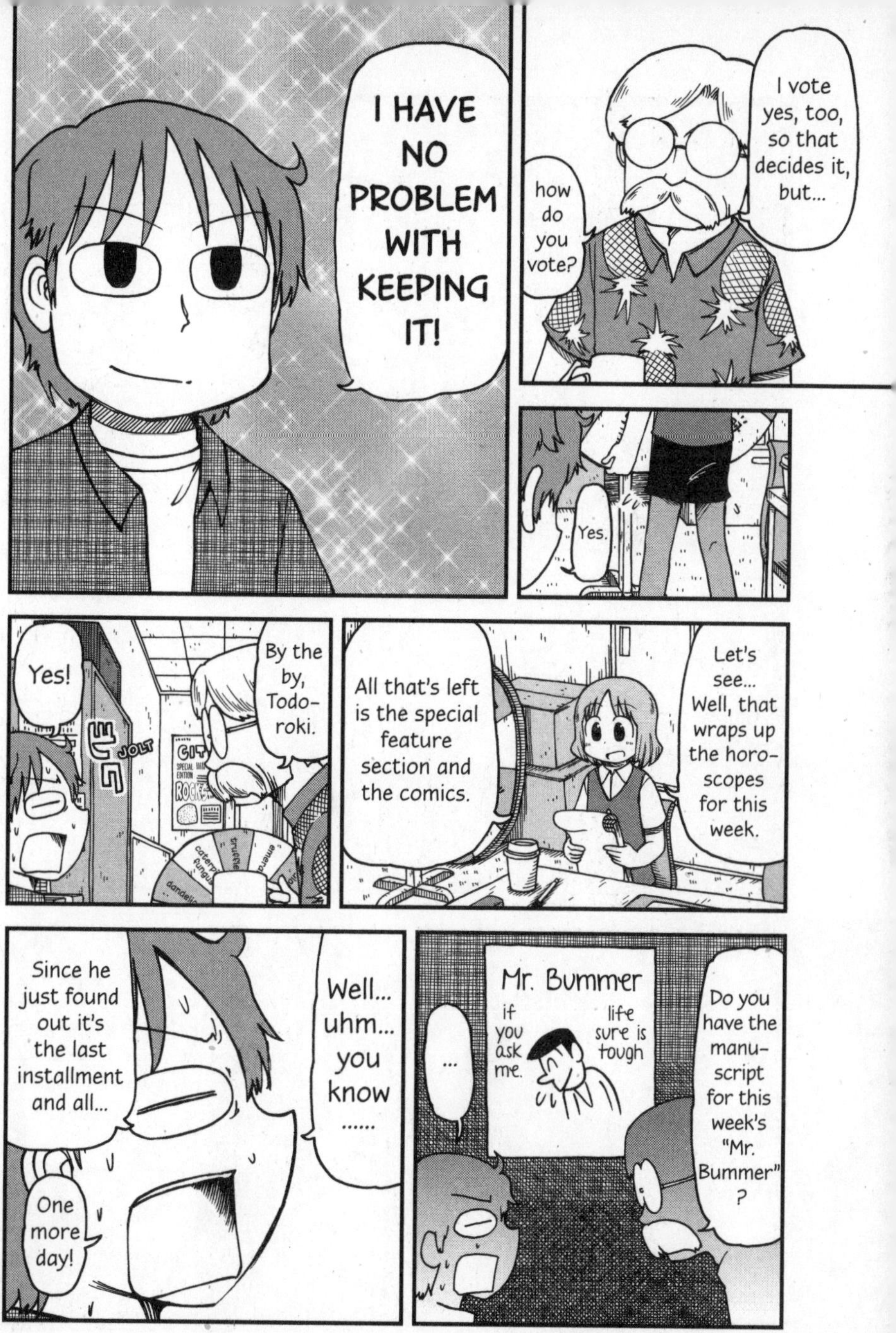
I vote yes, too, so that decides it, but...
how do you vote?
Yes.
I HAVE NO PROBLEM WITH KEEPING IT!
Let's see... Well, that wraps up the horoscopes for this week.
All that's left is the special feature section and the comics.
By the by, Todoroki.
Yes!
JOLT
Do you have the manuscript for this week's "Mr. Bummer"?
Mr. Bummer
life sure is tough
if you ask me.
...
Well... uhm... you know ......
Since he just found out it's the last installment and all...
One more day!

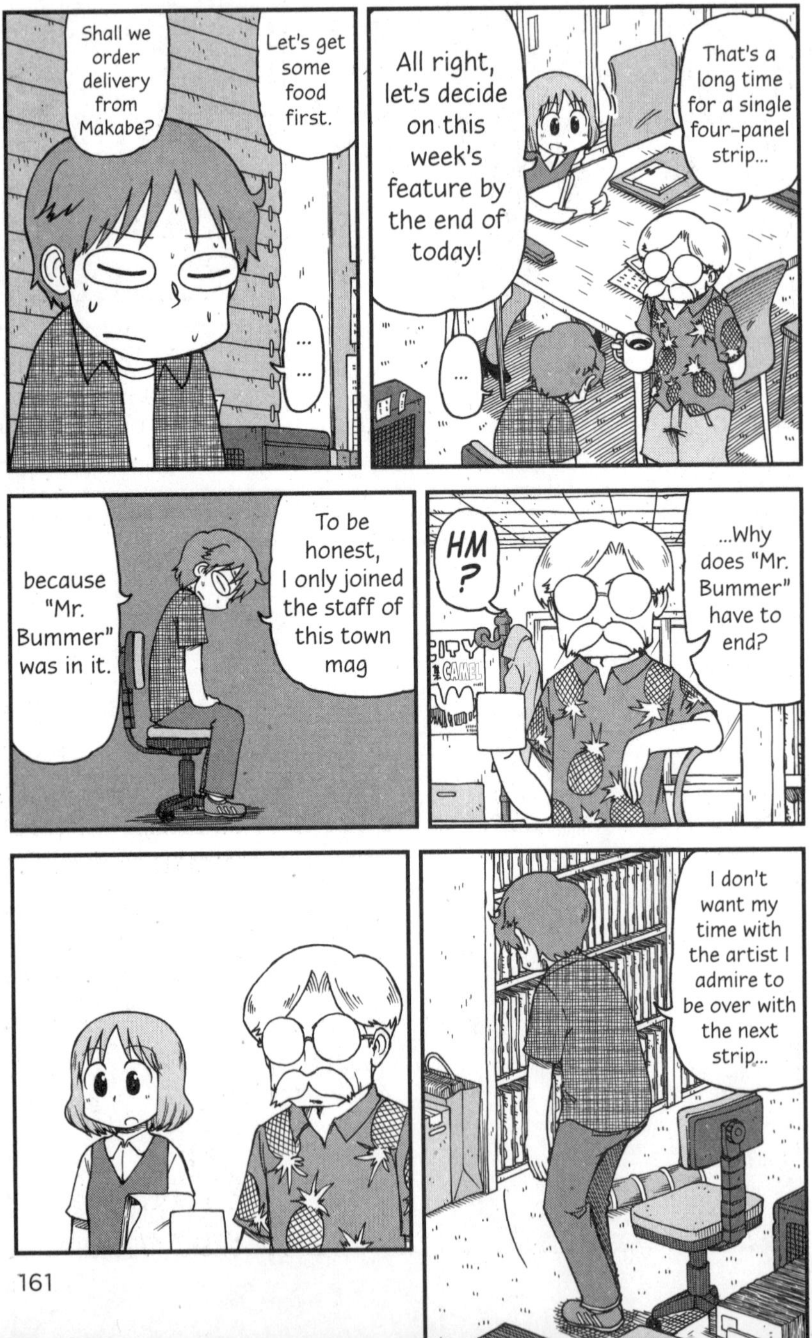
That's a long time for a single four-panel strip...
All right, let's decide on this week's feature by the end of today!
...
Let's get some food first.
Shall we order delivery from Makabe?
... ...
...Why does "Mr. Bummer" have to end?
HM?
To be honest, I only joined the staff of this town mag
because "Mr. Bummer" was in it.
I don't want my time with the artist I admire to be over with the next strip...

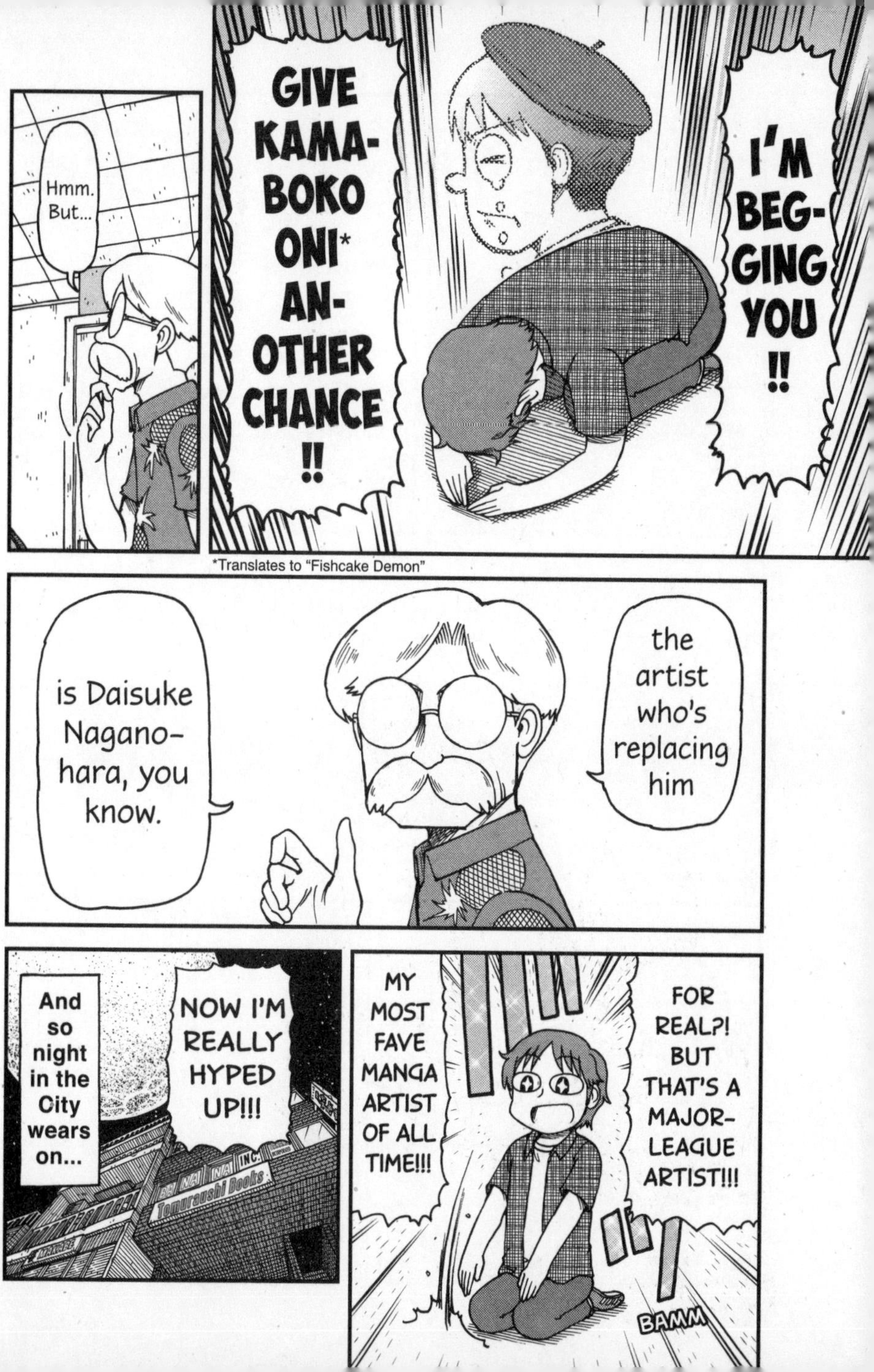
I'M BEGGING YOU!!
GIVE KAMABOKO ONI* ANOTHER CHANCE!!
Hmm. But...
the artist who's replacing him
is Daisuke Naganohara, you know.
FOR REAL?! BUT THAT'S A MAJOR-LEAGUE ARTIST!!!
MY MOST FAVE MANGA ARTIST OF ALL TIME!!!
BAMM
NOW I'M REALLY HYPED UP!!!
And so night in the City wears on...
Tomuraushi Books
*Translates to "Fishcake Demon"

define "ordinary"

in this just-surreal-enough take on the "school genre" of manga, a group of friends (which includes a robot built by a child professor) grapple with all sorts of unexpected situations in their daily lives as high schoolers.

the gags, jokes, puns and random haiku keep this series off-kilter even as the characters grow and change. check out this new take on a storied genre and meet the new ordinary.

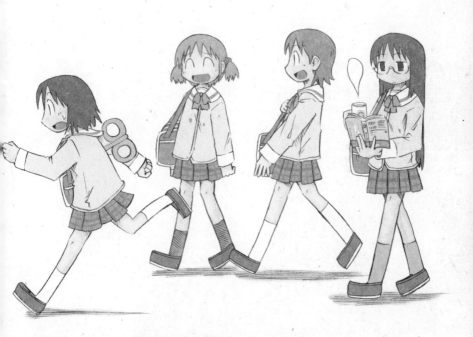

all volumes
available now!

nichijou

my ordinary life

keiichi
arawi

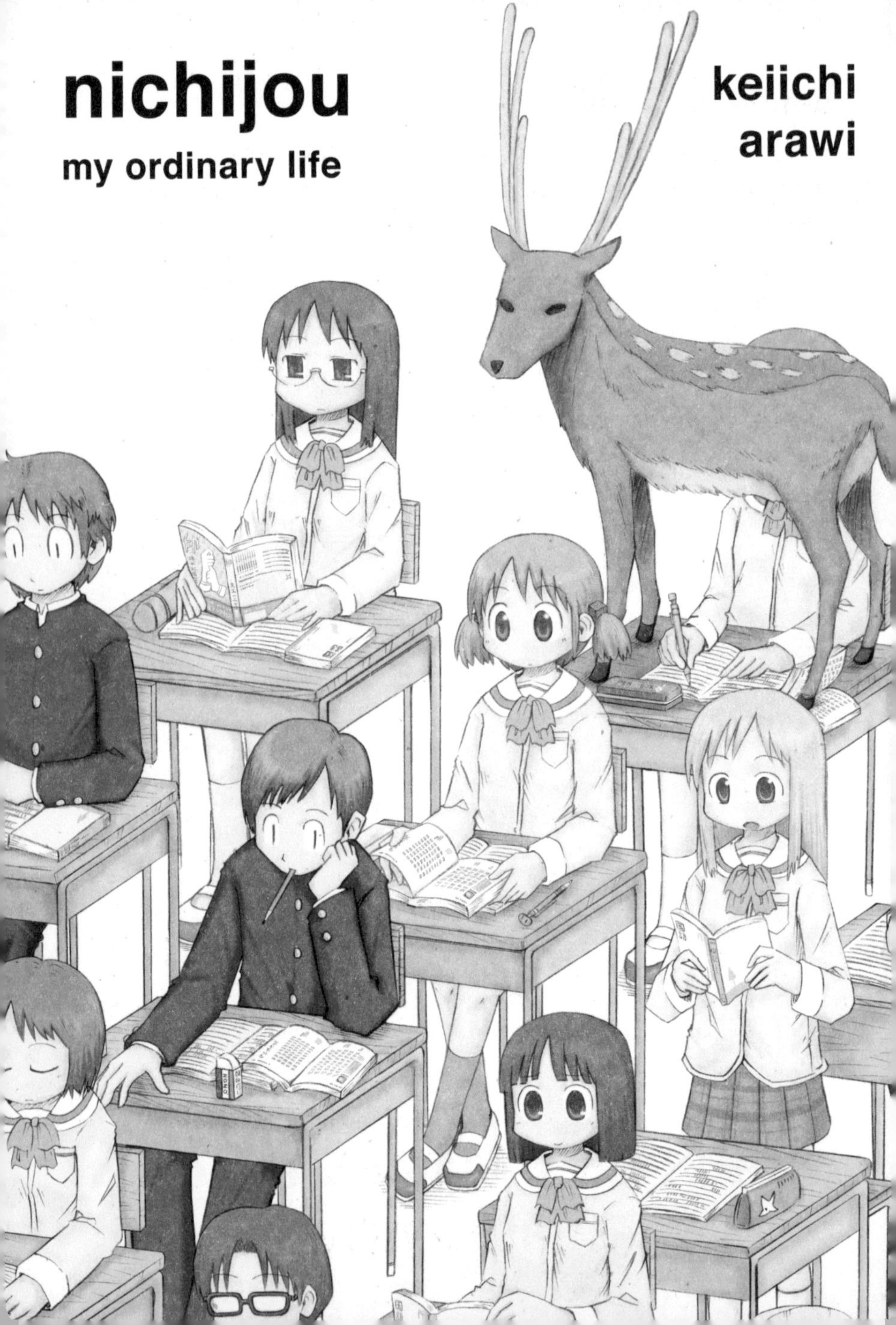

The follow up to the hit manga series ***nichijou***, ***Helvetica Standard*** is a full-color anthology of Keiichi Arawi's comic art and design work. Funny and heartwarming, ***Helvetica Standard*** is a humorous look at modern day Japanese design in comic form.

Helvetica Standard is a deep dive into the artistic and creative world of Keiichi Arawi. Part comic, part diary, part art and design book, ***Helvetica Standard*** is a deconstruction of the world of ***nichijou***.

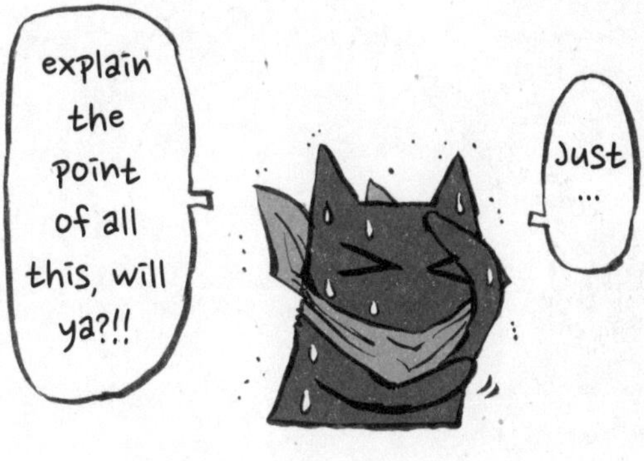
Just ...
explain the point of all this, will ya?!!

Both Parts Available Now!

Keiichi Arawi

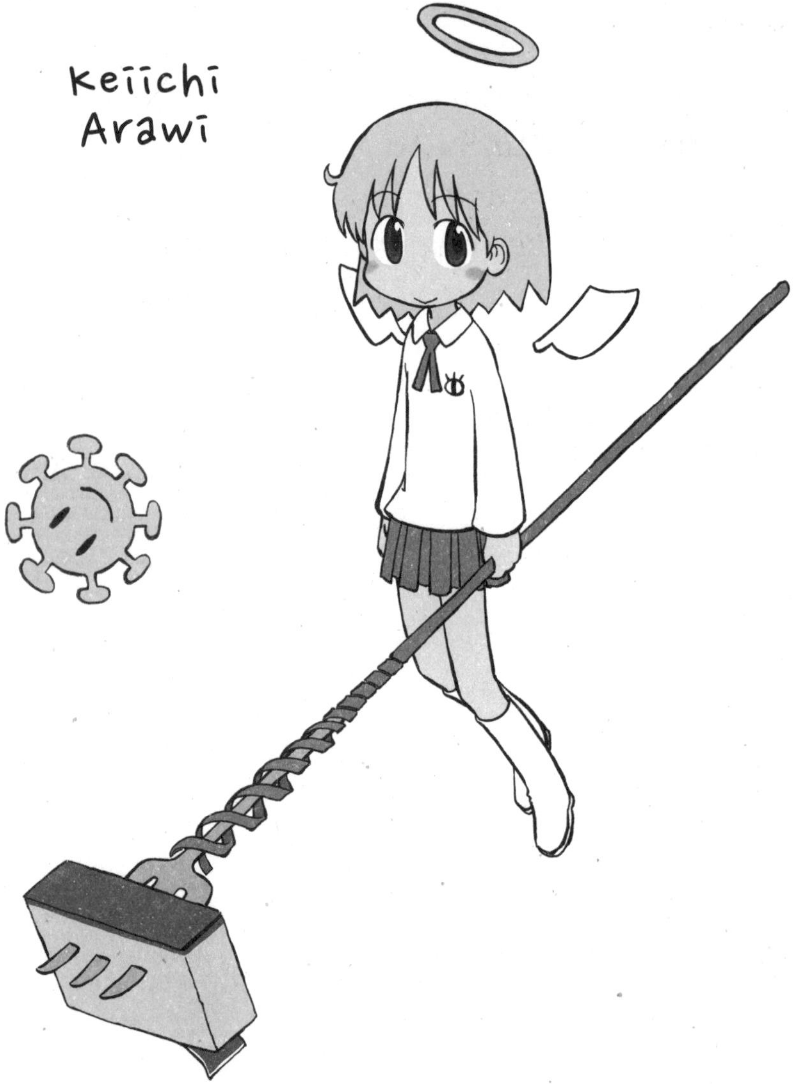

Helvetica Standard

CITY 1

A Vertical Comics Edition

Translation: Jenny McKeon
Production: Grace Lu
         Hiroko Mizuno

© Keiichi ARAWI 2017
First published in Japan in 2017 by Kodansha, Ltd., Tokyo
Publication rights for this English edition arranged through Kodansha, Ltd., Tokyo
English language version produced by Vertical, Inc.

Translation provided by Vertical Comics, 2018
Published by Vertical Comics, an imprint of Vertical, Inc., New York

Originally published in Japanese as *CITY 1* by Kodansha, Ltd.
CITY first serialized in *Morning*, Kodansha, Ltd., 2016-

This is a work of fiction.

ISBN: 978-1-945054-78-5

Manufactured in Canada

First Edition

Vertical, Inc.
451 Park Avenue South
7th Floor
New York, NY 10016
www.vertical-comics.com

Vertical books are distributed through Penguin-Random House Publisher Services.

define "ordinary"

in this just-surreal-enough take on the "school genre" of manga, a group of friends (which includes a robot built by a child professor) grapple with all sorts of unexpected situations in their daily lives as high schoolers.

the gags, jokes, puns and random haiku keep this series off-kilter even as the characters grow and change. check out this new take on a storied genre and meet the new ordinary.

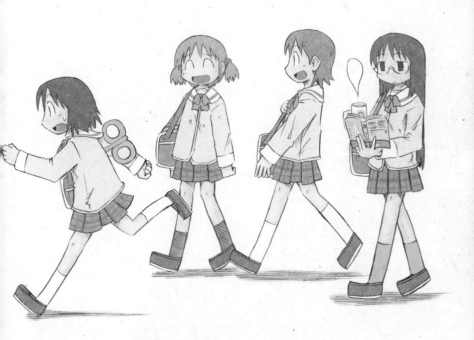

all volumes available now!

nichijou

my ordinary life

keiichi
arawi

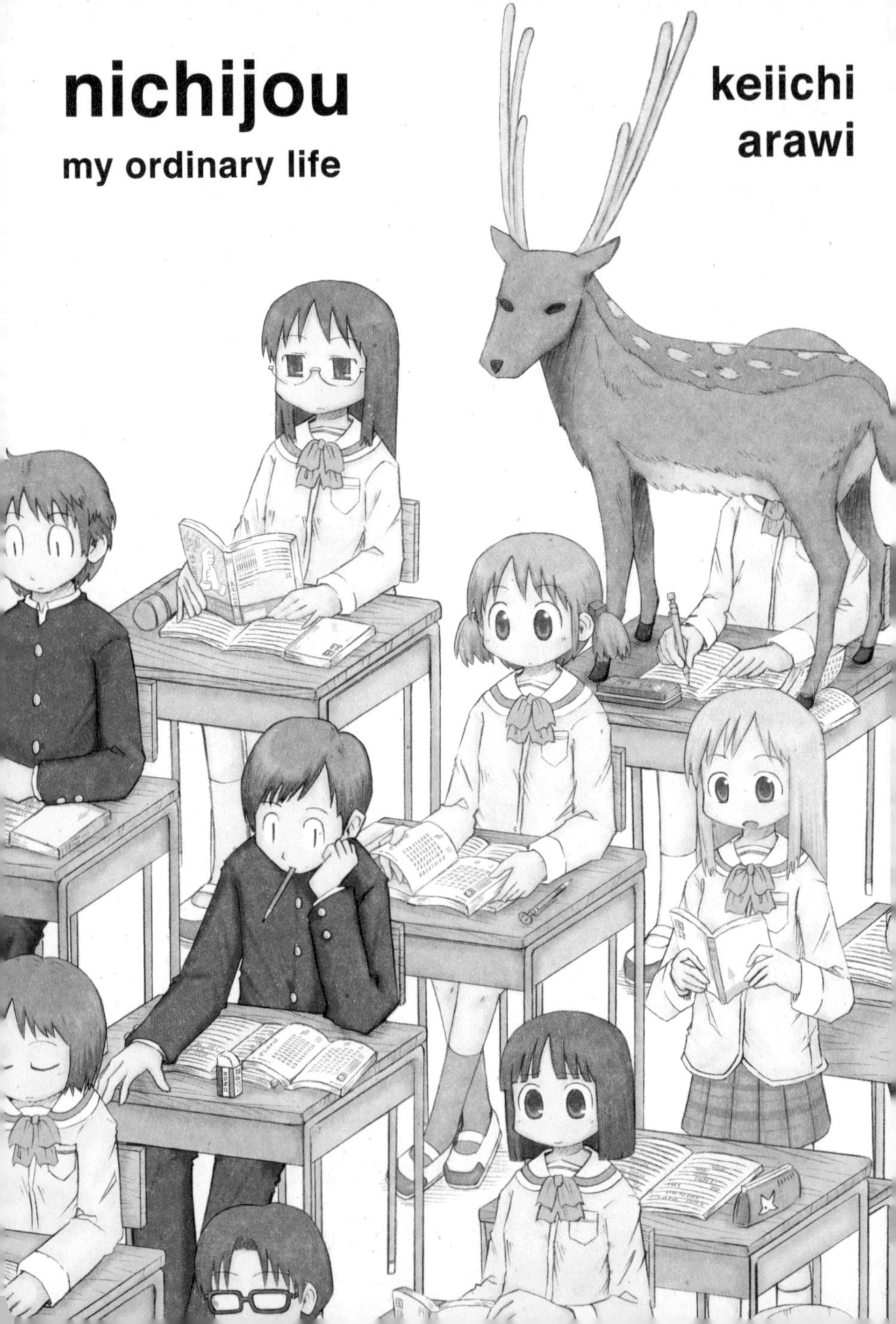

The follow up to the hit manga series ***nichijou***, ***Helvetica Standard*** is a full-color anthology of Keiichi Arawi's comic art and design work. Funny and heartwarming, ***Helvetica Standard*** is a humorous look at modern day Japanese design in comic form.

Helvetica Standard is a deep dive into the artistic and creative world of Keiichi Arawi. Part comic, part diary, part art and design book, ***Helvetica Standard*** is a deconstruction of the world of ***nichijou***.

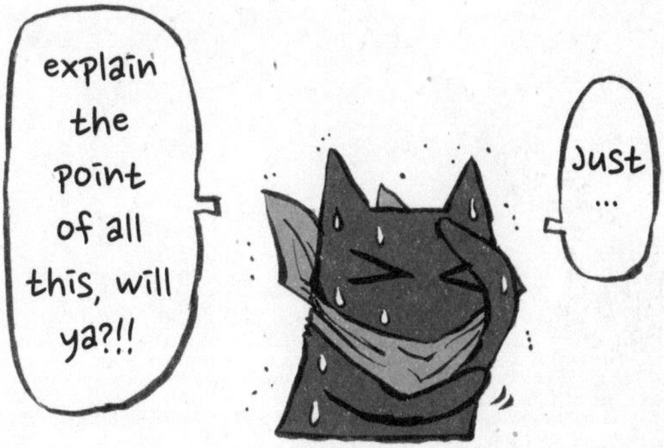
Just
...
explain the point of all this, will ya?!!

Both Parts Available Now!

Keiichi Arawi

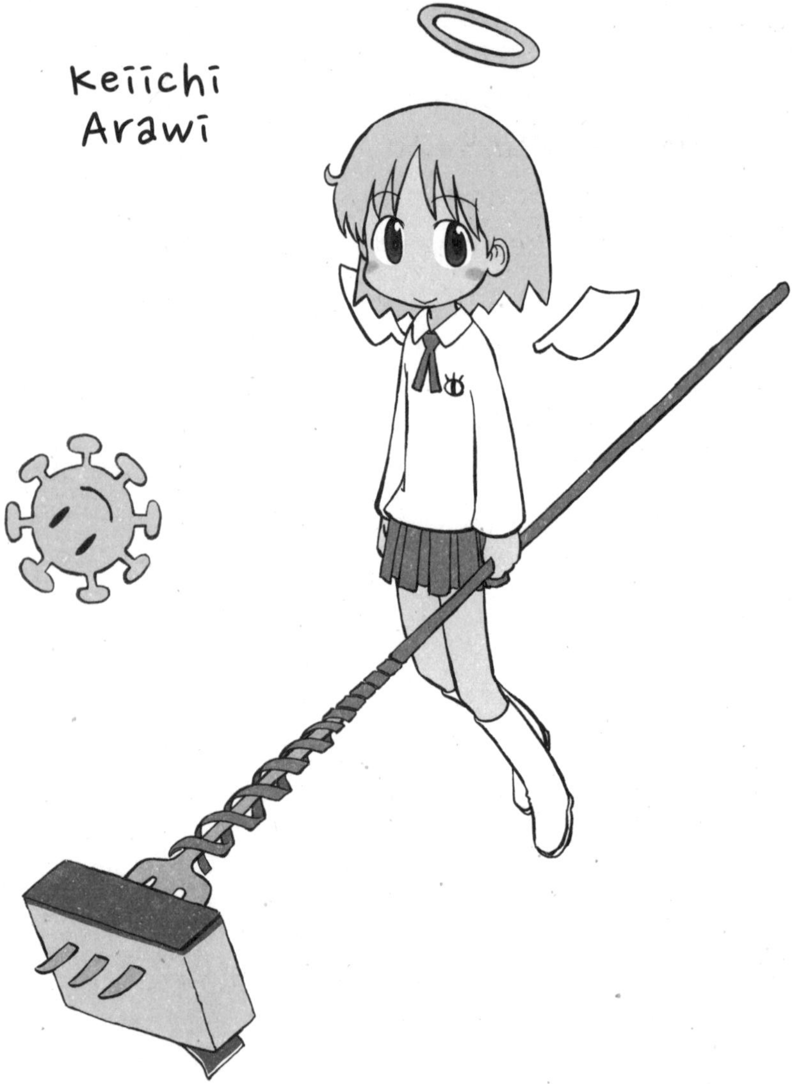

Helvetica Standard

CITY 1

A Vertical Comics Edition

Translation: Jenny McKeon
Production: Grace Lu
          Hiroko Mizuno

© Keiichi ARAWI 2017
First published in Japan in 2017 by Kodansha, Ltd., Tokyo
Publication rights for this English edition arranged through Kodansha, Ltd., Tokyo
English language version produced by Vertical, Inc.

Translation provided by Vertical Comics, 2018
Published by Vertical Comics, an imprint of Vertical, Inc., New York

Originally published in Japanese as *CITY 1* by Kodansha, Ltd.
CITY first serialized in *Morning*, Kodansha, Ltd., 2016-

This is a work of fiction.

ISBN: 978-1-945054-78-5

Manufactured in Canada

First Edition

Vertical, Inc.
451 Park Avenue South
7th Floor
New York, NY 10016
www.vertical-comics.com

Vertical books are distributed through Penguin-Random House Publisher Services.

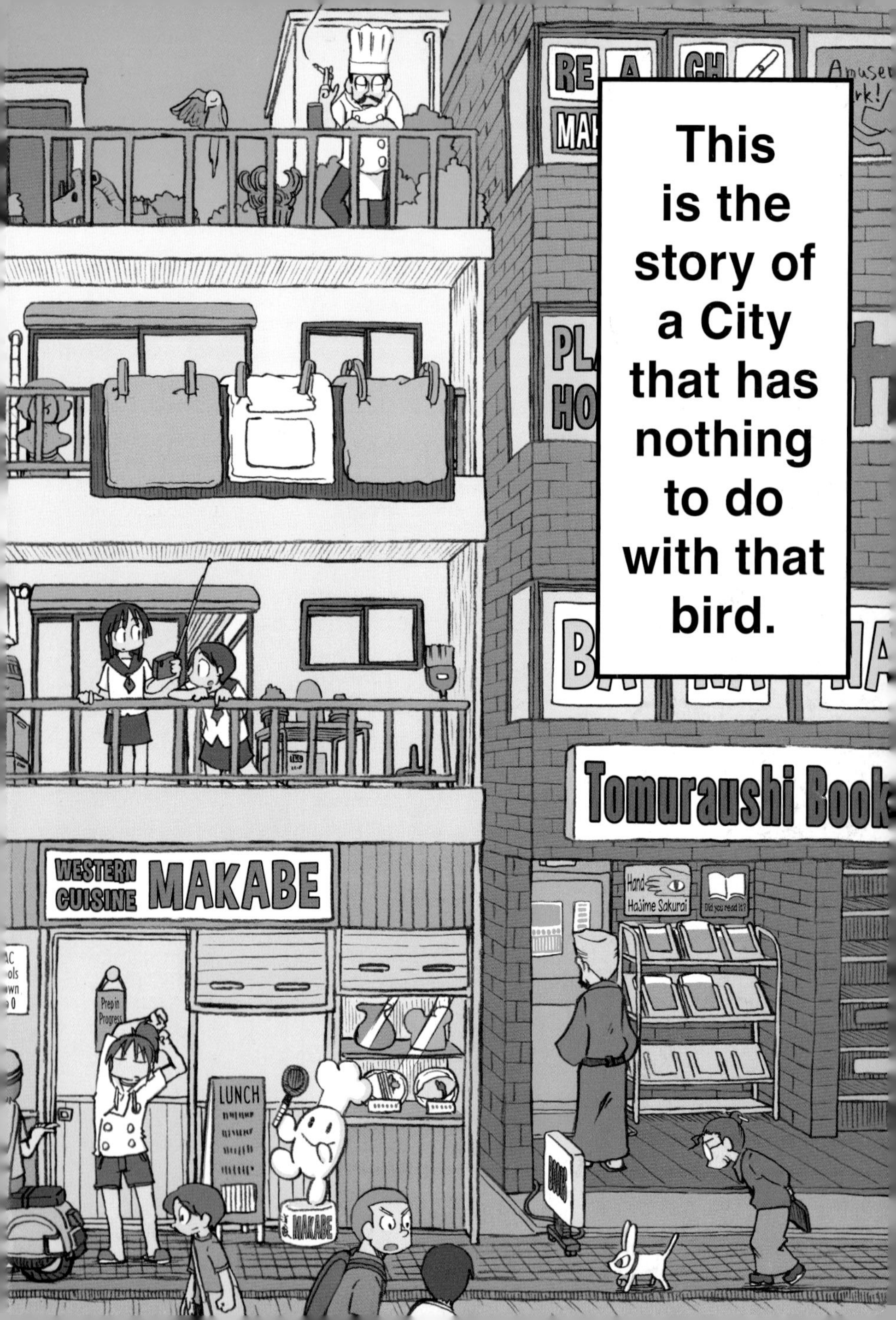
This is the story of a City that has nothing to do with that bird.
Tomuraushi Book
WESTERN CUISINE MAKABE
Prep in Progress
LUNCH
MAKABE
Hand
Hajime Sakurai
Did you read it?

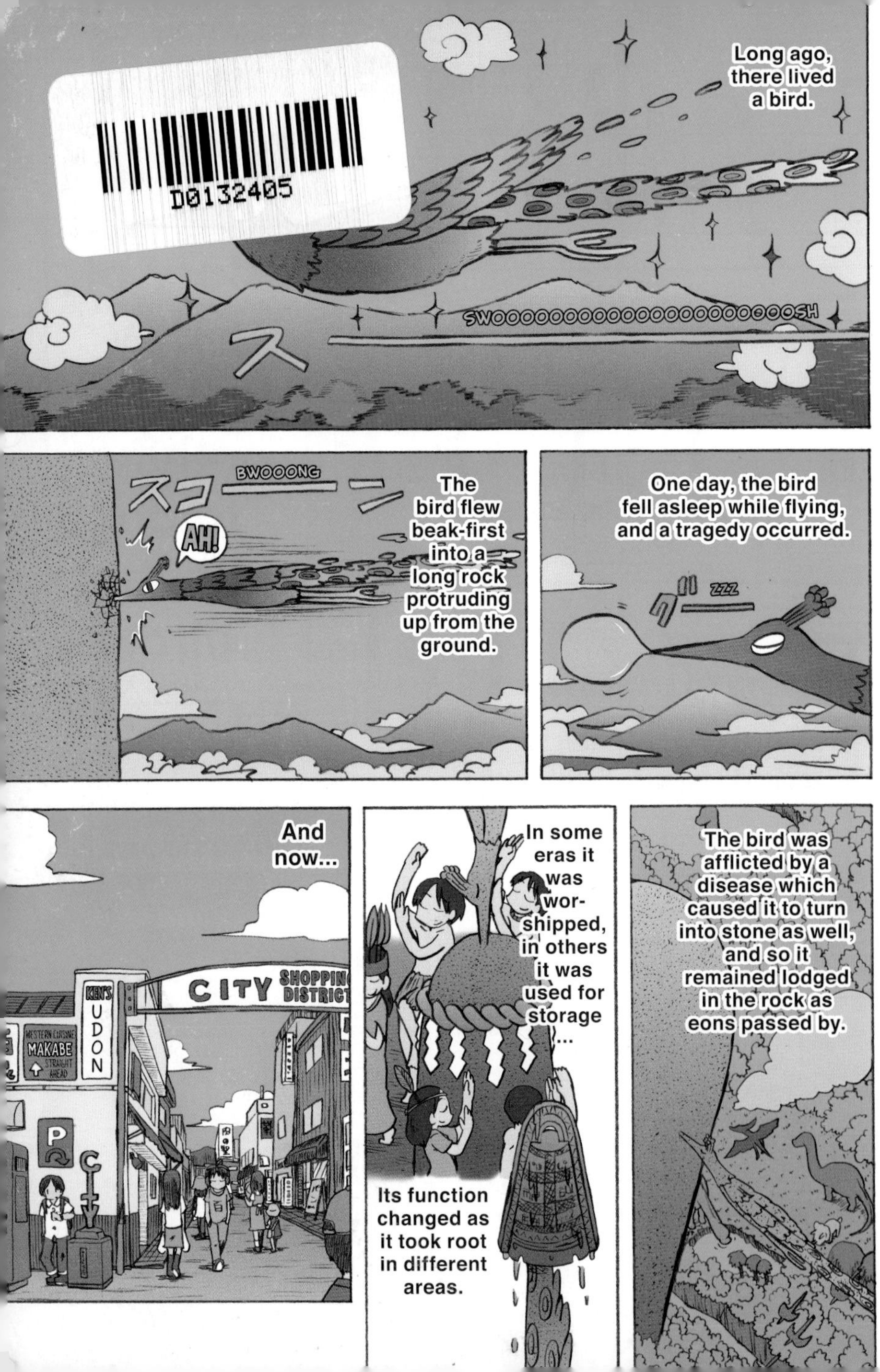
Long ago, there lived a bird.
SWOOOOOOOOOOOOOOOOOOOOOOOOOSH
ス
One day, the bird fell asleep while flying, and a tragedy occurred.
グー
ZZZ
The bird flew beak-first into a long rock protruding up from the ground.
BWOOONG
スコーン
AH!
The bird was afflicted by a disease which caused it to turn into stone as well, and so it remained lodged in the rock as eons passed by.
In some eras it was wor-shipped, in others it was used for storage...
Its function changed as it took root in different areas.
And now...
CITY SHOPPING DISTRICT
KEN'S UDON
WESTERN CUISINE MAKABE STRAIGHT AHEAD
P
CITY